I've Been Running for l

Jill

Keith Publications, LLC
www.keithpublications.com
©2016

Arizona
USA

To Sheila,
Thank you for supporting me on this journey.

Jill Hymel
2016

I've Been Running for Miles . . . and Found Myself

Copyright© 2016

By Jill Hynes

Edited by Isabella Dumon
isabella.dumon@yahoo.com

Cover art by Elisa Elaine Luevanos
www.ladymaverick81.com

Cover art Keith Publications, LLC © 2016
www.keithpublications.com

ISBN: 978-1-62882-122-2

All rights reserved.
No part of this book may be reproduced or transmitted in any form without written permission from Keith Publications, except by a reviewer who may quote brief passages for review purposes, with proper credit given.

This book is a work of fiction and any resemblance to any person, living or dead, any place, events or occurrences, is purely coincidental. The characters and story lines are created from the author's imagination or are used fictitiously, except for incidental references to public figures, well-known products and geographical locations, which are used fictitiously with no intent to disparage their products or services.

Keith Publications strives to release completely edited and polished material. Our manuscripts go through extensive revisions between our editors and the author. However, in the event the author feels as though the integrity of their writing has been jeopardized by edits, it is left to the sole discretion of that author to keep his/her manuscript as is. Any errors; grammatical, structural, use of Brand Names/Trademarked products and or historical are that of the authors.

If you are interested in purchasing more works of this nature, please stop by
www.keithpublications.com

Contact information: keithpublications@cox.net
Visit us at: www.keithpublications.com

Printed in The United States of America

Dedication

This book is dedicated to my parents for enabling me to be able to dedicate this book to my sons.

Acknowledgements

I want to thank my parents for seeing in me what I never saw in myself. Kathy Willis for editing me while allowing me to still keep my voice. To my friends and family aka my support system without whom I could not have accomplished my day to day and for encouraging my journey and enduring my stories. A great big thank you to anyone taking the time to read my first effort. This book was written for me, to you. I hope whoever reads this can see themselves in some of the characters and hopefully not feel so alone and take away strength, humor, encouragement, peace, and love. To John and Eddie who, be it good, beautiful, or horrible, independently influenced me to be who I am, be it good, beautiful, or horrible. From the sister you never wanted, I love you Mark Hudson. Thank you Diane Nine for believing in me and taking a chance on me. To Isabella Dumon and Keith Publications for giving me this wonderful opportunity. Anna, Kirk, Dawn, Felice, Francine, Donna, Josephine, Helayne, Annemarie, Anna W., Joyce . . . friendships that last forever. Philip, thank you for keeping my head on straight, somewhat. To Joey and Jack . . . my reason for everything. If you don't believe in yourself no one will ever invest in you. Teach people how to treat you. Never give up on whatever you set your mind to. There is nothing you can't accomplish. I love you always.

Reviews

I'VE BEEN RUNNING FOR MILES . . . AND FOUND MYSELF is a compelling book about a woman's journey to find herself through rock'n'roll, love, fantasy, sex, and family. I could be wrong , but it's so honest, it almost seems autobiographical. As if Jill Hynes possibly touched on the pain, pleasure, and humor in her own life, with a large amount of truth and passion, and transferred it effortlessly to Piper (the main character). There is an old anecdote: "Be careful what you wish for" and this story proves it. A sweet woman consumed with her turmoiled family, and her secret desire to be free and fall in love with a rock star! She gets addicted to love and the life style, but doesn't realize that every addict comes down, and Piper gets a huge reality hangover. However, through all her angst, Piper's slice of life is the real story. The kind of story that we all can relate to. There is not a lot of happy endings in the rock world. Fame, fortune, drugs, women, booze, can come and go in a minute, but this story does have a happy ending, because this beautiful, lost mother, found more than love . . . she found herself. Now THAT'S a happy ending.

Mark Hudson
"Hudson Brothers"
Singer, songwriter, producer for Ringo Starr, Aerosmith, Ozzy Osbourne, Hanson

Table of Contents

Chapter 1

I never intended to like him. I was not impressed or even interested when I first heard his name. Was it supposed to mean anything to me? I was twenty years old when I first heard his name and I never imagined that nineteen years later I would embark on an adventure that would end up changing me forever.

I was running late for work, as usual, because I was cleaning up the house for the painters. Mom always thinks the house is a mess, so now that Sean is getting married you can imagine what excitement lies ahead for Cinderella. Not only were we cleaning, but we had to call in the painters to freshen everything up. I was pretty frustrated because it seemed as though I am always getting stuck cleaning and organizing before some kind of event while everyone else's life goes on. After shoving the last of Sean's crap in his closet, I headed back downstairs to get ready again for work. I damn near fell over the trunk that he left in the hallway and had to drag it across the hall to the room that was hopefully not going to see a paintbrush today.

As I am now looking through my mess for my uniform, I am talking to myself. I don't know why, but I was annoyed at the painters for no other reason than they were coming to my house. My cleaning was their fault in some strange way. Pulling all of my clothes out onto the floor I called out, "Mom, where are my uniforms?"

Picking through my new mess to clean, I realized Sean left the wedding rings up in his room. Being the trusting New Yorker that I am, I flew out of my room and ran past my mother who yelled, "I said they were right here. Where are you going?"

I ran upstairs to find three painters covering everything in tarps. "Stop, I need to find the wedding rings before you start anything." As I'm lifting tarps, one of the guys caught my eye. He was really cute—long black hair, tall, like a painting rock star. *Focus, focus, I need to find these rings.* Luckily Sean leaves everything lying around just like me, so they were right on the edge of the desk. Rings in hand, I held them up, smiled, and said, "Carry on, gentlemen," and then went back down to my mother.

"What is wrong with you? Have you lost your mind? I told you I had your uniforms right here!"

"Uniforms? Who cares? That's old news. Did you see that guy up there?"

She started laughing and said, "I was waiting for you to spot him." All of a sudden, I didn't mind that the house was getting painted. I knew that Mom would get any needed info while I was at work, she was good like that. I grabbed my shirt out of her hand and said, "I cleaned the house, you get my dirt." And I took off for work.
I called home during the course of the day to get a progress update on my mother's information retrieval. The first call revealed a big blow. Mom picks up the phone and says, "He's married." Of course he is. Why wouldn't he be? He's hot, probably a musician, long hair . . . married. Oh well, maybe they're not happy. I know, I'm going to hell. Whatever!

Well, it was 5 o'clock, time to see if he can actually paint too. To my surprise, the hot one was still painting when I walked in. Honestly I wasn't expecting to still see any of them there when I got back. Hot boy was painting the fireplace?! What the hell was that all about? The other two guys had apparently left an hour ago. They figured they would be done around four and here it was about 5:30 and the fireplace was getting painted. Waving to the painter, I walked into the kitchen to find mom at the sink and I said, "The fireplace? What's up with that?" She shrugged her shoulders, shook her head and continued scrubbing the potatoes. He was very meticulous about his painting too.

Curious as to why he was still here, I walked back into the living room and said, "I wasn't expecting you would still be here."

"I noticed this needed to be done and I wanted to make sure everything was just right for the wedding. I saw all of your posters in your room. You're a big Satire fan, huh?"

What gave it away, the fifty-two pictures of Noah Anderson? Dad wasn't too happy about the nails all over my walls, and Mom wasn't too happy about Noah Anderson all over my walls. As it turns out my little painter was a musician by night. Now it is 1989 and Satire has been broken up for six years. There has been talk of them getting back together again, but without Noah. I really didn't see any point in them getting back together if Noah was not going to be in the band. Noah was a big draw so I couldn't even imagine going to see them without him. As much as I loved the music, the idea of them getting back together without Noah had me convinced that I would never go see them again. I mean really, who could possibly replace Noah Anderson? Whomever it was certainly could never be as hot as him.

I finally had to come to terms with the fact that perhaps I preferred watching Noah a bit more than I actually cared about the music. Oh God, I had become one of "those girls." I don't want to be one of those girls who just goes to shows to drool over the rock star. It's supposed to be about the music. There should be some emotional connection to the music and if there is a visual aid, well that's just a bonus. I listened to Satire all through high school. I was so into them that when I would run into people after graduation I was "the girl who always listened to Satire" or I would hear, "I heard SLAM HIM on the radio and thought about you. Do you still listen to Satire?" Now what was I going to say, I'm protesting Satire because Noah left the band?

So, hottie painter says, "You know, Satire is getting back together again."

I said, "Yeah, I know, but without Noah Anderson so what is the point?"

"I know the guy who is replacing him, played in a band with him. His name is Miles Baker and he lives in Brooklyn." Brooklyn? Ha. Is he kidding me? First of all, am I really to believe that a huge band like Satire has a nobody—from Brooklyn, no less—replacing Noah Anderson? Is this guy just trying to impress me, because knowing Noah Anderson's replacement does not impress me. In fact, it's pissing me off. This Miles Baker has to be a real jerk. I base this opinion on my vast knowledge of nothing. I guess I was just being mature and hating someone that I didn't know for no reason other than the fact that he was not someone else and filled a void in a band for someone who didn't even want to be in the band. Did ya get all that? I would have to say, that other than my painter telling

3

me about this Miles Baker person, the only other time I ever spoke his name for the next ten years was about two hours later when I called April, my partner in Satire crime, to tell her about this idiot who was going to try to take the place of our Noah Anderson.

****

The painter was a bass player in The Billy Mays Band and they usually played every Saturday at The Dock of The Bay. April and I were 20 at the time, only a year under the legal drinking age, but we had no fake IDs because we were "good girls." We were new at this "going out" thing, especially going out to see bands play. Luckily, we looked older than we were and the bouncers at the door weren't all that strict about checking IDs. It made it easy for us to make The Dock of The Bay our little hang out joint. We felt comfortable each week going in because we now knew we weren't going to get proofed and we felt like we at least had a place we could go.

Always keeping in the back of our minds that the painter was married, we would go see his band play every weekend and hang out with him after the shows, but we always kept our hands off. I think this was my first step to learning about men, particularly musicians. Just observing the environment we existed in, I was actually starting to feel morally compromised. The painter did have a name, but I have always found it easier to throw a nickname on someone, as it is easier for the poor bastard listening to me tell a story to follow it or even understand what I am talking about. You have to admit, you are going to be able to remember every aspect of the painter's actions as opposed to John's. What if there are two or three Johns? Let's face it, it's New York, all you're gonna have are Johns and Joes. It's just so much easier to be "the painter" or "the plumber" or "the pain in the ass." Trust me, this works and will make this a lot less painful. It's also a great way to protect the names of the guilty.

Since April and I were making a habit of going out each weekend to see The Billy Mays band, we were getting our first taste of getting the attention of musicians. It was not our intention. We were always into music. Satire was our first connection to each other; I guess you can say it brought us together. We were going to be Rock Stars ourselves. The whole music existence intrigued us; me more than April I think. We always talked and fantasized about hanging out with the band and just being a part of the music business in some capacity. We did not mean sleeping with the band, that task was reserved for the groupies . . . Which we were not. We did not want to be groupies. We also never talked about or thought about anything in a realistic sense. Clearly. The things we talked about were things that other people did, the fortunate ones. We never thought of ourselves as ever being the girl that gets the guy in the band. We didn't think it was possible, nor did we ever try. It was cool just to hang out with the band, and that was even more than we expected.

Since we were seeing the painter regularly, we really started to branch out in terms of our venues. We started to go into Manhattan, or as a typical Staten Islander might say, the city, and experience a lot of bars and clubs that we never would have done if we weren't going to see someone in particular. Not only did The Billy Mays Band play regularly at The Dock of The Bay, they also played clubs in Manhattan. As April and I started to become more comfortable in our own skin and going out in general, we decided to go see them play in the city. Although nothing ever happened between The Painter and us, if he was my husband, I would not be a happy woman. He seemed very flirtatious when we would show up at the shows. He seemed more interested in me, which was fine with April since she was interested in Billy May. When I was feeling obnoxious, I would often remind her that she could never marry Billy because then her name would be April May and that is just plain stupid.

April seemed to take on the role of my conscience these days. She would remind me each week that he was married. "I know, I know. I'm not doing anything," I would say. But she could see it was a potential problem. April knew me well enough to know that the tall, good looking bass player with the long black hair need only ask me if I wanted to go for a walk to have this situation take a turn to Piper going to hell in a hand basket. Needless to say, as a rule, April never left my side when we went out. I would also tend to have a couple of drinks which really meant April was on guard. Being a lightweight, anything past two was going to mean April was going to have to keep both eyes on my flirtatious self. On occasion, the painter's wife would show up at the shows. Those were the nights that we would get a nod hello from him when nobody was looking or if God forbid she went into the bathroom or left early, he would come over and kiss us hello. So taboo! For me it was sort of like out of sight, out of mind. When she wouldn't come around, it was easy to convince myself that she didn't exist. Childish, yes. Ignorant, perhaps . . . but I was also twenty years old. I feel as though if I really had tried at all to push the situation, something would have happened. Again, I was always feeling morally compromised. I knew I would not want my husband cheating on me, so I didn't want to do that to someone else. Boy, I'll tell you though, that painter was so cute. If I remember correctly, he was about thirty-three or thirty-five and I was twenty when we met.

After about a year of going to see Bill May's band on Staten Island, with the last couple of those months being in Manhattan, we were now twenty-one and hanging out in the city. We no longer had to pray that we wouldn't get proofed. It was a very free and exciting time for us. We could go out and have the attention of the band, yet nothing would happen between us, and we would not necessarily have the pressure of getting hit on too much while we were watching the band because the guys in the band would always pop over after every set. Yet we always had the freedom to flirt with other guys in the clubs because we were, in fact, unattached. We could use the painter and Billy as a shield, or not. It was a safety net of sorts. April was enjoying this as much as I was at this point. We loved going out and listening to the music and being the girls that the band came to sit with. It was very cool to us. We felt kind of special being at a club that was filled with people who came to see them, and then out of all of those people, they came and sat with us.

I don't really remember how it all began to wind down but I can say that of all the weekends that April and I spent in a two year span, my painter never once cheated on his wife, at least not with me. He may have been a little inappropriate for a "regular married man" but in my eyes, he was not a regular married man. He was a musician and some things go with the territory. I was young, cocky and naïve, and felt if his wife was going to marry a musician, there were certain things she had to accept and expect, and the women were one of them. If she was a good wife, she would be at every show, and then he couldn't stray. Again, this was an inexperienced twenty one year old talking who was only starting to bust out of her own Irish, Catholic, guilt-ridden world—and I was lovin' every minute of it. I do believe in karma—what goes around comes around. Keeping that in mind, again, I don't remember how this started to wind down. Other than going to shows and sitting with the band during their breaks and after the show, that was the extent of our big "sexual experience" with our big wanna-be rock stars. I'm sure to the naked eye and any one of those girls watching us in the clubs that wished they were us, things seemed different.

****

Since Billy's band didn't play as often as it used to, we started going over the bridge every weekend into New Jersey. We found a cool rock club called JJ Rockers. Our first night in the club, we sat at the bar and met the bartender and the bar back. The music in the club was great, there were cute guys everywhere, we were gonna like this. It was the early 90's so they played a lot of Warrant, Whitesnake, Guns and Roses, Skid Row and the like. April had taken an interest in the bartender who was blonde and a little chunky, and I was happy just to look around. Every now and then the bar back caught my attention. Not because he was cute, but because he was annoying. I kept hearing glasses slam, I would turn around and he would be doing a shot with a customer. I later came to find out that was some kind of shot that you slam the glass down before you drink it. I'm still not sure what it was, those days my drink of choice was champagne. As the night went on, April wanted to hang out with the bartender afterwards, but not alone. It was time for me to return the favor of keeping an eye out . . . or two.

As it turned out, what would turn into my ill-fated destiny, I had to hang out with the shot glass slamming, annoying bar back. See what friends do for each other! It turns out they were discussing us while we sat at the bar all night just as we were discussing them. As I recall, we ended up in a diner with them after the bar closed that night but where I thought I was serving as the company for my friend, it turned out that the bartender was not as much interested in my friend as the shot glass slamming, annoying bar back was interested in me. I figured if I can get through this night, next weekend was a new weekend and we could meet other people. We went for a walk when they were finished with work and while April talked with the bartender, I was stuck with the other fool. He was tall, lean, and sort of funny. That was his only redeeming quality at that point. I was really just not in the mood or mind set to get involved with anyone. The night went by quickly as we joked and laughed in the diner but I didn't have that feeling that I ever needed to do this again. The evening, in my mind, served its purpose. We had a few laughs, passed the time, now I was done. There was no love connection for any of us, at least that's what I thought, but it was a fun night. The guys sort of played off of each other so it seemed as though if we did this as couples, it would tank.

When we were parting ways that evening, Bar Back Boy asked me for my phone number. How far do my loyalties extend? I hung out with him, am I really responsible now for giving him my phone number? Come on, I draw the line. I'm not doing it. NO! I don't even like him, let alone want him to call me. I fulfilled my obligation to April, the night is over, I am in the clear, almost on my way home, where did this "Can I have your number" come from? I wasn't even nice. I was such a bitch with the few words I could actually get in because he never shut his mouth all night. I didn't know if it was his personality or nerves giving him IBS of the mouth. No, I don't want this to turn into a phone call or God forbid another night of hanging out. Envision this entire exchange going on in my head with foot stomping and all. I was adamant I was not letting this go past this night. I am standing strong!

This is how, to my recollection, it all went down, "So can I have your number?"

"Sure." I took out a pen and wrote it on his hand. Two things: one, I thought I was being sexy and clever by writing it on his hand and two, I figured it might smear off before he could transfer it to paper. Why didn't I say no? Didn't I have that whole conversation in my head? It's that whole Irish, Catholic guilt I spoke of earlier. Apparently I am the only sibling that seems to bear that burden. *Maybe he won't call,* I thought to myself. *They never call.* I figured at that point I had cleared another hurdle. Just because I gave him the number, doesn't mean I need to get on the phone if he actually calls. April and I could go back to the bar, not pay attention to this

8

guy and still be in the clear. That was at least the dream in my mind.

The following weekend, April and I were getting ready to go out. We were not going to JJ Rockers that night. We actually had plans to go into the city because some habits die hard, so I had a week that would pass to make Bar Back Boy seem like a bad dream. April was waiting in the living room with my mom while I was in the shower. When I came downstairs she had this half smile on her face and proceeded to inform me that Bar Back Boy had called while I was upstairs. You have to be kidding me. Shouldn't that shit have washed off? Oh God, now what? "I don't need to call him back right? Let's just get out of here." For some reason, she found this funny. Me, not so much. As she and my mom were having a good laugh at my expense, I said, "You know, this is all your fault!"

"My fault?" she said as her laughing curtailed a bit. "How is this my fault?"

"You had to hang out with the bartender. How did I get stuck with the other one?"

"Don't blame me. Why did you give him your phone number then?"

"Shut up."

I did not return his call that night because, well, I didn't want to, but he was also now at work and April and I were on our way out. There was a good possibility that if I blew his call off, he might just give up and not call back.

This guy was relentless. About two days later, he called back. Mom said, "He sounds nice, why don't you talk to him?"

It's more like listening, I thought to myself as I felt my face burning from frustration. *He doesn't shut the hell up. Ever!* As if I was doing my mother a favor and blaming her at the same time, I grabbed the phone from her like a five-year-old and, just short of stamping my foot, said, "Fine, I'll listen to him." I remember it being painful. I wanted to cry. I wanted off the phone. We were on the phone for about an hour of my life that I will never get back. He talked about everything and anything. When I finally got off the phone I said this is great, I at least got that over with. Now I don't need to talk to him again. We can go back to the bar and business as usual.

April and I worked together in a neighborhood restaurant. We spent the week working our asses off and looked forward to going to the club on the weekend. Often times we had to work on Friday and Saturday night, so we would fly home after our shift, shower quickly, and get to the club by about 11:00 p.m. The next weekend after that fateful phone call, we went into the bar and, with his eagle eyes, Bar Back Boy spotted us as soon as we walked in the door. Damn it! Oh well, I'm figuring he's stuck behind the bar all night so he won't be bothering us, and we could possibly even sneak out at closing and never have to speak to him.

April and I did our walk through when we got there and checked out all of the potential suitors, then found a spot to hang for the night. Every night that we were there, we would get hit on constantly. This, again, was not something that we were used to since we really only started going out to clubs about a year ago. We were late bloomers. Don't get me wrong, it was a real ego boost. We would flirt, just chat with any of the guys that came over, and leave at the end of the night. I came to find out later that this would drive Bar Back Boy nuts because he could see it all from where he stood. Did I tell you, we were constantly hit on. A slow night, which maybe happened once or twice in the year that we went there, was when we only got hit on by two guys in a night. I'm not bragging, just further pointing out how unusual this was for us. We did not go out a lot before our whole "painter" episode. The extent of our going out was hanging out at either April's house or my house, planning our fun existence, and of course our pending marriage to Noah Anderson. We never did determine who was going to get him. I felt I should have him because I saw him first on Don Kirschner's Rock Concert, and I introduced April to him and Satire. So of course, I would be the obvious choice.

****

The first time that I ever went to see Satire, I was twelve years old and my brothers took me to the show. We had an extra ticket and I knew April from school, but we didn't like each other. It was another case of knowing nothing about the other person and having a third party fuel the situation by constantly telling each of us how the other one hated them. But she lived down the street from me and we had the extra ticket, so I figured, why not? I called her up and, since we always did the phony smile and occasionally said hello to one another, it wasn't too insane to her that I called her. She said yes, and thus began the journey. After the evening of that first show, we went to every concert every time they came to the area.

We got our first taste of the backstage experience after a show about three years later, at the then-named Brendan Byrne Arena. As we were leaving the show with my brother Devon, we saw people leaving with backstage passes on. April and I were always looking at the scantily clad sluts down in the orchestra area from our seats on the side and we would say to each other, "are they serious?" They were thought of as the enemy because at thirteen and fourteen, we were decked out in our newest concert t-shirt and jeans and figured we would never lower ourselves to that level to get a man. They were disgusting in our eyes. Let me tell you, that was the first lesson in how it all works. I would watch the enemy and swear I would never do that, yet I was still intrigued and took it all in. My mind would be racing with all of these questions like "were they really getting what they wanted? What did I want?" I knew I didn't want to work my way through the roadies to get to the band. I mean really, isn't that gross?

As we were leaving, I said to April, "Let's see if someone would give us their pass if they're done with it." So began the cute attitude and flirtation. We had already started to change our wardrobe a bit and started to transition from the tomboy look to the girlie look but had not yet crossed over into what we might consider the garb of the enemy. Baby steps. I approached first as my conscience stood at a distance and watched with skepticism. I saw an unassuming gentleman come walking towards me and in my sweetest, cutest voice with a head tilt, asked if I could please use his pass if he was done with it, and voila – I had a pass. Was it really that easy? I grabbed April and we found the next victim. She was still somewhat uneasy about it but that didn't stop me from trying it again. I already had one pass and could not go in without her, nor could I let it go to waste because that would just be downright ridiculous. As I saw the next victim walk towards me, I showed him my pass and, again with a head tilt and flirtatious grin, asked if he was finished with his pass so she could come with me. Bam — two passes and we still had our panties on. Go figure. My brother Devon grinned and shook his head and waited outside. He may now have started to worry himself since he was witnessing the beginning of the wallflower starting to come into her own.

With two backstage passes in hand, we now had to figure out how to get back in to the arena. If you act like you know what you are doing, most people won't question you. We walked in where everybody was coming out from and found ourselves back inside the arena. Although we were back in, we still had to figure out how to get to the backstage area. I opened a random door, and we found ourselves in some back hallway. We followed this long, white hallway and went through another door. All of a sudden it was like Dorothy stepping into color. There was a whole other world going on—a room filled with people in line to meet Noah Anderson. Mike Richards stood out in the open just talking to people. Lou Volpe was standing next to him. They were all just standing around talking like regular people. April and I turned to look at each other in shock. We had made it. Now what? We were confused. We were assuming there was going to be all kinds of craziness going on and half naked women everywhere. Figuring rock stars had some kind of super powers and that they can't possibly do normal things like carry on conversations and stand around like normal people, they threw us off. Now we didn't know what to do. We decided to start with getting Lou Volpe's autograph, then sheepishly walked to where Noah was sitting and signing autographs. We were wearing our stylish, off-the-shoulder shirts, since we had now graduated from our concert tees and were trying our hands at sex appeal. We figured Noah would see us as the wholesome girls we were and appreciate us for that, rather than the usual cavalcade of sluts that hang around. We were going to be a refreshing change, catch his eye, and thus begin our future together.

This was the thinking of the fourteen-year-old. As we approached his autograph table, we saw he already had a little slut sitting next to him. She too had on a stylish, off-the-shoulder shirt. Well, we figured we must be doing something right. She was blonde though. Do blondes really have more fun? As I had auburn hair and April was a brunette, competing with these blonde bimbos was not going to be easy. After standing for about five minutes in the line in a room that looked no different from a conference room, I tried to come to terms with the fact that I was about to meet my idol, my future husband. All of a sudden the girl that had been hiding behind me all night channeled her inner Wonder Woman and, with the greatest of ease, April walked right up to Noah and asked for an autograph and a picture with him. They were both smiling beautifully. I was looking through the viewfinder and wanted to throw up. All I could think was, *this man is looking right at me at this very second.* I was praying to God these pictures were going to turn out okay since this was before the day of digital cameras. It was now my turn. I almost lost my nerve and wanted to throw up yet again.

As I begin my approach towards Noah, Willie Aames walked behind Noah on his way out and said goodbye. Willie Aames! This was so surreal. Celebrities just walk around like real people and here we were, two nobodies who basically scammed our way into this situation, taking it all in. As I dragged myself up to Noah, I don't even think I asked for an autograph. I just put the paper in front of him. Yet, I had the nerve to ask for a kiss (which I got on the cheek) and a picture. I got down on one knee for the picture, but people kept calling him. While I waited, I tried to take in the fact that I was seeing him so closely. He had blonde hair, electric blue eyes, and he was very tiny. He was about 5'6" and skinny. I was getting too embarrassed just sitting there, so I told April to just take the picture. She said, "He isn't even looking at the camera." I told her to take it anyway because I felt foolish. How long was I expected to genuflect? Upon developing that roll of film, we came to learn that Noah is not looking at the camera and I look like someone just killed my family. That was my big moment, the picture that I had to look at and show off to everybody. That photo was my incentive to meet him again so that I could get a better one.

We began to feel as though getting backstage wasn't going to be so easy. We were two naïve kids trying to live in a world that we were not prepared to live in. We thought we were slick and cool, but truth be told, we were not going to just sleep with anybody just to get to somebody else. We were not groupies and we certainly were not going to lose our virginity at fourteen to a fifty-year-old, married roadie. We also were at a point where we were too young to even be in those situations, let alone try to act on them. After a few years of concerts and that being our only meeting with Satire, we did start to branch out and see other groups. Satire broke up not long after that, certainly lessening our opportunities to see Noah, catch his eye, and marry him. Always keeping Noah on the back burner, we started to go see other bands. Duran Duran, Def Leppard, Styx, Aerosmith, REO Speedwagon, Paul Young, Journey, Jack Wagner, you get the idea. In the meantime, Noah released a couple of solo albums, and we would go see him open for other bands, but there were still no meetings.

Chapter 2

It was now the eighties, we were sixteen, Duran Duran broke up, but The Power Station was formed. April and I were now starting to change our attire and vamp it up a little more. I always pushed the envelope more than April did. Our friend had gotten us tickets for The Power Station one night. They too were playing at the Brendan Byrne Arena, now called The Meadowlands. Our friend really wanted to pull out all the stops and drove us in a limo. Now we really felt like we were something else. It was pretty cool to come out after the show and have a limo sitting there waiting for you. After the show, knowing how much we wanted to meet them, limo boy decided he was going to make that happen. He was a cop, so he drove like a lunatic. He thought like a cop too, so as soon as the band's fake cars came out, he spotted the real one and followed it. I remember pulling out of the parking lot and not much else about the ride. We followed them into Manhattan. He drove like a maniac trying to keep up with them. There was one point that with one turn, I flew from one side of the limo diagonally across from where I had started out and landed on my back on the floor. He pulled up next to them, lowered his window and flashed his badge. That maneuver got us a spot right behind their limo. We eventually got to the bar in Manhattan where they were going and we got out, a little nauseous from the ride but no worse for wear. We got out of the limo and acted like we were supposed to be there.

Right in front of us, again like real people, walked Andy Taylor, John Taylor, and Renee Simonsen. This was crazy. I know they are real people, but they are people that I watch on my video tapes and television and dream about. They are not people that I can actually meet—I thought. This was a life I yearned to be a part of but not just for the sake of being a part of it. We would only go to the shows of the bands we were really invested in. In our minds, you could only be a true fan if you knew everything about the band. It's not enough to just like and know the music. You have to love the band itself. Know facts about them. In our minds, only a true fan would. We didn't feel as though we just handed our affection and admiration out like candy. It was an earned privilege. To love one song did not a concert ticket purchase make. Besides the fact, we were going to see these other bands while we were biding our time until Satire got back together.

Skimming through the Daily News one day, I stopped dead in my tracks. Noah's name had caught my eye. He was getting married. How was that possible when he hadn't even asked me? I started to feel a little nauseous, as though the wind had just been knocked out of me. All I could think was, *this was not good.* Now I was faced with the fact that I might have to live my life as though Noah was not an option. *Wait a minute, he's a rock star, it will never last.* A wave of calm came over and I figured all was good. Nothing was any different than before I picked this newspaper up. By the time he gets divorced, I'll be old enough to marry him.

****

It was now 1990 and it turns out Noah was in a band that was going to be touring with Curtis Angel. Curtis Angel was another guy that, in my opinion, was not so hard on the eyes. He was cute and had the same build as Noah. They were both very tall and lean and had shoulder length hair that you could just die for. Curtis was also in a very popular band in the '80s, but it seemed as though all of the bands from that time were starting to split. Everybody was putting out their own solo album or trying to find their own way in this ever-changing music world. I was very excited. This was perfect. It wasn't Satire, but I still get to see Noah in some capacity. The name of the band was called Busta and they were awesome. Now that April and I were driving, we didn't need to rely on our siblings or parents. We loved summer concerts. Having no real responsibilities other than to work in the restaurant which gave me enough money to pay for my car insurance and gas and leaving enough to put away to save while still having enough for concerts, we had our nights free. For us, summer was a time to focus on concerts and having a good time. Traveling for shows didn't really bother us all that much either, since we needed to maximize our chances of meeting Noah. I still needed to get a better picture with him.

One of the things I love about living in New York is that when an artist comes to town, there are about four venues they hit consecutively. At one particular show that summer at Jones Beach, I was looking at the blonde standing a row in front of me. After a few minutes of trying to figure out if my calculations were correct, I hit April in the arm and said, "Do you know who that is?"

Rubbing her arm she turned to me and said, "Don't do that again. No, who?"

Leaning in as if anybody cared what information I was just about to divulge, I whispered, "It's Noah's wife." Curling her lip and shooting her the hairy eye, April just turned away and continued observing the crowd. *What were the chances that she would be here right in front of me?* I thought to myself. I guess it wasn't that much of a stretch that she would actually be there, seeing as her husband is in the band. I decided to get a little ballsy but tried to be slick about it. Figuring she must get bombarded with questions and requests about Noah all the time and may feel a little slighted since she is a "celebrity" in her own right, I decided to ask her for her autograph. Gently, I leaned over and tapped her shoulder and, acting as if I actually cared, said, "Hi, may I have your autograph? I watch you on The Nights all the time," which was an absolute lie. They also have a daughter so I asked how she was, to which she responded, "She looks just like her father."

All I could think was, *this bitch has a chip on her shoulder*, which made me question why anybody would want to be with her. I thanked her for her autograph and then I was about to reveal the big question and I was hoping she would not shoot me down. I asked her if she would take the horrible photo of Noah and I back and have Noah sign it, and she said she couldn't. She shares a bed with him but she couldn't get my picture signed? Again I thanked her and she turned back around, and April peered out of the corner of her eye at me knowing what I was up to. When I looked down at her autograph, it said "Allie Moss, Noah Anderson's Wife!"

My first thought was, was she kidding me? An exclamation point? Was she that insecure in her marriage that she had to further point out that she was married to my man? She was pissing me off too. I have gotten many autographs in the past and this was the first time I had a job description listed next to the name like it was a resume. I couldn't help but think that if I were married to him, everybody would already know. I wouldn't have to be throwing all kinds of punctuation marks all over the place. It didn't really matter much to me when I thought about it. What is the point in having an autograph you didn't acquire yourself anyway? There is no story, no history, just a signature. Again, this was more incentive to try to meet him again.

Minutes after the meet and greet with bridezilla, the lights went down and the show was about to start. Busta was made up of band members from various other bands. They all used to be in headlining bands and now they are almost starting over again in a band that will now serve as an opening act. Busta was going to be opening for Sierra, a band that never broke up, just had some interchangeable players. April and I decided to stick around for Sierra. We weren't all that familiar with their music but decided to give it a whirl. This was part of us trying to expand our appreciation of music. We stayed for the whole show and loved them. We figured that was a deal. We actually loved the opening act and the main act. Unlike most people, April and I were at the point now where we were seeking out the opening act. If you think about it, who really does that? Who watches the opening act then leaves for the headliner? We were not your typical chicks, as I had explained earlier.

Determined to try to meet Noah again, and just have fun at the show, we now started to travel a little bit further to see them. One particular show brought us to Westchester. This is around the time we were going to see the Billy May's Band as well. We were hanging around by our seats before the show and we saw a few people gathered around a blonde gentleman. We decided to go check it out. When we got closer we realized it was the lead singer from Sierra. April and I looked at each other then looked back at him and thought, *holy crap*. He was just hanging out and signing autographs. Naïve April and Piper thought, how cool, just wanting to meet his fans and sign autographs. Trying to play it cool we walked over towards him like we were completely unimpressed. If you think about it, we had been to about five shows but only stayed to see his band the last time we went. Feeling like we were breaking our own rule of not truly being a fan, it didn't seem right to get his autograph, but we were going to do it anyway. As we got closer, before we could say a word, he asked us to wait a minute, finished signing everyone else's autographs, then pulled out 2 backstage passes, smiled and said, "I'll see you later."

Again, looking at each other in disbelief and not saying a word, we took the passes and went back to our seats. Was that for real? Did that just happen? Am I still wearing my underwear? That only happens to the hot chicks at the concerts, the ones we are jealous of. Are the tables turning? We got back to our seats and the silence was broken when April retuned the arm punch from the previous concert. In a voice only dolphins could comprehend, she squealed, "Oh my God. How the hell did that happen?"

I had no answer for her. He seemed to be interested in April, so I said, "What are you going to do?"

"What are you talking about? I'm not going to do anything."

"What if he wants to sleep with you? You could sleep with a rock star."

"And how many people do you think he has slept with? I am not just having sex with a rock star because I can!"

Commendable, I thought, *but stupid*. But he was not Noah Anderson, so really there was no point. Like a scene out of Wayne's World, April planted her pass right up on her chest. I was a little more reserved. I didn't want to answer questions regarding how we got them or have anybody ask to use mine when I was done with it like I had done 10 years earlier. I was a little selfish in that I did not want to reciprocate with the whole backstage pass or info-giving favors. I kept my experiences sort of private for the most part because that's what made them special. I also was not doing any of this just as a notch in my belt. I did not want anyone learning from my mistakes because I was on a mission. I used the information that I got from everyone but kept my information to myself. I was grateful that everyone was not as selfish as I was.

Passes freshly pasted on our shirts, the lights dimmed. It was hard to concentrate now on the concert knowing we had passes. It was very strange not having to connive some kind of plan to get backstage . . . not only did we have permission, we were invited. This was new to us for sure.

When Busta finished their set, we were going to attempt to use our Sierra passes to get backstage for Busta. We walked as if we knew what we were doing and nobody stopped us. We kept waiting for the other shoe to drop every time we passed a security guard. I was sweating by the time we finally went into this big room where people were just hanging out. I saw Noah's wife sitting in the corner and felt like saying "Remember me, bitch? You wouldn't take my picture back to your husband to get signed." But I refrained.

After what seemed like an hour, he walked in. I couldn't believe it. Ten years later and I am getting to see him close up again. Forgetting for a second that he puts his pants on one leg at a time as well, nervous, I just stood there with April waiting. He talked to a few people and we were trying to be casual and wait until he was done. We were so casual we didn't look like we were waiting for him at all. I had my back to him because I was that cool, then April said, "He just left."

"What do you mean he just left?" His wife was still here, he had to come back, didn't he? My heart racing, we waited and waited, and then my heart sank as I watched his wife leave and take any hope I had with her. All I could think was, *Oh no, this did not just happen.* Sheepishly picking up our bags, we went back out to watch Sierra. Now it almost seemed like we couldn't concentrate because we were wallowing in our own stupidity. The show had already started by the time we got back to our seats and they were awesome . . . again. It didn't seem like there was much left of the show by the time we got ourselves back out there.

After their show we looked at each other with less enthusiasm than the first attempt and decided to go backstage. The lead singer was swarmed with fans but spotted us right away and came over. He said hello and immediately invited us back to the hotel to hang out. As if we were doing him a favor we said, "sure," then wondered what exactly we were doing. Oh boy, now what? The plan was to stay together at all times and make the most of the experience without compromising our morals. We got to meet the rest of the band and we took a liking to "Bucket." He was their guitarist and seemed very down to earth. We spent most of the time talking to him. April and I had already pegged the lead singer as a slime, but we were going to hang out anyway. We found out what hotel they were at and decided to head over while they were finishing their backstage shenanigans. In our minds we figured they were in the same hotel as Busta so maybe we could have another shot at running into Noah. We hung out in the hotel bar and before you knew it the whole band showed up. Bucket came over to talk with us immediately. The lead singer had a handler with him and his job was clearly to make sure Mr. Lead Singer had something to stick that night. He wasn't even discrete about it. We were, to say the least, a little turned off.

A few people were going to a local bar and Bucket asked us to join them. Without hesitation we got up and grabbed our things and were not even missed by Mr. Lead Singer. Bucket was more our speed. We wound up just having a few laughs and taking some pictures in the bar. He then took us over to the tour bus and let us in. He was a complete gentlemen the entire night. He was married and had a grown son. I realize that doesn't necessarily deter them from . . . anything . . . but I would like to think there are a couple out there that do not fit the stereotype. We looked around, and it was so cool but I was too embarrassed to ask if I could take pictures. I'm sure he would have let me but I didn't want to seem too star struck. I wasn't even star struck, it was more about capturing the experience. After five minutes with these guys, you forget they fill arenas and it's just like hanging out with a regular guy. April had a resume with her and gave it to him, since she was, at the time, trying to get into the music business having just graduated from college. He was an absolute gentleman and we told him we had to leave because we both had work in the morning and a long ride home. Without hesitation he got up and shook our hands and with his adorable British accent said, "It was a pleasure meeting you ladies and thank you so much for coming to our show this evening." How lucky were we? We said goodnight and rehashed the whole experience the entire ride home.

With Busta now touring, news was breaking that Satire was going to be touring. I was starting to feel like a kid in a candy store. I went from having Noah taken away from me completely to two of his bands touring at the same time. Hmm, how would this work though? Satire was going to tour without Noah because he was touring with Busta first. I was fine with that because at least we were able to see him in some capacity.

April and I were fitting in our concerts in addition to dating our boyfriends. I ended up dating Bar Back Boy and April was dating a waiter that we worked with. We made a pact that we would continue to be our own person, continue to go to our shows, and not let these guys change who we were. Bar Back Boy gave me a lot of freedom yet was very attentive. In retrospect, I guess he knew how to play the game. He wanted me but held back and let me do my thing. His plan worked because eventually April and I started to bring the boys with us. The boys became friends, which worked out for April and I because we could continue to scream and go nuts at the shows and they could hang out together. Satire had to replace Noah since he was touring with Busta and they also released a new album before their tour with the new guy, Miles Baker. Poor bastard, Noah fans are not going to be happy. I read some reviews in the papers and this guy was supposed to be a great replacement but the fans gave him a hard time because he was not Noah. April and I opted not to see them without Noah.

When life started to get in the way, we started spending more time with our boyfriends and going to less shows. We would still go together on occasion, but it was starting to change. April's boyfriend was the jealous type and didn't control it, and I can remember experiencing an incident going home one night after a show. Bar Back Boy and I were pretending to be asleep in the back of the car while they were in the front arguing. He was accusing April and I of having slept with Noah Anderson. She kept telling him he was crazy and he kept insisting that he knew what went on backstage. He knew we had gone backstage a couple of times and apparently there are just wild sex parties backstage. After listening to this idiotic conversation the whole way back from Jones Beach, I could feel my face starting to burn, and I guess Bar Back Boy was just as surprised as I was when I finally sat up and said, "Do you really think that I would have had sex with Noah Anderson and not had a t-shirt made up or a billboard?" Putting his hands over his face as if I had now just opened up a can of worms, Bar Back Boy rested his head backwards, preparing for an even longer ride home. After all the years of going to shows, meeting people, trying to just get one decent picture with Noah, I'll be damned if I am going to be accused of being a slut and not be able to reap the benefits. To date, the only person I had ever slept with was Bar Back Boy and I was in my twenties. Irish Catholic Guilt. A very silent rest of the ride home after those words of wisdom, I knew this was the beginning of the proverbial end of our socializing together.

Clearly, after that, we started to drift apart as a foursome. April and I were still close but the four of us were getting a little strained. April and Waiter Boy argued all the time and it was draining. I knew things were really changing when we all went to see Busta and Sierra and April and Waiter Boy left before the show was over. We had brought our passes from the previous show which was part of our routine because we were going to change the dates on them and try to get back again. She gave me her pass before she left and Bar Back Boy and I wound up going backstage. It wasn't the same. My partner in crime wasn't with me, and it was just a different feel. She had come full circle and was now the girl giving the pass to someone else that needed it because she was done. All good things must come to an end and with that, Busta had stopped touring, we were hanging out with our boyfriends more than each other, and the concerts were becoming non-existent.

Chapter 3

August of 1991, Bar Back Boy and I became engaged. We planned the wedding for September 13, 1992. I had actually told myself that if I get married, Noah is now no longer on the back burner. As ridiculous as that sounds, you have to realize that either Noah and/or Satire played a huge part in my development. I am primarily the person I am today because of my obsession or interest in Satire.

I can remember the first time I ever saw Noah Anderson like it was yesterday. I was in the seventh grade and I had no idea what I liked in terms of music. There were no boys in school that appealed to me in the least. When you don't find any of the boys attractive in school you begin to think there is something wrong with you. I felt like I had no interest and no direction. It was a Saturday night and Sean was watching Don Kirshner's Rock Concert when I walked into the room. Satire was on singing Meet Me at the Dock. That video was from 1977, so the outfits on these guys were not masculine to say the least. Up until this point, I was listening to whatever was on WNBC am radio. I had no other guide so that station came in clear. Noah wore a white jumpsuit, a scarf around his neck, and had long blonde hair.

As soon as I walked in the room and laid eyes on him, I knew this was going to be a defining moment in my life. I immediately showed an interest in him and, taking a deep breath, turned to Sean and asked, "Is that a boy or a girl?" This may sound ridiculous, but it was at this moment that my sexual preference was about to be determined.

He said, "A boy, that's Noah Anderson," as if I should know who that is. A sigh of relief and sensation of excitement and all I kept thinking was, *Thank God!* It was either going to be years of therapy ahead for me, or what turned out to be years of going to concerts. I finally felt like I had some kind of direction. Now I knew what type of music I liked. I didn't feel like a freak because I finally found a guy that I was attracted to. It didn't matter that he wasn't real because that just meant that everyone else was ugly (maybe therapy is still in the cards for me).

Immediately I started asking Sean questions about him. I wanted to know everything. Sean showed me all of the albums he had by them and, apparently, he did not have all of them. I had to know more. I ran to the candy store the next day, tore through the teen magazines, and pulled all of the magazines off of the shelf that had Satire and Noah Anderson on the covers. I started taking guitar lessons and doing a lot of drawing and writing poetry. It was as if a door had been opened for a creative outlet. It was at that time that I was really starting to find myself. I fancied myself an authority on all things Satire. I had a full time hobby.

Now that I was going to be getting married, what was going to happen to this creative, music loving person? I never got my better picture with Noah and also questioned if an affair with a rock star counts if you're married. This kind of psychotic thinking is not really a problem because I was not the type of chick who was literally stalking these guys. It was harmless fantasizing because I still went about the rest of my life. Sure, I imagined what it would be like to be Mrs. Noah Anderson, but why should that be any different than the girl who pictures her wedding day and a dude riding in on some equine? Shouldn't you be able to sleep with your celebrity dream without it counting as cheating? I think so. Let's face it; I had more time, money and emotion invested in my fake Noah relationship than I did in this new one. I knew nothing else for the last twelve years other than Satire being a very active hobby in my life, and now I have to change things?

I figured I would give this marriage thing a whirl, seeing as how I was twenty three and old. If I don't hop on this marriage thing, I don't know if there will ever be another offer down the road from anyone else. Probably not the best way to make an educated, informed decision that was going to affect the rest of my life, but I went with it anyway.

The yearlong engagement proved to be enlightening. While we were dating, Bar Back Boy proved to be very attentive. From the beginning whenever he took me on a date we always did fun things. He always seemed like he was trying to at least find different things to do all of the time and we were never really into a routine. Some of the things we did were going to the movies, taking a day trip to Atlantic City or Point Pleasant, going to county fairs, long drives to nowhere, dinner, miniature golf, you get the picture. It also didn't matter where I went because I was happy just to be with him. Once I let my guard down, we laughed a lot and had fun. While we were dating, he had a full time job and worked at the bar Thursday, Friday, and Saturday nights. Since April and I went out every weekend to the bar, it was great. I could see him without having him hanging on me all night, still hang out with my girlfriend, and have the freedom to hang out in the club. Every night he would have the rose girl bring me a rose. The rose girl's sole job was to walk around carrying roses and sell them to anybody looking to get lucky, be romantic, or beg for forgiveness.

After he was finished with his shift, we would go out to a diner, then maybe hang out at the beach. We had a lot of fun and got along great. There was nothing he wouldn't do for me. Everyone would always comment on how romantic he was and how much he loved me. It was nice to hear from other people too, especially people who hung out with him when I wasn't around. It had me confident that it wasn't just an act. In addition to his two full time jobs, he also had a side job. He was a juice and soda distributor. He didn't have a lot of accounts so it never really interfered with anything we did. If he got a service call that required him to go down to the shore, we would both go and then make a night of it.

Before we got engaged, his smart mouth got him into trouble at the bar and, thinking he would never get fired, he lost that job. Because he was doing it for fun rather than the money, he didn't seem to care. It put a little damper on the weekends for April and I now because we couldn't go back to the bar, so this changed some things. He had his weekend nights free, so he and I were hanging out more and April and I no longer hung out on the weekends. To backtrack a little, he lost his job while April and I were on our month long cross-country trip. We had planned this trip from high school, so boyfriends or no boyfriends, we were going. While we were away, our boyfriends spent a lot of time together. Turns out they weren't too thrilled with each other. I guess too much closeness without the girls around left them to really get to know each other so by the time we came home, they had a falling out. She and I had a great time on our trip but now that we were home, we separated into two couples. Bar Back Boy told me a few things that were said while we were gone and I sort of unloaded on April about her boyfriend. April and I swore we would always remain close, but there was no love lost between me, her boyfriend, her, and my boyfriend.

****

About two weeks after my and April's cross-country return is when Bar Back Boy and I got engaged. Unfortunately, April and I were not spending any time together anymore. We allowed to happen all the things we swore never would happen. Now that Bar Back Boy had his weekend nights free, he picked up some more accounts with his juice business. With him spending more time in bars, he was starting to drink a little more than usual. Trying to make arrangements for the wedding was a little unnerving since I felt like I was preparing an event to last a lifetime for two people, but I was doing it alone. As time goes on you start to see other sides of people. I guess the signs were always there, but I chose to ignore them.

About six months before our wedding, Bar Back Boy lost his full time job. That too was due to his obnoxious attitude and lack of respect for anyone else. He was not the least bit concerned because now he was going to do what he really wanted to do anyway — be his own boss. He easily picked up a lot more bar accounts and was making money hand over fist. I was starting to feel like I was taking a back seat to everyone that had his pager number. One problem with this job was that the service he offered was a 24 hours, 7 days a week. He was one person. He carried a pager that went off so often that if I didn't know better I would swear he was carrying a vibrator with him. I got to a point that I said, "You have to be fucking kidding me." I was concerned he would be answering it as we were saying our vows, or worse yet, on our honeymoon. He was clearly more interested in "servicing" every bar in New Jersey rather than me. He really had done a 180 from the time since I met him. What bothered me most was that it didn't bother him that we were constantly interrupted with his calls.

The Piper that first met Bar Back Boy never would have stood for this. Those walls that were up were there for good reason. It shows great work ethic that he took care of his clients like he did, but by being so focused on the money that was rolling in, he was losing focus of the big picture.

I contemplated canceling the wedding but, thinking logically as usual, I figured it was too close to the date and worried how I would I explain this to people. Thinking as a true twenty-three-year-old I told myself, *ah, he'll change.* Well, he changed alright. I started having trust issues as soon as we got married. There were too many instances of very late nights and I know his turnaround time with a page because I would be waiting in the wings while he returned calls to everyone else. Most nights my pages were not answered.

I got pregnant with our first son Bailey two weeks after we got married. I was twenty four. I got pregnant with my second child on Bailey's first birthday. I was twenty six. Three months into my pregnancy, after one of many, many fights while he was walking out the door to work, I held my stomach in pain and ran into the bathroom. I had started bleeding and went down to tell him. "Call the doctor. I'll be at work". It was a holiday weekend so the doctor had to be paged and my husband had a lot of bars to stock for Labor Day weekend. The doctor called back immediately and as I lay on the couch with my feet up as the doctor instructed and bleeding, my husband left for work and said, "I'll see you later." Without having to even ask, my oldest friend drove in from New Jersey to stay with me. We knew what this meant, and someone had to care for my one-year-old son.

Part of the problem with getting married when you are young, before you have really discovered who you are, is that when your self-esteem starts to take a hit. You don't have the maturity or life experience to make the right decisions. For me, once I had a child, everything changed, as it is supposed to. Your life is no longer your own. Everything you do affects someone else. Had I been a little older when I had gotten married, I may have handled things differently, but then again, had I been a little older I probably would not have been in this situation. Instead of telling myself that the best thing for my son would be for me to leave this marriage, the young bride told herself, I don't want to be a single mother. Seven months later, I became pregnant with my second son, Quinn. I was twenty-seven when I gave birth to him. It had been a tumultuous four years. Basically, seven nights a week he was in bars "working." The summers were the busiest season and now we had our Jersey Shore bars to consume all of our time. Funny how when I page him

I don't get a phone call back but if anyone else paged him, Smart would have his shoe up at his ear returning calls within seconds. Some nights he didn't get home until five in the morning, even though the bars closed at two. He had us living beyond our means, I was caring for two babies by myself, and I was growing very bitter and resentful.

Mornings I would wake up when my sons would stir and sometimes my husband would be in the shower and there was really no way for me to know if he had just gotten up or just come in. Either way, he left for work as soon as he came out. I knew what he was doing but had no physical evidence to prove it. Out of sight, out of mind. Denial. Mentally I was breaking down, yet I had to keep up a front for everyone else because I did not want to have to answer any questions. I was managing to close myself off from everyone. Although I would have loved any company, I couldn't really keep in touch with anyone because if they came over, they would know he wasn't there. In essence, in order to protect myself from the pain of discussing my reality with anyone and getting help, it was also helping to cover for him so that he was able to continue this charade and never have to answer to anyone. The whole marriage was like a scab that you just keep picking and picking and it hurts and you don't realize how much damage has been done till you rip the whole thing off and see what is underneath. It was getting to that point. Someone needed to rip it off. I spent more time alone so that no one knew that I actually was alone. I was too embarrassed to let anyone know that he was never home. He was very irresponsible and that careless behavior is what inevitably led to the end.

****

About a year before my husband's late nights really took a toll on us, his work truck was stolen out of our driveway. Surprisingly, I heard my husband on the phone with someone who saw it dumped on their corner, so we got it back later that day. I hopped in the car with him and we took a ride over to where it was dumped, only a few blocks from our house. Since my husband had bad credit, everything we owned was in my name, his truck included. When he got the truck back, the only damage that it seemed to have was a busted steering column. Since my husband was always looking for

29

a short cut and rarely did the right thing, he never got it fixed. He continued to use a screwdriver to start it each day.

Our relationship had declined to an uncomfortable point. The times that he was actually home we would strictly pass one another without speaking, and one of us was inevitably leaving the house at the time. After about a week of not talking at all, my world came crashing down. To assume something and to have to actually face facts are two completely different things. For quite a long time we were passing each other in the house, not speaking. I tried to call his bluff. I told him one night when he strolled in at three in the morning, "I know you're cheating on me and I'm telling you now to just stop."

He said, "I'm not cheating on you."

I said, "I'm not asking you, I know you are and I'm just saying, stop everything now."

He insisted he was not. I was hoping that what appeared to be my overwhelming knowledge of his comings and goings would curtail his reprehensible behavior. I guess the equivalent of me thinking that if I already have one child with this loser, what difference does it make how many more come after that is him thinking, *well if I have been cheating for a year already, why bother stopping now?*

On Sunday, May 26, 1997—seven years to the day that I met him—there was a knock on the door from the New York City police department. They asked me if I had a blue van. Heart racing a bit I said yes. The reason they asked for me when I opened the door was because the van was registered to me. "Very well, you have to call the New Jersey State Police," and they gave me their number. Almost in a daze, I took the number from the officer, trying to process what I knew was going to be a very bad phone call.

All I could think was that he was drunk and either killed himself or someone else. Either way, after I make this phone call, my life was going to change. Still in somewhat of a protective mode, I called the state police and they asked me the same question. "Yes, I have a blue van."

They said, "Do you know where it is?"

"My husband has it."

"Is there anything wrong with the inside of the car?"

"Yes, it had been stolen and they busted the steering column, but we never got it fixed."

With a sigh of relief the officer said, "Oh, okay. Because we just found it in a hotel parking lot and the interior light was on, we thought it was getting broken into."

Trying to remain unaffected as my hand shook holding the phone to my ear I said, "Oh really? What hotel?"

"The Mirage, on First and Ninth."

"Oh, okay. Thank you."

I don't know how I did it, but a switch flipped in my head. I got up, walked right over to the diaper bag, went to the fridge and filled it with bottles of milk, picked up the pace a bit and grabbed diapers, wipes (I don't know where I thought I was going), and a camera. Feeling more protective of my children than ever, I ran upstairs without turning on any lights other than leaving the already glowing television light, and scooped my one- and three-year-olds out of their cribs and went on a road trip.

I don't recall driving there, but when I arrived I found my car, interior light on just like the officer had said. I thought about smashing the windows, but that was somehow going to cost me money, so I thought better of that. Pacing back and forth I pondered, *what to do, what to do.* I was in a very precarious situation. I had two babies that I had to shield from what was going on but I could not leave them unattended in the car.

I peered over at the hotel and noticed all the hotel doors were inside. I couldn't leave the kids in the car and I so badly needed to catch him for my own sanity. The car was not going to be enough proof for me. This is where it was going to end. He could somehow talk his way out of that. I needed hard core evidence. Inspired, I got back into my car and drove around to the front desk. I pulled the car right in front of the door so that the kids were in front of me. Having experienced signing in at a hotel with Casanova when we were dating, I took a chance and figured he used his friend's name.

"Is Kevin Hunt here?" With one swift hand gesture and a warm smile the desk clerk held the card out for me. Sure enough, he was under his best friend's name. Not considering what kind of trouble that might cause between him and his wife, I saw the room number on the card and walked out, and then realized I still couldn't get in. I knew any move I made was with my children in the back of my mind, at the same time I wasn't really processing that they were actually with me. It was almost like I was mechanically responding to everything. The mind is an amazing thing. Somehow, I did everything I had to do and needed to do without emotion. I went back to the desk with my camera in hand. Now Desk Boy had lost the warm inviting expression and was looking nervous. I said, "Call his room and tell him his car is getting broken into now!"

You would have thought I had a gun on him. He never took his eyes off me while he picked up his phone and made the call. While he did that, I got back in the car and drove back by his car. The next thirty seconds that I waited for him to come out was spent looking in my rearview mirror, watching for him, still not knowing what I was going to do. His image appeared in my mirror and my shell shocked feeling left me. For a split second there was that feeling of familiarity, the warmth and comfort of seeing someone and knowing he was yours, but then immediately his image was of a complete stranger who had just turned mine and my children's lives upside down.

I got out of the car as he walked towards his car. His bustling gait took two hesitant steps and his face went white. It was at that very moment I knew that he was feeling exactly how I felt one hour earlier when I heard a complete stranger express a sigh of relief that my husband was in a hotel with another woman and not the victim of a crime. I started to beat him about the head and chest, forgetting for the first time that night about my children. My older son was awake and watching.

For the first time in four years, back in control I said, "Watch the kids." I needed to see her because he could still talk his way out of this. I went into the hotel, but as I was about to run up the stairs, I stopped short. There she was; a twenty-one-year-old skank sitting in the stairwell of the hotel. She looked right at me and I knew at that moment she knew exactly who I was. At that moment she was insignificant to me. What I need was to get to the room. When I opened the door, the first thing I spotted was Chinese food, but I still needed the proof. I looked in the garbage can and that's all I needed to see.

Confident for the first time in four years that I finally had exactly what I needed to end this charade with a clear conscience, I went back down and told him to get a good look at his, my kids because he was never going to see them again. I don't know what irritated me more, the fact that he had cheated on me or the fact that he bought her Chinese food, and we were sitting at home with no milk because he left me with no money. He was pissing all of our money away and staying out every night, claiming he was working to make money that he also claimed I wanted. I never wanted the money; I only wanted him to be home with us. He was always consumed with money and being the Joneses. I could care less.

I climbed back in the car and never looked back. I drove straight to Sean's and he and Jane came to my house to physically remove him. Figuring he would have gotten the hint when I left him at the hotel, I was not expecting him to come home. I brought Sean just in case he did. When we got there, he was sitting in the living room watching television as if this was a normal night. I walked in and said, "Get out." I could not believe he had the gall to come here.

He said, "I want to talk". After reminding him that the time to talk was months ago when I was trying to and he was ignoring me, Sean stepped in and told him he needed to leave. All he cared about was getting his checkbook. I said, "Take it, it's all you ever cared about anyway." I had to face the reality in order to deal with it. I had a new reality to deal with now. He took the checkbook, left me $30,000 in debt and $5,000 in monthly bills. I was giving pony rides twice a week for $5 an hour.

Always the conniver, he decided that since he was not living in the house, he didn't need to pay any bills. During our marriage, I had worked up to four weeks before giving to birth to both of my children, carried the health insurance for the family, and had only stopped working when my youngest was six months old because I lost my job. I was in a position I swore I would never allow myself to be in: asking for money from my husband. I felt like Lucy getting her allowance from Ricky.

Luckily for me, he decided to walk away from all of us and the visitation was short-lived. There were no Norman Rockwell shared holidays or alternate weekend situations.
I found myself at twenty eight years old with no money, no job, in debt, and a single mother of a one- and three-year-old. What the hell was I going to do? This was a far cry from the jet-setting rock star life I had envisioned. He was living the rock star life, but me, not so much.

****

I am very fortunate to have two incredible brothers. Both are very different, but also very caring always looking out for me. Devon and I were close, but since he was away at school most of my youth, I spent more time with Sean. Once Devon opened up his Veterinary practice in 1998, I was grateful that he gave me the opportunity to work for him.

I learned a lot about him as a person and a professional. He was always a very private person but now circumstances were such that he had to let me in, and we had to help each other. I had to learn quickly because he held himself to a certain standard and expected that same perfection from his staff and pretty much anybody he came in contact with. Having little experience in the medical field, coupled with a lot of stress from my pending divorce, my day to day existence with my brother was less than desirable. What made it worse was that he was tougher on me because I was his sister. That was a little tough to deal with since I would get in trouble for things that other people were doing or not doing every day. I'm always up for a challenge but this was ridiculous.

I had not been to many concerts in the last four and a half years. My husband had come with me to one Satire concert and I saw

April and Waiter Boy there. It was strange since she and I used to go together and now I was bumping into her there, not even realizing that she was planning on going. One reason that I went was because Noah was back in the band. It had been a few years and I know I had been out of the loop, but Bobby either looked very different or he had been replaced. With closer examination I realized it was not the regular bass player. His replacement looks like that guy who replaced Noah, that Miles guy. Maybe he's not such a bad guy if they brought him back while Noah was in the band. I didn't really pay too much attention to him or give it much thought because I was, of course, watching Noah. I believe we attended that concert during the first year of our marriage.

The next time I can remember going to see Satire was after I was separated from my husband and this time it was just me and April. It was like old times again. We had a great time and all I can remember thinking is that I still don't like that Miles guy—just because. It's the principle. It was nice to get out to a couple of concerts again, even if they were few and far between.

Slowly, once I divorced the excess 180 pounds that had been dragging me down, I started going back to concerts. There was a whole new dynamic now though. April didn't always go with me, in fact, I don't think we ever went to another concert together again once she got married. Yes, she did marry Waiter Boy.

Satire was touring full force again, and I had to try to find someone to go with me each time or I couldn't go. At least that was my compartmentalized way of thinking then.
I went to the Garden State Arts Center with my friend Donna. Donna and I met through our children at school. She has two gorgeous daughters that were best friends with my sons. When I purchased the tickets, I was limited with options as far as seating went and I always sit on the right so I could be in front of Noah. When we got there I said to her, "Now we have to sit on that jerk's side again." I knew nothing about the man, I just didn't want to know him or like him. But when it came time for the one song he sang, he was very funny and engaging, and I found myself laughing when he was talking. *Nope, not going to do it, he's a jerk,* I told myself. I found myself having the same argument in my head that I had some seven years earlier when I was not going to give my ex-

husband my phone number. I convinced myself that Miles had a good moment and that was it. He started to sing and I leaned over to Donna and said, "This is actually a good song." With my arms folded, as if I was doing someone a favor, I sat watching as he shook his ass all over the stage, ran through the audience, and got everyone pumped up. I turned to Donna and said, "He's such a jerk."

In my mind, getting to go out and socialize was not really an option. Having no money and two small children, I just didn't think I deserved to go out when I couldn't even pay my bills. Since I was now working for my brother, I focused on my children and taking care of them and just trying to get through each day. Luckily, when I would go to work my father would come watch the boys. It really worked out well for the boys since they loved their grandpa so much and he loved being with them. Everything was a struggle, but in some strange way it was still so much easier than having to wonder whether or not my husband was going to be home to help me. Knowing I was on my own made it easier in some way. I didn't have to rely on anyone other than myself. Bailey was in second grade and baby Quinn was in kindergarten. Luckily, my life had some semblance of stability as it was about to suffer the next blow. They say what doesn't kill you makes you stronger . . . right?

Chapter 4

On November 11, 2000, my dad turned eighty. We all went to Sean and Jane's for his birthday. We kept it pretty low key; it was just a chance to try to get everyone together. The boys love climbing all over their uncles and seeing nanny and grandpa is just like being with another set of parents. Devon seemed to struggle with the family togetherness a bit. He was always on time but also ready to make a break for it as soon as he could grab an opportunity. The night went without incident, which should have been an omen. Unfortunately, that was the last time we all got together for a happy occasion. About a week or two later everyone got together at my house for Thanksgiving, except for Devon, of course. He flew off to some foreign country and never gave us any contact info like he was some spy on a mission. This was not unusual behavior for him but just a bit annoying because, although it doesn't bother me all that much, my mother would sort of like to know if her children are in the country in case she should die. I don't know if that is an Irish thing, an elderly thing, or just a psychotic thing, but never the less, it makes a problem for me in the long run. Controlled chaos is another name for a holiday at my house. My cousins come over and there are children running all over, video remotes getting thrown around, and the faint sounds of a football game in the background.

As I'm trying to make some room in the kitchen for the dessert dishes to start coming in, Sean came in and said, "I think Dad had too much to drink, he's starting to slur his words." Being Irish and it being a holiday, of course he's been drinking but I never knew him to slur his words no matter how much he had to drink. I went in to take a look at him and he looked terrible. He was disoriented and drooling. I said, "Call an ambulance."
Turns out it was not the iron liver failing him, but the mini stroke he was having. By the time Sean had hung up with 911, his episode had passed. The kids resumed playing after dessert and had never realized the situation, and the adults were still drinking and laughing around the table. I corralled the kids upstairs as I heard the siren from the ambulance. After getting him checked out, it was determined that he should at least go to the hospital even though he seemed to have recovered.

Unfortunately, after they examined him thoroughly and ran the necessary tests, it was determined that surgery was necessary. One carotid artery was 100% blocked and the other was 90%. There were no options, unless you consider death via stroke an option. We were informed he could suffer a massive stroke during the surgery, but if we didn't do the surgery, a stroke was assured. Obviously we were nervous but had faith, knew we had to do the surgery, and hoped that his athletic history would carry him through. We were also warned that if he came through the surgery that the following twenty-four hours were critical. He came through the surgery fine, but seventeen hours after the surgery, he suffered a massive stroke. It left him paralyzed on his left side and in need of months of physical therapy.

I went in to see him in ICU and for the first time I saw my dad, the man who cared for me all of my life and now cared for my children, flat out and helpless. Not knowing how I would react, or how my reaction might affect him, I slowly walked up to the right side of his bed. He was staring blankly at the ceiling. Holding back my tears I touched his arm. "Hi Dad."

Without hesitation he responded, "Piper," then turned to look at me. At this point, all he could do was turn his head. I watched a tear flow down to the pillow and in a very low, hoarse voice he said, "I'm very lucky." Even if he was, at that very moment I couldn't even come up with a reason how. Then teaching another lesson he said, "At least I'm alive." What do you say to that? To some, that situation is not considered being alive, but I knew that it was his attitude that had gotten him through his entire life. When he asked, "What exercises do I need to do to fix this," I realized where I get my drive from.

Word had spread quickly of what had happened to him and a line of visitors started to form outside of the ICU door, which is unheard of. My dad was not only what you might call a local hero but also a well-known athlete, so he had many wonderful friends. This all really started to hit home when I saw our priest walk in to see him. My father's faith was very important to him but for me, being Catholic was only a childhood reminder of being pulled out of my friend's house or pool and being dragged to church kicking and screaming every Sunday, then getting the hairy eye from my father as Sean and I goofed around. As soon as he saw Fr. McCarthy, he became so emotional and started sobbing. The Father sat and talked with him for a while, and my dad cried the whole time. Apparently it is not unusual for the patient to be so emotional after a stroke or heart attack, but it was a big adjustment for all of us.

How does this work now? He had speech therapists come in to check if he could swallow properly. How does he go to the bathroom, how will he do anything? With visiting hours limited, we now had to leave but felt terrible leaving him. I told a nurse before we left, "he has to go to the bathroom." My father, who took care of everyone else, was now helpless.

"We'll take care of it sweetheart. Just go home and get some rest." As I walked out of the unit I took one last look over my shoulder and saw an orderly scoop my once strapping father up like an infant and carry him into the bathroom. Overnight my father went from what looked like an ageless, energetic man to an old, helpless one. Just like that. In the blink of an eye. Mentally I knew he was eighty years old but he was "Dad." He is not your typical eighty-year-old. Eighty-year-olds are old. When you take a step back and see people taking care of your parents, they now look old. Literally overnight, we switched roles. I was now going to be taking care of the man who was taking care of me up until yesterday.

We had no idea what we were going to do. This was when the family dynamic changed as well. My oldest brother Devon, who was already very withdrawn and private to begin with, was fading even more. Now it was going to be up to Sean and I to work through this. After five months in a nursing home, Dad finally came home. We had a 24/7 live-in for him. In the time that he was in the nursing home getting therapy, I basically wore myself down to a nub. My boys had no schedule, no routine; they would sleep on the floor at my parents' house while I ran between work, the nursing home, and Mom. They were up till all hours of the night, and it was very stressful.

I threw myself into caring for my father and helping my mother in addition to raising my two sons. As tiring as this situation was, it gave me the perfect reason to give up on men. I had no time to entertain the idea of a date nor did I really want to, and all I needed was an excuse. I was literally running all the time. To say I gave up on men was an understatement. I hated them. I felt that they were all cheaters and the ones that haven't cheated just haven't found anyone worth cheating with. I was bitter, jaded, and resentful. I blamed my ex-husband for everything. I could always manage to make it all go back to him.

****

The stress of being a constant caregiver to everyone, going back and forth to court for my divorce, working, and taking care of the boys took its toll. I had gone into Manhattan and started therapy with my husband when he first left, but he quit after about three sessions because he said that the therapist was an asshole and I was sleeping with him. I felt like saying, *believe me sweetie, you have ruined me. I don't want to have sex with anybody.* I continued with the therapy because I could not stand feeling the way I did all of the time. For years, I declined medication because to me that would certainly be the final straw. In my mind, I would have to admit that I was insane. I figured I could do this without medication because medication would only mask the real issues and I would feel like a complete failure because I couldn't handle my problems without drugs. Turns out, I couldn't. I had to finally admit defeat. I broke down, agreed with my therapist, and got them. What I did not realize as I continued my life of hell was that the medication was "notorious for weight gain." A little something a certain therapist failed to tell me. I think he just couldn't take me anymore and figured if I don't get on something he would have to.

Although now mentally I felt great, I was thirty pounds heavier and strictly caring for my parents, working, and caring for my children. In my mind, the way I looked didn't matter because I resigned to the fact that this was my life now. As long as everyone was being taken care of and was happy, that's all that mattered. My mother got very used to having me there all the time and loved it. She started to grow very dependent on me. She wouldn't let anyone do anything for her accept me, and if on some rare occasion someone else had to help her, she was not happy. Since I would never really go anywhere, it started to get to the point that Mom would start calling Sean to see if he knew where I was if I went to the grocery store for too long. Sometimes I would bump into a friend in the store and we would start to talk, and before you knew it—bam—panic stricken messages left for me on my phone. Of course these trips to the store were at about 11:00 p.m. because that was the only time I was able to get out. I had to wait until almost everyone was sleeping, or at least that the boys were worn out enough so that they wouldn't be running around the house making Mom crazier while I was gone.

****

In the summer of 2001, needing to get away before I had a breakdown, I took the boys and we got in the car and drove cross-country. Of course Satire was going to be playing in California while we were there so I figured, why not? I would now have my boys experience the music I grew up with. The purpose of the trip was strictly to get away from everything and spend some much needed quality time together. The concert, in my mind, was just a bonus. Satire was performing at a fair so there were other things to do besides just see a show. Since the boys were still a little young, I didn't want to shove a concert down their throats and not let them feed a damn pig too, if that's what they wanted to do. Luckily, they enjoyed the show but my younger son, the rebel, took an interest in the new guy. I said, "No, Mommy likes Noah Anderson, remember?"

He said, "No, I like Miles, he's cool." I was thinking to myself, *you have to got to be kidding me. Why him?* After the show, people were waiting by the fence right by their bus. Everybody was waiting for Noah to come out. My kids got excited because the one to come out to greet the fans was Miles. I said, "That figures."

He was very nice and talked to everyone. He took pictures with my sons and signed autographs. Management kept yelling at him that they needed to leave. Not rattled at all, he kept signing and said, "Okay." He slowly walked back as he continued to sign. There was more screaming from behind the fence. "Miles, NOW—we are leaving."

"Okay," as he continued to chat and sign. He did not get on that bus until he signed everyone's things. I was actually impressed and did take a couple of pictures of him. I did not want to admit that I was pissed Noah never came out.

Still hating Miles, for no reason, I filed in the back of my mind that he was the only one to come out, and he didn't get on that bus until he satisfied all of his fans. Before the show that evening, my kids were asking people, just as April and I had done some twenty years earlier, for their backstage passes. Both of my children got passes, I was so proud. It was too late though. Miles had come out and then they left.

Chapter 5

About a month after we returned home from our California trip, Satire was going to be playing at King's Dominion in Virginia. Since the kids seemed to do so well the last time at the show I decided to keep it a secret from everyone and I threw the kids in the car and we went on a road trip. The only hiccup was that it was a Sunday and my kids had school the next day. I couldn't have anybody saying I was irresponsible and let my sons miss school for a concert. So, they both understood we would do this but they had to sleep in the car on the way home and go to school in the morning. They agreed.

We set off for our eight hour drive. The only reason we were going to do this was because my kids had the two backstage passes from the last show that I was planning to change the date on. We got to the show just before Satire was to take the stage. Talk about cutting it close. The kids were a little annoyed this time because the concert was at an amusement park and there was not going to be any time for them to hit any rides. Since we got there as the show was going to start and it finished when the park closed, they were screwed. We watched the show and had a great time. I of course only saw Noah on stage. After the show, we made our way over to the back stage door. Since we only had two passes, I carried my little guy and told him to make believe he was sleeping. What I never anticipated was that twenty years later, things are done differently. There was only one other person in front of us with a pass and Satire's manager had a list of pass holders names that, low and behold, we did not show up on. He was a real Nazi too.

"Where did you get the passes from?"

Oh crap!

"A friend that works at a radio station gave them to us."

"Well you're not on the list," and he made a face like we were lying! Can you imagine? Lying, huh? Like we were common criminals, he said, "Come over and wait right here!" There was a state trooper standing and watching us. I guess I seemed like a threat, with the two kids and all. How would the band ever escape my clutches?

Quinn was getting pretty heavy. Since it was an outdoor concert there were a couple of trailers set up as dressing rooms and the infamous "back stage" area was a dirt clearing behind a ferris wheel. A far cry from what I remember envying at the age of twelve. He went in and got Dave and Snake, one of the guitarists and the lead singer. I guess that was an attempt at satisfying us. Noah came out but was talking to the only person that was actually supposed to be there. I kept peering over at Noah to see if he would sneak back in or if he was going to come over. The drummer came out and my boys got to take pictures with him and everybody else.

I peered over again and saw the guest walk away and Noah start to make his way over to us. With my heart racing all I could think was finally, after twenty years, I am going to get my picture. I was no longer going to have to look at that disgusting picture anymore. There of course was going to be an issue now with the new picture. I was now fat and I was not pleased. As Noah made his way over, he was smiling and my heart was racing. He was very nice and talked to us for a couple of minutes. Twenty years and I finally get to meet him as an adult, and out of the corner of my eye, I spotted Miles. He walked passed all of us. He sort of looked over, but kept going. He was actually the only one we didn't meet that night, which was unusual. He actually looked as though perhaps we wouldn't even be interested in seeing him since we were standing with The Apollo. In that split second, all of that went through my empty little head. Apparently after the twenty year wait, the anticipation, the excitement, the pure victory, I was sidetracked by this man that keeps entering my existence in some way. I can't tell you anything else that went on during my Noah encounter, no other distractions around me or even the conversation with Noah himself for that matter. What I can tell you is that I saw Miles walk from my right all the way over to the left and look over at us, then go in the trailer behind us. Noah was gracious, very sweet, I got my picture and now I could start home feeling victorious that I could replace that hideous picture.

I called Anna as I was walking through the parking lot. Anna is my best friend from the age of ten. She has been through all of this with me, but over the phone. I don't think we ever went to a Satire show together. She loved Rick Springfield; that was her "Noah." I told her how excited I was and how now I was "complete" so to speak. I finally accomplished the mission, I got the photo and got to see him again but now all I kept thinking about was how we didn't meet Miles. What the hell was happening? I figured he lived in Brooklyn, I could see him anytime. We walked to the car and started home again. After catching a quick catnap in the 7 Eleven parking lot and being awoken by a cop banging his radio on my window, it was time to continue our journey home. I got the boys home in time for school and no one was the wiser.

I slept while the boys went to school and had to talk my way out of having been unavailable when my mother called a hundred times. She was pretty cold to me that next day, since I didn't speak to her all day. Being out of touch was not good. Maybe the reason I feel like an irresponsible teenager at times is because that's the way I sometimes feel I am being treated. I'm a grown woman in my thirties with two children and I'm in trouble with my own mother if I'm not home when she feels I should be. See, I think in some way, although my mom seems to disapprove of my concert going routine, deep down she understands. She told me that when she and her sister were younger they had taken off from school one day and had gone to Frank Sinatra's house in New Jersey. When they got there, Frank was hanging out with his son in the yard who was still in a carriage and they took a picture of Ol' Blue Eyes . . . So please, don't tell me she doesn't get it. She also used to go see Martin and Lewis at the Tropicana. She just curtailed her behavior after she became a wife and a mother. I did not!

****

At the beginning of the summer, before we even took the trip to California, I had gone to see Satire at Six Flags in New Jersey. Donna came with her kids and I brought the boys. While I went to the show, she took them on all the rides. After the show, they came to meet me and I was waiting by the backstage gate. There was a bunch of people hoping for a glimpse of the band, or better yet a chance meeting. Of course Noah never came out but Dave and Miles were signing for everyone. I had to admit, I was standing there like a bitch because they were not Noah.

45

Miles had his back to me and I thought, *damn, why does he have to have such a great ass? Nope! Not looking.* I went from someone who would not acknowledge his existence to someone that could tell you he was wearing a black tank top, flip flops, and sweat pants with a white stripe going down the side that night. Lord have mercy. Having that same internal argument I often do in my head, I told myself I'm still not looking at him. The kids were all with me at this point. He signed autographs for all of them, spoke to all of them and was very sweet.

Noah never came out, and Miles was still a jerk, great ass, but still a jerk. I felt like I had too much time invested in Noah to feel negatively. How psychotic is that?

Historically, my closest friends, I have hated first—for no reason. I think subconsciously it is a defense mechanism. I must be subconsciously drawn to these people then don't want to like them so that I don't get hurt. Maybe we should get Freud on the wire.

****

It was 2001, and I had recruited a new concert buddy. Her name was Claire and she used to work with an animal organization that used my brother as their veterinarian. Whenever she came in the office I always had some '80s band playing on the radio in the background which always led us to talk about concerts. She said, "I would love to go if any shows ever come up." *Great*, I figured. With that, we saw Satire a few times and we had our friend Beth join us.

Everything changed for me after one show with Claire and Beth. While checking Noah out Claire turned and said to me, "Noah's okay looking," while I was drooling. Beth tapped me on the shoulder so I turned the other way and she said, "I don't know why you don't like Miles, he's hot and clearly one hundred times better looking than Noah. I figured he was more your type." Staring blankly at her all I kept thinking was, *what the hell was that all about?* I didn't ask her, but why would she offer that? Clearly she had no idea how much "Noah Time" had been invested. By the way, my mother was never a fan of Noah's. My mother was hip too. She was in her seventies but watched TV all the time. She would call me and tell me when all the people I liked were on talk shows or get the gossip on them from ET and Access Hollywood. She always had my celebrity back. She'd tell me about Satire too when she heard something, but still did not approve of my attraction to Noah.

Claire called one day, she was always looking for something fun to do, and said, "I found a show you might be interested in. Miles Baker does a big annual show with different acts, almost like a variety show and it seems like fun. It's for charity too so it's a night out and we're doing something for someone else." Maybe Satire will perform, since he's in the band there is a good chance they will be there.

We brought Beth and we went to Manhattan for the show. Apparently he does two shows back to back two nights in a row. Seems like a lot, huh? We brought some toys and canned goods as it was requested and we went on our way. I had surgery on my foot a month prior so I was on crutches this particular show. The show was at BB Kings. Many steps, mind you. The way it works at BB Kings is there are no reserved seats, it's first come first served. We didn't care much about our seats, because I don't like Miles. Because I was on crutches, they put us right up against the stage on the left side. Left side ring a bell? We were at the second show of the second night. The whole night Miles stood right in front of us. It was about three and a half hours long and it was all various types of music. It was the best show I had ever been to. I was shocked. I kept getting the eye from Beth all night as she kept checking Miles out. I was more impressed with the fact that he organized this whole thing. You never would have known that this was the fourth show they had done. We were already planning on coming back next year. Another thing I liked about him was that his children came out to sing and it was just a very family oriented show. After the show, I saw Miles come out on stage to clean up his own stuff; another humbling moment, and that's when I had hobbled over to him. I had a picture from our trip to California for him to sign and he was very sweet. Hmm. I don't want to go down this road.

Claire did some investigating and said, "Miles is playing at The Red Spot, do you want to go check him out and see what his solo music is like?" Not as hesitant as in the past, I said sure. Beth, Claire, and I trekked down to The Red Spot. We got there early and were just hanging out. It was time for Miles to start so we got on the side of the stage. He had a cute guitarist and we liked standing by him. Eventually we wound up over by Miles. We loved the music and then as a surprise, he brought Deanna Rose out. At this point, we never got the connection. It was great to see Deanna; she did a few songs with him. I took several pictures of him that night, which was very unusual for me. The music he sang just seemed like he loved his wife so much, and I was now really starting to admire him. I didn't realize at that point that you actually could reverse the meaning of his songs as I was initially seeing them.

After the show, my girls wanted to meet the guitarist. We did, but then Miles came out and was mingling. I decided to ask him for a picture and he was very gracious. After that night, we wound up going to see a few more of his solo shows. After a show in New Providence, New Jersey, I saw him outside talking to some people, and I, for the first time, was having butterflies as I waited for a picture. While I waited, I noticed he glanced over at me a couple of times. I decided to go over for another picture. As I walked towards him, he smiled and my heart started to flutter. I'm thinking this could start to be a problem.

After the photo, we went out with one of Miles's band mates, Tom, whom Beth had befriended at the Red Spot show. We went to a nearby restaurant and as we are passing appetizer ideas around, Tom looked up and said, "Oh, here comes Miles and his wife." I turned over my left shoulder, and sure enough, he was walking in with his wife. They sat a few tables away from us and they sat next to each other. I couldn't get over it. How romantic, I thought. He was really now starting to grow on me, in a different way. I was not jealous of his wife per se. I just felt that she was so lucky and respected in what appeared to be their perfect relationship.

Chapter 6

Not long after The Red Spot show, Satire had a CD signing. I took the boys with me and drove into Manhattan. We were the second ones in line and after waiting for a couple of hours outside in an ever growing line, they moved us inside. The store was closed otherwise. A quick scan of the store revealed an inconspicuous Miles Baker flipping through CDs. He was just walking around looking at everything in the store with his CD blasting overhead. He is so unpretentious. They were going to start the signing so the rest of the band appeared at the last second and got behind the table and they began. I had brought a photo with me from The Red Spot for Miles to sign. I was happy to finally see Noah but was intrigued to see Miles. We had passed the first three guys in the band and they pretty much just smiled and said hello. Miles commented that it was a great photo; he was the only one of them to personalize the experience. After the signing, as the band was on their way upstairs, I grabbed Noah who was standing next to Miles and asked them if I could take their picture. That is, to date, one of my favorite pictures. Miles got in this silly, sexy pose and, dare I say, Noah looked okay.

I unfortunately never got to see a Satire show with Miles in it after I started to pay attention to him. It seemed like not long after the signing I heard from that same friend of Miles that we went out to dinner with that Miles was leaving Satire. Now I was pissed about that. Sure, now that I like the guy, he's leaving the band. This is what I mean about your subconscious trying to protect you.

****

The night that I heard about Miles leaving was the same night I saw on Satire's website that they were going to do a festival-type show with Baggage and Clear View. I was excited about going but bummed that Miles was not going to be there. I recruited my younger cousin, Amie to come with me. Seeing as she was twenty one, it was not that much of a challenge. We wound up having a great time. The website for the festival stated that the bands were invited to stay on the grounds for the entire fest, but they did not know who would decide to stay. The only thing they guaranteed the bands to be there for was all of their scheduled events, but the rest was up to them. Since I don't fly, I booked a train from New York to Florida, roundtrip. Not long before the trip, I got a call that the train going there was cancelled. We were supposed to leave the day after Thanksgiving but there were no other trains for that day. Not even considering a plane, I now had to book Greyhound.

We had to get up at 3 a.m. to catch the train to the ferry. From there, we needed to get a cab to Penn Station. Then we hopped on Greyhound and started our journey. Since I get car sick, I popped some Dramamine and was down for the count the entire ride there.

While we stood in line to get into the festival, we saw some members of Baggage coming in. *Oh my God, this is gonna be great*, I thought. When we got to our room, there was a fruit basket waiting for us. We went downstairs and got our itinerary for the shows. Satire was going to be first. They had their meet and greet and show all in one day. The only members of Satire that stayed on the grounds of the festival the whole time were Bobby and Tim. Tim was now Mile's replacement in the band.

When Satire did their meet and greet, the whole band stood on the stage and their manager took a picture of you with them as well as the festival photographer taking one. I was pretty satisfied with the picture . . . this time. When I was walking over to take the picture, I of course went right next to Noah and he said, "Hi sweetie, how are you?" I'm sure I muttered some half-witted, unintelligible response. I'm surprised it doesn't look like I was having a seizure in the picture since he did have his arm around me. After the photos, they moved to the venue part of the festival and we waited in line for the show.

Amie and I sat in the second row on Noah's side. We met a couple of girls, Lori and Sue, that we became friendly with, but they had their own scheming that they do. They sat in the center. After the show, even at a festival we found where they might be coming out from. There were a few people that apparently had the same idea and were waiting too. With a quick push of the door, out they came. Snake signed a photo I had, and when it got to Noah, wife number three was standing behind and literally pushed him out the door. What a bitch. What a wimp. With the push came a "Let's go." Off he went.

To say I was a little turned off would be appropriate. I still, at this point, was not ready to come to terms with the fact that after twenty some odd years Noah was not the idol I had been following. Again, too much time and memories invested in one man. It was getting to be like a bad marriage, the only difference was there were no kids to be sticking it out for. I didn't know why I was doing this. The shows certainly were not as long as they used to be, the tickets were more expensive, and when you thought you might get close enough for a decent picture, he either was too good to come out or some bitch of a wife was behind him pulling his strings.

The push from behind was literally a push out of the festival. Now this is Bitch Wife #3, not to be confused with Bitch Wife #2 that wouldn't get my photo signed in Westchester. Everybody from the band left the festival except for Bobby and Tim. Now that pissed me off, even though I know they covered themselves by stating at the beginning that the bands were invited to stay but it was up to them. Clearly they didn't have any full band obligations because two of the band members remained at the festival. That was a $2500 a ticket — versus a $750 ticket if the bands were not there. I just felt that it was in bad taste that they left the festival since most of the people were there to see them.

I did get an opportunity to see what they were all about, so maybe it was a good thing. All things happen for a reason. The positives were that I went away for the first time by myself, I got to see three great shows, and it gave me an opportunity to see what the other bands were like "off the clock."

I found Kevin Stevens from Clear View to be a skank, as well as John Thomson. Here were two guys, not so attractive, walking around like they were two sex gods. I experienced first-hand Kevin's asshole potential. He was mingling after the show with people at the festival. Amie and I waited for the right opportunity. As he was walking away from people, we walked over to him and asked for a photo. Almost looking past us, like a cat on the prowl, he said, "Sure," then started talking to a girl and walked away. I thought, *What a dick.* I don't care if you're a "rock star" or not, that was just rude. Kevin stayed at the festival after the show, so this was his first night of seeing all of the action; it was also the last night. What turned me off about him was the fact that he talks about his wife on stage, everyone knows he's married, then he is clearly on the prowl after the show. It's his business, I don't care, but at least try to be discreet. I don't want to generalize but if my good for nothing, juice delivering husband couldn't keep it in his pants, what are the chances that a rock star with thousands of woman a night throwing their vaginas at him are going to remain faithful to his wife? I just think he could have been more discreet, then he would not have seemed like the dirt bag I now see him as.

The end result of this story was that I had gone to sleep and Amie remained downstairs in the bar. The next morning she said, "You missed it, Kevin was in the piano bar and he was singing and playing piano." That sucks because if I put my disdain aside for him, I would have liked to at least experience him playing in an intimate gathering and getting some photos. I was a little bummed about that but then she said, "He was hanging by a different girl and when they were standing there, he had his hands in her shirt." *Aw gross! That is just gross. What is he, 50? And he had to feel a girl up in a bar because he can? Would she let Joe the accountant do that, or is it just because he is Kevin Stevens and was in one of the three biggest selling bands of the '80s? Glad I didn't see it.*

After Kevin blew us off earlier that evening, we went over to one of the bars where we saw some of the guys from Baggage hanging out. The set up was such that there were some bar stools at a counter on the outside of the bar. On the other side of the counter was walking space between the next row of the bar stools that were up against the actual bar. Always preferring to be the wallflower, I sat on the outside of the bar; Amie was more outgoing so she was inside talking to everyone. I had taken a couple of pictures with the guys in the band. All of the girls were hanging all over Andrew Knight, another lead singer that did not impress me because he was a "replacement" singer. You have to understand my twisted, psychotic way of thinking. Andrew Knight did not join Baggage and kick the other singer out, nor did Miles Baker join Satire to kick Noah Anderson out. I have absolutely no basis for my way of thinking. These are two men that were sought out. They did not even initiate the call after the other two were gone, so what really is my problem? I don't like change, I can tell you that much.

I got a few pictures of John Thomson too. Again, not a good looking guy but apparently he is Brad Pitt in his own mind. This story I overheard while waiting in line to go in to the Baggage concert. A woman around my age (*oh my God, did I just say a woman my age?*), another fan around my age was standing in front of me with her girlfriends and I heard her tell one of them that she had gone up to John earlier in the day to ask for an autograph. Mind you, she was not babbling this for everyone to hear, which makes me feel like she was being one hundred percent truthful because she also seemed disappointed that she was so turned off and had just had this experience.

She said, "Hi John, I'm a big fan. Do you think I can have an autograph?"

And the eloquent response was, "Sure, if you suck my dick."

Hmm, I paused for a minute and thought, *if you want your dick sucked, you better be forking over more than a signature. Was he for real? If you want raw, I'll give you raw. You are an old, ugly, has-been who is trying to kick start your career again by playing an '80s reunion show at a five day festival.* Don't get me wrong, I enjoyed the entire festival, the whole concept, and think these guys are extremely talented. They played a huge part in my adolescence and have my respect, but when you act like you are on the top of your game and you're twenty-four with a seventeen-year-old's mentality, but you are in fact in your fifties with a family, you make me sick. Who do they think they are? Do they all have some enchanted mirror that the rest of us are not privy to? Again, if he was a notary public and I went into his office in the middle of Staten Island and asked him to please sign my contract and he said, "Yeah, if you suck my dick," would I drop to my knees? Because he has a guitar around his neck and doesn't sit behind a desk there are a different set of rules. Although, Bill Clinton did alright for himself sitting behind a desk. I can't help but feel I play a huge part in this deranged way of thinking too. I'm the jerk going to see them; this is where the bitterness of my marriage starts to rear its ugly head. John Thomson would be Jerk Number Two this trip. I haven't yet included Noah in there, but I'm sure his time will come. He only has time on his side at this point.

While sitting at the bar, I was watching everyone else mingle, talk, and drink with the band. I was not bold enough to do any of it. Even though I was a little nervous because of who they were, go figure, they seemed like regular guys. Since I was sitting alone and not really talking to anybody, I noticed Andrew Knight looking over a couple of times. I wish I could be the confident, chatty girl with the band like the rest of them but I couldn't. I just felt fat, ugly, and out of my league. I knew Andrew Knight actually lived on the same island as me, at least, that was the rumor. I had taken several pictures of Andrew during the show, many of which he posed for which was pretty awesome. Beth had always thought he was hot but you know me. Now that I was up close and personal, I was changing my tune.

Amie and I were hanging out with Lori and Sue the whole time at the bar; they were very nice. As I was about to take a picture of Lori with Andrew, I put the camera to my face and through the viewfinder I see this inquisitive face. Like a light bulb went off, Andrew said to me, "You're the paparazzi." I guess I took a lot of photos during the show. I wanted to die; I could feel my face burning. Not moving the camera, I just snapped the picture and hoped this would all go away.

Like I was just caught with my hand in the cookie jar, I moved the camera down to my side and Andrew came over and introduced himself to me. "You were taking pictures during the whole show," he said with a smile.

Mortified, I said, "Yes, sorry for all of the flashes." I was hoping that my face was not as red as it felt. Never really having anything to talk about with these guys, the only thing I could come up with to talk about was the only commonality we had: Staten Island. I asked him if he lived on Staten Island because that was the rumor. He said no, that he lived in Brooklyn. For some reason I think that was a cover just in case I was a stalker but that's okay . . . nice to see he is smart enough to try to protect himself.

"Where do you live?" he volleyed.

Oh God, was this now going to turn into an actual conversation.
Timidly I replied, "Staten Island." He said that he used to work as a

bartender on Bay Street. Now feeling a little more comfortable I said, "Oh really? Which one?"
"The Red Spot." It was a funky, alternative rock type club.

"I used to go there and I loved it."

"I probably served you drinks there, but you had to be very underage." *Underage?*

"No I wasn't. How old do you think I am?"

"I'm not saying, but you have to be half my age."

This now turned to more conversation and him asking what my last name was and if I knew a particular restaurant on Targee Street. I was not familiar with the restaurant, but he said his friends owned it and I should go in there and tell them that Andrew Knight had sent me. I now felt comfortable enough to ask for a picture with him and as we were posing, he just kept smiling and saying, "You are fantastic." I was feeling like I could get used to this.

Typically the wallflower, this was quite unusual for me. Just before I left, I whispered in his ear, "I'm thirty-six."

"No way, I never would have thought that. You are fantastic. I don't want to make you blush but you are fantastic."

Some girls I didn't know were poking me in the back and saying, "He likes you."

Enjoying the moment for what it was, knowing that he was married and still a gentleman and not wanting this moment ruined, I thanked him, said goodnight, and went to my room.

Andrew had to have been the biggest positive surprise of the whole trip. John and Kevin were the biggest disappointment. I did not want to acknowledge the inevitable about Noah. I was still making excuses for his bad behavior by saying it was his wife's fault.
It was very exciting to go away because, other than that trip with the boys, I had not been away or gone out socially in years. It was a little disappointing to go home on many levels. Now I revisited

what I was doing fifteen years ago and it was just like getting back on the horse, so to speak.

I missed my kids, who were staying with my parents and home attendant, and Noah was a disappointment. I loved the freedom of the trip, no cell phones, no phone, period. Nobody relying on me for anything, although I did feel somewhat responsible for Amie because she was only twenty-one and I was her big cousin. I know she was legal but my first instinct is to take care of everyone.

Ironically enough, I met a girl named Joyce at that festival that I had met back at Six Flags that night Miles the jerk had on a tank top, sweat pants with a stripe down the side, and flip flops. Not realizing this right away, I kept trying to figure out why she looked so familiar. It wasn't until I got the impression that she traveled to go see these bands that it hit me. I asked her if she had been to Six Flags in New Jersey and she said, "Probably". We exchanged information and when I read her card, it seemed familiar. I asked her if she remembered asking someone to send her a copy of a picture of her with one of the guys in Satire and not receiving it, to which she replied, "Vaguely."

That's when I knew and told her about the goings-on of my weak brain. I had taken a photo and she happened to be in it. She gave me her card and asked me to send it to her. I kept her card on top of my microwave because I had every intention of doing so. I'm not very diligent about cleaning and two years later the card remained on the microwave.

When I got home from my trip I compared the two cards; she had moved since, but I sent the photo out as soon as I had gotten home. Her story was that she was a Satire fan but more of a, dare I say, Miles Baker fan. She had his latest CD with her. I said, "Yeah, he's okay, but I'm a Noah Anderson fan." Apparently with this band everyone seemed to pick a guy. Lori and I were Noah fans, Sue was a Snake fan, and this was all new to Amie so she was just there for the ride. Amie wound up liking Dave from Clear View. Joyce kind of rolled her eyes at the whole liking Noah more than Miles thing. I said, "Sorry, I can't help it. Miles seems okay though." She had nothing but positive things to say about him, which I did file.

Chapter 7

That December things started to change. I had met great friends through my kids' school and I swear to God if I didn't have them, I wouldn't be here today. Donna, Felice, and Francine all took part in watching my children when it came time to go to a show or, in this case, a festival. We also had a perfect home attendant for my father. Home attendants are a dime a dozen; what we had was unheard of. She not only cared unconditionally for my father, she also cared for my mother. She was family. Because she was as great as she was, it was not so imperative that I be there so much.

The way things seemed to be running was that if things were too smooth for too long, the other shoe had to drop. Dad was healthy, just physically impaired. Mom was becoming increasingly dependent on me and her health seemed to now be failing. After a couple of weeks of not feeling well, she was really starting to look bad. We knew she had emphysema and chronic obstructive pulmonary disease (COPD), but she would not go to the doctor until the last moment. She was sleeping more and more and one night when I stopped by, I found her in a chair hardly able to move. I said, "You have to go to a doctor." Unable to argue, we went. Just trying to get her to the car was a task in and of itself. We weren't in the doctor's office for more than five minutes when the doctor sent her up the street to the pulmonologist. He was the one that called the ambulance.

After getting evaluated, it was determined that the COPD and emphysema had progressed. She was put on oxygen at the pulmonologist's office and she never came off it after that. After about a week in the hospital she was sent to a nursing home for rehab. She remained in the nursing home for about two months and I had to stop going out. Even though the couple of times I did go out were over a two-to-three-year period, I still felt guilty.

Once Mom came home, she completely depended on me. Our perfect home attendant took care of my dad and my mom wanted me as her personal caretaker. I knew this is what I should do, so I again resigned myself to the fact that I never should have been going out, and I just should have taken care of my parents. The routine was in full force. I was at my parents' house during any spare time I had. Any time free for socializing, which there wasn't much of, I spent at my parents'. My mom was a homebody to begin with, but now she felt like a prisoner being hooked up to the oxygen. There was nothing you could say or do; she was staying put unless it was for a doctor's appointment or a hair appointment that would, of course, accompany a doctor's appointment. I took her everywhere; I was always bathing, feeding, shopping for, dressing, and driving my mother. She was not a demanding woman by any stretch of the imagination. She was a nervous, now sickly, seventy-six-year-old woman. I felt it was now my place to care for her. I had my children, nobody wanted to date me, keeping my parents happy and making them feel secure was my priority; I hated men. My philosophy was they are all the same; they all cheat so you just have to find one that is the most physically appealing to you because they share all of the other qualities anyway.

Nothing really mattered because my husband had ruined me. I never ever saw any man that I found attractive, let alone someone I wanted to waste time having to actually do my hair, put make up on, and get out of my sweat pants for. Every weekend was spent at my parent's house. Having no desire to go out at all, this was actually a perfect set up for me. I had an excuse not to have to mingle with the outside world.

Claire would find a sporadic Miles show that we would go to. It wasn't that big of a deal because he was local and I just took care of everything for my parents before I left, put my brothers on alert that I would be off the island, and we would go.

Miles would always mention his wife, who was usually at his shows. I really was impressed because I thought, *wow, here's a guy who is a rock star and wears his wedding ring all of the time and really seems to love his wife.* It was still a little hard for me to swallow because of how much I hated men and how useless I felt they were.

****

At one of his solo shows, Miles's wife was sitting outside of the coffee shop that he played at that evening with their daughter and Claire and I sat in the back. I was trying to go unnoticed. Not that I would have any reason to stand out, but I just did not want to even

58

be seen by him. I had broken down and purchased a CD of his and I was blown away. He really was talented and his lyrics could just tug at your heart. All I could think was too bad there are no real men, real single men that actually feel like that. So Claire and I sat in the back of this coffee shop with Claire's friend Paul.

During the show, I had taken a picture and because of the red eye reduction, the camera flashed for what seemed like fourteen flashes before the photo was actually snapped. I wanted to die. Looking over at me, Miles leaned into the microphone and said "What, are the cops outside?" I could feel my face burning. I sank down into my seat and glanced over to catch him grinning at me as he continued with the show. It was at that point that I wondered what else could possibly happen that could make me never return to another show.

He closed the show with a song that he sang a cappella. Since Anna liked that song, I called her up and held my cell phone in his direction so she could hear him. Anna was now living in Arizona so we did this kind of thing often. Thinking perhaps I had gone the rest of the show under the radar, I sat quite relaxed for the last song. It wasn't until he put his hand up to his ear as if he had a phone in it while he was singing that I could feel my face burning again. Was the embarrassment never going to end? How did this turn into an interactive show? I didn't even want to be seen by him, and now he's mocking me. My fair skin tends to show my feelings immediately, so clearly, the burning sensation on my cheeks was a dead giveaway that I wanted to die.

At this point in my life, I was wearing clothes just to cover my large self. After the show, Miles, as usual, was free to talk, sign autographs, and take pictures. I walked up to him, mortified, and he immediately said to me, "I'm sorry, I didn't mean to embarrass you. I was only kidding." I assured him everything was fine and we thought the show was great. He signed a picture that I had with me and then Claire and I took off.

When Claire and I got into the car that night, I said to her, "Oh my God, he is so nice." Now I'm thinking he is kind of cute and so, so nice. I had him on such a monogamous pedestal; I would hate to think that he would cheat on his wife even if it was with me. How did I go from not wanting to hear his name to wondering how he kisses? This is bad. You know what was bad, without realizing it I had now logged a lot of Miles time under my belt. He crept up on me. No, no, no, this is no good. I'll tell you why, listen to this reasoning. Noah being married didn't mean anything to me because I started my infatuation with him before he met his wife, so I technically had dibs on him. I even had more time invested in my faux relationship with Noah than his own wife did. So if you think about it, it wouldn't even count if he slept with me because I really wanted him first. Hey, I'm not in therapy for no reason. Now the problem with Miles is that he has been married for about twenty-four years and has five children, and I have really only been seeing him for a few years. Years being my new invested time, but he came into this scenario married, so now I'm in a pickle. As much as I fear at this point that I could quite possibly want him, I would hate to think that he would ever cheat on his wife. Now I sit back and just gaze and think, *what a lucky woman.*

I would videotape some shows and watch them with my mom; my mother liked him. She actually said, "At least he's nice looking. He's better than that dirty Noah Anderson who looks like he needs a bath." Correct me if I'm wrong, but I don't think Noah Anderson ever killed her family or anything like that. I don't know why she hates him so much. But she always liked Miles.

It was February 2006 and we had gone to that same coffee shop that I was mortified in months earlier. Now we sat up in the front and this time I had my video camera. I paid a little more attention to him this time also. I guess subconsciously the obvious was kicking in. During the show he made a remark about Mike Richards and everyone was laughing. While videotaping, as I'm looking through the viewfinder, he looks right at me and says, "And look, she's videotaping. Are you getting the whole show or just the Satire stuff?" I thought I was going to die. He said, "I can see it now on YouTube. Did you hear what he said about you?" My face was on fire. How is it that this is happening again?

He sang a Deanna Rose song and I thought, *how cool, but unusual.* Then he sang "Can't Stop the Love," which he usually sings. I couldn't make the connection, why does he always sing that and always a Deanna Rose song? Towards the end of the show my battery was dying on the video camera and I figured I had enough taped anyway. I saved a little of the juice in the battery just in case something interesting popped up that I wanted to get. He was about to make another Mike Richards comment and then he looked at me and said, "Put your camera on." I thought he was kidding so I sat there. He said, "Go ahead, put it on." I picked it back up and put it on and he looked right at me and said, "Mike Richards and I used to cross dress together and boy has he got some fine legs." I was so embarrassed, you guessed it . . . burning cheeks. He said jokingly "Can I buy that tape from you?"

After the show, I went over to him with another photo for him to sign. As I approached him I said, "You're not going to sign anything for me are you?" He smiled and said, "I'll sign whatever you want." Boy this is really not good because I don't need my world disrupted. I don't like this feeling every time I see him lately.

****

About a month later, Claire called and said, "Hey, I just got something in the mail for The Event. Miles is in it, do you want to go?" With not much thought put into the decision, I said sure. I still had this whole admiration thing going on for Miles. The reason that he supposedly left Satire was to spend more time with his family. I thought that was commendable, if it was in fact the truth. He really just impressed me because he was so talented and nice and I respected what appeared to be the perfect marriage. Claire and I went to this Event thing and I brought my kids, Felice, and her daughter Kim. When we got there, we were just walking around and, lo and behold, who do we see walking through the place but Miles. As he passed us, he gave me a look out of the corner of his eye and looked back over his shoulder when he turned the corner. He must have just thought I was somebody else . . . Right?

The place was packed. Since this was the first time we had ever come to this show, we didn't quite know what to expect. We stood along the left side of the room for the show since we couldn't quite find seats for all of us. The band was really great, but my little guy was tired and starting to whine. We had already been there a few hours and it was enough for him. I left everyone inside and I took my baby outside into the lobby. I sat down in a corner chair and let him sleep on me. I could still hear the music, so it didn't bother me that I wasn't watching it. After all, he was not Noah Anderson and I hate men; nor do I have the desire to even be interested in another man as long as I live. There is too much pain involved and I have been quite content in my pathetic life.

Bailey and Kim came out to check on me while Felice kept their place inside. They wanted me to come back in but I told them I couldn't leave Quinn. Being kids, Bailey and Kim decided to explore. They went in the doorway behind me and were gone for a few minutes. Bailey came flying out and said the door opened up to the stage right next to Miles. "Go back there!"

I could see they really wanted me to do more than sit with my sleeping child, so I decided to entertain them and, since Felice had come out now, she sat with Quinn while I went to take a gander. I brought my camera in case I might be able to get a couple of good shots. I followed the kids back to their discovery. Well, they were right, Miles was right there. I stood observing for a few minutes, just taking in the different angle. Miles looked over as I was taking a picture and smiled. However I'm not acknowledging that smile. *What the hell was that?!* I looked around and no one else was there. That smile was for me. That was new. I never experienced that before. At least the type of smile that wasn't the generic smile. For the whole rest of the show he kept looking over at me. I thought, *well that was cool, I guess.* But when the show is over, that whole character gets packed up with the guitar so I should forget it as soon as the curtain comes down. Besides, I was not going to become some big Miles fan so why give it any thought? Why waste any more brain cells thinking about that great smile that the guy who wore the tank top, sweat pants, and flip-flops flashed me all night. It's forgotten already. Shake it off, shake it off.

When we were getting ready to leave, Bailey and Kim decided they want to wait and see if Miles comes out so they can get a picture. *What the hell is the big draw with this guy? Fine, I'll wait.* After a few minutes, that amazing smile walked out again. He was very engaging with the kids so they loved him. They got a picture with him and off into the night he went.

****

62

About a week after The Event, Claire and I were going to a Mike Richards concert because Miles was going to be sitting in with him. Lori, my friend from the Festival, was going to be there. We kept in touch after the Festival and this was going to be the first time we got together since then. We met at the show and Miles sounded phenomenal and actually looked incredible. Now I actually wanted the show to hurry up and end so I could possibly get a better look at him. After the show, we waited outside and I had two copies of the picture from The Event for him to sign for the kids. He was pulling out of the parking lot and saw people waiting so he pulled over. I was the first one to walk over to him. I wasn't really nervous since I really didn't like him that way. He took the pictures and looked at me and said, "I know you."

I said, "Yeah, I was the video chick from the coffee house."

He smiled and said, "That's right. So why am I signing their pictures?"

Oh my God. I know I've been out of the loop and completely uninterested in the loop, but did he just come on to me a little? And if he did, is that good or bad? Good if I'm interested, bad because he's married and I have him on that damn pedestal. Left speechless for the first time, I smiled, took the pictures back and gingerly turned around and walked, quite confused, back to Lori. I now had this grin on my face that I couldn't seem to shake. After that encounter I decided to go see him that next day at The Red Spot, which I was not planning on doing. I had to bring my kids because I had already left them with my parents the night before, and I don't want it to look like I'm always leaving them. I called The Red Spot and asked if my kids could come because they want to see Miles. They said, "as long as they stay by your side all night it won't be a problem."

Just the boys and I went to this show. I was scanning the area to see if there seemed to be anyone there . . . Like a spouse. I couldn't find anyone so it made it a little easier to concentrate on the show. While he was singing, his wife brought him a drink. A sure sign that this was now starting to be a problem for me was that I was a little unnerved that she was there. After his set, he came off the stage by the side that we were on. The kids asked him for an autograph after the show and he said, "Yeah, I'll be right back," and he grabbed some of his things and took it out to his car. When he came back in, he was with his wife and another couple. Wanting to now just get out of there because it was kind of pointless to just be standing around there, I told the kids just go over and ask him, then we'll leave.

We walked over to him and he was immediately attentive and they asked for an autograph and he said, "Sure." He leaned over and was talking to Quinn and then Quinn pointed to me. Miles's wife leaned over and said, "How did you get two underage kids into the bar?" I explained the phone call prior to bringing them and Miles said, "Cool." He then leaned into Bailey, and then Bailey pointed to me. *What the hell were they talking about?* I couldn't wait to get outside and ask them.

Miles looked at me and said, "You're the mother?" I said yes. "Boy you don't look old enough to be their mother." Oh my God. He leaned into my ear and in this unbelievably hot, sexy voice said, "When did we first meet?" I have no idea what unintelligible thing I muttered back, but it was so stupid that he had to rephrase the question and dumb it down to a multiple choice. I got through it though.

Floundering for something somewhat intelligent to say to recover, I said, "Do you know John Mason?" That was the name of the painter.

"He plays bass? We were in a band together. You have probably seen him more recently than I have." So the painter wasn't lying. Autographs in hand, we started out of the club. As soon as we got outside, I grabbed the boys and said, "What did he say to you?"

They said, "God Mom, what's the big deal?"

As if I was just about to take them hostage I said, "Give it up, what did he say?"

He had leaned into Quinn and said, "Where is your mother?" That's when he pointed to me. And when he was signing Bailey's things he said, "And where is your mother?" That's why I got the comment

I did. I must say I was feeling a bit giddy when we left but also a little depressed. I hate this excited feeling when there is nothing you can do about it. It kind of makes you feel greedy. You have these nice experiences that not everyone gets to have and you still want more. The only problem was once he leaned into my ear and I felt him that close and looked into his husky blue eyes, there was no turning back.

Eight years. Eight years I had kept all of my feelings at bay and now a married musician whose name I swore I would never speak seventeen years ago, has gotten to me. What sick plan did God have in mind, because it just seems like one more unfair situation being thrown at me.

Chapter 8

Since it was going to be a couple of months before our next outing, I had plenty of time to think. I thought about an Oprah episode that was on her fiftieth birthday. I was so jealous that she had Josh Groban all to herself. I thought about how awesome that must be to have a birthday party and have whatever you want. *If I could do anything, what would it be?* I would like to have a private concert with Miles Baker. Private with all of my friends, of course. While I was looking at his website one day, I saw a contact option. Just for kicks, I sent an email asking if he does private parties and if so, how much. I received a response back with his agent's phone number. I called her and she said $2500 for ninety minutes. I damn near dropped the phone. I could use my tax return, skip vacation, and have him all to myself for ninety minutes? Initially I was inquiring about a fortieth birthday because that would give me two years to come up with the money. When she said $2500, I asked if this April was possible.

She said, "So it would be a thirty-ninth birthday?"

I said, "Put whatever number you want in front of it, it's just an excuse to get him to sing." She started laughing.

I was a little nervous because this was a lot of money, and for a man, no less. My mother would kill me. That would be the most expensive concert ticket I ever bought. "Let's do it," I told her.

****

About two months went by before the next show. Claire and I drove about an hour and a half to Coney Island. We were very early so we were the first ones there. Miles wasn't even there yet. We sat at the picnic tables while we waited and it wasn't long before we turned and saw Miles walk in with his wife and daughter. I knew at this point that I was starting to fall because I was very annoyed that his wife was there. I have a lot of nerve too. I got up and got a drink, and I don't drink. Claire said, "Look, don't get drunk, just have a good time and don't think about anything else. He is married, you knew that." Yes I knew that, that's why I liked staying in my cocoon so I didn't need to feel this way. Why do I always feel morally compromised? No one else seems to. They can hop in bed with a complete stranger, married or not, never see them again, and go about their life.

I've never even had a one-night stand. Too much Irish Catholic guilt. Miles' wife and daughter left for a while as he was setting up. A little nauseated as I watched him kiss her goodbye, I turned my head when she left. Lucky bitch. My husband stopped kissing me after we got married, but twenty some odd years later he's still kissing her when she leaves the room, with the daughter there. Who is this guy? While they were gone, I got up and stumbled over to get my hand stamped since now someone was actually at the gate to collect the money. I think I was on my second drink, which was a mistake since I didn't eat all day knowing I was going to see him.

As I walked to the gate, I saw him coming out of the corner of my eye, walking with his cell phone. I heard him from behind me say, "Hey you." All I kept thinking to myself was, *that lucky son of a bitch on the other end of the phone.* Then I heard him again, "Hey you." I turned around half expecting him to look very animated on his phone. Imagine my surprise when I turned around to see him looking at me and smiling. I was actually the lucky son of a bitch. I almost died.

A little nervous because this was totally unexpected, I said, "Hi."

"The last time I saw you, you had two kids with you. Where are they today?"

"I only take them to bars, I leave them home when I go to amusement parks." That flew out of my mouth way before I had a chance to filter it, but it seemed to work so I went with it. "I booked you as a birthday present to myself."

"That was you?"

"That was."

I could feel my face burning the whole time we were talking, but the conversation seemed to flow pretty well. After some more small

talk, he smiled and gently ran his fingers up my forearm, I don't know how I kept it together, and said, "I'll see you later."
I walked back to the table where Claire had been watching this entire thing unfold, complete with a rash just short of hives. Like I was trying to sneak to my desk before the teacher noticed I was up, I plopped down at the table and blurted out, "Do you think he would cheat on his wife?"

Looking at me as if I had just gone and lost my damn mind, her face was contorted and she said, "He is a man and a musician. I think the chances are good." Claire still had her crooked brow working while she stared at me and said, "I saw the two of you . . . what are you doing?" I had no idea. This was just becoming an internal dilemma. I did not like feeling like this. Two reasons: I hate wanting something this badly that I really couldn't and shouldn't have, and I hate myself for wanting him to cheat.

I don't really want to feel anything. Just to be able to go about my daily chores of taking care of everybody else served me just fine. At least I didn't need to deal with the real world, and what was the point in feeling this way anyway? There is no chance with this and if there was, did I want to be with someone who cheats on his wife? That makes me no better than the girl sitting on the hotel stairs the night I caught my husband. I don't want to go back to that in any realm. I'm content being alone.

The sun was starting to go down as he started the show. Now the whole time he was on, I was replaying everything that had just taken place. At one point during his set, he introduced his daughter and she went up to sing while he went and sat with his wife. All I could think about was what a lucky woman she was. When I glanced over my left shoulder, trying to get a glimpse of what was going on over there, he was looking at me while he and his wife were talking. It must have been a coincidence. A minute later I looked over again and he was looking past his wife and staring at me. Quickly I turned back to the front. This couldn't be happening, could it? A few more times, like a child, I peeked again. He's still staring. I'm going to be one of those skanky girls that want a married man, aren't I? I sickened myself.

After the show, I honestly had one thing weighing on my mind about the party. I was still concerned with the cost and just wanted to make sure I was making the best decision. While he was packing up, I went up to him. He turned around, smiled, and said, "Hello again".

Always optimistic, I smiled and said, "My parents are elderly. In the event something, God forbid, happens would I be able to reschedule the party?"

"Don't worry about anything, of course."

Okay then, I no longer had this lingering doubt about the party hanging over my head.
After that show, I couldn't wait for the next one. It was exciting to have something to look forward to, but still, it was not going to be the end result I wanted, so it just ends up being painful. Unsure of what I really wanted as an end result, we just kept going to shows because we loved the music, it was fun, and, most importantly, it was an escape from my real world. This is why I like living in my cocoon under my rock. After the change of feelings I had for Miles, my mother must have picked up on it. I swear she could read my mind and it was scary. When I would go see Miles perform, it was no different from any time I went to see any other band. My mother must have known something because she said one night when I was going out, "What are you doing?"

"Nothing. Just going to a concert."

"He's a married man."

"I know, Mom. I'm just going to a concert."

What the fuck? I was doing nothing different, but she saw something. Something I didn't even see because she never questioned my intentions when I went to any other concert, and I had been to many. She didn't even question Noah Anderson and I did a lot of crazy shit involving him. What made Miles different? Now I was starting to worry. What could she know that I didn't? Even with the few little things that he did that I wanted to read into—like the smiling, the arm tickling, the whispering in my ear—

she didn't know any of that and I still never thought any of that would ever develop into anything. He was a rock star for God's sake. They bang blonde, hot, bobble headed groupies, none of which was me. Besides the fact that he always talked about his wife. This was nuts. She was nuts. Maybe she just wanted me to stay home more often and that's why she threw that out there.

****

About a month or so later, the boys and I had enough and packed up and went on our cross-country trip to California. They loved it the first time we did it and this time our friends were going to be flying out there. I had left a book for each of my brothers with care instructions for our parents and didn't wait to see if it was okay with them. Since I was going to be out there anyway, there was no harm in going to see Mike Richards and if Miles happened to be accompanying him, what the hell? I was not going out of my way for him; I was already going to be there.

We drove into San Diego and just relaxed the first day. Day two, we hung out with our friends all day in San Diego. We parted ways and made our way to Los Angeles the next day. Mike was playing in Agoura Hills; it was a small club. It was sort of set up just like BB Kings. There was one part during the show when Miles left the stage. He never stands still so he went into the club by the merchandise table and was talking to a few people. Not knowing if seeing me was going to seem strange to him, I walked over near where he was standing and waited. I saw him do a double take, smile, and quickly excuse himself. He had a huge smile on his face and gave me a big hug. My first of many to come. God was his cheek soft. He said, "What are you doing here?"

"We did the cross country thing again." In our conversation at Coney Island, I told him how the boys thought he was very cool when they met him in California during our first cross-country jaunt. There was some more small talk but now he had to go back up on stage. After the show, the boys went up to say hello to him just before we left.

Lori, aside from being a huge Noah Anderson fan, was a big Mike Richards fan. My original plan was to just see Miles in San Diego while I was there. It was Lori who called me and said why don't you go to Agoura Hills and see them too. This was actually going to screw me up because I could have stayed in San Diego and done that show and continued my vacation. But now I had to drive from San Diego to Los Angeles, set up camp there, and after that show, drive back down to San Diego for the show I was actually planning on going to, then drive back to Los Angeles because we were still planning on hitting San Francisco before heading home. This was the point where I started to compromise myself for a man, and I hated myself for it. I should have stuck with the original plan and gone to one show. Because I was greedy and wanted to see him twice, I drove around like Magellan.

We got to the San Diego show a little late. I still had to scalp three tickets from some fool on the side of the road. I was so twisted because I had even missed a minute of Miles that I threatened the scalper and told him, "If these tickets are fake in any way and I don't get into this show, I will come back out, find you, and kill you. I'm from New York so you know I'll do it."

He looked like he was going to shit himself. "No, no they're legit, I swear."

"Don't make me come back."

My kids at this point thought I had finally flipped, but they were laughing because they know occasionally I go "New York" on people. This was another sign that I was a little too interested in Miles, since now I'm threatening people for making me late to a show. We get to the gate; I can hear the music and the slow talking, yet perky, Californian tells me I need to check my camera. "Just take it." My kids really thought I lost it.

Like something out of Fargo, she says "Oh no, I couldn't do that. You need to go right over there into that restaurant and give it to the people at the coat check." *For the love of St. Nick.* The three of us ran into the restaurant. Those fools took it without question, no receipt, nothing, which actually, I guess, makes me the fool. I didn't care; I figured I'd deal with it later. We ran back to Fargo lady again, she took our tickets, and we were in. Luckily, my son, who is not known for his common sense, actually had a disposable camera with him.

Towards the end of the show, we moved towards the stage and my son took some pictures. Miles had his back to us and I said, "Take one for your mother."

"Oh Mom, don't make me do that." *The poor bastard.* I took the camera and did it myself. I had come full circle; the ass that caught my attention at Six Flags in New Jersey was now getting photographed on purpose in California. What had become of me?

The old me, the one that would go out with April, was trying to break free, but now I was too old and a mother. I had no business acting the way I wanted to. You can't go backwards, especially when you are in therapy. They frown upon that. After the show, we waited for Miles and he talked to us a few minutes, hugged me, and we went on our way.

The rest of our trip was great. We usually do a lot of crazy things, things we would never do at home, when we go away. When we got to San Francisco, we never took a cab. I damn near killed my kids making them walk everywhere. Quinn considers me an exercise Nazi of sorts. We rented bikes one day and rode all over, and we even rode our bikes over the Golden Gate Bridge.

A big step for me was when we went in a hot air balloon. I don't fly. Everyone knows that about me. It comes up in every conversation I have and inevitably the same person always says, "I just don't understand why you don't fly, you are so stupid." That comment coming from a highly educated individual no less. "Stupid," as it may be, there is just nothing I want to see badly enough that I feel the need to get in a plane. I have already been to California three times in my life so far, never needed a plane. "What are you going to do when the boys are in college and they are in California and it's an emergency?"

"They are nine and twelve, do I really need to think about that now? By the time they're in college I can teleport myself there and I won't need to worry about it."

"You are a jerk, I can't believe you don't fly."

Again, a little harsh, don't you think? I have found that this topic gets many people twisted. They get so angry with me, as if I have in some way kept them from going on vacation somewhere. I don't understand why what I don't do affects so many people. I don't fly, big deal. I still get to any destination I need to be at and I don't inconvenience anyone else.

So I, in my infinite wisdom, decide to book a hot air balloon ride over Napa Valley. I was fine up until the day before and the pilot had to call me and talk me off the ledge. He assured me that it was safe and we would not crash, and I assured him that I could not guarantee that I would not have an anxiety attack and that I could flip out. He had a very calm, soothing voice. I just hoped that he wasn't so laid back that we'd be hanging off the edge of some cliff somewhere. I don't remember what I took, but I think some Dramamine and an anti-depressant were involved. After we landed, they were chased with some champagne. I couldn't believe I had done it. I have the pictures to prove it too. To me that was not nearly as dangerous as a plane, though I later found out that was not true. You are literally standing in a God damn basket hanging off the ass end of a balloon. What made me think that was safe at all, let alone compared to a plane? Did I mention huge flames shoot up into the balloon? Again, I am not known for my great decision making. Never the less, the task had been accomplished.

Another psychotic idea that I thought would be safe for my allergy and asthma-ridden children was to horseback ride by the Hollywood sign. It seemed harmless enough. Did I mention that I left the Benadryl at the hotel? I had one son on a horse in front of me, the cautious, quiet son, then behind me I had Jesse James riding on the side of the cliff. He was riding with one hand because the other hand was wiping his nose and covering his mouth while he was coughing. I thought I would have a stroke. The entire forty-five minute ride I kept telling him, "get over by the mountain, if that horse jumps for any reason, you're dead! Right off the side of the cliff. Its over!" He is his father's son and stayed by the edge because he is, in fact, trying to kill me. This was by far one hundred times worse than the balloon. Watching helplessly as my son rode on the side of a cliff on an animal as his tiny little Mary Kate Olsen ass kept slipping to the side was killing me. There was no getting off like it was an amusement park ride either. Having a veterinarian for a brother, and working in an animal hospital, I know that even the calmest of animals can flip out at a moment's notice. They are animals, they are unpredictable. You can't just assume they will "follow the path" because they do it every day. That's what I told myself until we got to the bottom and I ripped him off the horse. He was so mad at me for nagging him the whole ride but hopefully one day he will understand. I myself was not all that thrilled about looking over the side at where my ass could end up. Again, another task completed. I knew I had to make the most of the vacation because when I go home, it's back to the grind. There is no social life. One concert every three months or so. That is the only time I would go out. I was slowly starting to work at my weight but figured, how fat could I be if Miles seems to be flirting with me?

Another stop in California was of course Disneyland. While we were in Disney, I was waiting for the boys to get off a ride when an older gentleman started to talk to me. This was not unusual because older people seem to gravitate towards me and I'm used to caring for them. We talked for a bit while he waited for his son to get off the ride. He was telling me all about his son and how he wanted me to meet him. His son was my age and he had his ailing friend with him. He was literally carrying him so that he could go on the rides. I forgot what was wrong with him but my understanding was he didn't have much more time. This man's son was his best friend and he wanted him to be able to do everything with him. He was a great friend, a great human being.

His dad introduced me to him and he gave me his number. It had been a long time since anyone had given me their number or talked to me. It was flattering, but I was still not interested. This was not something I was accustomed to since I had been focusing on caring for everyone else's needs. I continued to hide behind my ponytail and sweatshirts.

The only time now that the hair would come down and the sweats off was when I was going to a concert. Now I was starting to dress up a little, just a little. At least at this point, I cared what I wore. At the earlier shows that Miles had played, I didn't ever care. I was going for the music because I loved it.

74

****

After we got home, I guess it had been about a month or so later, Miles was playing at a fair. It was about an hour away, so Claire and I started back to the concert routine. We sat in the back but directly in his field of vision. A few times during the show, I moved to the side for a couple of pictures. He played for about ninety minutes, then after the show we stood off to the side while he talked to everyone. To my surprise he walked over and hugged me. He had such a great smile. "Hi, you made it back okay."

Giggling I said, "Yes." After a little small talk, we got a picture together, but it was blurry. I have the whole problem with now needing a decent picture with him. I noticed about three women waiting to talk to him before us. I never really looked at their faces but only noticed they were waiting, as was everyone else.

A few days later, on his website, a few pictures were posted. One picture had a cute girl in it and she had on low hung jeans. They were so low that about two inches of her underwear was sticking out in the front. She was very petite. Her girlfriends that were with her that night had posted comments about her jeans and about how pretty she was. "Jeans Girl" was born. Up until this point, I never noticed her. She is a thorn in my side till this day. Those cute, perky little bitches that get under your skin. She was a brunette about 5'0"—again, not your typical 5'10" bobble head. Her jeans looked like they were painted on. Even after we found out what her name was, we still called her "Jeans Girl." My friends that don't go to shows with me will still ask about her.

****

There were no shows for about three months. The next one was his annual show that I had gotten Claire and I front row seats for. I spent two months trying to figure out what to wear. This was probably the first time I was going to be wearing something that wasn't boring. I had on shorts with tights, ankle boots, and a button down blouse.

The day finally arrived for the show and again it was nice to have something to look forward to. We schlepped into Brooklyn for this gig. Miles never looked at me at all during the show, at least that's what I thought. I was videotaping the show and during one of the songs that he was singing backup for, he slowly approached the mic with a sly grin, he stared right at me, and sang, "I wish you were with me." Again, he tosses me a bone. *What was that? I'll take it, but what was it?* I didn't see him after that show because it was just so busy and Claire and I left right away.

Not long after the show in Brooklyn, he had another one planned in Manhattan. Between those two, he made an appearance at a show for his friend. He didn't come on till the end, but it was well worth the wait. He sang two songs with no instrument blocking his hot little body. He really sounded incredible. After the show I waited to go over to him. When he saw me, he came over to me and gave me a hug. While he was hugging me, he whispered in my ear, "I saw you last night, you had great seats."

Thank God he was holding me up because I almost passed out. Trying to seem cool and unaffected I said, "I still have dibs on you for April, right?"

He smiled and said, "Of course." I was about to do the boldest move I have ever tried to pull off. I pulled out my card and told him, "I think I gave Meg all of my info but if you need me for anything. . ."

He looked at it and said, "Piper," then looked up and smiled. Every time up until now, he would say "Hi, you" or "Hey, you." It was very cute and I liked it but at least he didn't need to feel awkward after a year to have to now ask me my name. As we were about to part ways, he said, "Are you losing weight?"

This was embarrassing for two reasons, one because clearly I needed to and two because clearly I needed to and he noticed. I said, "I'm trying."

He smiled and said, "You look great," as he walked away. *Holy crap.* The fact that he even noticed or that he said it, I was amazed. He personalized every conversation you had with him. He certainly knew how to torture women because I was starting to climb the walls. *What was all of this?* The last time I remember seeing his wife was at Coney Island. I didn't even see her at the annual show, which was unusual. Don't get me wrong, I'm not complaining, I just found it to be unusual. A few days after that was his NYC show. While we were waiting outside he pulled up and ran his stuff in. Emma was in front of us in line. She flew in from Texas with her husband for the show. She is a friend of Miles' somehow; she is always posting on his site.

Still thinking he probably forgets me from show to show, I was surprised after he parked his car, he came over, smiled and said, "Hi, thanks for coming." I hated that I got excited about any little crumb he would throw me. I felt like a weak woman. Who was he anyway? Just a man. Just a stupid man that probably cheats on his wife. Yet I wanted him so badly. We went inside to watch the show after a few minutes of standing in the crisp New York winter. Since it was in a club, there were no seats, everybody was just milling about until it started. Anticipating a long night standing on heels, I meandered over and stood by the stage stairs. Claire was talking to some friends that had met her there.

Miles came out and as he walked by us, didn't really look, which had me thinking that I was just reading into everything and that he is just friendly to everybody. But as he passed me he ran his finger up the back of my arm and I swear to God every hair on my body stood on end. Trying to be cool as if this happens to me every day, I didn't even flinch. He sat on the steps behind me getting his music together. He dyed his hair a funky color this particular night. Not knowing what else to say other than "fuck me right here, right now"—barely turning my head as if we were having an affair and couldn't be seen talking, I said, "I like the blue." Engulfed in the faux affair, he doesn't look up, keeps flipping through his music and responds, "I look like Papa Smurf." I laughed and mentally rejoined the conversation with Claire and her friends. Claire never even witnessed the entire exchange and she was right next to me. This was fun and very sexy.

I enjoyed this show a little more than the Brooklyn one and I think that is only because I love the city so much. After the show, we said goodnight. Nothing special, just a wave and goodbye. The hard part now was waiting for the next show. I had some guilt because I never told my mother about the party. I figured I would tell her closer to the time. I didn't want her telling me what a fool I was for giving some man $2500 for a concert. I put it all in perspective. Since I really never do anything for myself, this was going to be my indulgence. The only thing was, as of late, now my focus was starting to switch from just having a private concert to wondering if I would be able to seduce him. If nothing had happened yet, and he is a rock star, maybe nothing would. That would probably be the most embarrassing thing that could happen. Being out of my league and asking a rock star to spend the night with me and being denied. I don't know what would be worse, never doing it or being denied. Men are supposed to ask anyway. If I have to ask then I guess he really is not interested. The reason I am even thinking that I can ask him is because I don't think of him as a rock star. I keep saying that he is one but I don't think of him like that. If he was Miles the mechanic and I was interested, I would be fumbling just as much and I would still have hives when I talked to him. This had nothing to do with that. It was strictly about a woman being struck down by a man. I don't know. I wanted more reassurance that if I asked he wouldn't say no.

Chapter 9

About a week after that show, Mom was feeling sick and not willing to go to the doctor. She just sat in her chair. Each day she was declining. Sometimes I feel like she got depressed whenever I went out too many days in a row, weakening her immune system . . . Yeah, I know. I finally told her that I had to take her to the hospital. We were past the point of going to the doctor's office. She had been sleeping for days, unable to really get up. A clear sign that it was really bad was the fact that she agreed. However, she didn't know that I had already called the ambulance. She wanted to take her time getting ready before we went. When she heard the sirens outside, she said, "What is that?" I told her I had to call them so she could be seen faster. I also knew I wouldn't be able to get her there on my own. She needed attention before she got to the hospital but insisted she go to the bathroom first, and the EMS agreed.

She was so bad they had to go in and get her out of the bathroom. I felt very bad because she was angry at me for calling the ambulance. She is such a private person, to have the EMS in the house was bad enough, the fact that they had to come in and get her made it worse. Even though she knew she was bad, she was still angry; that was her Irish make up. Too weak to speak, holding her head in one hand, she waved to my dad with her other as they carried her out. Assuring a confused husband that his wife would be back soon, I ran out behind her and called Sean on the way. He met me at the hospital and I figured, like the last time, they'd give her some medicine, some antibiotics, and she'd be out in a day or two.

After they hooked her up to the IV, she seemed much better. Her breathing was regulated and she was alert. Unfortunately, like the last visit to the hospital three years ago, one of the medications they gave her made her a little wacky. She was very alert, and then thought she had super powers. Sean was on call for this because I was there for her last visit, and she was ready to kill me. She wanted to get out of bed, but we couldn't let her, and since she wasn't tired, this went on all night. On top of that, she didn't know what was going on and was talking crazy. You wind up getting crazy yourself and when you stop laughing, you want to cry. The last time she was in, she was stuck with me and Devon, which was no picnic. She always spoke properly and politely; she was spunky but never nasty.

Well this time she was so sassy; she kept saying to me and Devon, "You two are a couple of jerks. Where's Sean? I want him here." Devon and I couldn't stop laughing because it was so not her and because Sean was the calm one: reasonable, sweet, as close to a perfect human being you could get. Here she was stuck with us. Devon and I had similar personalities but so did Sean and I. I was a perfect mixture. I could be the sweet and caring, most understanding person ever, but I could be cutting and nasty if you got me to that point. That would not happen too often but I could tell it like it is in a raw way and Sean could make it sound acceptable in his way, driving the same point home. It's all in the delivery.

I was at the point where it was not funny anymore and I was tired. Just as Sean walked in the door, they gave her a shot and she went to sleep. *Are you kidding me? How does he get off the hook? I'm with her every day and he couldn't even get this?*

Three years later, guess who's in charge of crazy, because I'm leaving. We kept telling Sean how she was the last time, but he couldn't appreciate it until this visit. I left him around 4 a.m. We had both been sitting there holding down this frail, 110 pound, seventy-nine-year-old woman with superpowers. He said, "You go, I have this." Since I had to get the boys out to school in three hours, I took him up on his offer. When I saw Sean the next day, he looked like someone had beaten him and left him to die. He said, "She tried to get out of the bed all night." I almost pissed myself laughing. *You think?* His face was priceless. *No shit Sherlock.* He said, "She's a small woman but she was tough."

She looked good when we left. They determined she had pneumonia, but with antibiotics she would be fine. She was nervous when she heard pneumonia because with all of the television she watched, all she heard about were pneumonia-related deaths. She was so nervous about getting sick because of her weak immune system; she said a cold would put her in the hospital. Sure enough, a cold did put her in the hospital. The other thing she would say is, "I don't need pneumonia because if I get pneumonia I will die." I told her not to be so dramatic; she wasn't going to get pneumonia. I guess even at thirty-eight we should listen to our mothers because they do know everything.

I was confident because she was already breathing better and starting to look normal. Figuring the antibiotic would run its course, she'd be home in a few days. They moved her from the emergency room to a regular room two days later and, when I went up there, her sister was sitting with her. Mom was still talking a little wacky but not as peppy this time. At least she wasn't trying to get out of bed. When my aunt left, Mom was feeling a little tired so she went to sleep. I didn't think much of it, assuming it was just exhaustion from all the excitement in the emergency room.

The next day, she seemed less peppy and her breathing wasn't as good. I couldn't understand how she could be regressing while on medication. I found out they were just letting her sit there and not moving her at all. "You have to get up," I told her. Not really able to help much, I moved her to a chair and had her stand a little. After being in bed for so many days in a row, she was very weak on her feet. It took a while just to get her to hang her feet over the side of the bed before I could get her to stand.

The next day she was too weak to even try to get in a chair. I had her just hang her feet over the bed. A little pressed for time today, I had to leave to take Quinn to his drum lesson. I was trying to keep my kids lives as normal as possible while simultaneously doing everything possible for my parents. Obviously something would have to suffer because nobody can pull that off for a long period of time. I was gone for only thirty minutes when I got a call from the nurse.

I heard my mother yelling in the background, "I can't breathe!"

"What is going on?" I asked the nurse.

"Mommy wants to talk to you." Gasping, Mom gets on the phone and tells me she can't breathe and that they lowered her oxygen. I calmly tell my mom that I will be right there and to put the nurse back on. When Nurse Ratched got back on the phone, she tells me she just put the oxygen back up and she's fine. Counting the seconds until Quinn was finished, I paced back and forth between guitars and drum sets, trying to make sense of all of this. You can't even have peace of mind leaving for thirty minutes. The stress was starting to get to me and I felt like a horrible mother. As soon as Quinn was done with his lesson, I had to drag him back to the hospital while I tried to get to the bottom of the hide the oxygen game.

The ten minute ride back to the hospital seemed to take forever. Sitting in rush hour traffic on Hylan Boulevard, I kept replaying my mother's struggling voice in my head while Quinn rapped his hands on the back door to practice his drums. It was enough to make me think that they may have a bed waiting for me when I got there.

When I found the nurse, she said that by putting the oxygen up higher it was making her feel better temporarily, but since she couldn't expel the carbon dioxide, she was in essence suffocating herself. Frustrated by the sub-par care in the hospital, my stress, and fatigue, I figured the quicker she gets out of this hellhole of a hospital, the better she'll be. The next stop on this nightmare ride was supposed to be a nursing home for rehab. Since she seemed to be declining quickly, we moved her to the same nursing home she was in the first time. She liked it, we did not. We brought her there because she was the one that needed to thrive, even though we were not fans of this nursing home. Between this and the hospital, this seemed to be the lesser of two evils.

The transport alone took its toll on her. We assured her once her therapy started and she started moving that she would feel better. I don't know if we were trying to convince her or ourselves of this. Even after the move to the nursing home, she still seemed to be declining each day. Questions would go unanswered; comments would be swept under the rug. Since she was such a nervous woman, anytime she said she couldn't breathe she was told by the staff that it was because she was anxious. "Just take a Xanax and you will feel better," was the ongoing suggestion from the staff.

You know the paperwork that comes with your prescription that you take out of the bag and throw away so that you can tear into your meds quicker, especially if it's Xanax? My mother actually read it all. She would be taking her last breath as she read the side effects to her inhaler. "Who gives a shit? Take the medicine, at this point the side effect to not taking it is death, so just take it!" This was the usual exchange when it came to medication between my mother and I. Now that I started taking something to get through my divorce, I was all for it. The feeling was night and day. There was no hesitation on my part anymore when it came to taking medication. I, at this point, did not feel Xanax was going to make the difference between my mother breathing or not. Little did I know, it would.

She was still anxious for a few more days because she was having so much trouble breathing and was sleeping all the time again. Sean and I decided that we needed to go in and have a talk with her. When we got to the nursing home she was sitting quietly in bed and looked so tiny. It's weird when you see your parents out of their normal element. My mom was lost in a sea of white sheets and blankets and looked at us when we came in almost like her rescuers. Sean stood at the foot of her bed and I sat next to her and said, "Look, I know that you don't want to take any medicine that you don't know anything about, but all this will do is relax you enough to help you breathe a little better. At least you won't be worried about it anymore."

"I'm just afraid that if I take it I will die."

"You're not going to die, you will just be relaxed."

"Fine, but if I die, it should be on your head."

"Fine, it's on my head. Sean's here too, you know, but it's on my head." She did not look happy, almost like agreeing meant that she gave up her last right. I reached for a Mallomar and held it up to her mouth; she struggled to take a bite but did manage to finish it. I was happy because she couldn't even catch her breath enough to eat; it wore her out. Mallomar was her favorite so she battled through that.

Of course now I have on my mind that the Xanax better not kill her or I will kill someone. Feeling uneasy the next day, I went to see her around ten a.m. I'm not usually there that early but on Mondays I get out of work early so I felt I should shoot over. Hoping that the pills perked her up a bit and that we may be on the road to recovery, I got off the elevator at her floor. I got that sick feeling I usually got as soon as I got off the elevator. They have everyone lined up in their wheel chairs and everyone looks old. My mom was not old to me, she was just my mom. She was not the old lady in the wheelchair that you might see in the food store, restaurant, doctor's office, or lined up like cattle at the nurse's desk in the nursing home. She was Mom. When I got off the elevator that day, I looked around to see if she was there before I headed to her room. She was afraid to be alone and was so very nervous. I didn't see her, but an old woman hanging out of her chair and onto the nurse's desk caught my eye. When I looked again, I recognized her. I ran over to my mom. She could barely lift her head and I said, "Mom! Are you okay?"

She mouthed, "Help me." I went over to the nurse who was standing behind her desk, the exact desk my mother was clinging to the opposite end of, and said, "Can you go check on my mother?"

"She's fine, I just checked her an hour ago."

An hour ago? She's been suffering for an hour? This is a registered nurse telling me that in an hour, nothing can happen to a seventy-nine-year-old woman with advanced COPD, emphysema, and pneumonia? I went back over to my mother who looked at me with glassy eyes, helpless, just staring. I finally grew a set of balls, got into "Devon Mode," and was ready to throw down with the bitch. I said, "Get over here and check my mother."

The nurse walked over to my mother, put her hands on her shoulders, pushed her back in the chair, and yelled at her, "What's the matter, Ruth?"

As my mother sat helpless, unable to speak and blue, the nurse took her oxygen saturation (pulse ox) and it was sixty. All of a sudden she was concerned. I was done.

Call an ambulance, just get her out of this hellhole. While RN of the year was now feverishly running around trying to locate a doctor, I called Sean. Devon, the healthcare proxy, was in Switzerland. This was bad and I knew it. Something takes over your body at times like this and somehow I snapped into a mechanical mode and took care of everything. I pushed her wheelchair back to her room, but I didn't think she was going to make it before the ambulance got there. It's hard to keep it together, but you realize you have to so you don't upset the person suffering. I am a big believer in either denial or hope, whichever you choose to call it. If you don't keep the faith, you have nothing else. I kept telling her everything would be okay. Just before the ambulance got there she barely turned to her right and panted, "Pray for me."

While the EMS worked on her, I called her sister and told her she might want to meet us at the hospital. I never saw my mother look so bad. I was trying to prepare myself for the worst, but I was starting to freak. The EMS hooked her up to an IV and she was taken to the hospital. I don't remember how I got there, I can't even remember if I went with her or if Sean did.

She was barely breathing in the hospital and they wanted to put her on a ventilator. The healthcare proxy, who would pull her plug in a heartbeat, was in Switzerland, I want to be put on ice, and Sean is the reasonable, sane one. Between Sean and I, we needed to decide whether or not she should go on a ventilator. She had a living will but was barely conscious and going to suffocate. We couldn't get in touch with Devon; therefore, it was up to us.

I went out into the waiting room and all of the hospital noises were drowned out by this weight that was now taking over. There was a feeling something was about to happen that we no longer had control over. It was a terrifying feeling. I collapsed in the waiting room chair, overcome with emotion. The rational one decided to ask my mother what she wanted. He explained to her that she needed to have a tube put down her throat to breathe, or she was going to die. It is all well and good to have your paperwork state that you don't want any extreme means to be used to be kept alive, but most people assume they will be unconscious when this happens.

My mother lay on her side with her mouth half open, fully aware of what was going on but looking like she was staring into space. She was not; she just could not muster the strength to even move her eyes from subject to subject. Sean stood in front of her and explained, "They want me and Piper to make a decision. What do you want us to do?"

Slowly moving her glassy eyes to look into Sean's, she mouthed, "Help me".

At this point it was all on Sean. For the first time in six years, I couldn't handle it and I dumped everything, the worst situation we have had to face yet, on my brother and walked away. Thank God he picked up where I left off. I couldn't see her anymore. Looking drained, Sean walked over to me. I felt a hand on my shoulder and looked up to see a blank look on his face. "They are taking her up now."

After about half an hour, a nurse walked over and told us that she had been tubed, was in the ICU, and that we should go home now. I called Anna, hysterical, to tell her about my mother. Anna had been living in Arizona for the last year. Oddly enough, our mothers were friends and had the same condition. When I called her, she was boarding a plane back to New Jersey because her mom was also in the hospital with pneumonia. She went in about a week after my mother first went in. Anna's brother had just called her about an hour before I did and said, "Maybe you should come home." Standing in the darkness of the parking lot with nothing but the EMERGENCY light glowing at my back, she said, "I'll call you when I land."

The longest night turned into the longest day, followed by the longest week. Still emotionally drained, I couldn't bring myself to go back to the hospital after I left that night. Mom had been unconscious for a week and thank God Sean went every day. He sat there every night talking to her and told her I was there, even though I was home weeping. I had so much guilt about not being able to see her when she needed most me. She was so afraid of being alone and dying that I couldn't handle it when it got bad. I felt guilty leaving Sean to handle it.

About eight days after she was put on the ventilator, Sean called me on his way home from the hospital as he did every night. It is such a strange feeling to cry all the time and feel like it is never going to stop. You are physically and emotionally drained and you would think at some point, your body would just stop weeping . . . yet it doesn't. Just when you think you have nothing left to give, you reach in and find new tears to cry.

His voice was different this night, I could sense it. "The doctor came in to talk to me tonight and he feels that we should take her off of the ventilator and move her to a tracheostomy tube."

Well, why would we do that? Wiping my tears I said, "Has something happened? She never liked that commercial on television about that guy with the trach." The silence on the other end of the phone told me everything I needed to know. They said usually patients are somewhat responsive when they take them off the meds during the day, but she has been off them for a week and she's been unresponsive. The doctor had told Sean to "let her go with dignity and get the tube out of her mouth."

I hung up the phone and cried myself to sleep, as I had done the previous eight nights. Finally I got myself together and knew that I needed to go see her. Sean and Jane took me up, but I sat in the hallway for a minute. Trying to find whatever kind of strength I needed to face this, I slowly crept behind the curtain and saw my cousin Brian sitting at the foot of her bed weeping. I turned to my left and just lost it. She looked so bad, her mouth was all cut up from the tube and to see her chest only moving because a machine was doing it was killing me. My body moved on its own and brought me to her side where I leaned over, kissed her, and whispered in her ear, "I love you. Anna's mother is waiting for you in heaven." Anna's mom had passed the day before.

On autopilot, in the morning I called the hospital and asked them to send a priest in to see her before her surgery. They assured me they would.

The evening of my mom's procedure, I was at Anna's mother's wake. It just seemed so bizarre that as my mother lay dying in New York, I am now consoling my best friend at her mother's wake. What else did God have in mind for us?

My pocketbook was vibrating, so I reached in pulled out my phone to see that Sean was calling. I got up and walked into the hallway.

"I have something to tell you."

Since he knew that I was at the wake, I figured he wouldn't call unless it was important. "What's wrong?" Barely able to hear because of a bad connection, all I could make out was that my mom was awake. When I left for the wake I was told that she probably would not make it through the day, and now I am getting a call that she is awake.

Apparently moving her to the trach had the opposite effect than what they predicted. She was now alert and awake. I listened to my brother while looking into the other room. My friend sat in front of her mother, and I felt guilty for being happy that I just got mine back. We figured they would go together. I almost felt like my mom backed out of a pact and now I had to go in and tell them that their mom would be traveling alone.

After the surgery, Devon went in to see her and was beside himself when he saw her eyes open and she was terrified. He flipped out that no one had called to tell us that she was awake, annoyed that she would be sitting here alone and scared not knowing what was going on. Although she was now experiencing the one thing she feared the most, she was still with us. She hated the commercial of the guy with throat cancer who talked with the trach. Now here she sits in the same situation.

Although we were thrilled to have her back, now we had to face a new set of problems. She had been moved to a feeding tube after they put her on the trach. My joy from her being back now turned into fear from seeing her that way. Not only did I need to see her that way, but she was now awake and alert to see my reaction. I retreated back to my place under my rock at home and was unable to go see her again. What if I couldn't hold it together for her? I didn't want to upset her further, but I also didn't want to leave her.

Feeling like I really needed to man up, I made the phone call. We decided to take Dad up with us so he could spend some time with her. Every day I was greeted with questions about how she was and how she was feeling, and I lied every day. At least now he could see her for himself, but I really didn't know how I was going to handle it. I met Sean in the lobby of the hospital and he slowly walked over and, with a questioning look, asked me if I was sure I was up to this. I knew I had to do this for me but more so for her, so we took a seat in the lobby and waited for Dad. Preparing me for what I would be walking into, we sat and talked for a few minutes. Of course, in a moment like this it seemed as if time flew and, before we knew it, Dad had showed up with the home attendant and we were headed upstairs.

My stomach turned as I watched the elevator numbers climb. When the bell rang at four, I closed my eyes and took a deep breath. The doors opened and we all stepped off. As we proceeded down the hallway, I lagged behind. The others approached the door, but Sean looked over his shoulder at me, then turned to the home attendant and said, "I'll meet you guys in there." He walked back to me. "You don't have to do this you know."

I really did need to. If I didn't do this now, I would wind up avoiding everything. "Maybe I could just wait out here for a few minutes then I will join you?"

Smiling, he put his hand on my shoulder and said, "Take as long as you need, but I need to get in there before Dad starts slapping all of the nurses in the ass." I sent him in and waited in the hallway. After a few minutes, my aunt and uncle came out of the room and were on their way home. They said, "You have to do what's right for you, but she is asking for you." I hadn't realized that my aunt was here too, and it really set in that I had to do this. Slowly, I stood up from the hallway floor and stared at the swinging doors that housed the bold sign over them that read Vent Unit.

Gently pushing them open, before I knew it I had taken enough steps to get me halfway there. Passing bed after bed of machines beeping and watching everyone's chests move mechanically, I spotted a familiar face. Sean watched me with a reassuring smile as I approached. I poked my head around the curtain and I could finally see in her face. She was happy, so I knew I had to be here. It took about five minutes before I was right back to doing whatever I needed to do for her. Though I had stepped backed initially out of fear, I knew my fear paled in comparison to what she must be feeling, so it was time to shake it off, get my helmet on, and get back in the game. I felt like I had my two week breakdown and now I could handle this again.

As the days passed, she actually looked as though she was progressing. She was in a chair one day when I got there, which was so bizarre. They started to get her to eat a little with the trach but she was scared because choking was always another fear of hers. I went in earlier than usual one day to see her, and her face lit up. I was washing my hands in the sink at the foot of her bed when I looked over at her. She pointed at me and mouthed, "You're mine."

I said, "That's right." She was so happy that I was there. Having only a couple of days to process this change of events and relax a tad, now the hospital said we had to decide what we were doing. She was being discharged; this was our immediate future. We were told she was going to get moved to a nursing home but only two of them have a vent unit on Staten Island. Luckily, the one she went to was around the corner from Sean's house. This was not going to be like in the past where she would come home after a few months of therapy. This was going to be permanent. How do people just throw this information out at you like you just have to decide what meal you are going to order for her from the cafeteria. When your mother goes into the hospital, she is supposed to get discharged and sent home with instructions. Maybe there is not a gentler way of saying, "here's your mother with tubes coming out of everywhere, and she can't speak anymore. You have about two hours to decide where you want us to send her because she needs to leave tomorrow."

Even though this was not the life we planned, this was the way it was going to be. She was going to have to live in a nursing home. At this point, it was a temporary move until we could see what was to come of all of this. The day she got moved to the nursing home, Sean was with her. Since she seemed stable once she came out of the whole vent to trach transition, I was feeling comfortable. She had been fine, so the evening of the transfer, I went out locally to see Miles. Since I couldn't be at the nursing home at that hour anyway and it was going to be an early night because of the location, I went. Miles was opening for someone and the show was at a local college. Since I had never gone to a concert alone, I brought a friend with me.

After Miles finished his set, I went out into the lobby to call Sean to see if there were any new developments. It started ringing as soon as I had my phone out of my bag. Quickly trying to connect before he hung up, I think I hit every button on the phone. Sean was calling just to let me know that the transfer had gone smoothly, but it seemed to take a lot out of her. As he was giving me a play by play, out of the corner of my eye I spotted Miles walking towards me. Exchanging glances and smiles as he walked past me, I put my hand over my right ear to drown out the sounds of the next artist and walked to a quiet corner. "What does that mean? Is she okay?" He felt she just needed to rest tonight because it was a big day and tomorrow we would have a better idea of how she was.

After hanging up the phone, I walked back towards the center of the lobby and spotted Miles at the merchandise table. Feeling a little sexier than normal, I felt a little more confident. My attire was starting to change; I had a short skirt on and heels. As soon as he spotted me, he came over and gave me a hug. As he had his arms around me, I softly whispered in his ear, "Well you look incredibly sexy tonight," hoping that might prompt an interesting exchange. Just as he pulled back and we were about to start talking, a young man came over and started talking to him, like I wasn't even there. He was a little wacky, but Miles did not blink an eye. Even after he left he never rolled his eyes or said anything negative. Again, I was impressed. He did say, "I'm glad he didn't say what you said." We started laughing then he casually said, "Did you come alone?"

Damn it, why didn't I come alone? Short of stomping my feet like a two year old, I pointed behind me and said, "No, I have a friend over there."

In a tone that struck me as disappointment, he only said, "Oh." We didn't spend much more time talking, just some more small talk, and then I left.

I went to see Mom the next day because Sean said she was not looking good again, sleeping a lot, and swollen. He told me that I might want to come soon too. I sent Miles's agent a follow up email. She knew my mom was ill but now I let her know that this was touch and go, day to day. It was a month and a half from my scheduled party and I didn't want to goof his schedule up in any fashion.

Once I got to the nursing home, I was amazed at how drastically her condition had changed basically overnight. I sat there for a while with my mom before she started to wake up. It was horrible to watch them suction her. Feeling like I shouldn't have the option to look away, I watched every time they suctioned her even though she was cringing when they did it. I figured if she had to go through it, who was I to look away? At least it wasn't happening to me.

While she was awake, it was evident that she didn't want to be left alone. I promised her that I would sleep there with her. With that, she calmed down and fell asleep. It was torturous to listen and watch them suction her and change her every four hours. I sat next to her during the day. I don't even remember if my kids went to school that day. I had been there for over twenty-four hours before I told her that I had to go because Quinn couldn't miss any more of his religion class or he'd get thrown out. Now, of course, I wish I had taken my chances. She asked me not to go, but I told her that Devon and Sean were coming in a little while and said she'd be fine. My famous last words. That Xanax is still on my head. When I walked out that day to get Quinn to class, that was the last time I saw her awake. Apparently that night that my brothers were there was the last time they saw her awake as well.

Sean and I would pass by or meet each other in her room every day. He looked like shit. I know I didn't look any better. She was never awake, but we would sit there anyway. We felt guilty for hoping she wouldn't wake up while we were there because she was so uncomfortable when she was awake. We were looking worse, she was looking worse, and Dad was asking how she was every day. I thought we would be in the bed next to her if we kept this routine up.

Work was stressful because I work for a bunch of raging lunatics and I was getting scolded for not being friendly to the clients. I was getting temperature and breathing updates on my mother every hour and because I did everything but give a lap dance to these clients, the poor babies felt like I was a meanie. People really need to reconsider what is really fucking important. To tell you the truth, I couldn't give two shits about the whiny, rich, pretentious, asshole client who sat on hold on their phone for one minute longer than they felt they should. Sometimes there are more important things going on. Or the client that didn't get the really big smile they felt they deserved after they came in and complained about prices, then paid $80 for a visit that they think they were overcharged for. That because they graced us with their presence and the customer is always right, I should have to listen to what a bad day that they are having because they were stuck in the office twenty minutes longer than they should have been. In the big spectrum, do I care? Not so much. Apparently that comes across. I'm sick and tired of people not realizing what is really important. The people that you are making phones calls about and writing complaint letters about could be the same people that just took a phone call from a doctor telling them, "I think you should take your mother off life support." Now smile, a customer just came in.

I'm losing my patience. Even though everyone knows what's going on, I have to put on a phony smile at work because "you can't bring your personal problems to work." My paycheck reflects the position of a volunteer job but please tell me, what can I do to make your day easier for you?

Sean called to give me constant updates on my mom. "Hey Piper, Mom's temperature is really climbing."

"Okay."

"Piper, you know she didn't want this."

"So what are you saying?"

"I'm saying her temperature is 103 degrees no matter what they do."

"Is she suffering?"

"I think we need to make a decision. She authorized the intubation but now I think it's time that we step in. She never wanted to be like this. Yes, she is suffering at this point."

"Well we can't just euthanize her! What are we supposed to do?"

"We can stop all medication and just keep her comfortable. And then we would possibly have to take her off the machine.

I was drained. "I'll do whatever you guys want."

"We all need to be in agreement. What do you want to do? Are you okay with this?"

As long as she would not be in any pain, I was in agreement.

After making that decision, I had to deal with the irate client whose house was infested with fleas because she was too cheap to buy the Frontline when it was recommended the last time she was in. Now it's somehow my fault. *Let's prioritize here people.* I really started to put things into perspective as I watched my mother die.

After a week and a half of Mom being unconscious again, we decided to take her off life support. Because they don't do that in the nursing home, she needed to be moved back to the hospital. The plan was for her to be moved Monday morning and then a few hours later we would all be with her when they removed her from the machine. On Sunday I went to see her one more time and to set her hair for her and talk to her. I hated that we had to make this decision, especially since I second-guess everything I do. I would never want to sit on a jury, let alone decide whether my mother lived or died. That's why Devon was the healthcare proxy.

It was around 11:30 a.m. on Monday and we were all in different locations waiting for the call that she had been transported. My phone rang and I saw Devon's name come up. This was it. We were going to have to head over to the hospital now. When I picked up, I wasn't expecting to hear Devon say, "Piper, she passed away on the way to the hospital."

Caught off guard, I stood for a moment, hung up the phone and again, alone, I just wept. Knowing that she was no longer suffering didn't make it hurt any less. One thing I did know was that there was no way she was going to have us have to make this decision.

Right down to the end, she decided what was going to be done for her. She passed away March 12, 2007.

****

After talking to my sister-in-law about what the appropriate thing to do about the party was, I sent Meg an email. I let her know that my mother had passed away and, although we were profoundly upset, it was a month away and I needed something to look forward to, so I would still be having the party. The night my mother died, I wrote her a letter. In it one of the things I asked her for was to help me get through this. I was sorry that I never told her about the party, but I guess she knew now. I spent the entire next day copying pictures and making a board of photos. Clothes still had to be bought for the boys for the wake while Sean shopped for my father. Everything was accomplished fairly quickly, which was unusual for me because I am late for everything. Tuesday night, my choices were sit around doing nothing except wait for day one of the wake on Wednesday, or go see Miles in the city. Not wanting anyone to think I didn't care about my mother, I went to the city without telling anyone. Miles was sitting in with another band and I just needed to get out by myself. This was the first time I went to a concert by myself.

I didn't have a ticket, so I bought one from someone standing in line. I said, "If I take this ticket off your hands, how about letting me get in line with you?" I didn't know who I was anymore, but now I was the girl in the front of the line. When the doors opened, I walked right up to the front of the stage and stood on the left hand side.

To my surprise, Miles was on stage getting his stuff together. He saw me and came over. He knelt down and said, "I'm sorry to hear about your mom."

"Thanks," I said.

"I hope you don't think I'm crazy because I'm at a concert the day after my mother dies."

"Of course not, I understand wanting to stay busy. Do you know where I have been the last few nights?"

"No."

"I've been in the hospital because my dad is dying. I can't believe we're going through this together at the same time." With that, he gently ran his fingertips across my left cheek. I wanted him more every time I saw him.

Before the show started, I offered the couple next to me a piece of gum. They seemed really nice. "So, are you a City Lights fan?"

"Not so much. I'm more of a Miles Baker fan." Gum Boy looked puzzled. I didn't realize Miles' name wasn't on the bill so that's why he was so confused. When I tried to explain who he was, since people don't usually know, he said, "I know exactly who he is. I used to play in a band with him. He's here tonight?"

"Yes, he was just over here talking to me, didn't you see him?"

"No, but will he be out again later? I'd love to say hello to him."

"I'm sure he will, he usually comes out after a show."

"Are you his girlfriend?"

"No, he's married," I said. Gum Boy just grinned. If he was in a band with him ever, he knows he's married, so why would he ask me if I'm his girlfriend if he doesn't cheat? Oy vey. We hit it off during the show and wound up exchanging numbers and said we'd keep in touch. After the show, I went up to Miles and asked him if he would take any requests for the party. He said he would sing whatever I wanted. With that, I pulled out my list.

He laughed and said, "You have a list? That's good." After a quick exchange, we said goodnight and I walked out with Gum Boy and Gum Girl. As we approached the street corner, they spotted Miles and stopped to talk to him. Since I had already spoken with him, I thought it would be redundant to stop again, so I walked by him and tickled his back as I passed him. When I got to the parking garage,

I waited about two minutes before Miles walked in. He was parked at the same garage. Of course, as soon as he got there, some girls went over and started talking to him. Turning back towards the direction of the attendant, I hoped these girls would leave before my car arrived. Their giggling was a tad irritating.

The loser cruiser appeared around the bend so this was my cue. As the attendant got out of my car I could still hear the cackling, so I didn't even turn around. I gave a Lady Di wave as I plopped my ass in the car. I heard him yell, "Piper!" as I shut the door and drove out of the lot.

My sister-in-law and I had a lot to do before the party. I needed an outfit to assure me, how shall I say, of achieving my goal. I was now resigned to the fact that I would take my chances going to hell because I had to have him. Two days after my mom died, Miles' website's home page went black in memory of his dad that had passed that day. I couldn't believe we were in the same pain at the same time. Now the day after, Miles' Dad died, he was to start his concerts with The Event. I assumed he wouldn't be there. Friday was my mother's funeral and Saturday I got a call from Lori who was up from Florida and said, "I am going to Atlantic City to see Noah and Curtis. Why don't you come? I have an extra ticket. Don't just sit home being miserable." I agreed.

At least I would be able to see Lori. She is so sweet and the concert really was good; I was glad that I went. Sunday came along and someone had posted that they were pleasantly surprised to see Miles had still gone to the shows. Surprised that he had performed, I decided that I would go to his last show. Concert number two alone.

Exhausted from the week, I went to the show a little later than I normally would have. I sat in the lobby and waited till the last minute before I had to go in. Just before I got up, I saw Miles walking towards me. A little distracted and withdrawn, he was looking at the floor and didn't see me when I stood up. I called over to him. He came over and just put his arms around me and held me. We exchanged mutual condolences. It felt so good having his arms around me. He whispered in my ear, "I have to head in now. I'll see you in there."

During the show, I noticed for the first time that he didn't have his wedding ring on. What was that? I text messaged Felice immediately. In fact, I think I texted Kim too. The concert was a blur after that, since I think I spent most of the time trying to rationalize a missing piece of jewelry. After the show, I gave him a sympathy card and he hugged me again. Inside was a small card from my mother's wake with an Irish cross on it. He said, "You're Irish?"

"Yes."

"Did you do anything special yesterday?"

Forgetting he was asking because it was St. Patrick's Day, I said, "I feel like a traitor, I went to see Noah and Curtis."

"Oh that's right. Where were they playing?"

"Atlantic City."

He smiled and said, "You're not a traitor."

How is it that I feel like a traitor going to see my boyfriend of the last twenty-three years? A traitor to Miles—*what is happening?* The problem I had with Noah was that he was not as fan-friendly as Miles. Noah had become so commercial that he forgot his roots. Miles was this organic, home grown, genuinely nice guy. And a hot piece of ass to boot.

I got a call from Gum Boy that Monday and I was so happy. People always say they are going to stay in touch, but they never do. He did. He was saying how good it was to see Miles again and he shared with Miles that he had gotten divorced since Miles saw him last. Then he said that Miles had said he was going through a divorce as well. *Watchu talkin' 'bout Willis? Miles is getting divorced?*

"Was I not supposed to say anything?"

Trying to sound calm and cool I told him that it was okay, as I psychotically jumped for joy. To clear Gum Boy's conscience, I told him that I noticed he didn't have his ring on this past weekend. *Oh my God, my mother was going to make sure that I could have what I wanted without me going to hell.* This was too good to be true, but I felt bad too. I'm not happy if they are miserable, I'm just happy that now I'm no longer chasing a married man. I, of course, called all of my biotches. They couldn't believe it. The following weekend was now assured that Jane and I were going to go to the city to get the perfect dress and shoes. Now I had lost fifteen of the thirty pounds I had gained. We got a short dress and very high heels then she gave her stamp of approval.

Chapter 10

The day of the party arrived quickly. As I was on my way to go buy a curling iron, I got a call from Miles' agent saying that he lost my list and wanted to know what songs I wanted. I still could not believe that this was going to happen. I told her I felt bad for making requests, but she assured me that he preferred it because then he didn't need to make a set list.

Waiting for him to arrive at the party was absolute torture. The kids announced that he was here and I think my heart stopped. I went outside to meet him because I was also saving a parking spot for him. As I walked out, he looked me up and down with a smile and said, "You look great."

For some reason, my new natural instinct when a hot guy passes a compliment is to look at his hand. . .And he was wearing his ring. My heart sank. All of the street sounds were muffling together: the cars passing, the kids yelling, and all I could see were his lips moving but heard nothing.

"So I'm following you?"

Dazed, I looked back up at him and said, "Yes, I'm parked right over there." I motioned across the street. This was a monkey wrench I was not anticipating. *Who in the hell puts their wedding ring back on after it has been off for all of the waiting women to see? Huh? Tell me who!* We moved the cars and when I got out of the car I was still reeling from that albatross on his finger. Before we walked back across the street, I asked, "Should I pay you now or later?"

"Later is fine." And with that, we walked across the street together and into the bar. Not realizing he was going to start immediately, I found myself tripping over the folding chairs trying to hit the record button on the video camera. Since I was curious about the whole Deanna Rose connection, I looked at her CD case to see why he always sang these songs. *Ahh, he wrote them.* I had no idea that he was as connected as he was. He wasn't just the "replacement for Satire." He had written a couple of number one songs. He didn't sing them, so who knew?

Besides singing every song I requested beautifully, he sang a bunch of songs he chose. The night was perfect, but as it started to come to a close, I didn't know what to do. My kids were going to be sleeping at Felice's house. I asked Jane what I should do. "Ask him, you have come all this way, don't stop now. You'll never know unless you ask."

After the show, before I could give myself a chance to think about what I was doing, I walked up to him and said, as if I do this all the time, "Can you be coerced into going out for a drink?"

He smiled and looked up at me as he closed his guitar case and said, "Sure." *Holy shit. Now what?* I told Jane and Felice that he said yes but now I was starting to panic. I only rehearsed my anxiety attack about asking him, I never got as far as him actually answering me. Once word got out that he would go out with me, the place cleared like a room full of roaches when the lights were switched on. We started to walk to our cars and he was looking a little torn. *Oh no, please don't let him change his mind. How do I explain that?* I will look like the biggest fool, and if he says no under these circumstances, when no one is around, that has to mean no forever and I couldn't handle that.

Giving him an excuse, because I'm an asshole, I said, "Are you tired?"

He said bashfully with his head down, "Yeah and I have that wedding tomorrow."

Subconsciously somewhat possibly relieved, I volleyed, "That's okay." Approaching the car I told him I would just grab his money for him. Smiling with an aching heart, I handed him his money as the cars raced by us. The lights from the Italian restaurant that we were standing in front of made half of his face visible. As I handed him the money he leaned over and hugged me and then kissed me on the cheek. That was a first. He needed directions to the Verrazano Bridge, but I was having a blonde moment and couldn't help him. I said if it was the Outerbridge, I could help because I live near it.

"That works."

"Okay, then just follow me."

We got in our respective vehicles and I called Jane and said, "What do I do, he's leaving. Do I try again?"

She said, "Yes, you do whatever you need to do to get what you want."

As I drove, I passed a sign for the Verrazano Bridge. *Oh please don't go, please don't go. Yes*—he stayed behind me. I still had absolutely no idea what I was going to do. As I approached my house, I pulled over. Still not knowing what to do I decided to wing it. He pulled over and I got out and started walking towards him.

He got of his car with a big smile. Looking me up and down as I approached he said, "You have great legs." *Why is he doing this if he is not coming home with me? Why the torture?* It's been a year. That is the longest foreplay I have ever encountered. As if I didn't even hear what he said, I told him how to get to the bridge, but he didn't seem to be paying attention. Pausing, I gazed into his eyes and said, "Are you sure you're not thirsty?"

He said "No, but my car is. I really need to stop for gas to get home."

"Okay."

Staring another minute, he slowly leaned towards me and I felt the softest pair of lips barely touch mine. Then, ever so gently, I felt his tongue on my lips, then in my mouth. My heart was racing. Everything was so soft and gentle, I could barely stand it. Not wanting this to stop, I still could not believe it was happening. Slowly pulling back and looking in his eyes I said, "I live around the corner. Are you sure you don't want a drink?"

He smiled, moaned, and said, "Maybe one. Maybe for a minute."

After the breakthrough of a yes, I was a little shocked at the amount of time he was allotting for a "drink".

"A minute?"

With that, he smiled as I walked back, no, maybe I ran back to my car. Slamming the door, I put my hands on the steering wheel, took a deep breath, and tried to plan my strategy. First things first, I called my sister-in-law and said, "Change of plans, we're on our way to my house."

"Okay, call me in the morning. Good luck!"

Next call was to Anna, screaming. "Shit, I hope my house doesn't look too bad. Would he care? Do I even care?" It's like when you're going in to have a baby, you don't want anyone seeing you naked before you give birth but when you're in labor, you don't care who is in the room. If the janitor can make the pain stop, you'll let him in. Did I really care what the house looked like at this point? Maybe a little bit, but that's why I left the lights out. We pulled into my driveway and I looked in my rearview mirror. Miles Baker was in my driveway, sitting behind me, about to go into my house. This is so surreal.

I got out and waited for him to walk to my car. It was a warm, spring night and all you could hear were the trees gently blowing in the night air. It was almost like this was a movie the way everything was working out so perfectly, even down to the weather. We walked up to the back door and as soon as I walked in I tried to hang the keys on the hook but that wasn't happening, so I threw them on the counter and they made a crashing noise. So much for ambiance. Before I could turn around, I felt his hands come around my waist and his lips on my neck. My eyes rolled in my head so I had to wait a minute before I turned around so that he didn't think I was having a seizure. When I turned around, there was that beautiful smile in my kitchen. I put my arms around his waist and started kissing him. I could feel him pressing his body against mine and softly moaning. I actually thought, *if I had a heart attack before this happens, I'm going to be so pissed.* I didn't want to spend too much time in the kitchen because it was a little cluttered. Once I felt his hand gently go up my leg, I knew we needed to move because if I passed out, I didn't want to crack my head on the kitchen floor. We started to walk through the kitchen and I stopped at the fridge, turned with a perplexed look on my face and said, "You're not really thirsty are you?"

He smiled, "No." *Thank God.* He took my hand and we went upstairs. I figured if I get through this without vomiting, there is nothing I can't do. Reaching for the music I jokingly said, "Should I put you on?"

"Oh, please don't." *Radio it is. . .*I walked back over to him and put my arms around him again. As he kissed me, I heard his belt buckle hit the floor. *Oh my God.* I tried to unbutton his shirt, but it was too difficult and I was concentrating on acting like this is normal behavior in a non-slutty way. He had this unbelievable grin on his face as he stared right into my eyes then he started to unbutton his shirt. I could not believe this was happening. What if I didn't like it? He passed the kissing test with flying colors, though. I had never been kissed like that before. What if this sucked? Leaning onto the bed, I watched him take his shirt off then just waited for him.

Slowly he walked over to the bed, kissed me, then climbed on top of me and kept kissing me. Okay, so at this point, I'm quite confident that he can't screw this up. He sat up and the only light shining on him was coming in from the window behind me. I could not believe that I was looking at my fantasy right in front of me. Slowly, he pulled my tights off, then my panties, then leaned down and started kissing me again. He has the most beautiful brown eyes I've ever seen, and as he kissed me he said, "I want to look right at your face while I'm inside you."

Revive me when it's over because I can't handle any more. He lost me about thirty minutes ago, two blocks from my house when he kissed me the first time. After that, I went on autopilot. I tried to remember and enjoy every moment because I knew this could be a one-time thing. He just kept telling me how pretty I was and kissing me the whole time. As I lay next to him, I'm still freaking out that this man is in my bed. Resting my head on his chest, I ran my hand across his chest. He had a content smile on his face and said, "You've lulled me into a complete state of satisfaction." After kissing him for a few more minutes, he said what I dreaded all night, "I have to go."

I didn't know what to do with that. I've never had a one-night stand. Even though I have wanted this for a year, I felt like a whore. Why can't I do once without guilt, what everybody else does every day without a second thought? Hell, he does it. What is my problem? I had to act cool, like I was fine with it. He said, "You stay here and go to sleep." Go to sleep? I have calls to make. Watching him get dressed, I thought to myself, *so this is what it's like . . . when they leave.* He came back over to the bed as he finished buttoning his shirt. We were nose to nose as I kneeled at the edge of the bed. He was gently caressing the sides of my legs and ass as he kissed me. He said, "I must have a lot of will power to leave someone as beautiful as you."

I'm guessing this is the line that goes along with the get up and go. I wrapped my white down comforter around myself and, looking like a big marshmallow, followed him downstairs. As he opened the door, he turned back and looked me up and down one last time and said, "You are so beautiful and so sexy." He locked the door, and then pulled it closed behind him. Standing there dumbfounded for a moment, the sound of the trees blowing in the night air was interrupted by the sound of a car door closing.

Jolted back into reality, I was happy that it happened but I felt cheap. He was an absolute gentleman and did nothing to make me feel that way other than get up and leave. I wish it didn't bother me. Now I had to face the facts that this could be the only time it ever happened.

Picking the bottom of the comforter off the floor, I ventured back upstairs and called Anna. She had patiently waited by her phone for two hours. "Well?" she said.

"It is what it is. It was okay. No big deal. Bar Back Boy was better but it was fine."

There was silence, and then the Acme trumpet came out of my other ear. "What? Are you drunk? Now tell me the truth."

"It is what it is."

"Oh, we're doing that again, are we?"

I told her that I knew going into this that it was not going to be easy but I could handle it. What did she expect me to say, that I'm in love after one night? That's what everyone was worried about. I'm so cool, that I forgot it even happened.

My sister-in-law said that at around 8 a.m., Sean was fumbling around with the phone and she said, "What are you doing?!" He told her he was going to call me. She said, "Don't you dare. You're trying to find out what happened. She'll call when she's ready." You would have thought there was a telethon being held at my house with the phones ringing. My two brothers are the funniest because they are the biggest girls of all. They were my first two calls. Apparently Piper getting laid should be a National holiday.

I have to say it took about a week for the shell-shocked feeling to wear off. I couldn't actually appreciate anything for about a week. Anna got another call from me; this was the call she was waiting for. The ongoing joke now is, "It is what it is." I was too nervous to actually verbalize my feelings because I didn't want everyone saying what most of them wound up saying anyways.

A week later was the first time I was going to see him after the party. He was playing with Mike in Atlantic City. While hanging in the lobby before the show, I saw him come out looking confused. He saw me, came over and planted a kiss right on my lips. He said he was lost and late and had to run back in. That kiss was going to hold me over for quite a bit. I was good with that. Right out in front of everyone: a kiss. Now that we had sex, I've become an uneducated mute. I used to be able to talk to him with ease before, but now I'm stumbling over my thoughts. I've become the blonde bobble head.

I wish I could have just kept acting the way I did when he first started flirting, but I guess it's just natural to start changing your clothes and become a little more conscious of things, like the things you say and do. It's a shame because I think that's when we start to lose who we are. I must have been good enough before if I caught his attention. So why am I changing now? I'm changing into someone I don't even know—how do I know he'll still like me when I don't even know me?

****

The final nail in Noah's proverbial coffin was a concert I went to in the city about a month or so later. He and Curtis were playing at BB Kings. After the show, Claire and I waited outside like a couple of assholes in the freezing cold. There were only about ten of us. We were standing right by their bus, only because that was the only place to stand. The bus was parked right in front of the venue door. Noah came out and didn't even look at anybody and walked straight to the bus. Ten people? It would have taken five minutes of his time and he would not have pissed anyone off. I understand that they don't need to stop but this wasn't like he was out at dinner with his family. This was right after a show. You're still sort of on the clock. I was done.

After the festival thing that I tried to ignore, this was the final straw. After twenty-three years, I closed a huge chapter in my life. I mourned for about five minutes, and then I moved on. I never thought I would ever stop being interested in him but he is just not worth my time, which I don't have much of, or my money, which I have none of. Miles was someone who snuck in under the radar and has consistently been available and accessible to his fans. I have never heard one person say anything negative about him. Anybody I have ever crossed paths with have all said the same thing: "He's a great guy," or "He's such a nice guy." Why did I waste my time on someone who is so callous? I love his voice and his music and he is clearly extremely talented, but no more than Miles in all of these areas. Miles doesn't need to be out in the front all the time. He writes for other people and gives his time and money to charity and still lives in the hometown he grew up in. It was a no brainer.

****

About two months had passed and Miles was doing a show in his hometown of Brooklyn. I took my little guy and his friend Garrett. Claire was with us too. After the show, my son went up to Miles to have him sign a picture of them together from the party. After signing Quinn's photo and talking to him for a minute he looked past Quinn, smiled, then hugged me. He no sooner did that when someone started talking to him. Not waiting around, we just left. I saw Jeans Girl walking around like she was up to no good, then she went into a bar with a friend. I let Claire take the boys and then walked back to where Miles was. A minute later, he pulled up in his car and started to load it. As soon as he saw me, he came over. He signed the picture for the guy who owned the coffee house that I had the party at.

The night of my party, Joe, the owner, had introduced me to Johnny Simms. Johnny had played drums with Jefferson Starship. The photo Miles was signing was a photo of him with Joe and Johnny. After talking a minute he finished loading the car and left. Now I was starting to read into everything. Did he think I was a whore and now he was done with me? Was he now afraid I was going to be everywhere and was he going to pull back? Was he really still the same and was I seeing things that weren't there?

On one level, I missed the innocence and pressure-free faux relationship we had before, like it or not, for better or for worse, things would never be the same after my party. But I would never give that night up for anything, even if it meant it would never happen again. It symbolized a lot for me. I had achieved what, to me, seemed like the impossible. I put my mind to something and made it happen. A rock star wanted me. It blew my mind. I had lost fifteen pounds and was well on my way to losing the other fifteen. He still wanted me when I was fifteen pounds overweight. It was all too surreal for me.

Chapter 11

After the Brooklyn show, Claire and I went to a show in Philly. There was about a month or two between shows. I paid too much attention to what everybody kept telling me and was pushing things I should have just let go of. I blame myself for not having enough confidence to just go along the way I had been. I would have been okay with going to shows and not knowing what would happen each night. After the show, I went up to Miles and said, "You know, if you think about it, you never had your required meal at the party. I am contractually obligated to take you out to dinner. I wouldn't want Meg angry at me because I broke the contract."

He started laughing. "We can do that. I'll talk to you." He kissed me and I left. It wasn't a no, but there was nothing set. I would have been content to leave it like that but I allowed myself to get pushed by the people who were not there to see the actual exchange between us each time. Just going to the shows and having it remain copacetic would have been enough for me. Anything else would have just been an added bonus.

****

About two weeks later, Claire and I went to a show in Mt. Vernon. This was an eye opener and a sign of things to come. After careful planning with Jane, we decided that I would make two reservations for two different days in a restaurant in Manhattan. Since I apparently could have sex with him but was now unable to speak to him, I printed the restaurant info from the computer. The plan was to give him the info and ask him which day was better for him. What I was not planning on was for the girl that would be there. I was still at the point where I was sort of cold, trying to not have an emotional connection.

Claire and I were sitting at a table and behind us at another table was a red head sitting with a couple. I could not guess her age, as I'm not good at that. When Miles came in, his guitarist Paulie was sitting with us. Miles came to us and said hello, then motioned to Paulie to sit with him. Miles sat directly behind me, our chairs were hitting. He sat across from the red head. This was not going to be good. I was starting to get a little sick. Sick because I got to this point. I was safe in my cocoon. Why was this now happening? All of a sudden, she comes around the table and gets behind him, ass in my face, and has her arms around his neck. Claire looked like she was going to shit herself because she didn't know what I was going to do. I contemplated beating her ass down for about a half a second but realized he would not like that. Claire's eyes were like dinner plates staring at me.

"Let's just go," she said.

"No, I'm not running away." We drove an hour to see a show, so we were going to see a show. Some little bitch was not going to determine my night. How about a little discretion though? I always held back because, although I knew he was divorced, no one else did. I didn't want people to get the wrong idea about him. He had to know I saw all of this because her big ass was on my shoulder at this point. He never put his hands on her. I could play this two ways in my mind. It was nothing and she just is a whore, or she is a whore and he is leaving with her after the show. Before the show started, I ran downstairs and called Donna. Donna is my personal spin-doctor and my voice of reason. She is a mother of four daughters and does not get rattled easily. My infantile problems were a piece of cake for her to solve. "Do I go through with this whole thing or abort mission?"

"Well I think you will regret it if you don't do it and clearly, if anything, he is playing the field so there is no reason why you can't do this."

Okay, I'm doing it. After his set, he went out to his car and I followed. Holding my phone to my ear like I was engulfed in a very important conversation, I stood by the front door. As he approached, he smiled and walked over to me. He hugged me and said, "You look great. How long did it take you to get here?"

"About an hour and a half," I said. Wanting him to know that I knew hose bag was there for him, but that I am cool with everything, I said, "Listen, I know you are busy tonight so I just wanted to let you know I made two reservations for dinner." He started laughing. "I have to cancel whichever one doesn't work for you and I can cancel both. But I do need to call before Thursday." I gave him the paper and he kissed me.

"Okay, I'll let you know." As he walked back in, he turned around and said, "Where is it for?"

"The Gotham Bar and Grill." He looked impressed. I had written my home and cell phone numbers on the paper. Now I was about to endure the longest four days of my life. We decided to split after the mission was accomplished because the less I had to actually witness, the better.

****

Each day that went by, I grew increasingly stressed and depressed. I had stopped taking my meds the day my mom passed. I had been running every day so I never felt the need for any meds. Now I feared I would have to go back to them. I was more worried about him not contacting me at all rather than him saying no. I would have to acknowledge that he was a typical loser man and a jerk and certainly not the man I thought he was if he didn't call. By Tuesday, I was crying. I haven't cried over a man since I found my husband in bed with a twenty-one-year-old whore. How did I get to the point where someone whose existence I did not even want to acknowledge had gotten to me, broken me down, and made me vulnerable again? I swore I would never allow myself to be this weak ever again.

Wednesday night I was supposed to go to BB Kings with Claire to see John Waite. By Wednesday, I was sobbing constantly. My children were afraid to question anything. I dropped the kids off at my dad's and Sean was there. I had to hold it together, especially the way he felt about what I was doing anyway. He asked me if I was okay.

"Yes, I'm fine." While I was there, the restaurant called to confirm the reservations and I said to cancel both of them. I was hysterical and left. I picked Claire up and off to the city we went. I sat all night just praying he would make the call. Even if it's no, just make the call. I didn't want to lose faith in him. What was the point to this whole thing? Why did the painter tell me about him eighteen years ago, why has he continued to show up in every part of my life, why was he getting divorced, why did our parents die three days apart, our birthdays are eleven days apart? He has never disappointed me yet, but if he does not call, I will be devastated. Claire the optimist said, "Well, I'm sorry it didn't turn out the way you wanted. I guess he's not the man we thought. He should at least have the courtesy to make the call."

Okay I get it. Not helping. I said, "It's not over yet. The first reservation isn't until tomorrow night." She rolled her eyes. My heart was broken. I kept asking my mother for help. *Please don't make him like everyone else.* I cried myself to sleep that night. At 6:30 am on Thursday, my cell phone rang. I looked at the number and it was out of state. For a second I thought it was a bill collector but at the same time a calm came over me and I put the phone down, closed my eyes, and went back to sleep.

An hour later I saw I had a voicemail. "Good morning Piper, it's Miles Baker." Oh my god, now they were tears of joy. Thank you, thank you for not letting him be a jerk. "I've been meaning to call you. I'm at Newark Airport right now. I have a gig tonight in Indiana, so therefore obviously tonight's date I would not be able to make. I won't be home till Saturday so I can't make that one either. Thank you for your tenaciousness, if that's the correct word. I really am flattered that you have gone to all this trouble but I can't, at least not yet. I have to go now, but thank you. Bye Piper."

Who knew my faith in men could be restored with one man? A rock star that is supposed to be inconsiderate, self-centered, a player with no feelings—isn't that the definition?

I can't help but think there is a reason for all of this. I just pray the reason was not so that he would be a catalyst to get me back on track and out in the real world to meet a different man because that would just be cruel.

I was feeling better about the whole thing, as I just wanted the call, but now I was thinking about him with the other girl. How do people handle this? This was just a very distressing situation that I kept insisting I could handle. I wanted to believe I could, but I knew I was fooling myself. My therapist was on speed dial at this point.

With every setback, I had more inspiration. I kept telling myself that I had to work out more, so I was running like Forrest Gump. I figured if he was with another girl, I wasn't thin enough, so I should bump my running up. Again, in some twisted way, he was having a positive influence on me. I was getting healthier, back to the way I was before my husband. I let myself go for so long that I forgot who I was. In my mind I was a skinny tomboy in a fat body. I used the fat body to protect myself so that I didn't get looked at or asked out. I didn't want to be bothered. I also didn't think that I had the right to go out when I had two children at home. Feeling like I needed to be home with them and be a mother, I rarely went out. I got into a terrible rut that I accepted as the way that I was going to live my life. What's sick about the whole thing is that usually when someone gets into a rut, they are miserable and plan to get out of it. I was miserable and resigned to the fact that this is the way my life was to be and that I didn't really deserve to be happy. I don't really know why I was punishing myself. It was a lot of guilt again. I really just figured if I took care of everyone else, that if something did come up that I wanted to do, I could at least feel like I did deserve that one night out. Once Miles came along I did want to climb right out of the fat costume.

Maybe it's good that I thought he was a jerk for as long as I did. It's all about timing. I would have tortured myself watching him from the sidelines with his family, at least now there was some glimmer of hope. Hope for what, I don't know.

****

Since Miles's shows are broken up the way they are, sometimes there could be two shows in a month or six weeks between two shows. You feel like there is a fine line you walk between stalker and fan. I felt like I was in a different category. I know I'm not a stalker, but you worry about what you are being perceived as. Since there is such a span between shows, you don't want to miss any because it would wind up being months without seeing him. I hate to consider myself a fan because I am not just going to a show, appreciating the music and the view, then going home and going about my night. I have stepped into some other realm. I've been intimate with him. I don't want his autograph and I'm not star struck, I genuinely care about him. It's not easy for me to watch a show, get up, and leave like he's just any performer I would go to see.

My friends and family are very funny. They don't want me to emotionally invest myself in this "rock star that sleeps with anything that moves and doesn't give you a second thought," yet they want him to call me and take me out as if we're dating. They have said, "He is who he is." Well then you can't play it both ways. They also think maybe I should stop going to see him before I get hurt. I am going to get hurt no matter what at this point, so why not make the most of this dream? I was getting a little discouraged because, other than the night of my party, nothing has happened. Did I pale in comparison to everybody else he's been with? Does he regret it and now he's just being kind? Maybe he never even wasted a second giving me a second thought and I'm just nuts. I'm sure I've put one thousand times more thought into everything than he has.

Chapter 12

A show was posted that he was going to be doing down the shore. I was hoping there would not be many of his cult following there. This was not a solo show, tonight was a full band show. Claire and I sat at the bar before they went on. Claire spotted Miles talking to someone in the bar so she walked past him on her way to the bathroom so that he would know we were there. Smiling, he said hello as she went by.

We moved to the other side of the bar when they went on so we could see better. He spotted me immediately and I saw him grin. Thank God none of the usual suspects were here. Hopefully I would get a chance to talk to him tonight. Every time I see him someone inevitably interrupts us. I always wait until he's done talking to someone before I go over to him, if I go at all. Nobody gives it a second thought when they come right over and start talking to him when he is with me. It is very irritating but again, I am used to this and I let it go. My dad was a professional soccer player. He was the "local hero" where he lived. People were always talking to him, he was always out socially, people constantly around. I am immune to this on some level. I automatically put myself in the backseat and I know that is not good. I never demanded to be acknowledged, therefore I'm not. I have allowed myself to be a doormat for a very long time and I don't want to do it anymore. As strong as I am in some ways, I can also be so weak.

During the break, Miles went to the upstairs loft. I could see him from the bar. He didn't stay there long and often went in and out of sight. Again I was confused because if he did see me, was he not coming over on purpose? Claire said she was going to the bathroom so that if he wanted to come over he could. He had not returned back to view in the loft so I turned to look towards the ocean and I saw him outside on the back patio looking out at the sky. Nobody was near him, dare I go out there? With my luck, I'll get halfway there and someone will come over. Ever since my party it seemed as though I am the one that always goes over to him, whereas before he used to come to me. Since the chase was over, was he done? I don't know how this works and I am tired of games and trying to figure out if I'm supposed to get uninterested in order to keep him interested. This is just too much stupidity for me. I just want him, why can't I have him?

Oh shit, he's on the move. What do I do now? Oh I know, I'll act like I don't see him. I know, junior high. Turning straight ahead I stood at the bar looking in the opposite direction and all of a sudden I feel this gentle hand run up my back. My hair stood on end. Turning over my right shoulder like I would never expect to bump into him here, there was that beautiful smile and brown eyes.

"Hi," he said, as he leaned in and kissed me.

"Hi."

He asked me if I had seen Paulie. He said he was looking for him because, "He is here with his wife and he really should be out back because it is beautiful out."

I said, "Well ain't you romantic."

"Yeah, for other people, not myself."

He put his hand on my back, leaned in, and kissed me, then said he was going to go look for him and would see me later. I've noticed something since my party: he never looks at me from the stage. He used to, but I don't know what any of this means, if it means anything at all.

During the second set, it was business as usual. He was ignoring me. Out of nowhere, three guys came over and started talking to me. Two were brothers and one was a friend. I guess this was the "pickup artist" and his two "wingmen." As I glanced back up and over at Miles, I noticed he was now looking at me. In fact, he stared at me for the rest of his set. Not wanting to give them the wrong idea, I played it up a little, but I didn't want to get myself into another situation that I couldn't get out of (think JJ Rockers, circa 1990). After the show, one of them asked me for my number. Damn it. Having the spine that I do, I handed it out like candy. I of course now started the ritual of praying that he doesn't actually call. On our way out, we passed Miles in the doorway. He said hi as he passed us. What is that really? I feel like the biggest ass, standing around and waiting for him. Sort of like the women standing on a stage hoping they are handed a rose. Please! Give me a break. I hate that show, and myself for what I'm doing since it's no different.

Miles was carrying his stuff to the car, so were the other guys. Claire took the keys and walked to the car. She thought he might stop and talk if I was alone. He saw me and put his finger up indicating to wait a minute. That, I don't mind. It's the whole walking back and forth past me and saying nothing that irritates me. Clearly I am here for you. It's like the elephant in the middle of the room. Say something. Finally he came over and said, "Hey, what are you doing?"

Flying by the seat of my pants I blurt out, "Do you want to go for a walk?"

"Sure," he said. Not expecting that since he kept shooting me down, I motioned forward as a suggestion. He smiled and we walked over to the boardwalk and stood up there. It was a beautiful, almost perfect August night. There was a couple not far from us in the street fighting. We were making up all different kinds of scenarios that could be going on with them. She had bags; who is locked out of the car; who is yelling; the whole time I'm wondering how I can kiss him. I feel like I'm in limbo. I have no idea what's appropriate because I don't know what kind of relationship we have. I don't know if he ever wants to kiss me again since it's been four months since I slept with him. It's so silly that we've had sex and now I don't know what behavior is appropriate.

"So is your next show in Florida?"

Contemplating for a second he said, "Yeah I guess it is." Smiling he said, "You're not going to that though are you?"

I just shrugged and said, "I don't know." I had purchased my ticket the day they went on sale and about two months later bought a train ticket. I wanted to see what his reaction was before saying anything about going. I really wanted to go. It would be a little adventure and hopefully won't have the local fans hanging all over him. It was also going to be a sound check and meet and greet in addition to the show. Not that I need a meet and greet. What am I going to do, walk up to him and shake his hand and say nice to meet you? I'll put out of my mind that I've seen you naked and make believe we're meeting for the first time. This is what I mean when I say this whole situation is ridiculous. You're in limbo. You're not the girlfriend by any stretch of the imagination but you're not the fan waiting for the autograph or the chance meeting either. It sort of puts you in an awkward spot. I don't even like to ask for a picture now because I feel stupid—almost like I'm star struck, when in fact I could care less about all of it. I just want him, the man. Since my mother passed away and my father was well taken care of by our home attendant, I have the freedom to do things now that I haven't been able to do since I had my kids.

After the small, bullshit talk was over, he turned and looked at me. I wanted him so badly. He smiled and put his arms around me, it was so perfect. It was gorgeous out; we were on the boardwalk and all I kept thinking was I could stay like this in his arms forever. He just seemed so comfortable and content. I pulled my head back a little and we were cheek to cheek. His skin is so soft. I kissed his cheek, then moved a little closer to his mouth with another kiss, then the corner of his mouth. He turned his head and again, so softly and gently his tongue barely touched my lips, then he half put it in my mouth before gently kissing my lips again.

When he kisses me, it takes my breath away and my legs get weak. Since I was so shell-shocked the last time, I told myself to make sure I remember everything this time and feel it, even though I can barely stand when he kisses me. I ran my hands up his back slowly, feeling every inch of it, and down both his arms, feeling every muscle. I put my hands on his lower back before I ran them over his ass. He never flinched, so submissive, letting me explore everything I wanted. He never stopped kissing me slowly and gently the whole time, except for maybe two times when he pulled back and just looked at me, smiling. Other than that he just kept kissing me. I couldn't believe this was the body of a fifty-two-year-old man. He was so much sexier than anyone my own age or younger that I had ever met. When he first started kissing me my bag fell off my shoulder to the floor and we just kept kissing. At one point he put his cheek on mine and just hugged me firmly.

"We have to go," he moaned.

"Do we?" I asked.

"Mmm, I have to go back to Brooklyn and you have to go back to Staten Island." He kept holding me. I didn't want the night to end. He picked up my bag and put it on his shoulder.

I said, "It's not your color," as I took it off him and put it back on the floor and started kissing him again. After a few more minutes, he picked my bag up and put it back on his shoulder and took my hand.

"Where are you parked?" he asked.

"All the way down there," I said as I gestured ahead. We slowly walked hand in hand and as he passed the bouncers he said goodnight. He held my hand the whole time. In front of everybody. I couldn't believe it. As we walked, he turned to me and said, "You have beautiful eyes."

"No, you have beautiful eyes but I'm sure you hear that all the time." It's like telling Angelina Jolie she has nice lips. This man had the biggest, brownest eyes I had ever seen and they were caring, sexy, and warm.

He smiled and said, "I just think when someone has beautiful eyes, you should tell them they have beautiful eyes." He doesn't need to say any of this. I'm a sure thing. He knows that. I love "girlie men." To me they are so much sexier and one thousand times more masculine than any of these muscle-head Neanderthals. It was such a turn on that he thought it would be romantic to go outside on the beach and the fact that he carried my pocketbook on his shoulder from the boardwalk to my car, past the people that had watched him perform earlier that night and the bouncers from the club. Three quarters of the way down the street to my car, I remembered Claire was in there waiting for me. I stopped short and he looked at me. I said, "Claire's in the car." We stood there and kissed a little longer. Like a child I said, "Five more minutes."

He started laughing and kissed me again and said, "No, you have to go home." He held my hand till the last minute as he turned to go back to his car.

I had a big stupid grin on my face as I walked back to my car, which was further than I had remembered. Claire, to my surprise, was still awake. "Well, what happened?"

"He is unbelievable. I just can't get over the way he kisses. It's unreal."

"Well it doesn't surprise me, he is very sexy. I'm sure he knows exactly what he's doing."

Yeah, but what the hell am I doing? I don't know how long this night will hold me over. Luckily there's only about two weeks until Florida.

****

One of the things I worried about in Florida was that I had no idea if he was going to have somebody there with him. Since I didn't say I was going, he had no idea. I also worried he might think I am crossing the stalker threshold. I see many people show up at his shows that fly in from other states and they are not considered stalkers. Am I pressuring him or making him feel uncomfortable by coming out of the local setting? I worry so much about everything that I forget to actually enjoy the whole experience. My nerves have me physically ill before each show. I was also unnerved about asking him to hang out after. *What if he says no? How much of a dick am I then? Is everyone who knows I went there going to hate him then and think he's a jerk? Why do I even care about that?* I never asked a man out before in my life except my date for the senior prom, and that I had to take a running start at. This girl was not brought up to think that it's okay to ask a man out. The feminists of today would say, why should you wait around for him to ask you out? If you want him, ask him. Terrified of rejection I just do not have that drive in me. What person isn't terrified of rejection? It must be horrible for men. Society sort of dictates it's their place to put their neck on the line each time. Since the night at the beach, I felt a little more confident going into this. At least I knew he was still interested.

Since I absolutely refuse to fly, I was taking an eighteen-hour Amtrak ride to Florida. Before I did that, I had to take a thirty-minute train ride to a thirty-minute ferry ride to get off the God-forsaken island that I live on. From the ferry, I took my life in my hands and got in a NYC taxi to Penn Station, where I sat with society's elite, before getting on Amtrak. I got into Florida at 8:00 a.m. the day before the show. I didn't want to take any chance with the train breaking down or any other catastrophe. Not only did I go on this big excursion, but I swore my kids to secrecy. I don't normally ask them to do this, but I made them promise they would not tell my brothers. I know, I'm thirty-nine and should be able to go wherever I want, whenever I want, but like I said, I'm not in therapy for nothing. Jane was in on it. She lent me her ho boots for the occasion. My sons knew where I was going but I told them if my brothers called looking for me, just say I was out, then they should call me. Only one of my brothers was going to be a real problem, Sean. I talk to him a few times a day so my absence was going to be inexplicable. He also teaches in my son's high school, so my son had a little extra pressure on him to shut the hell up. That son is the weak link too. Book smart, but not much street smarts or common sense. He'd break easily. That is where Jane comes in. She could occupy my brother and distract him for a few days so he didn't call.

Remember what I said about my eldest. He was about two weeks into his freshman year in a new Catholic school, which was a far cry from his New York City public school upbringing. I told both of my sons before I left, "Do not do anything stupid to make anyone have to call me." My kids were staying at my dad's house with Rani, our home attendant. Rani was the best—any chance I could see Miles, she would say, "Go, go, leave boys here, go." She was in on the cover up as well. She was awesome. She was Sri Lankan, so if need be, she could act very confused and act like she didn't know what my brothers meant. She loved me and would do anything for me.

Sean is a math teacher and friends with all of my son's teachers, especially his math teacher. I had to leave two days before the show because of the train and was not getting home until two days after the show. I had three days of school to cover. My scholar decides he's not going to do his math homework before I leave. Needless to say, I receive a call while I'm in freakin' Virginia or some shit like that from my brother saying, "Boy Wonder didn't do his homework, call me back." *Call me back?* I'm what, a couple of hours into this and I'm already getting calls. Not good.

So I immediately call my son, screaming, "Are you kidding me? Did you think he wasn't going to find out? He wants me to call him now. You need to call him and fix this." I was like a lunatic. "Didn't I tell you not to do anything stupid?" For the record, this is stupid. He promised me he would talk to my brother and rectify the situation. I sent my brother a text, that way he didn't hear any background noises.

I know I'm a fag but I wasn't ready at that point to stand up for myself and say, "I'm going and that's it." Everybody, actually just my brothers, felt I was a groupie, letting myself get used. I, on the other hand, was having the time of my life and didn't understand why I needed to change my routine after we slept together. Devon would ask, "Are you still going to go to as many shows? Don't you think you should hang back now?" Why? I wasn't going to more shows after I had been with him than before. He is not a co-worker that I see every day and can play coy games with. I have limited opportunities to see him and I have to make the most of every situation. This was a situation I planned to make the most of.

After I arrived in Florida, I took a cab to the hotel. The hotel was adorable. As soon as I saw it I fell in love with it. I can't explain it, and this is the only time I have ever experienced this, but as soon as I opened the door to my room I was overcome with what felt like my mother's presence. So much so that as soon as I walked in the room I smiled and said out loud, "You're here Mom." I was hoping that was a sign that everything was going to go the way I wanted it to. The room was very quaint. It was a nice size and the only thing I didn't really like was the fire escape ladder right outside my window next to my bed. It was a little too convenient for anyone to just walk up there. I dropped my stuff off in the room then went downstairs to get directions to the venue. I knew it was only two miles from the hotel so I decided to walk there to get an idea of where it was and to find a nail salon. Luckily the hotel let me check in early.

I found a couple of immediate necessities: Dunkin' Donuts, Subway, a nail salon, and the venue. It was in a cute little area and it was a good walk, I'll tell you that. Peering in the front window I could see that the venue was very small inside. It was dark and all of the chairs were set up waiting for the next show. You need to know these things beforehand so you can plan your attack.

Although I never really know what the hell I'm doing until I'm doing it. On the way back, I stopped at the nail salon. Apparently down south, they don't have all the modern conveniences of New York, like Lady Godiva nail polish. I had to go with Baby's Breath White. After the manicure and pedicure, I went next door to get a twelve inch sandwich because I eat like a farm animal. I took that back to the hotel.

I know that this does not sound exciting or interesting but my plan was to go back to the hotel and take an uninterrupted shower, then go to sleep. After my shower I wound up lying down around 4:30 in the afternoon. It was a beautiful thing. No phone, no interruptions, no obligations. I put my headset on and fell asleep. At about 6:00 p.m. I awoke to a voicemail from Sean saying, "Boy Wonder had no calculator and no homework again." He's kidding me right? Is my son out of his alleged mind? What fool goes into his math class two days in a row with no homework when your uncle is a math teacher across the hall? An idiot does, that's who. This was how my son rectified this situation? By going in the next day with no homework, then also leaving a graphing calculator home just for shits and kicks. That's two unsolicited phone calls in two days due to the arrogance of my son's stupidity.

I called my son, yet again. Calmly, I tried to explain to him that he was killing me slowly. I said, "I haven't even gone to the show yet and you are doing everything to get my ass caught."

"I'm sorry," was the reply. Not helping. Thank God it was Friday. At least when he doesn't do his homework Monday, I'll be home for the call on Tuesday. Ironically enough, my pepper pot, Quinn, managed to stay out of trouble. After that phone call I did nothing but stay in bed until the next morning and was very excited that Pretty in Pink was on. How lame am I? It was so relaxing. I thought I might come back next year just to sleep in, even if Miles doesn't play here. The next morning I got up and ran downstairs and got some tea. When I go to concerts, I end up on the Mary Kate Olsen diet. Besides feeling sick, I got paranoid about looking fat so I didn't eat. Again I'm not in therapy because I can think rationally. I had lost seven pounds since my party. The outfit decided on for this excursion was a brown plaid mini skirt, brown tights, brown sweater, and a cream camisole. I didn't know what I was going to do but I took my time getting ready and called a cab around 4:00 p.m. because I didn't know how long they would take to get there. He came pretty quickly so I wound up sitting outside the venue for a while. Little by little people started showing up and they all kind of knew each other from the website. I read the site but I would never post anything because I would never put my business up there, yet I appreciate that everyone else does.

I was sitting on a bench a few stores away from everyone else. The promoter pulled up with Miles and his agent in the car. Miles had his aviator sunglasses on, jeans, and an opened shirt over a white wife beater. There was a set of stairs they came walking up to my left. As they approached me, Miles smiled, pointed at me as he passed, and said, "I am amazed." *Well*, I thought, *he's not freaked out so that's a good thing.* The crowd went in after him and we were handed our passes then sat and watched the sound check. He looked hot, as usual. The sound check took about twenty-five minutes and was followed directly by the meet and greet.

I sat on the end seat in the aisle and he had to walk past me to get to the meet and greet area. When he came by, he looked at me and said again, "I am amazed."

The girl behind me said, "I told you I was coming."

He looked at her and said, "You, I expected." He then looked back at me, smiling and shaking his head. He gently ran his fingertips across my left cheek and said, "I am amazed." Everybody lined up to see him and I was still unsure how I was going to handle this. I thought it might be difficult to just ask him because everyone was swarming around him.

This warranted a text to my sister–in–law. I said, "Should I ask him or maybe pass him a note like I'm in freakin' junior high?"

Her famous last words: "You do whatever you need to do to get him to leave with you."

Okay, I figured, there is no alternative. He leaves with me. I wrote a note on the bar napkin that said, "Do you want to hang out later?" I figured I had the note as a backup in case I could not verbally ask him due to the crowd. When I got up to him, my heart was racing, but I tried to act all cool and collected. He gave me a big hug and the girl behind me was going to take our picture. As we're posing, he had his left arm around my lower back and was seductively rubbing it. I rubbed his back and turned towards him. It was all I could do not to start kissing him. I was melting, it was almost torture. After she took the picture, he said, "How did you get here?"

"Don't ask."

"No really, how did you get here?"

"I took a train."

"How long did that take you?"

"Eighteen hours."

"I can't believe it." He sat down behind his table of pictures and said, "You don't really want one of these, do you?"

I said, "Of course I do." While he was writing out the picture, I bent over in his ear and said, "Do you want to get together later?"

Before I even finished the question he said, "Yes," almost with a "duh" tone. He gave me the picture, smiled, and I went back to my seat. Waiting till I sat down to look at the picture, I was like a child on Christmas morning ripping the picture out of my bag to see it. To Piper the Beautiful, Love Miles. Yeah, I want him. How was this going to work out, though? After the meet and greet he went back to the hotel to get ready. Everybody just hung out at the club and they were all very friendly and nice.

He looked incredible when he came back. He had on a white, button down shirt and black dress pants for the show. The show was better than I imagined and I was so glad that I decided to go. Now I'm sitting there wondering how this is going to play out. After his set, he went upstairs and I was standing by the bar. He came out and stood next to me, looking through some things in his pocket. He pulled something out and put it in my hand and said, "I'm always being watched." Tell me about it. I kept my hand closed tightly, dying to know what it was. He was smiling and said, "Well you're dressed provocatively tonight."

Since I had two layers of clothes on I said, "I'm covered, do I look like a whore?"

"No, no," he said, "You don't look trashy. It's sexy, I like it."

Leaning against his arm I said, "I have a problem."

He smiled, leaned in and said, "What's that?"

I said, "I can't stand to be this close to you without wanting to rip every article of clothing off your body."

He started to laugh and said, "I have to sing a couple songs with this guy." Jackson Bentley was playing after him and apparently Miles had to sing at some point with him. As much as I wanted to hear him sing again, I much preferred leaving early and ripping his clothes off.

After talking a little more I said, "Do you really need to sing?" He laughed, and then of course, he got called away.

I ran into the bathroom to see what treasure lurked in the palm of my hand: the coveted cell phone number. Oh no he di-int. I went back to my seat almost giddy and sent him a text saying, "I'm staying five minutes from here."

He responded back saying, "Where? A hotel? What's the name?"

I sent this long-winded text with the hotel name and directions (pretty precise since I had walked it the day before). After he sang with Jackson, he ran off the stage. I sat there watching most of the remainder of the show only because I never heard from Miles. Starting to get a migraine from the music, I went outside to get some air. While I was out there, one of the girls had come out and said she was going to leave since Miles had already left. Out of character for me, I joined their conversation and bellowed, "He left!"

"Yeah, a while ago."

Oh, well that's just great. I'm sitting here watching this guy and I could be with Miles. But why haven't I heard from him? I'm starting to get nervous. What if he blows me off? I already told Anna and Jane we were hooking up. How do I explain him being a jerk? Here we go again. I called and left a voicemail, asking if he had left yet and that I was still here. Then I sent a text saying, "Are we still meeting?" I called a cab because I figured there was no point in staying here if he had already left. While I was sitting outside for the cab, I was starting to get that same nervous feeling I had when I was waiting for him to respond about the dinner reservations. He has not disappointed me yet, so let's not lose hope.

My phone vibrates, I look down, Miles' cell. I read the message, "I'm at the hotel, same as mine." Oh my God. What are the chances? Where is that fucking cab? Hurry, hurry, hurry. "Okay, I'll let you know when I'm there." Finally the cab shows up and I throw all of my shit in and hop in like it's a get a way car. Let's go, let's go. As I look around as he's driving, it seems as though he is going in the opposite direction. Oh no, this cab driver is not going to screw up my only chance at bi-annual sex. Again, out of character for me, I actually spoke up and said, "Where are you going?"

"This is shorter," he tells me. I have to say. Asking him where he was going was ballsy for me. Normally I would just end up at the wrong location, pay, and I would somehow end up apologizing. I guess I wanted Miles badly enough to speak up. I flew up to my room and brushed my teeth and sent a text saying, "I'm back and I'm in room 1011."

A minute later, I get a text that says, "Are you ready?" With that, I almost dropped the phone in the sink. I responded back, "You have no idea." As I hit send, there was a knock at my door and my heart stopped. Taking a deep breath, I walked over to the door and when I opened it, he was smiling and reading my text. To open the door and see him standing outside, it was just surreal. He could be anywhere, with anyone right now and he's here with me. He had on jeans and a long sleeved t-shirt and he looked absolutely incredible. He stood in the middle of the room with his hands in his pockets.

"Wow, you have a nice room." I showed him my "peeping Tom" window that had stairs right outside of it. Then I turned and looked at him. He was smiling and I put my arms around him and started kissing him. Every time I kiss him, I do it as if it is the last time it's ever going to happen. I don't know when this dream is going to end so I want to make sure I enjoy every moment of it.

He started to unbuckle his pants and said, "Don't mind me," as his pants hit the floor, "I'm just taking my pants off." Christ, is this really happening again? I feel like I'm living someone else's life. Never taking his eyes off me, he pulled his shirt over his head then started kissing me as it dropped to the floor. I get absolutely weak useless when he kisses me. In one swift motion, he moved me towards the bed. He slowly got on the bed and I watched as he smiled and lay down, waiting. I took a second to just look at him lying naked in my bed, with his hands behind his head. Never forceful, never in a rush. Fully clothed, I laid on top of him, kissing him. Again, taking every moment in. He started to sit up so I sat next to him. He unzipped my boots and slipped them off. Stockings and panties were next. He lay back down, torturing me. I straddled him and started kissing him again. The moon was creeping through the side of the blinds and I could see his face and beautiful brown eyes. I kissed him again and then kissed his forehead and just looked at him. I am so calm when I am with him. It's a feeling of euphoria. I'm never nervous when I am actually with him, it's the not knowing if I'm going to be with him that has me shaking in my ho boots. It feels like I belong with him when we are together. Not knowing what tonight might bring, I just tried to go with the flow. Would he stay the night since he is in the same hotel? It's not like he has to get home.

After a couple of hours, somewhat abruptly he said, "I gotta go." He's kidding me right?
Sort of dumbfounded, again, I got up as he was getting dressed and said, "How about five more minutes?"

He laughed and said, "I'm old, you're young, and I'm tired." He kissed me when he was dressed and said, "Thank you for traveling eighteen hours by train to come see me. I can't believe it." We walked to the door where he kissed me some more and we discussed my fear of flying again. A few more kisses and into the night he disappeared. He was staying down the hall from me, what were the chances? This is another one of those signs I reflect on. Before he was even back to his room, I was on the phone with Anna. I said, "Oh my God, I love him."

"Oh geeze, here we go. You can't do that."

"I know. I love him, I just love him." We both busted out laughing because I sounded like Renee Zellweger in Jerry Maguire when she was telling her sister Laurel how much she loved Tom Cruise."I love him, I just love him. I love him for the man he is, I love him for the man he's going to be, I just love him." We couldn't stop laughing. Now every time I call Anna and I am having a "Miles moment," I either just say, "Laurel," and she says, "Oh God," or I'll say, "I love him," and she says, "I know, Laurel." Anna knows exactly what my emotional state is as soon as I say Laurel, and I really didn't love him. "So he just left?"

"I know, I don't know why. Maybe that's just the way it's gonna be because if he stayed, it would mean more than what he is intending."

I would rather him leave than stay and have that mean nothing. At least I know if he stays, things have progressed. I'm taking whatever I can get and I hate that I am turning into that kind of woman. Why am I so willing to settle for any crumb he will throw at me? Do I think that little of myself? Do I want him that badly? Clearly I want him that badly, so let's skip that question. I don't think that little of myself. I don't feel like he is the Mecca and I can't get anyone else. I think I'm just hoping if I play it cool enough and he gets to know me that this can progress. Of course I am putting way more thought into this than he is. I'm probably a forgotten thought already and he's sleeping, dreaming of his next conquest.

So wired, I could barely sleep. I think I got in a solid four hours. At the ass crack of dawn I got up and showered quickly and ran downstairs to grab food. This is another psychotic part of me: I can't eat in front of him. I know, he can see me naked but I can't eat in front of him. Maybe we can get Freud on the phone again. I can drink, I just can't eat. There was some strange relief when he didn't go to dinner with me over the summer. I didn't know how I was going to pull that one off. After I grabbed some food, I flew back up to my room to eat.

I still had several hours before I had to leave. Checkout was twelve, my train left at 6 p.m. It was only about 9:30 a.m. now. The boys called not long after I got back to my room so I walked downstairs and sat outside the hotel to talk to them. I was out there for about a half hour talking to them, then went back upstairs to get my sweatshirt. The two of them were starting to fight as usual. It's hard enough to stop a fight when you are in front of them, let alone over the phone. I'm telling them to stop, they're not listening. It's worse than being home. Frustrated, I grabbed my sweatshirt off the chair and start back down the hall again to go sit outside. As I'm yelling at them, Miles turns the corner, walking towards me. In an abrupt move, I hung up on my kids. The mother of the year award would go to me for that one. At that point I could care less if they killed each other.

He smiled, said hi, and said he was going to check out the coffee situation. We walked downstairs and found no one was in the little breakfast room. He walked around the room, looking at everything on the walls. I wanted him again. We sat down and he asked me if I ever met his son Jason. I said yes and stopped myself from saying, "He's hot." Instead I just said, "He looks exactly like you." We talked about him, then Miles asked me where my kids were. I told him they were home with my dad and his home attendant.

He said, "Who normally watches them when you go away?"

"I've never gone away before. This is the first time. I couldn't tell my psychotic brothers either." He asked why. I couldn't tell him it was because they think I'm an asshole, that he's using me, that I'm nothing more than a groupie that he doesn't give a shit about. So I said, "I have overprotective older Irish brothers that worry about me traveling alone." I cleaned that one up pretty well, huh? There was some truth to that. Devon had said that he wouldn't worry so much if I flew. He worries about me driving alone. If he knew I took a train to Florida, I would have to listen to his mouth for eternity and it just wasn't worth it.

After a couple of minutes of talking, he said "I have to meet Meg in a half hour for breakfast."

"Okay."

"Why don't you join us?"

Very hesitant I sort of shook my head no and said, "I don't know." I know this was a no brainer. In the back of my mind I'm thinking, *how am I going to eat in front of him, yet how do I go home to my therapist and tell him I said no, especially with that reason.*

Thank God he pushed it and said, "I think you should."

I smiled and somehow when I opened my mouth, "Okay," flew out. Thank God I can eat like a man because, if you recall, I already ate to avoid this whole situation. He was going to take a shower and meet me downstairs in thirty minutes. Thirty minutes is a long time to have a nervous breakdown. Now I was also going to be nervous sitting with Meg. I've met her several times before but never spent any time with her. Was she going to check me out and report back to Miles? You know women are ruthless.
I sat outside the hotel and Miles came down five minutes later. Very nervous, I tried to be cool, like this happens to me all the time. I guess I didn't look as calm as I thought because Meg came down looked at me and said, "What's wrong?"

Oh shit. This was going to be a long breakfast. "Nothing," I said and smiled. Was she thinking, was this last night's flavor of the night? If I were just a whore, I wouldn't be at breakfast with him, would I? I don't know "Morning after groupie etiquette." This situation is very unnerving, but it doesn't have to be. We went to the restaurant attached to the hotel and sat outside. It was a perfect fall day. I tried to pick something I wouldn't drop on myself or make a mess with, and that was not too involved to eat. I got a fresh fruit bowl. What a fag, such a girl. I could have gotten a full plate of anything and finished it before the two of them but no, cop out. I sat like a pansy eating a bowl of fruit. This was a second meal too, but they didn't know that.

I know this sounds ridiculous, but we were sitting around like normal people. I had actually wondered how it was that Miles had no tattoos. Every rock star has tattoos. I don't particularly like them so I was impressed that Miles didn't have any. Out of nowhere Meg starts talking about tattoos. She said to Miles, "You have one right?"

"No, I don't like the idea of anything being on my body permanently. Actually, I almost got one but Noah Anderson saved me. I was going to get a heart, like the old sailor tattoos with an arrow through it with my wife's name on it," then he turned to me and said, "We're getting divorced by the way," turned back and said, "but then Noah Anderson comes in with the exact one, but it says 'Momma.' I was so pissed off I said, 'fuck you, now what, are we both going to have one?'"

So the divorce is real. Yes! It was so surreal sitting there talking with Miles about Noah Anderson, like I'm in the inner circle of sorts. I didn't want this to end. After an hour, Meg said, "You have to get ready. Mike will be here in fifteen minutes to take us to the airport."

He said, "I don't want to go yet."

"Well, you were the one who told him what time to come," she said.

The bill came and Meg said, "Can I help you with that, Miles?"

"No I got it."

I took a twenty out and put it in front of him. He said firmly, "Piper, no," and pushed it back. I pushed it back towards him again and he looked at me sternly and said, "Absolutely not, put it away." So he is perfect. It's the little things. We walked back to the hotel and Meg said, "I'll see you back here in fifteen minutes," leaving us to have a moment together. Miles and I walked upstairs and he said, "I guess I'll see you in fifteen days," and I laughed. He kissed me at the top of the stairs then went back to his room.

Although he was leaving, I still had six hours to kill. I got my stuff together and put it downstairs. Once again, I found myself on the bench. About a minute later, Miles came down with all his stuff.

Meg followed about two minutes later. Miles was doing a coffee run and I stayed with Meg. She went online to check Miles' site and asked if I wanted to check my email. She is very sweet. We talked a little longer, and then Mike showed up while Miles was still in the coffee shop. Another thing I loved about him is that he was always late, just like me.

While Mike loaded Meg's things into the back of his truck, Miles made his way back over. This was the end of the line. He hugged me, thanked me, and told me to be careful then off they went. If only I wasn't too scared to fly . . .

I didn't know how things would be once I got back. I figured even if it is only sex, how could he feel nothing as time goes on? If he didn't have children and had not been married for thirty years, I'd say it is possible to stay completely unattached, but he does have the ability to connect and commit on some level, so as long as I stick this out, something could come of it.

****

About two weeks later, he was playing in his hometown. I sent him a text saying something along the lines of, did he want to get together after the show. "Sorry baby, very close to home, too close actually." That was fine. I respected that. He wasn't doing anything in front of his children or wife even though they were getting divorced.

I arrived at the show a little late and he didn't see me until towards the end. After I got there, Jeans Girl showed up. He spotted her immediately and grinned at her. She shook her little ass and planted it right in the center of the seats. After the show he came and sat next to me and he smelled so good, I couldn't stand it. He didn't sit with me long before he got up and went to sit with her. I was not liking this one bit. Everybody kept warning me that I did not have the skin for this lifestyle. I insisted I could handle it because 'it is what it is.' After a few minutes the seats started to clear and she hung around with a couple of friends. What I don't like about her is that she seems to chat with the close friends of his, or she at least tries to talk with someone so she's not alone. She's a user. I go by myself and make no bones about my purpose. She strikes me as a phony bitch and I don't like that. Besides the fact that she is either married or, at the very least, engaged. He will never see what she is because what does he care, as long as she is a hot piece of ass?

Another thing I noticed was that she has noticed me and she has been trying to figure out my deal. After the show I went up to him to say goodbye after she left. There was still his normal, eyeing cluster of females mulling about, watching every move of the other females near him. I could feel the hole burning in my back from the stares. He came over to me and kissed me right on the lips. They must have been fuming. I said, "If your plans change, call me." I left but I spotted Jeans Girl in the parking lot.

Between shows I spent most of my time working out. I kept telling myself that if I got thinner, then he will be interested. It didn't matter whether there was any truth to that because I needed whatever motivation I could get my chubby little hands on. These days I also spent a lot of time arguing with Devon. I guess I shouldn't say I argue with him as much as I just hang up on him now. I used to listen to him until I got upset, but it is so freeing now just hanging up. The hang up does not come without warning: "If you continue to verbally abuse me, I am going to hang up on you."

Every time he gets into some kind of mood, he calls me and tells me I'm a "groupie loser, chasing some asshole that doesn't give a shit about me." How long can someone listen to that before eating lead? What was a bit amusing was the fact that he was living in a glass house and throwing boulders. He accused me of lying to my therapist because if I was telling him the truth, I wouldn't be doing what I am doing. I didn't really see what was so wrong with what I was doing. It really was no different than what many guys do. Because I am his sister, I guess he felt things should be different. It doesn't work that way. I was never made any promises, I was not the other woman at any point during his marriage, but my brother hated Miles and apparently felt his way of talking to me was acceptable and warranted because "he cared."

I still managed to care for my two boys on my own and take care of my father. I never went out socially, so if my only form of entertainment was going to see Miles every few weeks or sometimes months, that was my business. The stress in my life started to somewhat lift when I stopped taking his calls. I guess he noticed a change in me as well. I used to call him after a fight and he'd still ignore me, but now I was the one hanging up and not looking back. The next day he would call and send apology texts. It became so frequent that the apologies were too little too late. I always promised my mother that I would remain friends with my brothers but not at the expense of my pride and self-esteem. Unfortunately I have had to come to terms with the fact that although we are blood related, we could never have an open relationship.

The next show coming up was going to be upstate and I figured no one from his regular group would be going. He was going to be sitting in with another band and opening for them as well. I sent him a detailed text explaining what I'd like to do to him and asking him if he might want to get together. I didn't really want to make a five-hour trip without knowing. He said that he "doubted that he would be up for my sexy offer, but he sure does appreciate it." What does that even mean? How does he know a week before that he won't be up for it or that he doubts he would? I thought about it and said to myself, if I don't go, it looks like I don't care about his craft and I only care about his ass. I opted for the trip. I booked the adjoining hotel to the venue.

The room was nice and I was third row for the concert. I'm not sure if he saw me during the show, but afterwards I sent him a text asking him to come out. Everybody had pretty much left the arena when he had come out. I had on a black sweater and a black and white plaid skirt. He came walking over with a smile and he hugged me. He circled me like a shark as he looked me up and down and said, "Where are you staying?"

Smiling, I said, "Next door. Where are you staying?"

"Next door. What room are you in?"

"748. Hmmm, sure you're not up to it?"

Grabbing his head, clearly conflicted and staring at my legs he said, "I was going to go to sleep."

"You can sleep anytime, I want to rip your clothes off now."
"Oh God, you're killing me. I'll call you."

We kissed goodbye and I went back to my room and waited. As I literally watched the time pass on my cell phone, I started to get a bad feeling. Five minutes turned to ten minutes then thirty, and after one and a half hours, I gave up. I never heard from him, he didn't show up, I was heartbroken. All night I kept talking to my mother, begging her not to let him be a jerk. Again, I had in the back of my mind that everything had always worked out in the past. That next morning I got up and put some stuff in the car. On the way back up to my room, I looked next to my hotel and there was another hotel. Holy shit, I told him I was staying next door instead of upstairs. His car was in the parking lot next door. I flew upstairs and sent a text saying I am at the Park Ridge Inn, not the Hampton Inn.

After a few minutes I sent another message saying goodbye and that I was leaving and sorry for the mix up. I never heard from him. As I was pulling out, I saw him walking to his car. I couldn't figure any of this out. All of a sudden I get a text from him saying, "My phone ran out of juice. I'm just getting your texts now." I apologized for all of the texts and assured him I was not psychotic. He said, "I almost knocked on 748, good thing I didn't." Well, at least he almost came to the room?

As I was driving home, the rain was brutal. I could barely see anything in front of me. We texted for quite a while as we drove home. It was nice. I asked him if I should send him an occasional text asking if he would want to meet in the city or not. He said he wasn't sure because he liked spontaneity. I said, "So . . . what are you doing at the next rest stop?" He laughed. With that, I changed lanes and I looked at the car in front of me, and it was him. I texted him and told him to look behind him.

"So . . . what *are* you doing at the next rest stop?"

He said, "You are killing me." I did need gas too, so it worked out well. We pulled over and while I got gas, he ran into the bathroom. After filling up I pulled over and ran in too. He was walking towards me and he gave me a big hug. I was lost in his arms. He didn't let go, it was so nice. I told him to wait a second while I ran into the bathroom. I looked like a drowned rat in the mirror. When I came out and we walked to my car. After talking for a second outside we decided to hop in. I looked at him in my back seat and thought, *is this man really sitting in my car right now?* He was sick and that's why he didn't think he would have been up to getting together. Sitting next to him I just put my arms around him and we sat there. He moaned and said, "This is nice." I started kissing his neck, then I just put my head on his chest and we sat there again. I felt like we were hiding from the world and I finally had him all to myself. No fans grabbing at him, looking for something from him, just a second of his time. He was mine with no interruption. Nobody knew he was here. Not moving, but having to face reality, he said, "We have to go."

I couldn't help it, I had to ask, "Do I just not turn you on, or do you have a lot of self-control?"

"You do turn me on, and I have no self-control. That's why we need to leave now."

Reluctantly I let him out of the car and it was going to be back to reality. He hugged me again before he went back to his car and motioned to text him. Since he had divulged a little secret to me on the way to the rest stop, I decided to divulge one to him. "I knew about your divorce before my party. I didn't want you to think I was some whore who only sleeps with married men." I waited with baited breath for a response. I looked down.

"I don't think you're some whore that sleeps with married men. No judging." That works for me. We were parting ways and he wrote, "Bye, pretty."

Although we didn't hook up, I felt it was a successful trip. I'm glad we were texting. We never talk, so it was nice. I wish I could have more, which I guess is unrealistic, but how do you stop yourself? Here I am living a fantasy and it's a little difficult to imagine anything else.

****

Other than a show coming up that I knew I wouldn't be able to talk to him at, there was nothing on the horizon. I hate when that happens because that means I have to get back to the real world where there are no concerts. I feel like when I am living in the real world, the stress that I am under warrants the break I get when there is a concert. It also helps to consume myself with taking care of my father, kids, and work because then it seems to make the time between shows bearable. I also don't have any guilt when I go out because I know I have done everything for everyone prior to my night out. Don't get me wrong, I'm not rushing through my life with my kids. I love every minute I spend with them, but I thoroughly enjoy my escape time.

I have to say, I find the men that post on his site to be more like yentas than the women. They are like a bunch of washwomen. I appreciate the heads up about a show but if I know something that no one else does, I can't stand when they post that. I guess that would be the definition of a greedy, selfish bitch, huh? I checked the calendar part of his website and there were shows posted there that were not on his board. I figured maybe nobody realized he was playing. I called Gum Boy and Gum Girl, the friends that I met at the City Lights show, and asked them if they wanted to go see him in Jersey. They were on board.

I was happy there were no familiar faces or jeans there. After the show he came over to talk to us. He was standing next to the table and I said, "Why don't you sit down." He came and sat next to me and we talked for about five minutes. Although we were sitting next to each other, we were turned in to each other. I said, "Guess what."

He smiled and said, "What?"

"I know a short cut to Brooklyn through Staten Island."

He started laughing and said, "I have to have a drink with Paulie and his wife, then get home. I have to pack and get ready for a five day gig in Philly." As always, someone came over and started talking to him like I, the wallflower, wasn't even there.

"My husband and I would like to buy you a drink." *Are you fucking kidding me lady? I am right here!* Always courteous, he got up and thanked her, but declined and looked as though he was going to walk over to meet Paulie.

"I'm leaving." I said.

Now looking conflicted he said, "Oh, you are?"

"Yes. Do you want to walk out to the car?"

"Yeah."

Gum Boy and Gum Girl had walked out to the car as soon as he sat next to me and started talking to me to give us some time. While we walked towards my car, they were still warming up theirs. I said, "Well, you look incredibly sexy tonight."

He was parked nose to nose with me. He looked shy with his hands in his pockets and his head down. He looked over and said, "Our friends are still warming up the car."

"Well, he is killing me."

He looked at me and said, "You look great."

I was leaning on the hood of the car and I couldn't take it anymore. I said, "I don't care if they're still here." I walked over and started kissing him. It was so hot, so intense. I felt his hand go in my skirt as he ran his hand up my left leg. I almost collapsed. I ran my hands over his ass, and then as I went to open his pants, he had already opened them. My bag fell off my shoulder to the floor and I said, "Come home with me." I could barely catch my breath and he whispered, "I can't tonight baby."

I opened the car door and said, "Get in."

He looked around, grinned, and said, "This looks a little obvious."

"I don't care," I said, as I climbed in. He got in right behind me. What the hell was I doing? I started kissing him. I don't know where he gets his willpower. I wanted him so badly. No matter what I do at this point, I am going to feel like a whore. I am in the back seat of a car for God's sake. Am I thirty-nine or nineteen? Who cares? He is amazing and this is getting more difficult as time goes on.

He said, "I have to go get this over with." I pulled back and looked at him strangely. "No, not you! You I want to do. I have to go in and have drinks with Paulie and get that over with." I continued kissing him and it was getting very hot and intense. "I really need to go." I sat back down next to him and watched as he fixed his clothes. Now is when I started to question my own stupidity. I couldn't even use alcohol as an excuse. I am absolutely sober, thinking clearly, opting to rip this man's clothes off in the back seat of my car because I would rather that than nothing at all. I justify this in my own mind by saying that I don't do this with anybody else. Although he doesn't know that. So . . . am I a whore in his eyes? One might say, who cares what he thinks as long as you are enjoying yourself and getting what you want. I care about him too much for me to make poor choices that might make him think less of me. I know in the big spectrum I'm not doing anything that is so horrible, but it's that whole Irish Catholic guilt that I am riddled with.

As he got out of the car I said, "I thought you were supposed to be an irresponsible rock star?"

He smiled and said, "I'll see you soon," and walked back in to meet Paulie. I sat for a minute before I started my journey home and I replayed everything that just took place in my mind. Parts of my body still literally tingled from his touch. There should be laws against being allowed to drive after a session like that. Anna called, of course, as I'm pulling out of the parking lot. I think she has a lojack on me. As soon as he left me, my phone rang. "What happened?" she said. After a brief synopsis, she laughs and says, "You slut."

See, that's exactly what I'm talking about. Quickly she says, "I'm only kidding. I'm living vicariously through you."

"Good, because now we are both lost." I managed to somehow get lost on my way home. I was so preoccupied thinking about him, I had no clue as to where I was. Turns out, going there, I went over the Outerbridge, but coming home I went over the Bayonne Bridge. That was a first. I had never been over that bridge before.

Confident that I was well on my way to getting home, Anna said that she would talk to me later. After getting off the phone, I see a text from Miles. An unsolicited text from Miles. "Thank You." I was ecstatic. Then I thought, *is that a thank you for being a whore?* I don't care, I'll take it. Planning on seeing him in a month, I sent him a response that said something to the effect of pleasuring him all night. I tend to send what appear to be drunk texts when I am sober. I don't think I've ever used the word "pleasuring" in my life. What was that? Now I had another month to work out and try to focus on looking better.

****

I have always taken pictures from the time I was a kid. Not really concentrating too much on it, I just did it. Everyone always commented on how good they were, but I was always drawn to the pictures Devon would take. Through the years, I had taken pictures at all the concerts I had gone to. Claire approached me one day about calling a local bar that wound up housing my birthday party, and inquiring about hanging some of my photos there and maybe getting some work. Always dragging my feet with everything else, this call I decided I better make. Surprisingly, they told me to come in and see Joe. I was told over the phone there was a three to six month waiting period. I went in with my portfolio and Joe said I could come in the next day with my pictures and have the entire right wall in the front. What? I brought my stuff in, pictures of friends, family, and musicians. He really liked them and was most interested in the musicians. Usually you get three months to hang up your work. When my three months were up, he had me move them to a different wall in another room. After those three months, he had me move them back to the front room on the left wall. This time it was strictly musicians. He said a lot of people came in and commented on them. That was a cool feeling.

Throughout this whole Miles escapade, I have been taking photos. Getting pushed from my friends to do something with it so I can get out of my current job and do something I love, I started putting a little more emphasis on my picture taking. I had a photo I took of STYX published in a music newspaper. The editor had photos from their photographer on file but used mine instead and I got photo credit, which was pretty cool. People tend to be amazed at what a procrastinator I am. They can't understand why I would not try my hand at photography rather than stay at a low paying job I don't really like. Neither can I. I just don't have the confidence. I'm working on it though. I do wish that I could make a go of this so at least it seems as though I have some kind of brain in my head and that I'm not just "some receptionist." I can sell anything I believe in, I just need to believe in myself enough to get this going. It seems I have always succeeded in anything I have put my mind to, I just need to put my mind to more things.

What I would really love to photograph is Miles in a more casual setting. Other than your typical concert shots, I would like to start getting some off stage candid shots.

****

The next show to come up was the Philly one. A couple of days before, I sent him a text to remind him that I planned to abduct him that night. He responded with, "Sorry baby, I don't think I'll be able to be your boy toy after the show." Well that sucks. But let's see, if we read into everything, he said, "I don't think." That's not definite. There's room to work with, therefore I refuse to lose hope.

I ran into him before the show and he kissed me hello. I didn't mention anything about getting together because one, I'm an ass and two, when he pulled up, he let his agent out of the car first. Clearly, he needs to drive her back first so I don't have much hope tonight. As we were talking and walking into the joint, someone, of course, came over and started talking to him as if I wasn't even there and walked him in. I really don't understand what is wrong with some people.

Claire and I sat against the wall toward the middle of the place. As if my nerves weren't shot enough, Jeans Girl walks in and plops her ass right in front of me. Claire just looked at me, waiting for a reaction. She had her typical smirk on her face as if she had some kind of advantage she was rubbing my face in. She does this all the time and I don't get her point. She's either married or at the very least engaged. Why won't this bitch just buzz off? Miles should only know the childish bullshit that surrounds him. After the show, I waited for the opportune time to go over to him as I watched Jeans Girl calculate her move. She came out of the bathroom and walked right between him and the person he was talking to and grinned while she slithered her ass between them. She wound up taking a picture with him and I left before she did.

At the time, when I left, I had no reason to think she would have left with him, but as time has passed, I found myself looking back and questioning everything. I really dislike her. Knowing he had his agent with him was the only consolation. Just before I left, I had gone up to him and asked him if there was anything now impeding our going out to dinner one night. He smiled and said, "We'll talk." I'm sorry, what the fuck is that? It's not a yes or a no. It's leaving his options open as I hang on to hope. I hate myself for that. It makes me feel like a pathetic, weak woman. He has some kind of hold over me. I find myself getting upset or reflecting the night I see him, then by the next morning, I shake it off and just plan on making the next time successful. The time between shows I work out harder and clear my head. I feel defeated sometimes the night of the show, but then tell myself it's a new day the next day.

The next show was not posted officially on his site. One of the yenta men posted that he would be sitting in with a band at The Red Spot. I stood for about three hours inside, enduring other bands and waiting for him to come out. To make matters worse, as I walked in, Jeans Girl was walking out. Great, I have to deal with her all night. It was getting late, and I hadn't spotted him at all. I had Jeans Girl standing off to the side of me with her Amazon friend. She had this stupid smirk on her face all night and she kept looking at me. One smack, that's all I want to give her. Just one, right in her fat gob.

Every time she went into the bathroom, she walked right passed me. She had no reason to walk by me at all. She either had a bladder problem or was trying to piss me off. She reminded me of Florence Cosentino, the girl who went from kindergarten to fifth grade standing behind me in the line every year in school doing the same shit. Florence should have been in front of me because we were lined up by height, but she stood behind me so she could laugh at, point at, and try to mentally torture me with her two taller friends. Grammar school bullshit.

As I walked to the bathroom, I spotted Miles at the bar, but then I spotted a girl with him. She actually looked like the girl from Mt. Vernon. I couldn't pick an elephant out of a lineup of ligers so I'm not one hundred percent sure it was her. Either way, I'm not pleased. I went into the bathroom, which they were standing right next to, and my heart sank. I got myself together and realized when I walked out that I would be literally facing him. I didn't know how I was going to play it, so I just walked out and played it by ear. He saw me come out and walked towards me, hugged me, and thanked me for coming. Out of character for me, I said, "No problem," and walked back to my spot.

I now realized Jeans Girl's stupid smirk certainly meant nothing because she hadn't yet spotted what I had just seen. She was walking back there for her tenth bathroom run and as I turned, I noticed she sat at the end of the bar with Amazon and they were having a meeting of the minds regarding the new development in our common bond. Feeling satisfaction at her pain, I turned back toward the front and noticed something else. Miles' ex-wife was now standing in front of me. Was this a fucking joke? I'm now looking around for cameras. For a half of a second, I felt a little bad for him. A half of a second, I said. Although he is getting ass thrown at him like extreme Frisbee, it has to be uncomfortable having everyone in one room together. You can't really fault him. What man is going to say no when everyone wants you? It's one of the perks to his job. It sucks for the ones that actually care about him though. I'm sure he knows that too. He is up front and I'm sure it's for reasons like that. He is a very likeable man: always polite, sexy, funny, and a great entertainer. Now single, who wouldn't want him all to themselves? Of course after being married for so long, and I'm sure burned in the end, why wouldn't he want to live the now guilt-free, rock star lifestyle?

This night was certainly going to prove to be interesting. After the brief intermission between sets, Miles joined the band for two songs. He looked great and was very rambunctious, as he usually is when he is only singing and it's a guest spot. I was too hurt to actually enjoy it because I knew for sure he was leaving with the girl I spotted him at the bar with. This is another one of those times when I feel like a whore. I always give him the benefit of the doubt and say he's not "socializing" with anyone, just sleeping with them.

Clearly, he came in with her, so what is that? Am I only good enough behind closed doors? She's nothing special, but now of course, I need to work out more. Why is his wife here? She was smiling and laughing during his performance, but I think she is dating the singer of the band he is sitting in with. This business is very incestuous. I don't know if I can handle it.

After his performance, I was going to take off. Jeans Girl and Amazon stood behind me the whole time he was on, talking so I could hear them. Right in the fucking gob I tell you. I felt like saying, "You're married, bitch, go home to your husband!" I digress . . . I heard Amazon tell her to take her time. I guess she was now going over to say her goodbyes as well. I beat her to the punch. I did not want to watch this nightmare unfold before my eyes. Let me cut my losses and get the fuck out of here. I walked over to him where he was standing with "her" and another couple. I poked him and waved goodbye. He came over, smiled, and hugged me. "Thank you so much for coming."

Half smiling, that was all I could manage to muster, I said, "Goodnight," and turned around and left. He had to realize that it was unusual for me to act like that, but I'm tired of acting like nothing bothers me and everything is just picture perfect. I realize he never made any promises or commitments, but it still hurts. A lot.

****

My therapy sessions seem to consist of planning my non-psychotic means of landing this man. I am ninety-eight percent truthful when I go to therapy. I'm okay answering any questions he has regarding this situation, except when he says, "What are your feelings towards him?"

All of a sudden, I get blonde and say, "What do you mean?"

"You're not in love with him, are you?"

"Of course not, that would be stupid." Meanwhile my stomach is in a knot.

"Good, because you can't do that."

Well of course I can't, that's why I am lying and saying no. According to my compact Oxford dictionary, the definition of Love is, 1. Deep affection. Fondness. 2. Deep romantic or sexual attachment. 3. Great interest and pleasure in something.

Do I love him? Sure. Am I terrified that I have gotten myself into this situation? Absolutely. Now I have to deal with it though. I can't just stop, I am in too deep already. I honestly did think before the first time that I slept with him that I would be able to handle this, that I wouldn't have any feelings for him. I thought I could just use him, as he would me, and that would be it. I never expected to start to fall for the man that I didn't even want to acknowledge twenty years prior. Maybe use is not a fair statement. My intention was not to use him, but I kept telling myself that I would be the one getting used and that he would never feel anything other than lust for me, so I didn't even want to go there. Enjoy your experience with him and let it go. It is what it is. It all sounds good. It all sounds like a plan. A year later, it ain't happenin'.

I had really started to bump up the running and working out and had to find a positive in all of this. At least I had a focus. After my mother died, I realized I had no idea who I was. I never allowed myself to figure out what it is that I like to do because it didn't matter. There was never an opportunity to do it, so why bother? My mind was always focused on music and art when I was younger but I allowed a part of me to die after I got married. I always kept music alive with my children. My husband was never into music like I was, so he never would make a connection to it. He could never understand why I always wanted to go to concerts, he could never appreciate it. I guess that was maybe another sign that I never should have married him. I never stuck to my own rule of never losing myself just because I got married. Not only did I lose myself, I became somebody I never wanted to be. It wasn't until I became involved with Miles that I started to feel alive again and started to rediscover who I am and was. I actually liked the person I was evolving back into. To my new friends, I was a different person. To my old friends, I was coming back. I was a tweaked version of the old me. For my kids, I guess this was the biggest change. I was always frumpy mommy to them. There were never any men brought around and they always had my undivided attention. Well, them and my parents. Most kids at least see their moms interacting with their dads or some man at some point. My husband left when my boys were babies, so as far as my kids are concerned, they were born in a cabbage patch. To see their mother getting dressed up and knowing and understanding what it means that men are asking her out, is a big adjustment. That is just gross to them. Nowadays we always hear doctors and therapists saying how you have to be open and honest with your kids. I came from a generation where parents were parents and kids were kids. Now we are supposed to be closing the gap. I don't know how comfortable I am with that. I fault my parents for nothing and can only learn from my upbringing. I'm sure I have fucked my kids up on many levels. There is no rulebook on how to raise kids, that's why I can never fault my parents. They did what they thought was the right thing just as I am trying to do with my boys. Times are different and so are the circumstances. I was raised in a two-parent home by a stay–at-home mom and a father that retired when I was in kindergarten. We didn't discuss sex, even though we were told to go to them with any questions. Who the hell was going to do that? My sex talk was being told not to ever let any boy put their hands on me as I was walking out the door on my first date.

Fast forward to a fucked up adult sex life. My boys are being raised by a single mother that has been working anywhere from one to three jobs at a time their whole lives. They never see their father and their mother now goes to overnight concerts. They have physically taken care of their own grandparents to the point of toileting and dressing them. I never knew my grandparents, they passed before I was born. My mother was forty-two when she had me. I was twenty-five when I had Bailey. Although my children have a completely different upbringing than I had, I'm trying to give my children a modernized version of my upbringing. There is a fine line. A two-parent household discussing sex with their children is one thing, but for a single mother with two boys, it's a bit more involved. You can fool yourself into thinking your parents are old and not having sex, and only did that a bazillion years ago to procreate and that's why you are here, and the sex questions and discussions can go much smoother. No child wants to picture or even discuss their parents having sex, even if your mother is Pamela Anderson or Heidi Klum. Now, you're a teenage boy whose friends tell you that your mother is hot, that's one thing that grosses you out, then you know she is going to concerts, sometimes for two or three days to see a guy that you know she's into. Do you really want to have a sex talk with your mother? Not so much.

The first time I realized that my son was more mature than me was when he asked if I was sure that I wanted to be involved with Miles. I don't give them enough credit. I didn't think they would assume I was having sex with him just because I go see him. To me, it's still the impossible dream so I don't know why everyone assumes it can happen. I said, "Yes, and why are you asking me that?"

"Well, he is a rock star and probably has STDs."

I was dumbfounded.

"Are you aware of gonorrhea, syphilis, and AIDS?" he said.

"How do you know about it?" was my mature comeback

"I learned about it in school, do you know about it?"

Sad to say, my son probably knew more than I did. I knew enough that I didn't want to contract it. I said, "I don't think we should be talking about this." I realized after that comment, it was my opportunity to talk to him about sex. An opportunity missed. Of course my therapist told me I was an idiot. I promised myself the next time this came up, because it would, that I would talk to him. In fact, I did tell him that if he had any questions, I promised I would answer them and be more mature. Talk about turning the tables.

Chapter 13

The next show to come up was another local show about three weeks after the last one. In fact, it was the three day event that started this all. Always unsure if I should buy all three days tickets or get them each day, I hesitated. I didn't want to commit to all three days. I don't want to look like a stalker. Meanwhile, almost everyone who attends goes all three days. I, however, would feel like I looked like a stalker.

I decided when I walked in, day one, to buy all three days. I got my ticket and sat in the lobby. Yeah, I could look like I was browsing or was interested in the memorabilia, but not so much. I'm tired of playing games. I was there to see Miles and the concert and that was it. While sitting in the lobby wasting time, I was on the phone with Claire and didn't realize Miles was walking up behind me. All of a sudden he planted a big kiss on me and then kept walking. I said to Claire, "Oh my God, he just kissed me. I gotta go, I'll call you back."

I went into the bathroom, which was right in front of where I was sitting. As I'm getting ready to walk out, who comes walking in with an obnoxious smirk on her face, but Jeans Girl. You couldn't plan this shit. I completely ignored her and walked right passed her and out of the bathroom and sat back down and waited. Two seconds later he came walking by and I said, "Hey, after your show can you come to my car so I can give you something?"

He smiled and said, "Sure." He walked back toward the auditorium. Satisfied, I sat down. To my right I saw Jeans Girl come out of the bathroom and walk toward the auditorium. He comes walking back again and they were about to cross paths. I watched with anticipation. Who will acknowledge who? He grabbed her arm as she went to pass. They hugged, chatted a moment, then went in opposite directions. She just puts a damper on everything, for me at least. Not him. The show was great. She was nowhere to be found after, thank God! I went up to him and said I would wait outside. He said okay and that he would be right out. I waited in the lobby and when he came out he had a big smile on his face. He came over and said, "Where are you taking me?"

"Are you really going to leave that up to me?" He laughed and we took the short walk to my car. "What did you do?" he said as I gave him a little gift bag. His birthday was in a few days so I just framed a picture I had taken of him and his kids. He put it back down then hugged me and started kissing me, right out in the middle of the parking garage with everybody walking by. Well that didn't suck. "Why don't you pass by my house on your way home?" I said.

"I have to go back in for a party. I don't really want to go. I have to stop by and I'm staying here this weekend."

"Oh."

"I'm not the big wild rock star. I'd like to pass on the party."

A few more kisses and I was on my way back home and he was on his way back in. The boys called as soon as I got back in the car. "Well, did you see him?"

"Yes, I saw him."

"Well?"

"I'm going home, and he's staying here."

They were disappointed for me. I said, "It's okay, don't worry, I had a great night."
I picked the boys up on the way back home. Bailey was going to come with me tomorrow. Quinn was going to Dad's.

When I woke up, I had a text from Miles that said, "Thank you." When I finally got out of bed and got a few things together, it was time to go. I was feeling old. I wasn't even the one performing and this was wearing me out, and it's only day two. Holy crap. I picked Kim and Felice up and we started over. We got there in the afternoon because there were things there that the kids wanted to see. As I was walking around with Bailey, coming toward me was none other than Jeans Girl, with that same stupid, fucking smirk on her face. I want to slap it right off her. I felt like screaming, "I fucked him too, bitch. You haven't cornered the market on his affections." I don't know if she did, but I figured I'd cover my ass by throwing "too" in there. She had a child with her this time. I guess she was trying to show a maternal side other than the scheming, conniving, cunty side that I am so used to seeing. I know it may seem as though I am always scheming, but I am not married! I refuse to let her ruin my day. By this point I had not spotted Miles at all. Felice found me and was so excited. "I just saw Miles upstairs." With that, Bailey and I ventured upstairs. Miles was talking with some people so I went into a room with artwork and Bailey said, "Why did you do that?"

"Do what?"

"You completely ignored him. Why are you such a bitch?"

"He was talking to people. Why, he saw me? And don't call your mother a bitch."

"Yes he saw, he nodded his head at me and was looking at you."

"Oh, geeze. I wasn't even looking."

"Nice going Mom, now I know why your plans never work out."

Out of the mouths of babes. When we came out of the art room, he was gone. We went back downstairs to meet Felice. Bailey was hungry, so he got in line for food while I walked toward the front of the line to see what they had. Looking ahead I noticed Miles was walking towards me. He had a big smile on his face and walked right up to me and kissed me. "Hi, you look great," he said as I drooled on myself.

"I saw your son upstairs, he's huge."

"I know."

He said that he was late for rehearsal and had to go. "I'll see you later."

I turned around and he was talking to my son and my son was laughing. I walked over to him when he left and I said, "What were you laughing at?" He said Miles had come over and shook his hand and said, "You got big. I bet you could kick my ass."

After the food escapade, we went back over to where Felice was waiting. We wound up doing a few things the kids wanted to do, then went in to see the show. Since it was Saturday, the concert was packed. The kids found a spot on the floor to sit but we wound up standing for the show. All of a sudden, I saw Jeans Girl with her faux child plop her ass down right in front of him on the floor. It seemed like I didn't even exist when she was around and it was very irritating. I was happy to see that she left before the show ended. Good riddance, bitch! Bailey and Kim wanted to get their picture taken with Miles again since they had one last year. They waited for him after the show but he never came out. I texted him and asked him if they could get a picture, but I didn't hear from him before we left. After I dropped Kim and Felice off, I took Bailey to the diner. While I was there, I got a text from Miles apologizing for missing my text and he said he was very tired and going to bed. At least he acknowledged my text. Not to sound like a pessimist, but I'm always waiting for him to fall off the pedestal that I have put him on. It's going to be a hard fall, too, I'm not looking forward to that day. For now, I'm good.

Day three and I am draggin' ass. I am absolutely exhausted, but there is still some kind of rush doing this and seeing him. I'm also in a lot of pain because I sprained my ankle walking out of the door to the first show. It is swollen and painful. "Wrap it tighter, play harder" is my motto. Standing for two days on it has been rough and now my other ankle hurts too because I sprained that one running and never let it recover. I kept running on it just like I can see myself doing with this one. Off I went with my two sprained ankles and some wishful thinking that perhaps tonight, something might happen. Luckily, since it's Sunday, it's not as crowded but it's still a full house. I did not give Miles a birthday card with the picture because I didn't know what I wanted to write in it at that point. I brought it with me tonight and in it, I included the photo of his son I wanted to use in the frame. Jeans Girl did not show up for this one, which was nice. I sort of had a feeling she wouldn't so I took my seat in the lobby again. This time I was more relaxed and brought a book with me.

As I was sitting there, I had on a short skirt, I had my legs crossed and was reading. Before I knew it, Mr. Wonderful walked by and as he passed me, he ran his finger up my thigh and kept walking. I think I slid off the seat. After I recovered and shook it off, I started reading again. This was almost like a replay of Friday. He was doing a lot of walking back and forth. As it got closer to show time, he went upstairs and got dressed. When he came down, I had hoped that the drool running down the side of my mouth wasn't too obvious. He looked so good, I tried to act unaffected. The rest of the band had come out and they were taking a group photo. Not wanting to interfere, I missed out on a perfect photo op and just sat and watched. They were doing this right next to me. Occasionally I glanced up from my book like this didn't interest me in the least. All of a sudden Miles stood directly in front of me and started adjusting his shirt in the mirror above my head. I think it was at that point when I realized how much inner strength and willpower I had. "You need some help with that?" I said, as he continued to torture me.

He just grinned and straightened out his suit. I think he found himself to be amusing. Photos complete, chaffing on my chin, and it was just about time for the show. I was sad that this was the last night, even though I was exhausted. I couldn't imagine how he felt. When the show was over I went up to the stage to give him the card. He bent down and kissed me right on the lips. The place was still full. That didn't suck. I gave him the card and told him I forgot to give it to him the other day. We never really seem to talk and I don't want to just be a fuck to him. I feel like if at least he knew some things about me, it might make it a little more difficult to just brush me aside. Not to compare him to Hannibal Lecter, but if he can at least see me as a person, it makes it a little more difficult to not have feelings, or in Hannibal's case, eat me. You get the picture. I said, "Do you want to meet me outside and say goodnight?" He said he was going to have to pack up and get out. I waited in the hall and sent him a text saying, "I'm outside if you want to say goodbye quickly." I could see him packing up from where I was. There were still a lot of people in the hallway and I was sitting on the window ledge. I was wearing a red plaid shirt with black tights, a black top and black boots.

He started to walk towards me with a smile and said, "You look cute." He gave me a hug and a kiss. I told him that I wanted him in his ear while he was hugging me. He giggled and moaned and said he had to leave tonight. He kept his arms around me while we talked which was pretty awesome since everyone was still milling about and he didn't seem to care. I tried very hard to coerce. He seemed conflicted but I didn't want to push either. Some guy walked over and started talking to him and he still kept his arms around me. He gave me a few more kisses then said he had to meet his lawyer in the morning, and then I knew to forget it. Remembering the way I felt when I had to go to court or meet my lawyer, I decided to drop it. Although, I did want him terribly. He held my hand and walked me to the door and told me to be careful going home. I was honestly worn out. Physically and emotionally. Tomorrow my week was just beginning. I don't know how these guys do it. Although there was no "love connection" this weekend, I wasn't discouraged. This is what carries me through to the next event. It is a sickness, but it inspires me to work out and that is not a bad thing.

****

Every time I talk to Anna and I tell her something that happened with Miles, she says, "You have the Secret."

"What the hell does that mean?"

"The Secret, you have it."

"Okay, again, I heard you, but what the hell does that mean?"

After about four more exchanges like that, verbatim, she said, "The Secret from Oprah."

Oh my God, this was going to be a long conversation. "I never saw Oprah, I know there is a book called The Secret, I know it was on Oprah, but what is The Secret? How do I have it?" She proceeded to tell me how it was about being able to get whatever you wanted with positive thinking. Why she couldn't have said that ten minutes ago I'll never know. She then informed me that she does not have it nor will she ever, but I have it. I said, "With that attitude how would you ever expect to have it?"

I decided to go get the book and see what it was all about. Honestly, I think I was in better shape before I read it because I was doing everything naturally, but now I felt the pressure of doing everything with the right attitude. All I told myself before was that there was no alternative to what I wanted. I wanted him and I was going to do whatever it took to get him. A few good things did come out of it. I decided after I read it that I was going to get on a plane. Not only was I going to get on a plane, but I was also going to see Miles in Vegas for three days and I invited Devon. I thought he might want to join me on my first plane ride since he was the one who pushed me the most about it. I thought he would faint when I told him. I said, "I can go see Miles and you can go see Cher."

I thought this would be a great way to bridge the gap between us. The first time I told him about the book he was very open to the idea about it and said that his friend Mike said he should read it. I think Mike would suggest Devon use any means to change his attitude. He was on his way out the night I mentioned the book to him. While at dinner he asked the people he was with about it since he only heard of it when I mentioned it.

They told him it was like scientology and a cult and so on. Needless to say, I got a phone call when he got home. Since we had such a nice conversation before he went out, when I saw his name on the caller ID later that night, I thought we were going to continue our conversation. Wrong. I picked up the phone all happy, and then he laced into me. I'll spare you the details and just say words like loser, whore, has-been, and groupie were used. He also said if I'm going to follow the book, I would be homeless, Bailey would drop out of school, and Quinn would be in prison. Clearly things he has in the back of his mind anyway and the alcohol just brought to the forefront. "I'm not going to that stupid, fucking concert with you to see that loser and you better realize you're getting used like a groupie. How many other people is he gonna be with when you are there?" This was a very defining moment in my life. I hung up, and never looked back.

No matter what he feels about Miles, which he has no reason to judge him anyway, he has no right to talk to me like that. He would hang up on me and I would call back like a battered woman. No more. He continued to call and I let it go to voicemail.

In the morning I had a couple of vile voicemails waiting for me. I sent Sean a text saying, "Your brother is an asshole and I'm done with him." Poor Sean, always the mediator, always gets caught in the middle of everything. Devon and I are usually like, "Fuck you—Fuck you" and Sean is all about the whole, "Can't we all just get along." That is usually responded to with, "Fuck you too." Poor bastard. So Sean responds back with, "Geeze, what happened now?" I told him and he understood my feelings. This was nothing new. While I was on with Sean, I got an apology text from Devon. You know what? Too little, too late. I didn't respond. This was all totally out of character for me and it was very empowering. I did promise my mother that we would always remain friends. I intend to honor that promise, but I don't think she meant for that to happen at the expense of my pride and self esteem. We can be siblings, but the dream of a relationship like I have with Sean is simply that, just a dream.

A couple of weeks went by and I never spoke to him. He sent me a text saying, "I know you're not talking to me but I'm in Vegas and was wondering if Satire was here because I think I just saw Noah Anderson walk past me." I responded back with a "Yes."

I realize the issues on the table are not mine. I know he needs to fix whatever is going on with him but I will not be his punching bag. I got divorced for that reason. I'm not going to take it from anybody, especially my own brother. He thinks Miles is so horrible, meanwhile he has never spoken to me the way my own brother has, nor has he ever made me feel like the dirty whore my brother has. I need to let time pass before I speak to him, but will stop him dead in his tracks when this attitude flares up. He is also notorious for throwing comments around after I say something like, "Did Oprah say that?" or "Did you get that from The Secret?" Those are other instances that warrant a hang up too, just for the record. I resent the fact that when he can't get in touch with me to be verbally abusive, he calls my sons. They then think I am mean because I won't talk to their uncle. I take that as an opportunity to let them know that I will not be spoken to that way and that they should never speak to people that way. I also tell them if I am to remain friends with my brother I must not speak to him when he is like this. They should see that I am strong woman and stand up for myself.

I was still planning on going to Vegas. If he changed his mind, I was not allowing him to come with me. I couldn't chance him embarrassing me in front of Miles or God forbid have him say something to him. In order to get myself on the plane, I just kept telling myself that my mother would not let the plane crash. I would tell myself whatever I had to, to get on that plane. Everyone was shocked that I was doing this, but very excited for me. My excuse for not flying was that if I drove to California and Canada, there was nothing I wanted to see badly enough that I had to fly to it. At the time, it was true. There is nothing I had more anxiety about than flying. I couldn't even talk about it without stammering. I really was terrified. Everything about it terrified me. Miles knew how much if freaked me out because we had discussed it.

****

I felt great about my decision until I called to order the tickets. I did it from work and my friends were all there and they were relieved that I did it. They were also there when I hung up the phone with Continental and they said, "Now call the doctor and get Xanax." First call: Continental, second call: Xanax. Hm, "I'm sorry, what?" There is something very wrong with this. I turned to them and said, "Why am I doing this again?"

"Miles, and it's empowering, now pick up the phone and get the Xanax."

Ah, shit. I called the script in and they said, "Now you're set." I came to find out after I got the tickets that everybody that encouraged me to do this also hates to fly and they all take pills or drink and are terrified. That's not good. Miles even said that he hates it. That's just great. Now I start to worry that if anything happens to me, I will have orphaned my children for a man. I now have more guilt than fear and I think I am going to start the Xanax early.

The few months leading up to this I was surprisingly calm. That should have been the clue. I had a countdown going to everyone in my cell phone with a little message. Most of them seemed to look forward to it each day. Miles did a show in Brooklyn about a month before I was to leave for Vegas and I decided at the last minute to go. I thought maybe no one else would go since it's a Thursday night. This was one of the cover bands that he plays with. Mike and Stacey were going to come but they couldn't make it at the last minute. I was very nervous going there because I can't really figure out how he feels about me. At least, I freak myself out thinking he's not interested and I'm a nuisance. Clearly that's not the case. I'm always second-guessing myself. I was also going back and forth with the idea of letting him know ahead of time that I would be going to Vegas. Too many issues. He shows up, sings, has his choice of who he's gonna fuck that night, then sleeps like a baby and does it all over again the next day. I'm plotting, planning, starving myself, running, finding the right outfit, getting physically ill, then hoping like The Bachelorette, that he'll pick me. By the way, I hate the premise of that show. It's nauseating and yet I continue to do it show after show. Doing a quick walk through, I didn't see anybody familiar at the venue so I was happy. I sat in the front and he looked amazing as usual. Just before the break, between sets, I turned and saw Jeans Girl at the bar. The typical place to find that drunk. I think if you ever took the drink out of her hand she might just topple over. It must be helping her keep her balance, yeah, that's it. Again, must be a social turn on to some. Whatever. I saw him look in that direction and smile, it never fails.

During their break I thought Miles would come over but he did not. Paulie sat with me the whole time. He does occasionally do that but now I can't help but think tonight it is a diversion. Miles spent the whole break with drunky Jeans Girl. I saw him introduce his nephew to her. I was hoping she'd fuck him too and get her out of my hair. Just watching her talk, she looks so phony. Such a shame that he will never see that or even care. When the show started again, I was getting a little nervous. So what else is new? I didn't know if they made plans or what. During the last song I sent him a text that said, "I want you. Leave with me."

He sent one back that said, "I can't tonight baby. I have my nephew with me." That was fine with me. I figured that, but I threw it out there anyway. After the show, as I was walking up to him, he was smiling and looking me up and down. He hugged me and said, "You look great."

"So do you. Listen, if I were to fly out to Vegas, any chance we could spend some time together?"

"Sure. You're going to get on a plane?"

"Maybe."

He kissed me and said he had to run.

Now I was really on a mission. I didn't want to fly out there for nothing to happen, although just getting on the plane should be glory enough. Everyone kept telling me not to focus on that. "You have to enjoy yourself out there no matter what. Don't sit around waiting for him. See Vegas!"

"I know, I know."

It's hard not to think about it though. That was the main reason for going.

I felt good now. At least I know he will hang out if I go to Vegas. I was freaking a little because I figured everybody in Vegas is probably hot and scantily clad so naturally that bumped up my running regime. How could I compete with that? Not only am I going to have to compete with the normal little bimbos that show up to see him, but also I have to deal with the scantily clad residents of Vegas. Too much pressure for me. But I keep running.

About a week before I was to leave for Vegas, a show was posted in Seaside Heights, N.J. Again, I was hoping no one was going to this show. By no one I mean no threatening parties, obviously I'm not hoping he has no audience. I am not that much of a twisted, psychotic, Sybil bitch. Beth came with me this time. We hadn't been out together in a long time and when we got there it was a little crowded. It was a small bar. I did my normal scoping of the situation and saw none of the usual suspects. Beth and I took our place at the end of the bar. Unfortunately, where we were standing left us no room for viewing. There was a huge pole blocking our view of Miles. A couple of guys came over to us immediately and started talking to us. Miles of course did not see any of that because we couldn't even see him. There was nowhere to move in the bar since there were tables and people everywhere. He sounded great. At one point I went into the bathroom and I think he may have seen me at that point but I was still unsure. After the show Beth said, "Are you going to go up to see him?"

"I guess. I'll see." Then as Beth and I are going back and forth, Jeans Girl literally came up skipping. Where the fuck did she come from? He stepped to the edge of the stage and she stood there, ass pushed out (did she know he can't see that from the front?) and bobble heading. After their conversation, she walked into the bathroom. What the fuck was that? Where did she come from? She is like an STD. She creeps up on you when you least expect it, irritates the shit out of you, and when you can't see her, you know she's still there making you sick.

He was getting his stuff together on stage when Beth said, "What are you gonna do?" Now I didn't know what to do. Beth was going out for a cigarette and I saw him go out the side door. I went out the front door and told her that I was going to catch him at the side and say hello. He walked out to his car and I tapped him and said hello. He was loading his car. He gave me a hug and we made small talk. I told him I was starting to freak a little about going on the plane next week. "I can't believe you're going to do that for me." Neither could I, to be quite honest and I told him anything could happen in a week but as of now I was going. He said he was going back in to meet his friends and go see another band. A couple of kisses and we walked back to the club. Beth was in front, so he said, "I'll see you," and went back in. That did not sit well with Beth. "What the hell was that? It's like you're just anybody. I don't like that. He's pissing me off." We decided we were going to walk around for a while before we went home. Jeans Girl came out and walked down the street. "Good, she's gone for the night."

He was standing in front of the bar with some people. Beth and I started down the street the same way Jeans Girl went. We weren't following her, she just so happened to be going the only way there was any bar action on the street. Big surprise. We lost her quickly and figured she was gone. We continued walking around because it was a cute area. Just as we decided to leave, we saw Miles outside a different bar with his friends. Not wanting him to think we were following him, we decided we were going to leave. With that, he goes in the bar for a second and comes out with Jeans Girl. My heart sank.

Beth immediately turned to me and said, "Just stay calm, just stay calm." It was too late. I thought I would throw up, for many reasons. Now I was in such a spot, literally, that this whole thing was going to be out in the open. They started walking up the street toward me. It was Miles, his friend, and Jeans Girl. I was on the phone with Beth trying to look busy. Meanwhile I was holding back the tears and the vomit. I did not want to give her the satisfaction of having her know that I knew. As they walked passed me, Miles did not even look at me. I made believe that I didn't see them but we were the only ones on the street so it was pretty obvious. I had to pass his car now to get to mine. This was getting worse by the second. As Beth and I got closer to his car, she was getting in. They had parted ways with his friend right about the time they saw me. Not thinking clearly, being hurt and pissed off, and the drinks didn't help, I sent a text message. As I crossed the street in front of his car, I sent him a text that said, "I guess Vegas was a bad idea," in hopes to put some kind of damper on his night. I wanted him to know for sure that I knew he was leaving with that fucking pig. After I sent it, of course, I was second-guessing that decision.

This now warranted a call to my therapist. "I think I did something stupid," was the message left for him. And something along the lines of, "You need to hurry up and call me back before I do something else stupid in an effort to rectify it." In the meantime, the next day I went to Sean and Jane's house because it was my niece's birthday. As soon as I got there, I told Jane what happened and she said not to worry, it could be fixed. She said, "Just send him another text that says, I was caught off guard, still looking forward to Vegas." That sounded fine with me. It certainly does take a village.

My therapist called me back and I told him what I did. "What have I told you about the text messaging? Stop doing it when you are emotional. If it's not something that needs to be addressed immediately, wait till the next day when you have calmed down. If you still think after that it is a good idea, call me and I'll let you know." He agreed with Jane's response. That was the plan. I typed it up, showed it to Jane and she said, "Do it." Send—now I wait. I didn't have to wait long. About five minutes later I got a text that said, "I don't think I can give you what you want, and deserve."

Jane and I looked at each other.

Well now this was a sticky wicket. We could pick each word apart. "Well, now what the hell do I do?"

"Ask him what he thinks you want," Jane said.

"I most certainly will not say that. Are you crazy? Oh my God, you're drunk." She started laughing. "I can't be sending texts from you when you are drunk. What are you doing to me?" She kept giggling. She was killing me now. I had to take her advice with a grain of salt and I was obviously on my own at this point with giggles by my side. I sent him a text that said, "Was booking this trip a mistake?" About an hour later I got, "Sigh." What the hell does that mean? I left it alone and went to therapy the next day.

"Well, you did it again."

"Oh for God's sake, what did I do now?"

"You pressured him by saying, was booking this trip a mistake?"

I feel like I have to walk on eggshells with everything I say. Are you freaking kidding me?

"Fine, now what?"

"Just send a light text saying something to the effect of, I would love to hang out with you when you're free, no strings attached."

He has this somewhat look of disapproval on his face. "What is the problem now?"

"I just can't believe, I need to send another text."

"Just send this one and be done with it and stop sending texts without asking me."

Geeze. I hate this. It's like a big fucking production. You'd think we were splittin' the atom here or something. I'm just trying to get laid. Say this, don't say that, text this, don't text that, look over here, don't look straight at him or you'll turn to stone. Give me a fucking break. Who knew you'd need a Ph.D to get laid by a rock star. Don't they hand it out like candy? I had to find a somewhat morally conscious, sensitive, yet fucked up, rock star. Is that actually the definition of one? I could be on to something here. It just seems like it should be easier than this. I leave the office of getting my head examined and as soon as I get to the car, I send it. I simply wrote, "I just want to enjoy you if you're free, no strings attached." Off into cyber space it went.

Now I find myself getting ready to embark on a journey that involves therapy, Xanax, possibly some vomiting, and I'm not even sure if what I want to happen will even come to fruition. I didn't leave feeling all that confident, even though I was remarkably calm the weeks leading up to the plane ride. I didn't start to bug out until the Monday before my flight. I woke up feeling anxious, and I could feel it building all day. There was no controlling it. By the time I got home from work, I started popping the Xanax. Why was I doing this again? I figured if I am taking these pills six days before the flight, how am I going to be on the actual plane? I thought one day of Xanax would help but it did not. Monday was followed by Tuesday, Wednesday, and let's not forget Thursday. Friday came around and I was fine. That alone made me nervous. I was anxious because I wasn't anxious. It's at this time that I am thinking maybe weekly therapy appointments might be warranted. Could this be the calm before the storm? What would the storm be? Crashing? If I could have, I would have smacked my face left, then right, and shook my head like the Stooges and gotten myself together. Not wanting to inflict any more pain than I was already going through, I took a deep breath and said, "Mom would never let the plane crash." She, if nothing else, certainly would never leave my children in a situation where they had to go to live with their father—excuse me, sperm donor. I would tell myself whatever I needed to in order to get my ass on that plane.

Of all my biotches, I chose Donna to drive me to the airport. Lucky her. She drew the short straw that day, let me tell you. I needed someone who would not be emotional and who would make me get on that plane. Donna is my voice of reason, my spin doctor if you will. She can spin any situation you throw at her. It's amazing to watch, really, and she always spins it in my favor. She does play devil's advocate, but by the end of the conversation, whatever it is, you always feel good. When I was morally conflicted before my party, Donna actually spun the whole situation in my favor and blamed Miles' wife for causing the whole thing. I said, "That is so wrong, but so working in my favor, I will take it." The only problem with Donna at the wheel is she will do anything you ask of her. She's a good egg that Donna. So if I were at the airport and told her to take me home, she would. I had to warn her ahead of time that, no matter what I said or did, she had to make sure I got on that plane. Even if she needed to involve security. Under no circumstances, was she to drive me home. She was only allowed to drive me there. No matter how much I cried, and she doesn't do well with crying, or however emotional I got, I knew she would do a slap, snap out of it thing. Sean was on pick up patrol, so I had to reiterate that she was drop-off only!

The morning of the trip was my niece's preschool graduation. I was thoroughly distracted for the better half of the morning, but I guess I was starting to stress a little towards the end of lunch. I think my sister-in-law knew it too. Now it was not only the plane, but also the lack of confidence going into this whole thing. As we were parting ways from my niece's celebration, my sister–in-law took her bracelet off and put it on me and said, "Wear this with your white dress, it'll go perfectly." I, of course, started to tear up at this point and she looked at me and said, "You'll be fine." She had gone with me two weeks prior into Manhattan, just as we had done before my party, to find the perfect clothes. There was a torrential downpour while we shopped but we still went store to store until we had at least six outfits, two for each day. I stopped at Francine's after I left Sean and Jane to say good-bye, and to bide time before the plane situation. Francine was very positive. "You're gonna do this and you're gonna have a great time. Don't sit around and wait for him, see Vegas and enjoy the flight."

I know this must seem like I am certifiable. Why I need so many people and prescription meds to walk me through this situation, but if you don't have the fear of flying, you cannot understand. It is a debilitating fear. Anybody that knows me knows flying is not, nor would it ever have been, part of the equation. This is the one thing in my life I could stand firm and say no, I am not doing it and everyone knew not to mess with me. Until now. This one man has me doing things I have never done in my life or ever imagined I would. To any normal person, the things I am doing are not that big of a deal. To me, they are life changing. I always said my fear of flying is not any fear I feel the desire to overcome. I feel no need to put it on a bucket list. I just didn't care enough. However, if I get on this plane, I will be very proud of myself and have such a huge feeling of accomplishment. Isn't it strange how something left undone has no meaning either way, but should I challenge myself and do it, it could change my life.

It was huge that I was getting on a plane, but throw in the fact that it's a evening flight, I'm not happy with that, and when Donna and I were driving to the airport, it started to downpour. All of my fears bunched into one big 747. Fuck it. Let's do it! If I'm going to do this, bring it all on. I decided to call my credit card on the way just to double check and, as my luck would have it, it was maxed out. This was going to make for a challenging three days. Maybe the plane would crash and I wouldn't need to worry about it. Just kidding. Double checking, I had enough cash for the room, and the Mary-Kate Olsen diet was sure to start tomorrow so I wouldn't have to worry about food. I guess I'm good. Donna managed to get me there in time considering there is no one later than both of us, except maybe Sean.

She brought me up as far as she legally could and got a little nervous when she saw them take me aside and go through my bag. Apparently, I forgot about that whole no water bottle in the carry on thing. I was supposed to take the Xanax an hour before the flight but I sat waiting to board and felt okay. Hey, maybe I didn't need it. For the record, if ever a doctor is okay with writing out a script for Xanax, you're not a candidate for opting out of taking it. Just thinking you're okay and don't need to take it is a sure sign that you're crazy and need to take it. Fast forward to the flashing sign that says: "Now boarding." I sent my universal text to everyone that I was about to step on the plane. With that, my foot hit the plane, and I started crying hysterically. My phone started ringing. It was Devon. He had a bunch of people in the background cheering. He said, "You did it! You did it! No, no, why are you crying?"

Like Lucille Ball I started blubbering, "I'm scared."

"Didn't you take your pill?"

"No, because I didn't think I needed it."

"Take it now."

In true Lucille Ball style, I bellowed, "I have no water!"

I thought Devon would need a pill. I hadn't even reached my seat yet while this entire exchange was taking place.

"Ask the stewardess to get you water, then take your pill."

"It takes an hour to kick in and I'm on the plane now."

I have to say, Devon was very calm and comforting (he must have thought I was a dog or a cat). I asked the stewardess for water. She saw me crying, said okay, and then I never saw her again. Panicking, I took the gritty, nasty, bitter pill without water and waited. Luckily they were waiting on a part that would only take five minutes to install, but we wouldn't be able to land without. So the hour and a half wait, gave the pill time to kick in. I didn't give a shit if Fred Flintstone and Mister Slate were rolling a big ass, square wheel out to install it at that point. I really couldn't care less if we crashed either.

I did find it troubling that it would only take five minutes to install something so crucial, but as I said before, I couldn't care less. I have to say, I actually enjoyed the flight. I was stoned and had my iPod on the whole time, and didn't have a care in the world. We landed fine, not crash landed, just landed. When I got to the hotel, since it was so late, they said they gave my room away. It was about 1:00 a.m. when I had arrived. They said they were very sorry and that they were going to put me in another room. It really didn't matter to me one bit. As long as I was not home, I did not give a shit what room I was in. Room 2011.

I schlepped my bags to the elevator and went up to the second floor. I couldn't find the room. Thinking my vision may be poor but I know I can count, I could not see the room anywhere. Before I schlepped back down again I left my stuff in front of the door that my key would not work in and looked at the surrounding doors. Everything seemed correct, so I went back and jammed my key into the door again. Why, oh why does the light keep coming up red? With the time change, my body was really hanging by a thread at 4:00 a.m. Resigning myself to the fact that I needed to pick these bags back up and go downstairs and claim insanity, I almost contemplated leaving two behind and taking my chances. Since I am such an experienced traveler, my bag felt like I was dragging a body from floor to floor. I made it back down to the lobby and tried again. Looking like an absolute tourist with a suitcase dragging behind me on my left and my right side bogged down with three totes, I just kept staring around the ceilings hoping an elevator sign would appear. I'm looking around and I still can't find the proper elevator. In a final effort to end the madness, I retraced my steps back to the desk. I tried explaining to the lovely, patient woman behind the counter that I just couldn't figure any of this out. Apparently Goldilocks forgot her room number by the time she gotten upstairs and had been looking for the wrong room. I'm sure the people in the room I was trying to break into didn't mind. Making another go of it, I headed for the elevator again, this time with the room number written down. The elevators were visible, however none of them had a floor to match my room. Still unable to find the proper elevator, in a pathetic plea, I asked a gentleman who resembled a hotel employee, "Where is the elevator?" He smiled and pointed behind my head, I was standing right in front of it but did not think it was for me because it said Penthouses. No freakin' way. He said, "You need the key for the elevator and your room."

"Shut up!" It kinda slipped out.

He smiled and said, "Really."

Barely able to contain myself, all of a sudden I had superhero strength and could not get up to my room fast enough. When I got up to my room and opened the door, I swear the freakin' bathroom was bigger than the second floor of my house. All I kept thinking was I wish Miles was here now. It was 3:00 a.m. and I didn't know if he was here yet. The room was beautiful and I was sorry that at this point it was only going to be for a few hours. Check out was 11:00

a.m. My second thought when I saw the refrigerator was that Quinn would have cost me forty dollars by now pulling all of the candy out of the slots. Just so I could say I went out in Vegas, I walked outside for a couple of blocks, but then I quickly got back to that room and into the tub. I was like a ten–year-old that you can't get out of the pool.

A little jumpy, because again this is a rare occurrence, I kept waiting for my sons to come barreling through the door in some intertwined, Looney Tunes array of a Catdog fight. It never happened. After the uninterrupted bath in my private lagoon, I moved my ass into my very large bed. Again, I was waiting for Quinn to come jump on the bed and bounce me off like a tiddlywink. Didn't happen. I could get used to this. I don't know at what context of my life that I would actually, ever have to get used to it, but I was certainly prepared to do so if need be. I was a little stressed to say the least when I got up because I did not know what my day had in store for me.

10 a.m. rolled around rather quickly, and I found myself reaching for the phone to call the desk and asked what the absolute latest time was that I had to move. Happy I made that call because then I rolled over until 12:00 p.m. At noon I moved to my new/old room, which was nice, but it was not the penthouse by any stretch of the imagination. I could stand in one spot and see the whole room, unlike the penthouse which I could have driven a golf cart around.

I made contact with my friend Jay. Jay is a very old, dear friend that I have known since I was nineteen. We have a very strong bond and are very much alike. He dated a friend of mine while I dated his friend when we were twenty. He and I were the masterminds of that plan. He was interested in my friend and said, "You like Kevin, and I like Dina, let's go out together and we can help each other." Sounded like a plan. He and Dina hit it off and wound up having an affair for about four or five years. He always liked her but all along, she had a boyfriend. This was his intangible fantasy. Intangible in that, although he had her in a sense, he never had her fully. Such is life . . .

Kevin and I went out a few times but it quickly faded as he was also a musician, like Jay, and he liked to drink and sleep around. Jay and I talked all of the time and I think he and I were the closest in that foursome. He would whine about wanting Dina and I would whine about wanting Kevin. We were a good team. The day I dreaded was when Jay had moved out to Vegas. The only visits in the last three years or so were on his part. This would obviously be the first time I would be visiting him in his hood. We had planned that the evening before the show we would meet at some point. He couldn't wait for me to meet his girlfriend. Jay had gotten divorced a couple of years prior—we really had more in common than I care to discuss. He is Hannibal Lecter to my Clarise, two characters we could channel at any time and incorporate into any conversation we were having. I really didn't know what I was going to do during the day while I wasted time. I'll tell you one thing, it was hot as hell. We Irish people do not do well in the heat and sun, so I just walked around the hotel a little and tried to relax. Subconsciously I think I was trying to accomplish things so that when I got home I could actually say I did something other than sit in my room. That first morning I didn't contact Miles at all during the day. Unsure if I should give him a heads up or just hope that when he saw me he would want me, we went with the hoping he would just want me thing.

Before the show, I met Jay and his girlfriend down at the bar. It was so good to see him and very comforting. He is my comfort food. Seeing him was exactly the stress relief I needed before I went into the show. We didn't get to spend too much time together before I had to head over, but it was perfect just the same. When Jay's girlfriend got up to go to the bathroom, he turned to me and said, "You look great."

I said, "Thanks, but would you fuck me?" He almost spit his drink out. Not that we don't talk to each other like this anyway, but I think I caught him off guard. I said, "Not you, per se, but . . ."

Cutting me off, he said, "I know what you mean, I think you are going to be just fine."

When she came back he was still shaking his head from the last comment. Our time together was short but sweet, and when Amber came back, we got up and started to walk over to where I had to go in, and that is where we parted ways. They were going to dinner and I went into the show.

During the show I did not sit in the front. It was not crowded at all but I still hovered around the center of the room to blend in with the wood work. I had on my hoochie shoes from my party, black shorts, and a black shirt. After the show I waited in the lobby outside the ballroom and hoped he would come out that way. Quite a stupid plan, but it was all I had at the time. The double doors opened and I saw Luke Michaelson come out with a few of the other band members. He smiled and tilted his head in an acknowledging way as he walked passed me. I figured I was in the right spot. Then the door opened again and out he came. I stood up and he was walking toward me with a smile. There were two other guys with him that walked away from him as he came over. As he hugged me, he asked, "How was the plane? I can't believe you did it."

I said, "I cried for an hour but then I was fine after that."

He was just smiling and staring and he said, "You look hot."

You know, I'm standing on stilts, trying to act as though that's normal, trying to be cool and natural, then you gotta say something like that? That's not right. I almost keeled over. "Do you want to hang out?" I said.

"I can't, I have to go out with everybody to a piano bar."

He's fucking kidding me right? Build me up, and then push me over on my stilts. Acting like it doesn't bother me in the least because I told him before the trip I could handle this. I said, "Okay." Okay? What am I, a whore? Okay. I shook my head to myself, replaying my words of wisdom in my head. O.K., the two dumbest letters in the alphabet. That's what I come up with. A five hour plane ride, therapy, Xanax, declining relationship with my brother, and I say, "It's okay if you don't want to have sex!" Okay. What a dick I am. He hugs and kisses me and shakes his head and says, "You really look hot." And then he leaves! At this point, quite honestly, I don't know which one of us is the bigger dick. You know what, I'll take this hit because the arrogance of my stupidity never ceases to amaze me.

Just for the record, it's not okay. I'm not okay with it but I have to be because I said I was okay with it. I also said, if I'm not mistaken, "Anytime you want to hang out, no pressure, no strings attached." Since when did the prude become such a raging whore? Sometimes the shit that flies out of my unfiltered mouth amazes even me. You may catch me on occasion flailing my hands around as if trying to swat a bug, but don't be fooled, that's usually me trying to grab the words back that have started to escape my mouth. "Okay," would be one of those times.

Who says it's okay to treat me like a piece of shit? I'll let you do that and then come back for more tomorrow. That would be me once again. I go back to my room feeling defeated, and then I get a brainstorm. I don't know if brainstorm is accurate, maybe a final act of desperation. I send him a text saying, "If you'd like to hang out when you're done, let me know." Wanting the night to either end or for the new day to just hurry the hell up, I went to sleep. When I got up in the morning, I checked my phone. Nothing.

****

I texted my sister–in-law and told her what was going on. She said don't worry about it. "Why don't you send him a text saying something like, since the evenings seem to be difficult for you, would you like to meet this afternoon?" That was a good idea. I was a little nervous about sending another text. I was equally nervous about having any sunlight come into the room for him to see my fat ass. A dilemma, but a plan nonetheless. She said, "But once you send it you have to go about your day and don't think about it, otherwise nothing will happen."

Easier said than done. "Fair enough" I told her. I sent the text, then went for a walk around the area. I walked down to the Bellagio because Devon has a friend that works there. He used to be a client of ours, so I figured I'd go say hello to pass the time. Let me tell you, I had never been to Vegas before but it was July and hot as balls. The walk to the hotel damn near killed me, and then when I got in the Bellagio, it's another schlep. Finally making it over to the concierge desk, I ask for Michael. "Oh Michael is off on Tuesdays." I laugh to myself and say of course he is, why wouldn't he be? After writing him a quick note, I did an about face and started back.

Dreading the walk back in the heat, I was afraid I may start to hallucinate like Bugs Bunny, and I don't care to hear about this dry heat bullshit. Hot is hot, dry or not. Luckily Anna called while I headed back and broke up the monotony. She could also serve as my emergency contact if I passed out. She asked what was going on so I filled her in on all of the gory details. "Do you think he'll call?" she said.

"I have no freakin' idea but I'll tell you one thing, I think I'm a little lost."

The sun was so bright I couldn't see the time on my phone and I was sweating like a farm animal, so you know this is the perfect scenario for a return text. Anna said, "Do you see anything familiar?" I walked a straight line, who gets lost? My phone vibrated, I look and it says Mile's cell. I almost fucking fainted. I said, "Anna, he just texted me."

"What does it say?"

"Holy shit, the sun is too bright, I can't read it."

"Read it! Read it!"

I'm bent over, hovering over my phone like I have a pocket full of kryptonite and she's screaming, "What does it say?"

My hands were shaking, "Oh my God, it says what room are you in?"

"Oh my God!"

"What am I gonna do, there are fifty fucking hotels here and now I'm really shaken up and don't know what I'm doing?"

"Alright, just calm down. Stop, look around, do you see anything familiar?"

"I can see the hotel!"

"Okay, text him back and go back."

I sent him a text that said, "I will be in room 4837 in twenty minutes." The walk back seemed a hell of a lot longer than the walk there. I got back and washed up again, then texted my sister–in-law. She was very happy and said, "Keep in touch and have fun." I wound up lying in bed for about an hour. I sent him a text saying, "You're killing me." A half hour goes by and still nothing. This has to be a joke right? I hate jumping for him then being left like a loser to wait. Don't get me wrong it's not about being late, because I'm always late, but I shouldn't have to wonder if he'll show up at all. That's what makes me nervous. I sent a text to my sister–in-law. She said, "Don't worry, send another." I sent the same one again. Immediately he responded, "I am sorry. I will be there soon." I was good after that. I texted my sister–in-law and she said, "See I told you, just calm down and enjoy it."

I said to her, "What do you think the 'coming down the hall' text will be this time?"

She said, "I don't know but I'm sure it will be good."

About twenty minutes later I get another text. For a split second I got nervous because I thought it could be him saying he's not coming. Miles' Cell. *Oh crap. What is it?* I open it. "Are you ready to get fucked?" The phone almost flew out of my hand like a greased pig. *Oh no he di-int!* I responded back, "PLEASE!" I thought I would die. I heard talking outside the door so I walked over and I heard him say, "I don't know, I'll ask her," then there was a knock. Curiously I peeked out the door and there he stood looking back as he pulled his aviators down to reveal those brown eyes. T-shirt, sunglasses, shorts, flip-flops, smiling—gorgeous. "The maid wants to know if you want your room cleaned," he said as he came in.

"Not by her," I said as I closed the door. He put his phone, key, and sunglasses down on the table behind him and put his arms around me and started kissing me. It was heaven. His left hand ran up the outside of my right leg and pulled my panties off in a second. Starting to get weak, I got lost in the moment. He stepped back and took his flip-flops off as he was taking his shirt off. It's all I can do but stand and watch him. He took his shorts off and I started kissing him. I couldn't stand anymore, "Get in the bed," I said to him.

Smiling, he got in and lay on his back. I left my dress on and got in next to him. There was enough sun coming in so that I could see his face as I leaned down to kiss him. His eyes were closed and as I leaned down he opened his mouth slightly and I saw his tongue start to come out slowly. He gently moaned as his mouth barely touched mine. He is so hot, I feel like I'll never get enough, yet he is so restrained. In the moment, I don't reflect on the fact that he is as amazing as he is because he has had so much practice, I am just going to remain in the moment. All I know is that I don't want this to end. I straddled him and was staring in his eyes. He slowly and gently reached his right hand to my left shoulder and slid my strap down, and then he did the same with my right. I felt his fingertips go down each arm slowly and gently.

Every inch of his body was tended to. We were cheek to cheek as I collapsed on him. Embracing me, he flipped me over and started kissing me. Smiling as he stared in my eyes, I could not stop quivering. He held me closer, but then what was the most amazing time was interrupted with a softly spoken, "I gotta go, baby." For the love of St. Nick, is he shitting me? I locked my legs around him tighter and he kept kissing me. As he went to get up he moaned and came back and started kissing me. Wishing that he didn't have to go, I just laid there as he attempted to get up. He was unsteady on his feet and said, "I feel like I'm stoned." I knew how he felt, that's another reason why I didn't even bother to get up. He got dressed then came back over and sat next to me on the bed. Since I was happy that I had gotten what I wanted, I didn't focus on his most recent asshole maneuver. Leaning down and kissing me again he whispered, "I'll see you later, baby." I never got up and let him walk out on his own.

After he left, I had to just lie in the bed. I couldn't move. Of course I called the girls from my headquarters. Headquarters being the station in which I lay in the center of the bed, unable to move due to what feels like a seizure. I could quite possibly be making the rollover phone calls while I was still experiencing the aftermath of the quake, if you will. My legs were like rubber, in fact my whole body was not unlike Gumby. Although, it was the most unbelievable experience I've had.

Since I have been popping Xanax since I landed, I decided to go down to the little coffee shop and get something to eat. See, now that I had sex, I could eat something. Psychotic, I know. Again, not in therapy and popping Xanax like Valley of the Dolls for no reason. I got a tea and a small container of chicken salad. I was feeling ballsy. I ventured past four chips and went for completely fattening. The hallway was very busy but I grabbed a seat on the edge of a waterfall and called Felice. While I was talking to her, I saw Miles walk by. He smiled, I waved, and he kept walking. Still floating, I was hoping that was just an appetizer and that I was going to get a second round after tonight's show. After sitting for a few minutes and people watching, I realized I was going to have to venture back upstairs and start getting ready for the show. Not having much time, I made sure I still had some time for a little nap.

The outfit Jane and I had chosen for tonight was a long white dress. It was almost a mesh with a silk slip under it, with spaghetti straps. This was her favorite of the three. It almost looked like a dress you would wear to a beach wedding. Even with the nap, I got down there a little early and stood outside the ballroom peeking in at the event going on. Luke Michaelson was onstage and someone was with him. It may have been one of his brothers, but I wasn't sure because I was really only making believe that I was engrossed. I saw Miles walking towards me but pretended I didn't. I'm very mature. He ran his left hand down my left arm, moved my hair with his right hand, and kissed my neck. To know I had just spent the afternoon with him, and now this just before his show . . . In fantasy world, this is perfect. This was the kind of greeting I liked.

Tonight I stood up front, and the only bad thing about that is hearing the girls around you talking about him. You sort of want to hear, but then sometimes you're sorry you did. There was a guy standing next to me the whole show and he kept talking and flirting with me. He was on a business trip for the weekend and last minute heard about the show and decided to go. As he's flirting, I throw the whole, "Are you married?" question out there. Guess what? Ding ding ding, we have a married man. Do all men suck? I wasn't interested in him, I just felt like throwing that out there for shits and kicks to confirm what I already assumed. During the show, when he wasn't on stage, I sent Miles an inappropriate text, explaining what I would like to do to him after the show. He didn't respond and tonight's show seemed very long. I don't know if that's because I just wanted to get out of there and attack him or what. After the show I waited in the lobby and watched him talk to all the women waiting for him. While I was waiting, two women near me seemed a little giddy and whispered to each other, then came over to me. One woman said, "Are you with the guitarist?"

Caught off guard, I stammered and said, "No."

The other woman said to her, "See, I told you," then the first woman said, "I'm sorry, I could have sworn you were." Smirking to myself, I thought, *well that was cool!* I'd love to know what gave them that impression. There were a few times that he kissed me out in the open, maybe they were there. I never paid much attention to what was going on around me when he was there.

After everyone had cleared away, he went to go back in but was locked out. He tried the other doors, which brought him down the hallway further. I walked over to the end of the hallway and he started walking back toward me. We were the only ones in the hallway and as he got closer, he said, "I'm locked out." He put his arms around me and kissed me and said, "You look like you're going to a wedding."

"God no," I said.

He kept kissing me and said, "Today was fun."

"Yes it was, would you like to do it again?"

He smiled and said he couldn't, there was another party. "But I had fun today."

That's great, I'm good enough to fuck when no one is around but he has to go to a party two nights in a row with people he sees all the time. These are the signs I should pick up on that I refuse to accept. I see them, I just don't accept them. I guess that would be the definition of denial. I'm the queen of it, baby. "Well, if I'm locked out, I guess my equipment is safe for the night." He took my hand and we started walking back toward the elevator. Some guy came over and started walking with us, right between us like I wasn't even there. I swear a lot of the men are worse than the women. It's like they have a man crush. The guy finally left at the elevator, which didn't help me much because that's where we were parting ways. We kissed goodbye, then got on two different elevators. Hoping again for a middle of the night knock on the door, I went to bed.

I texted my sister–in-law the next morning and asked if I should do what I did yesterday. "Sure" she said. I went back to the coffee shop and repeated my message from yesterday afternoon. I tried to distract myself by going out and walking around. Ducking into a hotel to escape the heat, I found myself in what I think was The Venetian. It was so freakin' hot, I don't know how people live there. So my sightseeing was dictated by the weather. At least I was able to see some things, even if I really was wasting time till he responded. Again, sweating like a whore in church, I tried to make my way back to my hotel as quickly as possible without incident. It had been longer since yesterday's response so I started to worry. I texted Jane and said, "Should I send another one?"

She said, "Yeah, go for it."

"I don't want to be a nuisance though."

"You went out there with a purpose, send the text."

Okay here I go again. I sent it. Another hour went by and still no response. Now I was starting to really worry. Wasting time by walking around the concert area, I spotted him. I walked up behind him and hit him in the ass. He finished making a purchase, then turned around and came over to me. He sort of had his head down. He kissed me hello, then said, "I know I frustrate you."

"In a good way," I said. We were standing very closely and talking and I said, "Do you want to go back upstairs?"

He pointed over to Luke Michaelson and said, "I'm supposed to be hanging out with Luke. Maybe I could blow him off."

"That sounds like a good idea."

With that, again, as if I'm not even there, a male fan comes over and starts talking to him. It's almost laughable at this point. If I didn't know any better I would swear there was a camera somewhere. That's another reason why when he is actually in my room it is so private, because there is no one to interrupt. Yet by the time I have him all to myself, we immediately have sex and there is no talking. I have never had sex with anyone who's like a stranger. I constantly struggle with the decision I made. I feel like I know him from shows, interviews, his music, talking minimally after shows, but we don't really know each other at all. In his eyes, am I a whore because he really doesn't know anything about me. If he chooses not to know anything about me but still fuck me, is that truly the definition of groupie? Have I allowed myself to be perceived that way? I saw things differently than him. Does he realize that if it wasn't him, it wouldn't be someone else? I can't help but feel there was no way this situation could end well. When things were simpler and I went to the shows because I enjoyed the music and it was a night out, a night to just escape my life of being a mom and a caretaker, it felt different. The problem with putting someone on a pedestal is the only way off is down. Once the line was crossed, things would never be the same and I could never go back to the innocent enjoyment. I was now going to step into his world and maybe see more than I should have and feel things I'm never supposed to feel. The choice to cross the line may seem like a no brainer to most, but to the wallflower that could potentially lose her only outlet to sanity, it was a big deal. This is the difference between the groupie and the fan. I was not a groupie, but I wanted him. I was not looking to sleep with anyone else at any other concert. I only wanted him, but so does everyone else.

****

Feeling like yesterday was all I was going to get, I got ready for the last night. Tonight's outfit of choice was "the little black dress." I have to say, I was surprised at how many people looked at me as I walked down the hallways. But how can they think I look good if it's like pulling teeth to get Miles upstairs? I can't figure it out. Trying to keep it a no strings attached situation, as soon as I saw him, each time I cut to the chase. Clearly he does not want to chit chat so I am making it easy for him . . . or so I thought. How can it not be me if he won't even take me up on that?

I sat in the lobby outside the ballroom, the same spot where I started this mission two nights prior. I saw him coming towards me but he didn't see me. I got up and started walking towards him with my head turned like I didn't see him, but I could see him out of the corner of my eye staring and smiling. He walked right up to me and kissed me.

There were many people milling about. Much to my surprise, I asked one more time. I only asked because of his reaction when he saw me. "Do you want to stop by and say good night after the show?"

He had a big smile and said, "Yes, probably," and shook his head as he looked me up and down and said, "Wow," as he walked away.

It was about fifteen minutes to show time and I had to continue walking even though I was heading in the opposite direction. Feeling rather confident now, I walked down to the infamous coffee shop and sat there to text Jane and Francine. While I sat there, I noticed a table of three gentlemen sitting two tables away looking at me. Being the anti-social bitch that I am, I put my head back down and kept texting. It was getting close to when I had to head back and these guys kept staring. Fumbling through my bag, now looking for a pen, I could still see the boys peering over. A fruitless effort now caused me to have to pass my friends to get a pen from the counterperson. As I approached, they all stood up at once like The Stooges and the self-appointed leader stopped me and asked if I was a professional photographer. Reluctant to be truthful, I told him I was not. Noticing they all had staff buttons on, I was afraid for a split second they might tell me that I am unable to photograph tonight's show. "Oh, we thought you were and we were going to ask you if you would photograph us." I assured them I could do it anyway.

"Where do you want us?" the leader asked.

"Right there is fine" I assured them.

As I was about to take the picture, one of the guys had a silly look on his face. Lowering the camera I said, "Why are you laughing at me? Is this a joke?"

"No, not at all. Go ahead, we are ready." Raising the camera back up to my eye all I could see was this ass laughing again. Lowering the camera and putting my left hand on my hip, I looked at them again and he said, "Okay, we don't really want our picture taken, we just want to look at you." With that, we all started laughing. They really did seem harmless and they seemed like a lot of fun. I took two pictures and two of the guys gave me their business cards and asked if I could send them copies. I thanked them for the laugh and was about to leave when they invited me to sit for a few minutes. They seemed very nice, so I sat even though now I was starting to get unnerved that the show was starting and I was missing it. These are probably the little signs I should be listening to. I should take the time and sit with these guys that took the time to acknowledge me and make me laugh and invited me to sit with them. Instead, I am far too worried about getting back inside to check out a guy that gives me a definite maybe every time I see him. The leader looked very familiar to me but I could not place him, then it hit me: he was Brad Parks, a television personality. We were talking and laughing for a few minutes and I got the impression that they were pleasantly surprised because I think they thought I was some bobble headed whore. Not that there's anything wrong with that. Who knows, they were probably disappointed that I wasn't a bobble headed whore. I was actually sorry that I had to break this little get together up but it was time to start to head in.

Brad asked me if I wanted to join them after the show and I apologized and said I had temporary plans at the point. He said, "Wait a minute, you told us you don't fly, yet you flew out here for a concert, you stayed in your room every day, and that's why we never saw you until tonight, and yet there is someone here you have plans with?"

"Pretty much."

"There is more to this story than you are letting on."

Unwilling to give any information because I would never do that to Miles, I said, "I'm sorry. I would have loved to meet you later but at least at this point, it seems as though I have plans."

Brad seemed intrigued. He said, "Please tell me it is not with Luke Michaelson because he must have fifty diseases."

"Okay, first of all, uncalled for. Secondly, it is not with him."

"Alright, well I hope whoever this mystery person is follows through, otherwise they would be a fool."

I thanked them for their company and promised to send them the photos.
Heading back towards the ballroom, I was feeling confident. Still a little worried that there was a chance we would not hook up, I still kept the faith. For the first part of the show I sat down. My feet needed a break since it had been a long weekend and I still had the rest of Sunday to go. Eventually, as the show progressed, people started to get up and some moved forward. This was now when I moved up and stood in front of him for the rest of the show. The last song of the night everyone came out on stage to sing. Luke decided that for the chorus he would take the microphone into the audience and go up to certain people. Historically, I am always chosen under these circumstances. If there was a huge clown in the middle of the mall looking to pull foreign objects from a selected orifice, I would be the chosen one. Every time I put my head down and try to hide, avoid, retreat, it never fails, it's like a red flag. Luke makes it down about two people away from me and, sure enough, the mic is put right in front of me and there is silence. I could feel my face burning. Shaking my head no, he smiles and goes to someone else. Not off the hook, he smiles and comes back to me again. Same scenario. Silence, purple burning face, and he has a big smile. Apparently the third time is the charm. One more time he attempts—no go.

When the show ended, he came over to me and says, here's the kicker, "If you were younger, I'd ask you to call me." If I was younger, he'd ask me to call him? What, if I was a fetus? I guess the twenty year age difference wasn't good enough for him. Then he tried to put something in my hand but it fell to the floor. As I'm looking for it, he puts his finger up indicating to wait a minute. He walked away and came back, put something in my hand, and closed it. I kept thinking about when Brad said he had fifty diseases (that he has since told me he was kidding about because they are friends) and now he has his hand wrapped around mine. He walked away and I opened my hand. It was a guitar pick. I had to know what was on the floor so I kept looking. Finally I spotted something: another pick. That one had said The Event. The second pick was just a generic pick. I went outside and waited in the hallway. Luke came walking over smiling and said, "I remember you," looked me up and down, turned, and left with his entourage. There were a lot of people around since it was the last night. I decided to move out to the lobby and wait by the wall. Perfect place for a wallflower.

Tonight was a long wait for me with a lot of running around for him. I stood and waited while all of the woman went over to him again. When everyone finally left, he came over to me and kissed me as if that was it. I said, "Are you coming back with me?"
"I have to pack all my shit up and get out of here." We started walking back toward the elevators and since I had the ho shoes on, I was unable to walk briskly. He said, "I'm gonna have to walk faster now."

I said, "Okay, I'll watch." With that, he shook his hot ass and started running a little. Of course someone with a man crush attached himself at his hip and kept up with him. He was on his way to get a luggage cart and I was going back to my room alone. I was pissed at myself because I always do this and I knew my mother would have been furious with me. What I should have done was hung out with the three guys that I had met earlier, that I had fun with, and that had the decency to invite me to sit, go to dinner with them, and go to the casino with them after the show. No, I was going to hang on to the probably and wait and see if I was thrown a bone, no pun intended. The guys did say that if my plans had changed I could meet them in the casino, but I did not want to now start looking for them, nor was I in the mood to do anything.

I let myself believe that he had to get his stuff together and by the time that was done, get to sleep because he probably has to get up early to fly out. If that's what makes me feel better and gets me through the day, then so be it. I'm sure he could fit some "fucking" time in there somewhere, but then I would have to accept that he did fit it in, just not with me. I didn't see him hanging out with anyone else during this trip so my scenario is possible. Who am I kidding? Anything is possible. I went to sleep rather upset and I was hoping to get some kind of text before I left, but nothing. I had to get up early for my flight. Another stressed filled day. I would have felt a little better getting on the plane if at least it had ended a little better. However, the day I did spend with him was probably the most unforgettable day I have ever had. Therefore, I will try to concentrate on that and forget about the blow off. It wasn't all that bad considering I met other people and had a lot of guys staring and flirting. It was a very flattering weekend. My three amigos from the coffee shop were trying to encourage me to go to the Memphis show because, according to them, "That is the best one." I didn't know about all that. All three shows? Another flight? Although, this Xanax thing is kinda workin' for me. If I did go, at least I could hang out with these guys and have fun. It was certainly something to consider. I was absolutely physically, emotionally, and mentally depleted after this weekend. So many emotional highs and lows, so much Xanax, a few drinks, no food, and throw in a pair of heels three days straight, and you got yourself a problem. I basically stood for three days in those ho shoes so my legs were killing me. I wound up crying on the plane, again, because I'm a big, fat loser. This time, I think it was a combination of things. Flying and second-guessing my choices again. Am I slut and that's why I don't get a text or any contact after? I really don't know. By the time I get home, it's right back into mommy mode.

****

I got home July second around 6 p.m. The kids were waiting and their friends were over and I was still on a high. A twisted, confused, psychotic high, but a high nonetheless. By the time I schlepped everything home, since of course I needed to stop at my dad's first for a while, it was after midnight. Bailey's fifteenth birthday was the next day. I actually got to sleep in a little on the third, but then I had to unpack and get my pictures developed. Priorities.

My whole body hurt. I was running five miles a day regularly, no problem. Put me in heels for three days and I'm like a quadriplegic afterwards. All I kept thinking was, *okay, tomorrow I can rest.* Then it happened. The phone rang. It was Anna Welsh. I figured she was calling to talk about Vegas since it is her favorite place and she was so excited that I went. I had been texting her from there but now she wanted all the juicy details. Anna is my own personal Jillian Michaels. She's the one who makes me run to get to the start of the race. The one who wants two more miles, and when you tell her, "fuck you," she says, "I don't care what you say. Give me two more miles," and you give her the two extra, otherwise she drags your carcass the last two and adds more for a bad attitude.

Aside from myself, she has trained with my two brothers. There is quite a bit of history here though. My dad and her dad are best friends. Both were world-class athletes, top of their game back in the day. My dad was a professional soccer player and her dad was a runner. They had been friends for fifty years and used to train together. I only recently learned that my dad, who believed soccer was the only sport to exist, used to call Anna's father a wimp. He said, "running is not a sport, it is a girl's past-time," which I think is hysterical. Sean told me that my dad was known for his speed, but when he and Billy would do sprints together, Billy would sprint next to my dad backwards. They were no joke back then.

At seventy nine, Billy is still running and comes to sit with his friend who can no longer walk. Billy always comes over after he finishes a race and brings my dad a t-shirt and the trophy or medal he always wins. After my dad's stroke, Billy came to the hospital and nursing home every day and sat with him, spoon-fed him, and on more than one occasion transferred him to a chair, then told the nurse that he had no idea how he got there. They are the brothers that each of them never had. I think I get my determination and drive from my dad. The whole "no excuse is acceptable" attitude. However, my mother was no slouch. She was very sassy, which I loved.

Anna claims that with the second generation, the shoe is on the other foot. The Evans's are the wimps. Sometimes we don't pick up the phone if Anna is calling because it could mean a painful couple of days. Once you pick that phone up, you are locked in. There is no telling her no. Avoidance is the key here. Anna has been extremely instrumental in my total body transformation. She has pushed me mentally and physically, and given me the encouragement I needed especially when I was at my lowest. I know when she tells me to do something I need to do it, but sometimes you would just rather kill yourself, like July 3, 2008. After we discussed Vegas thoroughly, she said, "Okay, I'll see you at the start tomorrow at 9:00 a.m."

"What? What start? You're kidding me right?"

"The Pepper Martin Race is tomorrow at 9:00 a.m. I'll be there at 8:15 a.m. to meet you at the start."

"What the hell are you talking about? I just got back from Vegas last night and I'm sore."

"That's nice, vacation is over, see you at the start."

Click.

That's one of those times when you just look at the phone and try to wrap your brain around what just took place. I couldn't wrap my little brain around it though. The Pepper Martin Race is a five-mile bitch of a race. The first two and a half miles are uphill. The first time I did this race was last year and I thought I passed away and no one told me. I got home from the race and my children found me on the upstairs hallway floor outside the bathroom. Apparently I fell asleep there, face down. It must have happened on my way in because I was facing that way. I figured the race starts right next to the cemetery that my mother is buried in, so maybe I should just dig a hole next to her because I did not know how I was going to do this. She is such a raging cunt to run with too, because she talks and keeps a brisk pace and if you try to slow down, you get scolded. Have I mentioned that I won't run in the rain? When I woke up that glorious July fourth, it was gross. Overcast, wet, nasty, and I was hoping it would get called, or at the very least Anna Stalin would call and say, "Fuck it." No such luck. Runners are historically psychotic and run in torrential downpours and freezing weather. It's nuts. She runs in crazy weather too, obviously.

I got my usual call forty-five minutes before the race started, asking where I was because I'm "not gonna get a spot." Good, then I can go home. I was so late for a race one time I was putting my number on while I ran to the start after the gun went off. Oh, she was not happy with me. While standing, waiting for the gun to go off, all I did was complain. Complained that I was there, complained about the weather, complained that I hated her, and then complained again that I was there again. "Good, I don't give a shit. Do you want to be fat or do you want this guy?"

"I'm here, aren't I?"

"Yeah, but your brothers are punks, a couple of pussies. Their sister is here, out in the rain, and they are home sitting on their fat asses. You should be proud of yourself."

Although I felt physically abused by that backhanded compliment, I was proud of myself. If I did this last year and finished it, I have to be able to do it now. I have jogged so many miles since then, this should be a cinch. The gun went off and the torture began. I stayed with Anna further than last year, but I assured her I would do this and she could go. Off she went. My standards are not high. I just want to complete the race and not pass away. That's it. I got to the worst part of the race. About two and a half miles into the course is this steep incline for a quarter of a mile. Most people walk it, that's how stupid it is. I refused to walk it this year. I got to the top and who was standing there but Billy. "Hey, whadya take, a cab? Anna's ahead of you."

More pressure, that's all I needed. "I'm going, I'm going." I managed to complete the race and I actually cut a lot of time off of last year's time. I was very excited. After the race, I filled Anna in on what I left out yesterday. I told her how I was toying with the idea of going to Memphis. She said, "Go for it. You met a lot of people this time, you'll meet more in Memphis. It's a great opportunity. Pass some cards out and start to sell yourself and don't be there just to fuck Miles Baker."

I actually loved the idea of going. I primarily wanted to see him, but anything else would be a plus. The more I thought about it, the more inclined I was to go. I told my brothers too. I didn't care what they said. I was feeling more confident in my decision-making and consequences as far as they were concerned. Feeling ballsy, I sent an email off to my three friends, thanking them for their company that night and to let them know that I looked forward to seeing them in Memphis, as I was strongly considering the trip. They all responded, actually two of them responded and said they would pass the message on to Joe as he was the only one that didn't give me a card that night. He was quiet also. I sent the picture out to the guys and they liked them. Pete and Joe have a radio program and posted the picture on their website which was very cool.

Now, since I was pretty much decided that I was going, I put that call in to Anna. "Anna, what do I need to do to get a Jessica Biel ass in only one month?" See, I complain about Anna, but then I ask for miracles in a small window of time. Clearly, I don't even think it is physically possible for anyone to achieve a Jessica Biel ass, no matter how much time you have, but these are the types of requests I make of her. You have to aim high otherwise, what's the point? "Stair master, every day," was the response. So I did it. I spent the next month working out like an animal. I had to go get a couple more outfits. This time my sister–in–law did not come with me and I swear every time she is not involved, things do not work to my advantage. One of the dresses I got just covered my ass. It may actually have been a shirt, I'm not quite sure. So I definitely continued on the stair machine to make sure my ass stayed in my shirt-dress.

Chapter 14

Again, not wanting to catch Miles off guard, or to be caught off guard myself, I sent a text a few days before the trip. I said something to the effect of, "I hope you'll be up for a little afternoon delight in The River City." I never heard anything so I assumed that was a good sign. If he already had plans to hook up with someone, or was bringing someone, he might respond back with something. I felt okay, so I took a cab to the airport this time because I was a "big girl." My flight was at about 7:30 a.m. and it would bring me there with enough time to settle in and not be stressed that I am late.

When the plane landed, I went up to the information booth and asked them where I could get the shuttle to the Hyatt. Not realizing the absence of one word like Memphis after Hyatt would make a difference, I was directed "over there to the right, and it's $50." *Fifty bucks, huh?* I thought it was a free shuttle and five minutes from the airport? The difference between indicating Memphis and not, was $50. Being the dick that I am, I paid and got on the shuttle. He never asked me which Hyatt. Apparently there are three, and I was on my way to one of them. The wrong one. What kind of asshole information guy are you that you point to a $50 shuttle without asking me which hotel when you know there are three of them. You are the keeper of said information, I am the unknowing tourist. If one does not ask the proper questions, isn't it your job to offer the information, hence the title over your head? I got in the shuttle and I was taken downtown to The Hyatt. Not mine. I asked the now Mr. Hyde turned Dr. Jekyll driver where the correct hotel is as I show her the paper. She now offers, "You on da wrong bus." No shit, Sherlock. Can someone help me out here? Work with me people. "You gotz to git off dis bus and git on anotha cuz I aint goin back, mmhhhmm."

I took a moment to tell myself to shut up, and then I said, "What about the fifty bucks?"

"You paid, I drove. It ain't my fault." To avoid slapping the everloving shit out of her, I "gotz off da bus" and she directed me to the bellman, who was actually very nice and helpful. Go figure. Two for the price of one.

After explaining in a civilized tongue what had just happened, he said he would send me back on another shuttle. "Hide your ticket and tell them it was a mistake."

The shuttle driver gets on and asks me for my ticket. Unable to lie convincingly, my ass clenched and I said, "I don't have it because they put me on the wrong shuttle."

"They," who the hell are "they?" I'll tell you who "they" are: "they" are the people that get blamed for everything when we don't know what the hell we are talking about. Now would be one of those times. Seeming unconcerned about my excuse, he looked at me in the mirror as he took the other tickets and moved on. At this point I was sweating like a farm animal, nauseous from all the driving around, and couldn't help but think this is not a good start to the trip. I hope this isn't a sign of things to come. *The Secret* would say you can't have that kind of attitude, otherwise you will invite that kind of day. Let me tell you a little secret about *The Secret.* After this trip, *The Secret* can kiss my ass. Yes, I personally have invited groupies to a concert and I invited Miles to fuck them. I am a powerful woman. Supposedly the things you worry about are the things you are giving strength to, so in a sense I guess I did invite Miles to fuck everyone but me. I digress. The shuttle brought me back to where it all began, the dick at the airport's information booth. Although I am nauseous from driving around downtown Memphis for an hour and a half, I am not too sick to not go all New York on someone if I don't get my fifty bucks back for that unwarranted tour of the city.

I went up to yet another shuttle information booth. This one had a female at it. I'm not saying it, but it just seems like I get more information when I approach a woman. However, my first shuttle driver was a woman. I explain the situation to her and she tells me to wait a minute, she needed to call her supervisor. Prepared to flip out if she did not come back with the correct response, I waited patiently. She gets her return call and I hear her say, "Should I give all of it or just half?" Since I returned the ticket I claimed I didn't have, oh this bitch better believe she is giving me the full fifty at this point or I am going over the counter. I should get it back just for having to deal with that stupid fool on the first shuttle and the moron at the information booth. This in not rocket science people, we are

189

not splitting the atom. I am in front of you with my luggage, having just gotten off a plane, though now it was an hour and a half ago at this point, but do I look like I have been joyriding around at your expense? Open the drawer and get the cash out. People do it all the time. Clearly there was a mistake if I bought two tickets, I have one and I am at the start line. Someone dropped the ball. You don't give round trip rides. I'm here because there is something wrong. She hangs up the phone and says, "Okay, I can give you a full return." Is she kidding me? I was leaving with the full fifty or the info booth was going to be empty, indefinitely.

"Oh, thank you," I said.

She pointed to the fucking hotel from her stool at the kiosk. Not realizing I'm at my breaking point, she throws salt in the wound and says, "Oh boy, it's only five minutes from here and you went all the way downtown?" *Shut up, bitch, not in the mood.* I gather all of my shit again and head off to the correct shuttle. *Hmm, look at that, five minutes.* I thought I would vomit by the time I got to my room.

Good thing I got the early flight. Although, maybe a different flight would not have lead to the imbecile at the information booth. I took a shower, got in bed, and sent Miles a text saying, "I just got out of the shower, why don't you come to room 834 and fuck me?" What was that? Who the hell am I? I debated for about forty five seconds then I sent it. Is he going to think I'm a slut? I guess we'll see. I decided to lie down and rest since I was still nauseous. About an hour or so later, I got a text from him. It read, "That was a sexy text." Ding ding ding, we have a winner. But now what? I respond back with "I could go back in and you can join me." I don't hear anything and it is also close to the time the show will be starting. He won't go on until 5:00 p.m. though. I got myself ready and decided to go downstairs and walk around. Tonight's outfit of choice was the one I wore the first night of the Vegas show, I just changed the shorts. As soon as I walked in the concert area, I saw him. He was talking to a vendor so I waited off to the side as if I was looking at something. I saw him checking me out as he walked towards me. He came over and kissed me and said, "You look cute."

"I only cried five minutes this time on the plane so I'm getting better."

"I was wondering how you got here, so you did a plane again. You're unbelievable."

We chatted another minute, then I said, "Would you like to get together later?"

He smiled and replied, "Yeah, probably." We said goodbye and I walked outside.

****

This is when it all started to go bad, quickly. I spotted a girl, whom I have seen pictures of online from The Event page. She is usually standing right in front of Miles when he is playing. She also looks like the girl from Mt. Vernon and the girl from that horrible night at The Red Spot. You see where this is going now. She was with her partner in crime. She looked like she was looking for someone, how ironic. I went about my night and ran into Joyce. She and I went into the auditorium and sat in the back just talking. Miles came in and said hi as he walked passed us, coffee and hot dog in hand. Some combo. "Caffeine and beef," as he put it. We took our seats just before the show started. We sat in the front row. I saw that girl, let's call her whore, walk past us. This would be the redhead I saw in the hallway. Joyce was on her cell phone and saw her walk by and told whomever she was on the phone with, "Yeah, I saw her, she just walked passed me." Apparently, Whore has a reputation. As what, I don't know yet. I didn't want to pry but I did want to get the scoop on this girl and her friend. Drinks in hand, they sat in the middle of the room, but not for long. As soon as the show started, they took their already-inebriated asses front and center. I asked Joyce who she was, to which she responded, "the one who does the band."

I channeled my inner Gary Coleman and said, "Whatchoo talkin' 'bout, Joyce? She does the whole band?"

She just looked at me as if to say, "Do I really need to spell this out for you?"

Well that sucks, I thought. Now I'm watching the interaction here and not liking it much. She and her drunk friend are standing in front of him dancing like two drunken, uncoordinated, out of work strippers. I'm looking at him look at her and he is smiling. Is he kidding me? This is what he likes? I don't get it. It just seems like he should be over this already. He's fifty-three and these two clowns have to be twenty-five, what the fuck is going on? This put a damper on the evening to say the least. At one point I looked over and they were gone. I turned to Joyce and said, "Hey, they left."

"No they didn't." she said.

"Sure they did, look, they're gone."

"They're on the floor."

Lo and behold, the two drunk asses were on the floor in front of their chairs. I'm thinking they're looking like fools but apparently he is still smiling. During the intermission I went to the bathroom and to get some air. As I'm on my way back, I see Miles walking with some other woman. She looked like an older woman and I thought she was perhaps someone's mother. They walked back into the auditorium together. The plot thickens. As the show begins again, Older Woman now goes in the "back stage" area to watch the show. Hmm, I am at a loss. After the show I saw Miles and asked him if we were going to get together. I don't even remember what the answer was but it was something along the lines of, "I'll let you know" or "I'm not sure yet." Fast-forward three days and that just means, let me weigh my options. I went to my room feeling like a jerk and waited, like a jerk. I convinced myself that getting to sleep early was a good, responsible thing to do, as if now was a good time to start being responsible. I was sugar coating the fact that I was waiting for him in hopes that he would call and I was making myself sick. Needless to say, there was no call. I also saw him leave with Older Woman.

Waking up that next morning I decided that I was going to start over. I went down to the coffee shop to get a drink and to pick up shot glasses for my boys. Anytime I go somewhere I have to get them shot glasses. Yesterday when I was checking out the coffee shop I picked up two shot glasses, but as I was about to head over to the register, something told me to put them down. More in tune with my inner voice or other personalities, however you want to look at it, I put them down. Figuring there was no rush to get them I told myself I could come back any day before I leave for them. Something told me to grab them today.

While I stood in line, in typical Piper fashion, I stared at the floor and did not familiarize myself with my surroundings. After about two turns over his shoulder I did notice there was a guy standing in line in front of me. Never wanting to talk to anybody, I turned away hoping to not invite any conversation. It's almost like I am socially retarded. It had nothing to do with him. It was me. Each time he turned around, I looked away. My bitchiness shocks even me sometimes. All I wanted to do was get from point A to point B with limited human interaction. Was that too much to ask? Wrapped up in my own Miles saga, I was not even going to consider looking at anyone else. How could I? All I wanted to do was pay for this drink and my kids' shot glasses, go back to my room, and feel sorry for myself. Now, if I can just complete this transaction without any verbal exchange between me and this guy in front of me, I will be golden. It seems like I will be able to pull this off because most guys just look, smile, and don't have the balls to take it any further. This guy was probably an accountant or a lawyer on a business trip and look at that, I already have him pegged as boring and all he did was look over his shoulder. I've also already put far too much thought into this guy. When I got up to the register he was next to me at the left register. He looked at me and smiled and I had no choice but to reciprocate. Not that it was painful, I just don't ever want to get involved with anyone because it can only end up painfully. I know it's only a hello but isn't that how it all begins? Totally catching me off guard and not following my unspoken prediction, he touched my bracelets and said, "I like your bracelets."

Slowly turning towards him as if he just insulted me, I gave him the look and said, "Thanks," as I took my change and left. I got outside and immediately felt like shit. Why did I do that? Why am I such a bitch? He was cute, seemed nice and friendly, and I just had to keep that wall up. No matter what I do I feel like shit. This was his fault, not mine. Why did he have to say anything? Why this was bothering me was an even more important question. I've never given it a second thought when I have acted like that before, until this guy. Like a child short of stomping my feet in anger at myself, I went up to my room to get my phone that was charging and went back downstairs to the desk to ask them a question.

As I got off the elevator I saw my mystery man. He was standing between the elevators and the desk and looked like he was perplexed with his phone. I thought, *let me try to remedy what I had just done.* Again, I have never in my life attempted to remedy a harmless blow off but something kept calling me back to this guy. I saw he had bracelets on so as I passed by, I touched his wrist, smiled, and said, "I like your bracelets."

He looked up and smiled and said, "Hey!" I kept walking as I looked over my shoulder in my best attempt at flirting. This time it was actually quite natural. He held his phone up and said, "I can't figure this thing out."

I smiled and said, "I can't figure mine out either," and I kept walking. Now I felt a little better. He was cute too.

Thinking a run might take my mind off Miles, I went upstairs to change and decided to get some fresh air. I'm trying to do things other than wait around for him, but who am I fooling? He is the primary reason I came, I'm not here to sightsee. The run only lasted about two miles, just enough to clear my head and be able to say I left the hotel. After the run, I went upstairs, took a shower, and then decided to walk around the concert area. As I was walking out, I saw Miles. He was walking towards me and he came over and hugged me hello. I said, "Do you want to go for a walk?"

"Sure, where should we go?" he asked as we walked towards the escalator.

"Do you want to go outside?"

"Yeah, it's freezing in here," he said.

We went upstairs and out the front door. It was very sunny out, a very warm August day. We found a bench and sat down. It was so weird. Sitting and talking like normal people about normal things. I know it sounds stupid but this is a man I go from two extremes with. I watch him on stage like a starry-eyed fan and he's the rock star, then he is my lover. There is little time for anything else. Shall I say, no time is made for anything else. Now I'm actually sitting face to face and talking to him. This is the opportunity I've waited for. Most people wait for the opportunity to have sex with him, I wait for the opportunity to talk to him. I still feel ridiculous talking to him like he's Joe the banker because I respect the fact that he is somewhat in the public eye and would never want any of my normal questions that I would ask a normal person to be perceived as a threat. I know that is stupid but I cannot emphasize enough, not in therapy for no reason. We talked about his brother and daughter and my brothers and sons. We talked for a few more minutes and I just wanted to savor this moment that I had him all to myself. We were sitting there, out in the open, but nowhere that I need be concerned with anyone with a man crush or some whore coming over to him. It only lasted a couple of minutes and then he of course said those words I love to hear, "I better get back in." We stood up and I pulled him back to kiss him. He smiled and we kissed a little bit more before walking back. He said with his head down, "I'm not acceptable."

"What?"

He looked at me and said, "I'm not acceptable."

Was this a foreshadowing? "What are you talking about?"

"You've taken a plane all the way here, and you don't fly. Am I really worth it?"

I stopped him in his tracks. I looked at him and said, "Look, I'm a big girl. I went into this with my eyes wide open. I don't want you to not hang out with me because you think I can't handle it. I can handle it."

"Okay, that's good to hear."

We walked a little further and just as he was about to go back into the hotel, I grabbed his arm and said, "Wait, before you go back in there and everybody starts grabbing at you again, I just want to let you know that this is not me. I'm not a whore."

"I don't think you're a whore."

"I just wanted you to know that I am not flying around to see anybody else."

He said, "I know," and with that, we walked in. Before I could say goodbye, as soon as our feet stepped in the hotel, a man crush came over and I looked back at him as I walked away. I was satisfied in that I felt like I said what I wanted to say and also felt that finally, maybe, at least he knew where I was coming from. Even though I mentally felt like I was satisfied, as I have tried to tell myself in the past, I knew in my heart I wasn't. It really didn't even have anything to do with him directly. Everything always felt like work or trying to plug a dam. When things were copacetic, they were uneasy. Nothing was ever right but I never knew any better. I knew all along this was strictly sex, which was fine, but I did not like the way I felt before or after. During was great, I just didn't like compromising my self-worth, but I did that any time I interacted with him. As soon as I walked in the hotel, I decided to walk around a little more. Feeling lazy, I took the escalator this time and as I was going up, my coffee shop man was coming down. This time he wasn't alone. He was with a woman but she looked like "people." I waved and he smiled and waved and I heard them talking and say something along the lines of, "Yeah, but let's get Luke this time." Luke? Was he talking about Luke Michaelson? Tell me my cute coffee shop man had something to do with Luke Michaelson. Was he in his "posse?" I heard the woman call him Brandon, and then it clicked. My coffee shop cutie was the brother of obnoxious Luke Michaelson. For crap sake! I can't catch a break. If Luke is obnoxious does the apple not fall too far from the tree? Well that was a downer. Guess he wasn't a boring accountant or lawyer.

There were a few things I wanted to accomplish today, one being to look for Joe from the radio station since he was the one that talked me into coming here in the first place. Finally tracking him down, he looked a bit busy. I waited off to the side for a few minutes and as soon as he freed up he came over and hugged me. He was shocked to see but equally happy. Joe was the quiet guy from the table in Vegas, the one with no business card. We talked for a few minutes then he asked if he could record a sound bite and send it to Pete and Brad. I said, "Sure." I, of course, was nervous as hell because anything that puts me on the spot makes me nervous, but I pulled it off okay. He said he was going to the show that evening so I said I would look for him. Pete and Brad weren't here but those two clowns were the biggest promoters of me coming. I knew they weren't coming because we have been e-mailing a lot since the Vegas trip. More so, Brad and I.

Feeling a little more relaxed than normal, I hung out a little more before I decided to go upstairs and get ready. Tonight I was wearing the white dress that I was a little concerned about my ass falling out of. I got ready and went downstairs and waited outside of the auditorium. Not wanting to go in too early, I found a chair right outside the auditorium door and just sat there and waited. At least this way I could see who was coming and going. Peering to my right I saw Brandon walk by and he said, "Hey, hi. How are you?" He was with someone again that looked like "people." Returning the greeting I smiled and watched him walk into the auditorium. I had to have this whole relationship right. Brandon went in and I waited outside for a few more minutes. No Miles. While I was sitting there, a woman came over and said she loved my shoes and that I looked fabulous. "Thank you," I said.

"May I take your picture?"

Looking around, I pointed to my chest and said, "Mine?"

"Yes, you look great."

Feeling awkward I said, "Sure."

That was bizarre, but flattering. And no, she wasn't looking for my number. She got her picture, thanked me and went into the show. I continued to sit there for a few more minutes taking everything in and watching all of the musicians start to head in.

Not wanting to wait for Miles anymore, I decided to go in and stand in the back of the auditorium. Brandon was a few feet away talking to some people when I went in. Out of the corner of my eye I saw him look over a couple of times—here we go again. He walked over to me and stood next to me while Luke was performing.

"Hi, beautiful. Nice to see you again"

"Hi. I trust you got your phone up and running?"

"These phones are too complicated. I love your dress."

"Thank you. I'm glad we bumped into each other again."

"Not as glad as I am. Are you going to stick around for the entire show?"

"I am."

It was only few minutes but talking to him was like talking to someone I have known my entire life. There was no effort and it was the most relaxed I have felt the entire weekend. This was the feeling I had lacked with Miles. Damn it! Damn it for so many reasons. A couple of people came over and talked to him on occasion, so clearly he was somebody. Shit, here we go again. He introduced himself as Brandon, so I was right. He told me that was his brother on stage. Damn it, right again. I made believe I had no idea who he was when he introduced himself, which was partially true. When I first saw him in the coffee shop I had no idea and had I not heard him say something about Luke as he passed me, I never would have known. When I saw him in the coffee shop and thought he was boring, I almost wished he was a regular person. As we talked there was a lot of physical contact as far as arm touching, bumping arms, and hair stroking. The longer we talked the physically closer we got until our shoulders were touching while we were watching Luke. We were probably standing and talking for about a half hour before the usual someone came to get him and said he had to go. Smiling to myself in total disbelief that this could actually be happening again, I turned back to watch Luke. And then there was one.

As it got a little closer to show time, I moved my ass up front where I saw Joyce. Just before I came in I spotted Older Woman and Miles was not with her. While sitting with Joyce, I saw her go sit in the back stage area and tonight she had a staff button on. What is going on? I leaned over to Joyce and said, "That other lady is sitting back there tonight."
"Yeah, I saw that," she said. Neither of us knew who she was. A few minutes after the show started, the Toxic Twins from last night

198

came prancing passed me. Too many available pieces of ass circling around him. This was too close for comfort and I was not feeling very confident. This entire evening was starting to feel like a horror movie or a comedy of errors and I was sitting in the audience. I had brought photos with me of Miles' last two shows that I had taken and I put an envelope with a note in it reiterating our conversation of how I could handle this and that I was glad that we finally got a chance to talk. I also added that, because of him, I have gotten on a plane and done things I never thought I would ever do, so in answer to his question, yes, he was worth it.

Towards the end of the show, I moved towards the stage since this is where I can get my best pictures. While I was up there, I saw Joe walking by and when I got his attention he came over and stood behind me. Miles, who did not look at me the whole time I was up there, was now all of a sudden interested. After about five minutes, Joe said, "Do you want to go backstage and watch from there?"

"Sure," I said. I was not trying to get under Miles' skin; in fact, I was hoping he didn't feel as though I was starting to invade his world, I was just taking a nice guy up on his offer. It's absurd for me to even think that any thought would go into this at all on his part. Joe and I went back stage, in the same area as Older Woman. Feeling like I was now back as a player in this comedy of errors, I spotted Brandon, Older Woman, and then Whore, half of the Toxic Twins. Joe told me to take all the pictures I wanted. I tried to keep my cool but I really was a stressed out mess. All I kept doing all weekend was trying to hatch some type of natural circumstance to fuck Miles. As I stood snapping photos, Miles had no expression. I can't read him anymore. Joe stood next to me the whole time and at one point I got to talk to Brandon for a few minutes. It came to the point where Brandon was going to go onstage and switch places with Miles. This was going to be the true test, if I in fact pissed him off, and I was hoping I did not.

Standing at the foot of the steps gave me the most opportune advantage for photos but that was exactly the same set of steps he was about to come down. The boys did the changing of the guard and then Miles came off the stage, walked right up to me, grabbed my face and kissed me right on the lips. Guess he's not mad. Wait a minute, in essence, he just pissed on me. What the fuck is going on? Instead of being annoyed about that, I watched the rest of the show thinking now perhaps we may get together tonight. After the show I walked over to give him the photos I had brought for him and he smiled and said, "What is this?"

I told him, then all of a sudden got a sudden physical sensation and blurted out, "This isn't happening tonight is it?"

He looked at me and said, "Probably not." I couldn't explain my emotions. Already anxious going into this trip, anything else just adds to it. If I was my friend, I would have slapped me a long time ago but sometimes it is not enough to hear it from someone else. You have to go through it before the lesson is engrained forever in your soul. Standing there, cold and unresponsive, mentally I rejoined the controlled chaos when Joe said, "There is a party afterwards. Would you like to go?"

Angry and hurt, I said, "I'd love to," and I picked my bag up and followed him. Joe invites me to a party, but the man I've been intimate with blows me off for parties. I know this is already something I should walk away from, but he has some kind of hold on me or I am allowing him to. I can't believe after all of these years, I've reverted back to the same girl who stands by hoping to be the "chosen one."

****

Bailey and I went up to the suite where the party was. It was so surreal sitting at a table with the band that was just playing for an auditorium full of people. Stage personas left in the auditorium, normal everyday conversations being carried on. We were sitting amongst people that have played with and slept with The Fury, the greatest rock band of all time. Miles was not there when I got there. He showed up about twenty minutes later with Older Woman. I could see him looking over on occasion, but my heart was broken and I was trying so hard to carry on conversations with the new people I was meeting. At one point we gave each other acknowledging glances. I fight with myself constantly, thinking, just hang back and let him do his thing, but then I say, why do I have to act like we have no history at all?

All of a sudden the Toxic Twins came in, and after a few minutes Miles parted ways with Older Woman and gravitated towards the

Toxic Twins. In the meantime, Brandon came in and sat down right next to where I was standing. Joe introduced me to another friend of his named Tom. There were too many things going on at once and it was all happening too quickly. I had taken some pictures of Tom downstairs during the show, so Tom asked me if I would take a picture of him and Leyna. I said sure. He had been very nervous and he waited the last two days to get the nerve up to talk to her and ask for a picture. With the mood I was in, I was maybe not the best person to be giving him a pep talk. "Just do it. Who the hell is she? She is no one special. Just do it!" He had a staff button on so clearly he was not a psychotic fan, so he went over and introduced himself to her and asked if he could take a picture with her. She said, "Sure, just give me a minute." With that, she took her plate, walked away and started talking to someone else. What a cunt. I looked at him and said, "Is she kidding me?"

Lowering his voice in the hopes that I would lower mine, he said, "It's okay."

"No, it's not. Who does she think she is?"

Even softer he said, "She's Leyna. She had two of the greatest love songs ever written, written about her."

"I don't give a shit. So she fucked a couple of rock stars and they wrote a song about her. Big deal. Everybody in this room has fucked a rock star. That's why most of us are here in the first place. She's a bitch. She's special because of who she fucked? That's her claim to fame? Are you kidding me? She should be lucky to take her picture with you. She's a cunt."

Tom, probably now very sorry that he asked me to photograph him in the first place, tried to reassure me that all was well. Sometimes — okay, often times — things fly out of my mouth, past that broken filter, and my inner New York comes out. The accent I try so hard to keep under wraps escaped. She really pissed me off and I was like a ticking time bomb. Then I thought about Miles and he really pissed me off too. The whole room was starting to piss me off. A bunch of "Fuck me because I'm a rock star and if you don't, I'll find one hundred others that will," pretentious assholes. With that, Miles and Older Woman were Elvis. Trying to concentrate on what I really should be concentrating on, I planned on turning my attention towards Brandon just so that I didn't close myself off to everyone. I wasn't planning on getting involved with him, I just figured I should talk to people other than myself, my dead mother, and four sentences every twenty-four hours with Miles. That being said, since Brandon was sitting behind me and he made the first move all the time, I decided to turn around and see if he was still interested in talking to me or if that was just him passing the time before a show. I excused myself from Tom and turned around, but at the exact moment two girls plopped themselves on each of his legs.

Staring for a split second, I was really starting to get nauseous. Turning back over my right shoulder I spot Miles coming back in without Older Woman. He made his quick rounds, then he was gone and the Toxic Twins were missing also. Joe put his hand on my shoulder and said that he had to go because he had an early flight in the morning. He said I could stay but I had really had all that I could stomach. Quite confidently I stated, "No, I'm ready." I thought it would be rude to stay since he is the one that brought me. Just as abruptly as I grabbed my things to go to the party, I grabbed them to escape it. I met quite a few very nice people and was happy that I went but now it was time to go. Joe and I said goodnight to everyone, I never even looked at Brandon, and he walked me back to my room. I hugged him and thanked him for a very nice evening and for being such a gentleman. He was not going to be around tomorrow for the last day of The Event because he had to get back to work in Florida. Look at that, a man can walk a woman to her room, not go in, and leave. Who knew? I'm sure that entire party made assumptions when we left, not unlike many that I have made. This is not the lifestyle for someone with self-esteem issues . . . or is it? Does every last one of these performers have such low self-esteem that they need to surround themselves with an endless array of ass so that they feel better about themselves, and then they can feel confident when they treat others like shit? Or do they in fact have very high self-esteem and are confident enough to sift through all of the low self-esteemers hanging on and pick what they want? All of these people should be put in a cage and studied, except inevitably they would all end up fucking each other. There is your case study.

I went to sleep feeling very depressed and at this point I figured that Miles had left with Older Woman. I call her that for lack of a better term. I felt like such an asshole and yet my assholishness has no limits. The next morning, I sent Miles a text asking if he could meet me where we sat yesterday. No response. I went down and waited on the bench just in case.

While I was waiting, I called Anna and told her everything. I even told her about Brandon and that I hoped I'd see him today. Where that came from, I have no idea. I haven't so much as even looked at another man since I started going to see Miles, and not because I wouldn't allow myself, just because no one has caught my attention. Brandon caught my attention and intrigued me. As I walked back into the hotel I headed upstairs. Cheating again, I took the escalator. That is my personal treat to myself while I wallow in self-pity. Almost as if it was planned, when I got off the escalator, I saw Brandon talking to about three women. This was starting to be the theme of my existence. I decided that I would say hello as soon as he walked away from them. The women never left. It was such a long period of time that I actually sat down in the lounge while I waited. Not wanting to be annoying like everyone is to me, I also didn't want to just stand there waiting my turn. Since it started out looking like a passing, casual, unplanned meeting, I didn't think they would be talking this long. Before I realized it, I had been sitting in the lounge for forty minutes. When it looked like they were breaking it up, I got up and started walking over. Just as I got close enough to be in a precarious spot, it reconvened. This new development caused me to have to walk straight past them and down the hall to the bathroom. When in doubt, go to the bathroom. Properly named the Thinking Room, I paced back and forth trying to decide my next move. Since I was so nonchalant the first time, I was thinking I could go right back to my original spot and start over. Again, as if it was scripted, as soon as I opened the door and walked out, Brandon was standing there. He smiled and said, "Hi."

A feeling of calm swept over me and I said, "Hi." Stepping out of the bathroom, I stood in the center of the hallway, which was actually quite private. Immediately he started a conversation with me and there was nothing contrived about it. We stood in the hallway and talked for a few minutes, but people would pass and stop to talk to him or stare as if he was some kind of attraction at the zoo. I felt like saying, "He's not gonna do a trick if you shove a quarter up his ass. Keep movin'."

We must have been there about twenty minutes when he said, "Please don't take this the wrong way, I'm not being fresh, I was on my way up to my room but would love to continue talking to you. Would you like to join me?" Still reeling from the last two days and thinking he was cute and sweet, I said yes. Miles couldn't see this though, could he? Although, I wasn't doing any of this for revenge, I genuinely wanted to go. We walked down the quiet hallway to the elevator. Even the ambiance when he is around is tranquil, a polar opposite of everything surrounding Miles. While we waited for the elevator, we talked the whole time with never an awkward silence. There were windows surrounding the area we were waiting in and you could feel the warmth from the sun wrap itself around you, making you feel safe in a way only the sun can do.

The bell rang, breaking up our conversation, and the doors opened. He smiled the most incredible smile I have ever seen and extended his left arm, which was holding his newspaper, gesturing for me to go in ahead of him. Immediately picking up the conversation where we left off when the bell rang, we went up twelve floors to his room. It was a perfect Sunday morning in a perfect world: he had his newspaper under his arm and a coffee in his hand and we were engulfed in the quiet of the morning. It's so weird, it's almost like seeing vampires during the day. There is this whole exciting, evening, rock star persona at night, and then during the day, they are regular people walking amongst the living. No offense intended, but when you see them during the day, they look like anybody's dad walking through a hotel on vacation. You just wouldn't want to imagine your dad getting laid left and right at night like they do.

When we got to his room, it was not some rock star suite with groupies all over. Not to say it wasn't like that in his heyday, but today it's the same room as mine. Bed unmade, a regular room, and a regular guy. Clearly not expecting company, he pulled his blankets up to cover the bed and gestured for me to have a seat while he sat on the chair across me. It was so easy to talk to him. I felt like I knew him my entire life. He turned on his computer to show me his website that documents his recovery. He told me less than a year ago he had been diagnosed with a heart ailment and was told to go home and get his affairs in order. Unwilling to accept that diagnosis, he sought other means of treatment and went elsewhere on the advice of his friend and neighbor. He said right now, he was completely healthy. He had a heart transplant almost a year ago. It was strange but knowing all of this didn't make me think or feel differently about him. It never once occurred to me that he was unhealthy or ever in danger of getting ill again. We must have talked for about an hour in one sitting. That is about fifty eight minutes more than Miles and I have spoken in a year.

Brandon asked what brought me to Memphis for The Event. Casually I said, "I usually go to see Miles Baker, so I came to see him."

He smiled and said, "So you're with him?"

"No," I quickly responded. "I just came to see the show."

He looked at me, clearly not believing a word I said. "Does he know you're here?"

"Yes, we've spoken."

"Why don't I believe you?"

"I don't want to talk about it."

"No, wait, he knows you're here, you know him, and you haven't spent any time with him?"

"That's correct."

"Why is that?"

"Well it wasn't my choice. I guess there are too many whores to choose from."

See, now that's why I didn't want to talk about it. When pushed, the uncalled for, cunty response comes out.

"Well that's not nice. He should spend some time with you, knowing you came all the way here just to see him."

Giving him the same look he got from me in the coffee shop, I said, "You are not helping. He has no obligation to me."

He smiled and said, "But you care about him."

Where did this guy come from and how the hell did he get in my head?

"Listen, I'm fine. I'm enjoying talking with you." He smiled and said he was enjoying himself as well. I was still feeling very guilty about the way I treated him in the coffee shop, though he did not seem bothered by it. He said, "I'm glad I bumped into you today."

"I had been waiting forty-five minutes to bump into you."

"What do you mean?"

"I came upstairs and saw you talking to some girls and I figured I'd wait a minute, then say hello, but they never left and before I knew it, I was sitting in the lounge for forty-five minutes. When I thought it was breaking up, I went over and it reconvened, so I went into the bathroom. When I came out, there you were."

He smiled and said that he was glad I waited. So was I. I really felt much better after talking to him. He shook his head and said, "You are so beautiful. Miles is a fool."
Embarrassed and broken hearted again, I put my head down and said, "No I'm not, but thank you. I was hoping to get to talk to you at the party last night, but you looked a little preoccupied."

"Did you see those two girls? They just sat right on me."

I laughed and said, "Yeah, I saw it. It didn't seem to bother you too much."

"Oh please, I couldn't get them off me. You know, sometimes girls think that just because you're a rock star or celebrity, then they can do whatever they want. Not everybody likes that, you know. I wanted to talk to you but you left with your friend."

"He wanted to leave, so I thought it would be rude to stay."

"You could have come back if you weren't too busy."

"I didn't think I could just come back, and for the record, I didn't leave with him. He walked me back to my room then he went back to his. I don't just hand it out like candy, contrary to what this may look like. You really don't know me at all!"

He smiled and said, "No, I think I do."

He looked at his watch and said he had to go downstairs and do an autograph session with Luke. Sad that this had to come to an end, I stood up and he grabbed his room key and turned to me and smiled again. "You really are so beautiful." Emotionally I wasn't in a place to handle hearing that from him or anyone at this point. He opened the door and we walked down the hallway to the elevator. Never at a loss for conversation, we kept it up until we got down to the entrance. The constant conversation we were having wasn't that whole new relationship, getting to know each other conversation. It was different. It was a continuous, you have always been a part of my life conversation. Just before we walked in I panicked when I realized I left my bracelet to get in upstairs.

He gave me a silly look, took my hand and said, "You're with me." We walked into the meet and greet area with no problem. It took about twenty seconds before a family saddled up next to him and started talking. In typical Piper form, I stood off to the side like a wallflower and waited. Spotting bottles of water, I walked over and grabbed one to waste time and grabbed one for him as well. Watching him talk to them, I was feeling a little ballsy and really wanted him all to myself, but not like I wanted Miles. As a gentle reminder to the folks that he was not alone, and feeling like being acknowledged, I walked over and handed him the water and his face lit up. No more interruptions were going to be tolerated.

They talked to him for so long that there was, of course, no more time to spend with me before he had to meet his brother. I walked him to where he had to go and he said, "I'll see you later." Something told me that he would. I walked out and back up to the lobby and while I was sitting there, I saw Miles come down. He was on his cell phone and I know he saw me. I think he tried to bypass me as I walked towards the elevator and he was coming towards me. He stood by me, waved, and continued on the phone. I made believe that I was talking on my phone, and then when I turned he was gone.

Now, I was actually a little pissed. This was the first time I actually witnessed, or allowed myself to witness, this immature behavior. I know you could say he owes me nothing, which is true, but would he treat any friend of his this way? Am I not a friend and just a fuck? I can't imagine that he necessarily categorizes everyone like this because he has four daughters and I would like to think that there is some part of him that thinks of them before he treats or would treat a woman like shit. I know men and woman are wired differently, but like I said, I would like to think he tries to respect women, as he would want his daughters respected.

Feeling very irritated, I walked downstairs and waited outside the room Brandon was in, and while I was waiting, Miles came around the corner. He came over and hugged me. I said, "You could have just told me you were with somebody, so I didn't make a fool of myself."

"First of all, you've done nothing to make a fool of yourself. Secondly, I'm not necessarily with anybody."

"Fair enough."

He said that he had to run inside for a second then go meet a friend for lunch. Whatever. He owes me no explanation, nor do I care. After that encounter, I just wound up going back up to my room and I didn't see him again until the show that night.

Before the show I didn't see Brandon, which made me a little nervous. I was afraid today may have been it, but I really did like hanging out with him. Older Woman was at the show but no Toxic Twins, starring Whore. Still trying to figure this whole thing out, I just sat back and observed. Miles made a comment during the show that he was "getting feedback from his vibrating ass, if that's any indication as to what is going on in my personal life." Apparently a lot of texts were coming in. Shocker. The show was great as it had been the previous two nights, and towards the end of the show I moved up to the front. Since I was in front of the stage tonight I got to see Brandon perform too.

Tonight was it. How was I going to go home and face everyone? I can hear it now, "Three days, and he couldn't manage any time?" The thought of going home made me sick, the thought of staying here made me sick. I almost wished somebody would fuck me so I didn't have to go home and say my hymen grew back. Lori wanted me to get a good picture of me and Miles for something that she's not telling me about. When the show ended, I asked him if we could take one together. He jumped off the stage, took the picture, and hopped back up. A bit shell-shocked, all I could think was that this could not be happening. Grabbing my stuff, I got ready to leave and walked to the side of the stage. Brandon was about to walk out and I waved. As he was being pushed like cattle with the rest of the performers, he yelled, "Hey, where are you going to be?"

I smiled and, holding back tears, said, "Around."

"Don't worry, I'll find you." I was so hurt by Miles at this point, I was literally numb. It was like a switch flipped. As I made my way to the escalator, lo and behold, who was going up as well but Miles and Older Woman. We were right next to each other on separate escalators. What the fuck is he doing? Getting off at the next level, I made my way over to the banister in the lounge. From there I could see down to part of the first level, and Miles going up to his room. I heard a lot of people coming up now. All I could hear was people yelling, "Luke, Luke, Brandon, Brandon." I figured, *good, at least he's in the vicinity.* I walked over to take a look. It was them. A large party. I made believe that I didn't see them and looked over the balcony. All of a sudden Brandon came running over. "I told you I'd find you." I was very happy to see him. He said, "What is going on with you and your friend and all the drama?"

My ass clenched. "What are you talking about?"

"I thought he was with you."

"No, I told you he was not with me."

"Then I guess you were not the one they were talking about."

"Who? That older woman is with him."

"What older woman?"

"The one you were talking to earlier. Right there — she's over there." I pointed behind him.

"He's not with her. That's Peter's agent. He is with some red head and her blonde friend is flipping out because apparently he is usually with the blonde, and phone calls are being made everywhere. It's like high school."

The Toxic Twins! He's banging them! Whore, the red head, was apparently the star. So this poor Older Woman was a distraction and these two drunks were the problem all along. Trying to unravel all of this in my little brain, I immediately didn't care when I noticed Luke calling Brandon over. The thought of him actually leaving right now bothered me. Brandon waved him off. I said, "I don't want to keep you from your brother and friends."

He said, "I see them all the time, I want to hang out with you." *Wow,* I thought. My own husband didn't even want to hang out with me.

"As long as we are going to hang out, can we sit somewhere because my feet are killing me?"

He laughed and we walked over to the lounge area. We sat on two separate hassocks. As we're sitting there, Miles walked by texting. We kind of acknowledged one another but I have a very expressive face that often gets me in a lot of trouble. If I'm pissed, there is no hiding it. Brandon is just watching all of this. He walked by again, and then stood near us. Brandon said, "Go talk to him, he wants to talk to you."

"First of all, I absolutely will not go talk to him. Secondly, he does not want to talk to me."

After a few minutes, Miles went back upstairs. I told Brandon to go in the elevator with him and, "see if you can get any dirt. Channel your inner feminine side and do something for me. You wanted to change your clothes anyway, go, go."

Off he went. In the meantime, Whore walked by without her blonde friend. She now goes up where Miles went. A few minutes later, Goldilocks walks by almost crying. This is the point in the show where I am in the audience watching all of this unravel around me and trying to figure out how I was ever involved in this in the first place. Then came the icing on the cake. Miles came down with Whore and walked right past me. He kind of looked at me like he knew he was ripping my heart out, but that it wasn't intentional. Brandon came down a minute later and tried to warn me, but I told him I saw the sickening sight already. Abruptly I got up and said, "I'm going to change my clothes too. I'll be right back." Being the tomboy that I am, what took me about five minutes, took him about fifteen. Not much in the way of clothing for this time of night to choose from, I threw on a tank top, capris, and sandals and called it a day. I wasn't all that concerned about what I had on as long as I didn't look fat. When I got back downstairs, there were four girls sitting with him. *You have got to be fucking kidding me*, I thought. Five minutes, that's all I was gone, five minutes. This is going to grow old quickly. Ballsy Piper joined them, but then after a few minutes of this torture, ADHD Piper got up and moved. He kept giving me the hairy eye like I should help him. In an effort to not waste another minute of these last few hours together, I went over to get him and finally, he escaped. "Thank you."

Yeah, yeah. "How about you open your mouth once in a while and stop letting everyone monopolize your time instead of waiting for a bail out?"

"It's not that easy. There were four of them."

"Wimp."

He smiled and we moved to the other side of the lounge where Luke had been earlier. My ass no sooner hit the chair when one of the girls came over and asked if she could talk to him for a minute. He looked at me with puppy dog eyes, held up his finger and said, "One minute. I swear."

"I'll be gone if you're not back in a minute."

About forty-five seconds later he came flying around the bend looking at his watch. "Aha, I made it!" He smiled that all-knowing smile of his. He sat next to me and we picked up as if no time had passed. We were there for about an hour and a half then the fire alarm went off. Everyone had to evacuate. All I could think was that this was awesome. Talk about cock block for Miles. But now I thought, *am I going to have to watch them outside?* Brandon and I stood right outside the door of the hotel, which was obviously very crowded. He stood close behind me and I could feel the heat from his body against my back and it felt safe. As wonderful a time as I was having with Brandon, I was still obviously torn up about Miles. I turned to Brandon and said, "Listen, if they come out, I'm grabbing you and kissing you, just so you know."

"No problem. I'll throw you into this big romantic dip."

"Well don't get carried away."

They never came out and I thought, *I hope she fucking burns.* Oh, I know, I'm going to hell already. That last comment isn't assuring anything that I didn't already know. We were allowed back in after a few minutes and all of a sudden I spot them before he spots me. I grab Brandon and lean into him and start laughing because he's much too tall for me to spring a surprise kiss on. I then spotted Miles staring at us. Brandon, being a man, is still oblivious, until all of a sudden the light bulb goes off with him. He said, "Oh, there he is. Oh my God, he is pissed."

"Don't look, I saw him, just get on me."

They walked away and we sat back down. "He was pissed, did you see that?"
"I saw him, but that was it."

"He was glaring at us. I can't believe you didn't see that. Wow, he's mad. He has some set of balls, let me tell you."
"Was he really mad or are you just trying to make me feel good?"

"No, he's mad and I will bet you that the next time you see him, he will ask you about me."

I gotta stop you there. "I really doubt that," I said.

"Mark my words, he will ask."

Fine, I thought. I'll mark your words and my mother's Xanax is on my head. All duly noted. We sat back down and continued talking. He wound up getting in my head to the point where I almost started crying. How could he know so much about me, especially when I was playing coy with my typical, huge wall up? I didn't have to sit there and worry that he thought I was some slutty groupie. He knew, he thought, exactly who I was and it was pretty powerful. My eyes started to fill up and he said, "What's wrong?" I finally snapped and was so hurt and angry.

"I don't know what I am doing! I don't just fuck people. I don't fuck anyone."

"Then just stop. You don't need to do this. You are too good for him. Look at all the turmoil that has been caused with you, those two friends, and all because of his dick. Who is he anyway? Stop this, please! Do your photography and don't go see him anymore. The only way anything is going to change is if you stop going to see him."

I knew he was right, but I was not yet ready to accept that part of it.

He told me all night that I was beautiful, yet never tried anything. There was no topic that was off limits and we spent most of the night laughing. Before we knew it, it was 6:00 a.m. We both still had to pack before our 9:00 a.m. check out. I didn't want the morning to end. Wishing tonight was Friday, I wanted to cry that I was going to leave Brandon. I never felt a connection with anyone like I felt with him, and that was with my guard up. When we decided it was time, he looked at me and said, "Listen, if we never see each other again, and you're ever feeling down on yourself, I just want you to promise me you will always remember tonight and that there is someone out there that thinks you are the most beautiful woman he has ever seen."

What do you say to that? "Don't say we'll never see each other again, why would you say that?"

"You never know."

I couldn't imagine never seeing him again.

With a tear streaming down my cheek, I smiled and asked, "So am I the same bitch you thought I was the first time you saw me in the coffee shop?"

Staring into my eyes, he wiped my tear and softly said, "The coffee shop wasn't the first time I saw you."

"Sure it was, when we were in line."

"No, I saw you the day before, going up the escalator while I was going down. You had on a black dress and your hair was down and straight. You caught my eye and I thought, boy, that is a beautiful woman. I hope I see her again. Then, the next morning in the coffee shop was when I turned into the luckiest guy in the world."

And here we have it again. A great guy, getting on a plane in four hours to go to California, while I go to New York. It's almost comical. We walked over to the elevator and he hugged and kissed me goodbye and said, "How can I get in touch with you?" I gave him my cell phone number, never expecting to hear from him or see him again. Different worlds. I went up to my room feeling exhausted and my emotions were running wild. I called for a wake-up call in two hours and I expected this to somehow get fouled up and that I would miss the plane, and then wouldn't know what to do. It's been that kind of weekend. Five minutes later my phone rings. Are they kidding me? I knew they would screw this up. "Hello Piper, it's Brandon. I figured you probably have already forgotten how beautiful you are so I wanted to call to remind you. I also wanted to tell you that I had a great time last night." Well, that made my day. I was torn up. My heart was absolutely broken on so many levels because of Miles and now here is this great guy going three thousand miles away. I can't figure out this great scheme God has in store for me. It just seems very unfair. With tears streaming down my face, I barely got out, "Thank you."

"Don't ever forget." And he hung up. Sobbing, I crawled on top of my bed and closed my eyes for two hours. When I got up, I had that

sick feeling when you wake up the morning after something terrible happened. I thought for about fifteen seconds and realized, *yup, the Miles thing did happen, but the Brandon thing happened too.* I had mixed emotions and this trip was definitely bitter sweet. Dragging myself out of bed, I got my stuff together and took one last trip down to the coffee shop for yogurt. Empty. No Miles, no Brandon. The same place that was filled with excitement two mornings prior now echoed loneliness and pain. It isn't the place, it is the emotions brought into it that fill the room and, at this moment, it no longer symbolized anything happy for me. I went back up to the room and saw that Claire had called. Keeping her abreast of the comings and goings of the weekend, she said, "He sounds like such a nice guy. I'm sorry to say, I know how much you like Miles, but this guy sounds a heck of a lot nicer."
I couldn't even speak.

"I know you don't want to hear it, but I'm sorry."

After we got off the phone, I went down to catch a later shuttle than I had initially planned. Since I told Brandon I was taking the earlier one, I decided to call him and let him know that I was leaving later since he was planning on the later shuttle. The desk rang his room but there was no answer. Feeling defeated, I left a message telling him I was leaving and thanked him for last night then hung up, hoping, by chance, he might be leaving too. On my way downstairs, I called Anna and walked to the front of the hotel and put my stuff outside with everyone else that was waiting for the shuttle. Too hot to be outside, I left it and went back into the lobby to catch her up about last night. Of course, anybody that I talk to at this point is just listening and wishing that I would just walk away from it all. This was one of those times I just want to climb up on my mother's lap and have her take all the pain away.

Really I just wanted to get out of here without seeing him. That was a first for me. Usually, no matter what the circumstances, I don't mind a chance meeting. Not today. As I'm talking to her, I look up and see Miles at the top of the escalator with his stuff. Oh my God, not only do I have to see him, but I am going to share a shuttle with him. Well that's just great! Normally I would get off the phone if I saw him coming, but not this time. Turning away from him, I continued to talk to Anna. He got down to my level and slowly seemed to be walking towards me. I was surprised because normally if I'm on the phone, he wouldn't come near me. I told Anna I would call her back and hung up. He came sheepishly over, kissed me, and said, "Hi."

"Hi." I didn't really want to do this right now, or ever for that matter. He sort of had his head down. Did he know that he absolutely broke my heart? Did he care? I felt like a dick just being there and let us now throw salt in the wound and speak to each other? Now he wants to talk to me? No one else around here that he knows?

"Did the fire alarm wake you up last night?" Oh my God, Brandon was right. He impaled this fucking whore, slut, tramp, pig, lush, garbage, trash for three days — *three days* — and I talked to someone in the lobby and he is beating around the bush — no pun intended — as to my whereabouts?

"No, I was still up."

"Oh." he said with his head down.

What? What does he want from me? I was here and you chose to discard me. You can't have it both ways. You can't fuck the world then be pissed when I talk to a guy. And still not having sex, mind you. If you want me, I am here one hundred and ten percent. Is that the problem? Why is everything always a game? Why is it so wrong to wear your heart on your sleeve? Am I to be kept on the back burner because he knows I will always be there?

Thank God the shuttle came and we went outside. He was flying American and I was flying Continental. Could you imagine if I had to share a plane? It would be sure to crash after this weekend. You can't make this shit up. As he sat there, there was a couple crying and kissing each other goodbye outside the door. Miles was watching the couple outside as I bumped my bags into every seat until I got to mine. I must have given him the dirtiest look before dropping in my seat. Engrossed in this visual he said, "that's a love story out there." I didn't know who I wanted to slap first. After this fucked up weekend, Mr. Sensitivity is going to sit there yearning for this "love story" outside the shuttle? Arranging my bags under my feet, I looked over my shoulder said in my ever so mature, intelligent way, "Ew, gross." He looked somewhat sad that I seemed so jaded. Is he fucking kidding me? Nobody is more of a sap than me, but to see him like this on the heels of this weekend, I would like to vomit. I know he is sappy, I love that about him, but it's almost like he channeled his inner 'Inconsiderate whore, my penis is my number one priority' attitude. It's hard to swallow—again, no pun intended—after I just had the weekend that I had. This obnoxious behavior now moved on to the shuttle. Part of me wanted to cry because on one level it is sweet, but on the other hand, I'd like to smack Miles over the head with the guitar he is sitting next to. He asked me if I had anything for the plane, and I said, "Yes, Xanax."

"That's good, but you have to be careful because that can be addictive." I'm sorry, is this you actually giving a shit or passing the time, because I don't know anymore. The seven minutes to the airport were the longest seven minutes of my life. Facing forward I just wished somehow this could be made right. My stop was before his. As we approached, I grabbed my things and never looked back. I heard him say, "You're going to be okay." He said something else but I never heard it because I got off the shuttle. As I'm standing in line to check my bag, I opened my pocketbook to get my Xanax. Nothing. Where the hell was it if? Oh, this can't be happening. I don't have enough time to get out of line to search my bag because the line is too long and if I get on the end of it I'll miss my flight. I dropped my suitcase on the floor and like a lunatic started tossing clothes everywhere. Thank God I found it in the bottom of my bag. In my haze this morning, I must have thrown it in there because normally it would be with me at all times. You never know when you're gonna have to pop one of those babies on one of these trips. I check in, popped my pill, then it happened. The sign up above said: CONTINENTAL TO NEWARK DELAYED 3 HOURS.

Resigning to the fact that this weekend completely ended up in the shitter, I picked up my bag and dragged it over to a seat. I have low battery on my piece of shit new phone that doesn't hold a charge, a cab scheduled to pick me up at the airport, and I just took this pill that is going to knock me out in about twenty minutes. In case I had a problem, I wanted to see if Miles would be around. I text him and asked if he was delayed and he said yes, one hour. No sooner after

217

reading that, my phone dropped to my lap and I was out cold in the waiting area.

When I eventually came to, I still had about another hour before we were to board. I sent him another text asking him if he was still here. "Yes, now delayed three hours." Something was going on at Newark, causing the delay. Now the pill wore off and I didn't know when to take another one. This weekend has been horrible, beginning to end. Little did I know that I could make this bad situation even worse.

Another delay. My 11:00 a.m. flight now turned into a 5:00 p.m. flight. When I was finally able to board, I sat down and started to cry immediately. Oh, the poor bastard next to me. This time I had a window seat and I tried to figure out my equivalent spot on the LOST plane. After this weekend, I figured it would probably crash, but I couldn't see exactly where I was through the tears. Would I be with Jack, Kate, and Sawyer and at least stand a chance or am I gonna be with the "tail group" and be all fucked up? Probably all fucked up.

As upset as I was, I still managed to take some awesome pictures out the window. I think I cried the whole time I was awake and I kept praying when we landed that when I turned my phone back on, there would be some kind of message from Miles. As much as I wanted to avoid any questions at home, I still wanted the comfort of my home and kids. As soon as the wheels touched down, I turned my phone on and I had a bunch of texts pop up and one voicemail. Not concerned with the voicemail because he has never called, I opened my texts first. None of the texts were from him. As I walked off the plane I checked the voicemail and heard, "Hi Piper, its Brandon." Smiling just from hearing his voice, I soon broke into the laugh-cry combo. It doesn't make for an attractive photo but the emotions say it all. "I just figured I'd call you because you probably miss me. I know, I know, you're already laughing, I can tell. I just wanted to say hi and to remind you not to forget what I told you. Bye Piper."

I was floored and so happy. He is so sweet. I just hope this at least meant we would keep in touch. It was going to be all up to him as I had no contact information of his. It was also a good way for me to try to keep my emotions in check regarding him. Since any contact made would be on his part, it would also show me how interested, if at all, he was in me. I was still very upset about Miles and just wanted to get home and cry in the privacy of my own bed and misery. Unfortunately, after things like this, you still have to go back to the real world. I still had to play mommy once I got home and go to work in the morning. It's hard to function when you're trying to wallow in your own self-pity.

Luckily I also had to go to therapy the next day. There were a lot of emotions running through me at this point and I hoped that he could put this all in perspective for me. The next morning I got an unsolicited text from Miles saying he is still in Memphis. Now I got a little nervous.

"Are you okay?"

"Yeah, my flight was cancelled."

He wound up going back to the hotel and he was going to fly out today. I was feeling a little better because we were texting. Of course this should not make up for anything, but you know sappy me. I wanted to hint a little towards the weekend in hopes that he would go with it since he seemed very responsive. You have to strike while the iron's hot, you know? A few more texts exchanged and I said, "This weekend was not what I expected, but I had fun." I thought that might seem like I had fun with Brandon, but also give him the opportunity to elaborate a little on blowing me off. I got, "Good. I'm glad you had fun. I'm glad you got home okay." Not what I was hoping for, but it was time for me to leave for therapy. A well-deserved therapy session.

He let me talk and I told him everything. Now he just looked at me. I didn't like that. When I heard myself saying out loud everything that had taken place, it sounded even worse than experiencing it. So, he looked at me and said, "Well, now you are done correct?" I didn't know how to answer that.

"Now I don't like him."

Again, didn't want to hear that either.

"I have said all along, as long as he is nice to you, you can continue this whole thing, but now he showed you that he is an asshole."

I explained that as miserable as I felt, I still was not ready to just walk away.

"I feel like crap and wish I could forget about everything that has just happened."

"So, does that mean you are going to stop this?"

"I'm not ready yet to accept the obvious."

"So you're going to let him treat you like a piece of shit?"

"No. I would like to just ease into it for my own sake."

"How so?"

"Can I at least send a text sort of expressing my disappointment?"

"Sure."

With some input from my therapist and Claire, I came up with what I thought was a nice way of letting him know I was hurt and an opening for him to at least apologize so that my therapist will no longer think he was a jerk, and so this charade could go on.

Chapter 15

I would like to emphasize that meaning, tone, and emotion are all lost in text messaging, but when you deal with some people that will only text message, you have to be super careful how you word things. Usually I am, especially when I text Miles. I guess because I hit a nerve, everything got all fucked up. I don't think he realized that it was coming from a defensive position and not an offensive one. Later in the day, I sent a text asking if he got home first. He said, yes. Then while I knew that he still had his phone in his hand, I sent:

"I don't understand how you couldn't find any time to be with me this weekend. It seemed very hurtful and inconsiderate and totally out of character for the way you've ever treated me."

If ever a text message could generate silence, that would be the one. I tried to get the point across that I was hurt, not implying anger or aggressiveness, in fact, the complete opposite. I used the word inconsiderate as opposed to "not nice" so that it didn't seem like I was five. I also tried to get the point across that he has always been sweet to me by saying that this weekend was totally out of character for him. Apparently all of that put together in text form comes across a lot differently than intended. That text was sent at about 5:45 p.m. on Tuesday. I still heard nothing by 7:00 p.m. Wednesday. This warranted a call to my therapist. He said to send another text Thursday saying something clever like, "cat got your tongue?"

I said, "I would never say that normally. It sounds like I'm looking for a fight."

"I didn't say to use that, I said you come up with something cute and clever." What the hell is cute and clever under these circumstances? I thought about it for a while. Unable to wait until Thursday, a mere twelve hours away, I sent one at 10:00 p.m. I wrote, "I thought you might prefer to text than talk . . ." At 1:00 a.m. I got a text. I had been sleeping, but Devon sent me an unnerving text that woke me up followed by Miles'. I'm surprised I didn't vomit that night. Good thing I was already lying down. It read, "Quite frankly, I really don't know what to say to you. I think I shall suggest you give up." This weekend I didn't think that I could feel worse than I did. I was wrong.

I called my therapist the next day. He said, "You didn't listen."

"It was a couple of hours, what's the problem?"

"No, your text is the problem. Not when you sent it. You totally put him on the spot. You fucked it up."

He's kidding me right?

"I told you to come up with something clever."

I can't do this anymore. No matter what I say, it's wrong. Everything has got to be done through texting. I can't talk to him in person too long because there is always something going on. What the fuck?

"You have to send another one to fix the last one." Oh my God, no, please, not another text. It's like quicksand.

"Try not to fuck this one up." Thanks for the confidence boost.

He had a show coming up four days later. We agreed that I would send, "Things seemed to get blown out of proportion. I don't want to end off this way. Looking forward to seeing you Sunday." That was it. Now we let it be. I figured I would feel better one way or another after at least seeing him. The first meeting was going to say it all. My therapist said, "This is it. You can go on Sunday, but if he ignores you, that's it. No more."

"Fine."

I was praying to God that he would not ignore me because I didn't know how I was going to handle it.

Every weekend, I cover my dad's home attendant's day off. I was covering Saturday and supposed to go to the show Sunday. Saturday night, the home attendant shows up and I thought, *this can't be good.* He said, "I forgot that I'm supposed to go to Pennsylvania with my family tomorrow and I'll be back on Monday."

Ha, ha, of course he will. Was this another sign? I told him it was fine and not to worry about it. The show was at a fair so I figured I would take my dad with me and give him a chance to get out. Claire was going with me. How mad can he be with me if my dad is with me?

It was a beautiful day, a perfect day to take Dad out. We got there and sat in the front, but off to the side because I had the wheelchair. I spotted Miles before he went on and I saw him standing off to the side of the stage. I wouldn't look directly at him but he kept watching me. I figured if he truly hated me, he wouldn't even want to look at me, right? I'll take whatever I can get. I rationalize however I need to. A few minutes after the show started, I scoped out the area and did not see Jeans Girl. I figured at least I had that working in my favor. My father actually liked the music; he was very happy. Believe me, he's not afraid to say he doesn't like something. A few more minutes later, I turn around again and there she was. The old flare up. I saw him look over at one point and smile. I was sick, but there is really nothing I can do about it, especially with the thin ice I am skating on. Claire, being eternally negative, said, "So what are you going to do after the show?"

"I don't know."

I secretly just kept praying he would not ignore me. I understand in the big spectrum, I am nobody to him. He can sleep with a different girl every night. That's clear. I can't grasp how one statement can just erase anything that happened. There was nothing really even wrong with what I said. My feelings were the ones hurt. Is he pissed because my being hurt didn't let his unattached, sleeping around go as smoothly as it usually does? Because I am "just a number" that spoke up, now I can be cast aside for not following the rules of non-committed, non-emotional sex. I'm a human being. How do you get angry with someone for caring? I could see if I was a bitch and made his life a living hell and bad-mouthed him, but all I did was fall for him. I would still never bad-mouth him, no matter how this goes. I have friends that are all about throwing him under the bus, but that is not me. I did and do care about him and am not about an eye for an eye. To me, that would mean I never really cared about him if I could flip that switch so easily. You can't blame people for the way they feel. No one should judge me for falling for the rock star, but no one should fault him for not being able to reciprocate. My therapist doesn't usually agree with me, clearly, but I don't fault Miles for this situation. He was always up front and never made any promises. In fact, he actually did say he didn't think he could give me what I want and deserve. I only fault him for starting this whole thing. I don't even really think I would hold that against him because I would never have passed this whole experience up, pain and all. I just don't get it.

After the show, Jeans Girl looked like she was walking away. It couldn't be that easy, no way. I waited off to the side and watched him interact with a lot of people. Not once did he walk over to them. Each of them had gone up to him. In my twisted, not wanting him to fail me way of thinking, I thought, clearly I need to wait on the side because if he doesn't come to me, it's because he went to no one. His agent Meg came over to me and said hello. We talked for a few minutes then she walked back and joined him. At a distance I saw Jeans Girl with Amazon and some guy. I had a bad feeling. I watched him keep glancing over as if he was just talking to people, but distracted by her. I knew I had no leg to stand on today. I was defeated. Eventually, I took a few steps away from my dad and left him with Claire. Miles kept looking over at me. Eventually he walked over, hugged me, and said hello. He said, "Thanks for coming," and walked back. Well, what can I say? I wasn't ignored. It was a very generic, mechanical, "Hi, thanks for coming." At least the ice was broken. There was nothing more I could do. I said to Claire, "Let's go."

As we started to walk away, Jeans Girl ran up behind him. Keeping in mind what my therapist told me, we did not stick around to see what was happening. I took one more look over my shoulder as I pushed the chair and knew this was it. When I got back to the car, I loaded my dad, the wheelchair, and all of the other shit we had with us into the car. As I pulled out of my spot and approached the red light, Jeans Girl walked across the street in front of me. Immediately Claire looked at me like a deer in headlights. Turning to her I assured her I was not going to hit the accelerator and she should relax. Not that it didn't cross my mind. I just smiled and shook my head. "Well," I said, "At least she is leaving. That's a good sign." No sooner had I said that when, as I looked straight ahead, facing me was Miles in his car. My heart started to race as if something was about to go down. What was going on?

Panicking I said, "What am I going to do Claire, are we going to pass each other?"

"Just go."

I went straight. He made a right, pulled over, and Jeans Girl got in his car and they drove off.

"Oh my God, you didn't need to see that. That was horrible."

Horrible it was. What was even more horrible was that I had a forty minute drive ahead of me and my dad kept asking me the same two questions the whole ride home over and over again. All I wanted to do was cry. I couldn't cry until I got my dad home, fed, and put to bed. I didn't have any allotted cry time until about 11:00 p.m. I was sick and I know Claire felt horrible. When I dropped Claire off she said, "Listen, I know you're hurt, but try not to think about it. It's not going to help."

I did exactly what I said I would. I fed my father, he watched TV with Bailey and Quinn, and I got him to bed. My dad lay there, smile on his face, with no recollection of our day. Sometimes I think he may be the lucky one. I wish I could talk to him or my mom. I sure do miss my mom. I miss my dad too. Physically he's here. It's all very sad. Very strange the way things work out. Before I shut his light, I said, "Did you like the show today, Dad?"

He smiled and said, "What show?"

"I love you Dad. Good night."

Now it was time for my cry.

I waited for the home attendant to get his lazy ass back. It was Monday and it was beautiful out. Bailey had marching band rehearsal, so he was unavailable today. When the home attendant got back, I took Quinn and went to Point Pleasant. Again, even though I feel like shit, life goes on. I still have a twelve–year-old looking to do something fun on his summer vacation. Though I was sad that Bailey couldn't come, he didn't mind that we were going without him which made me feel better. Quinn and I spent the whole day at the beach hanging out. Being with my kids always makes me feel better. They are starting to totally be able to read my moods. I try to act like everything is fine, but I am no actress. My face is very expressive and they are not dumb. They know when I am going to a show, and they know how the night went when they see me for the next few days. Sometimes I get an unsolicited hug and an, "it's okay Mom," which of course makes me cry more. It's moments like this that I draw from when my son plays a show with his band and I remind him, "Don't ignore any girl, Bailey. The quiet girl in the corner could be getting her heart broken and you wouldn't even know it. Don't just sleep around because you can either."

"Mom, I know. I'm also only fifteen."

"Yeah, I know. That last part is for when you're a rock star."

That's usually followed by a kiss on my forehead and a very soft, "I know Mom."

It's very difficult trying to raise two boys on my own. Two musicians, no less, when I am doing what I am doing. I don't even know what I am doing half the time. I pray a lot these days.

My new plan was now to go to shows but not go up to him after them. I figured I would be showing him that I could give him what he wants. I didn't think I should have to stop going to see him perform if that's what first drew me to him. I thought it would look like I only go to the shows if I am going to have sex. This would make me look mature and that I could handle this. There was another local show coming up at a fair that Claire and I had been to once before. This was going to be the first time I put my plan into action. It was a rainy day and he was supposed to perform twice, once with his band and the second time would be a solo show. The first show was very good and the rain stopped before he went on. I stood in the back center and I could see him watching me the whole time. Again, how mad could he be? After that set, Claire and I immediately walked away and got some drinks. It started to rain before his second set. Really rain.

We waited under a vendor's tent that was set up near the stage he was to perform on. Thank God there had been no sign of Jeans Girl. I guess she melts in the rain. A golf cart came by with Miles in it. He saw Claire and waved to her but I stood off to the side where he couldn't see me. We moved out from under the tent and into the rain. Claire only lasted a few minutes before she said she was going to stand off to the side under the shelter. I had an umbrella, but the rain was so bad that it didn't really matter. I even took my shoes off because I was drenched. I stood on his side of the stage and he saw me because there were not many people there. After the show, Claire and I never looked back and went straight to the car. I was very proud of myself.

I was due to go to therapy in two days and when I got there I told him of my ingenious plan. I got the look. "How is that plan working for you Piper?"

"Well I don't know yet, I just implemented it."

"You want to know what I think as a man?"

My ass clenched. "Well, I don't know, do I?"

"I think you're a bitch."

Am I actually paying for this verbal abuse each week?

"How in God's name did you come to that conclusion — aside from the fact that you know me better than anyone?"

"If I'm Miles, I'm thinking, she's not getting what she wants so now she's not going to talk to me. Bitch."

I tried to explain that I thought I was giving him what he wanted, therefore making him feel like maybe I could handle this and that in time, he may miss me. He said, "No, I'm still thinking bitch." How did I fuck this up too? This is ridiculous. Egg shells, egg shells. How do I fix this now?

"You have to be completely normal. Well, normal for you. If you would have talked to him after a show, go talk to him." I can't handle all of these bullshit rules.

"Why am I jumping through hoops for him?"

"You tell me."

"Oh, shut up."

There was one more show coming up before the Florida show. I wanted to try to mend everything before that trip. He was going to be playing at a very small bar near his house on the Wednesday before his Saturday show in Florida. This was going to be it. Do or die.

****

I decided to wear the outfit I wore in Florida last year to the bar. When I got there, he was not there yet. I thought I would throw up. It was probably about an hour that I was there before he showed up. He got there in just enough time to take the stage. He didn't see me. He had two of his daughters with him. At least I knew he wouldn't have any whores with him. He played all new songs and they were great. One was about his father and the others about his divorce. All very powerful, yet sad. I stood in the back but in the center where we could see each other. Thank God there were none of the usual suspects there. After the show of course all the man crushes had to shake his hand and he had some of the chickies hanging around. I waited. He walked back to me with a smile and hugged me and said, "I'm shocked that you're here."

I returned the volley with, "You shouldn't be." He looked at me and smiled and I said, "I'm gonna take off."

He hugged me again and said, "Thanks for coming." This was a complete 180 from that day at the fair. This was genuine. Now I felt better about going to Florida. I gave a coy smile and slinked out and drove home feeling successful.

Now I had one day to prepare myself for my trip. Like last year, I planned on getting there the day before. I was also hoping if I did the same things as last year, I would have the same results. This big girl was taking her third plane trip in five months. Or will it be my fifth? How do you count that anyway? Felice's husband drove me to the airport this time. I still get anxious, but not like before. Still, I definitely need meds—no question there.

This whole Miles thing was now starting to feel like labor. I used to have these great experiences with a span between shows. The more involved it got, the shows seemed to get closer together like contractions. Towards the end the beautiful experience was coming down to a screaming, bloody mess. I just didn't know whose vagina was going to explode since there were so many involved at this point. According to the sundial that I mark my sex by, it shouldn't be mine because I think at this point it has sealed itself shut from lack of use.

I got on the plane, pill ingested, and I was feeling good. The plane could go down and I'd never know the difference. From the airport I took a cab to the hotel. Cab drivers are funny in Florida. They pull prices out of their asses the likes of which I could not believe. You're initially told one price, but there is another price on the window—and honestly, who the hell can ever understand them, they're like parking garage signs. You think you're paying fifteen dollars then you pick your car up and it's forty dollars. Then all of a sudden nobody can speak English. When you get there, we're all on the same page. Leaving—two completely different worlds. When you finally get to your destination, it is a different price and it is more than what is on his timer. Whatever, just get me off this nauseating carnival ride of a cab before I throw up. Again, was that a sign? As fabulous as the Xanax is for your desired effect, it fucks you up. At least it fucks me up for the entire day.

I checked into my favorite hotel from last year, same room too. The weather, again, was absolutely perfect. I pretty much followed the same routine as the last time. This time, I ran the route instead of walking since I have been running so much now. Quite a few inclines in that run, by the way. This time I brought my own Lady Godiva when I stopped at the nail salon again. It was a beautiful thing, I was able to take an uninterrupted shower and nap again. Still a little worried about what might happen tomorrow, I tried to just relax and think positively. It sort of made sense that he would stay in the same place as last year too. I did explore the hotel and area more this time than the last time because I was a little more relaxed. I wound up talking to Felice at about 11:00 p.m. while I sat in front of the hotel. The restaurant next door was hopping. It was such a beautiful fall night. I was wishing that he was here now. It was getting late and I figured I better get to sleep since I have a nervous breakdown scheduled for tomorrow and it takes a lot out of me.

My routine consisted of my normal, flying down to grab some sustenance before anyone sees me. Utilizing my free time, I took my time getting ready. This time I knew I could leave a little later, I also knew to keep my eyes peeled for a certain rock star. Unfortunately, my cab came before said rock star was spotted at the hotel. The only difference between this year and last was that I waited outside without realizing that they had let people in already. Unlike last year the seats were labeled in the order that the tickets were purchased. My seat was in the front row, right in front of his mic. This could be interesting. I tried to just sneak in under the radar. There were some people checking me out which made me very uncomfortable. When I say checking me out, I mean in a "what's her deal" kind of way. The first person I spotted when I walked in was Emma. She makes me uncomfortable. She has a very strong personality and is a friend of Miles. I just sat in my seat and tried to keep a low profile.

Finally the man of the hour arrived. He didn't see me right away. Once he got on stage, I got a smile and a hello. That felt good. This could be okay. He did his sound check, which didn't last very long. After that was going to be the moment of truth—the meet and greet. This was going to be the first real time I would be talking to him since the ordeal I choose not to think about. I asked the girl in front of me if she would take a picture when I got up there and she was very sweet and said sure. It was finally my turn and as I walked toward him, he smiled and hugged me. In his ear I said, "Do you want to get together later?"

He said, "Hm, maybe." Maybe was good. It wasn't no. No is bad. Maybe, I'll take it. We sat down and talked for a little bit. He signed a picture and the girl asked if we were ready for the picture. "Sure," he said. We stood up and she took the picture. I don't know what made me check it, but I took a look at it. She didn't press hard enough and the picture didn't take. I wanted to die because now I had to ask him to take another one.

I turned to him and cringed and said, "It didn't work, can we do it again?" He smiled, put his arm around me again and we posed for yet another picture. She gave me the camera and I checked it and there was nothing again. An error sign came up. I don't know why I decided to do this but I opened the battery door and shut it, then took a shot and it worked. Now, I had to ask the girl behind me to take a picture. I was mortified. As we posed again, before she took it, she said, "Is this gonna work?"

I said, "God I hope so," and with that, we both busted out laughing. That was the moment she took it but it worked. Not the picture I was hoping for, but I gathered my shit and got the hell out of there because my face was burning from embarrassment.

I went back to my seat and looked at my picture that he had signed. To Piper With Love, Miles. If he hated me it could have said something more generic than that. I'll take the "Love." He had a couple more people to see after me. This time he didn't go to the hotel between the meet and greet and his show. He had come straight from the airport to the venue. When I had seen him Wednesday, he was performing with his daughters. He had gone Friday to Mississippi to go visit his son, and then flew in today (Saturday) for his show. I was very turned on and impressed with the attention he gives his children. He may be a shitty spouse or boyfriend, but he is certainly a great father. After his meet and greet, he went upstairs and I moved back by the bar and sat down. I saw Emma out of the corner of my eye and my ass clenched. She was talking to someone and looking at me. God, she hates me. *Please don't come over here.* Turning away so as not to make eye contact and turn to stone, I looked around the bar. Just like in a horror movie, when I turned back around, she was standing right in front of me. "Hi, I'm Emma."

"Hi, I'm Piper."

"Have we ever met before?"

"Yeah, last year when I told you your daughter was beautiful and you asked me how I knew that and I said because I read, but don't post on Miles' site, and then you called me a lurker."

She gave me a stern stare, almost as if we were at a stand-off, then we both started laughing.

"I remember you now." It looked as though I passed the test. "You never post huh?"

"Well, I posted the other day making song requests," and I knew she would know because she replied to my statement.

"What's your board name?"

"Ruby."
"Yes, I know you. So do you live around here?" Here we go. This is when the evil eye and questions are going to surface.

"No, I live in New York." I got the eye, then the question.

"You live in New York and you came all the way to Florida just to see Miles . . ."

"Yes, I know I can just cross the bridge to see him but I enjoyed myself so much last year, I wanted to come back. I enjoy the peace and quiet at the hotel with no children."

"Children? You have children? How old are they?"

What, am I so repulsive that nothing could have lived inside me? What was that? I was also a little defensive now because I didn't know if she thought I was a bad mother leaving my children while I went to a concert.

"They are fifteen and my little one will be thirteen in December."

"You're kidding me right?"

What is the problem? "No. I'm not kidding."

"You must have been a real slut in high school."

We both started laughing. I liked her.

"That was a backhanded compliment if ever I heard one." She asked me how old I was and I told her forty. She couldn't believe it. Wow, I thought to myself, this is good. We talked a few more minutes then she returned to her friends and I went back to my seat. I didn't want to walk around too much because this was definitely another case of "my ass may fall out of my dress again" because I could quite frankly be wearing a shirt.

It wasn't long before Miles came out and started the show. I'm sure I gave him a show myself. I was in the front row and like I said, I'm not quite sure if it was a sweater or a dress but I was wearing it as a dress. Well, hopefully it would increase my chances for laydom. I love watching him play, and I found myself not wanting the show to end, but on the other hand, I want it to be done and him in my room. The problem with wanting it to be over when you haven't gotten a confirmation for an after show rendezvous is that you have now wished away the hour and a half you have planned for, for the last eight months. It's a delicate balance. I sent a couple of racy texts during his performance because he will check them during the show. Still, trying to up the ante.

After the show, he went to the back of the bar. I saw that the promoter remained so I wasn't concerned that he was leaving during the break between his performance and Brett Hanson's. I went to the back to get in line for the bathroom, which was in the meet and greet area. Trying to keep my ass literally under wraps, I sat down while I waited, then he came down the stairs. He spoke to some people that were hanging out at the bottom of the stairs, and then he came over and sat next to me. I felt stupid asking him again, so we just made some small talk. He looked really good. There was so much pressure, I know it sounds stupid, but I didn't want to nag him and ask again. He could have said no right away but clearly he was waiting it out for a reason. He made his way back to the front to see the show and I went to the bathroom. Assuring the security of my ass, I made my way back to my seat. Brett Hansen and his cohort were cute. He used to be in Addison's

Fire. I watched his whole set and his meet and greet was after his show but I wasn't staying for that.

Since this was the time to make my exit, I saw Miles after the show and decided to ask him again. Emma and another girl were standing together and watching me. As Miles walked toward me, I said I was going to leave. He hugged me, and I said, "So do you want to get together?"

"I think I'm just going to take off myself."

"That's fine."

We said goodnight then I was going to pass Emma on the way out. I said good night to her and said it was nice to meet her again and then I went out and called a cab. I was only out there about a minute when he came out with all of his shit and the promoter. I'm sure there was a lot being talked about now back in the bar. I know what I would have been thinking. Again, here is another case of me being accused of having sex but it couldn't be further from the truth. He passed me and gave one last look and got into the car that I was standing in front of. I was hoping my cab would come quickly so that I could see if he was staying at the same place again. About three minutes later my idiotic cab driver showed up. I say idiotic because we were back to the whole, different price being charged from the meter thing. The meter said twelve dollars but the very clear spoken cost was, "$18.75."

"18.75? But the meter says $12."

He pressed a button and it flipped to $18.75.

"Now it's $18.75" He removed his finger and it went back to twelve dollars. Is he fucking kidding me? I could see Miles standing at the front desk. If I had exact change for either $12 or $18.75 I would have given him that just for being a dick. Unfortunately, I only had a twenty and had to give it to him. I'm holding it over the seat but looking at Miles. He wasn't paying attention either so I eventually just dropped it.

"You don't have to throw it at me."

Let me explain something to you. I am a very warm, loving, giving, non-confrontational woman. However, I have zero tolerance for stupid people. Stupid, ill-informed people. Believe me, if I was going to throw that at him, it would have been attached to a brick and it wouldn't have landed on the seat. But because Miles was at the desk, I did not entertain this exchange of wit. Otherwise I would have told him exactly what I thought and he would have driven away with his testicles in his nasty, grubby little hand. Miles saved his ass.

Slamming the cab door and praying I left nothing in there, I headed up the stairs. Miles was still at the desk with the promoter. I looked at him as I went up the stairs to my room and I was so hoping that he would change his mind. I really love this hotel. It feels like it's our little secret only. Everyone else seems to stay in town. I went to my room, brushed my teeth, and sent him a message that said, "If you change your mind I'm in room 341." Then I let it go and called Anna. I got in bed and just prayed he would change his mind.

I kept telling myself that this was still new. This was off the heels of the last trip so he may proceed very cautiously. I think it's a good sign that at least he didn't say no right off the bat, at least he entertained the thought. I fell asleep with the phone next to me and wound up waking up at around 6:30 a.m. I checked my phone immediately. Nothing. A second after I put it back, a text message came in. It was from Miles. I opened it and it said, "I'm sorry baby." Before I was disappointed, I was relieved. He at least acknowledged me and threw a "baby" in there, so I figured things are well on their way to going back to the way they were. I asked him what time his flight was and it was at 8:30 a.m. Well, this trip was a bust as far as sex goes, but I knew going into this trip I was taking a chance. I have no problem going through the baby steps to regain his trust again if I know the end result is going to be what I want.

I blame myself for this whole thing. I blame myself for not having enough faith in my own beliefs and decision making to just go at the pace we were going and for paying too much attention to everyone else's opinions. I let myself get upset and I felt pressured to push him, a man that is not looking to commit or be pushed into moving this into something he didn't want, just because everyone kept egging me on. I should have let it be. It's really kind of ridiculous if you think about it. Everyone kept saying, "He's a rock star and fucks everything that moves, you'll never be the only one," then in the next breath they are saying, "He should be doing this, he should be doing that." How about he should be fucking me and he's not even doing that now because I listened to everyone and not my own heart.

Ironically when I got up, I walked downstairs. I ate whatever I wanted, then I walked over to the coffee shop next door, the same one he went to before he left last year. I collected all of my things and said goodbye to my favorite room and hotel and hoped next year would be different. I sat out on the top steps for a while since it was so beautiful out and called Lori. She always loves to hear about Miles. Unfortunately, I didn't really have anything to tell her. I never told anybody about the text he sent me. Everyone knew it was bad but no one knew exactly what it said. I didn't need either of us being judged, especially since I didn't know what the future held. We are all guilty of saying to people, "well you should just do this. . ." but it's not always so black and white. I'm all about the gray area.

I called a cab and prayed that dick from last night didn't show up because I had nothing but time on my hands now. I could fuck him up the way I wanted to last night. My cab ride back was uneventful and Felice's husband was picking me up at the airport.
About a month before this trip, Miles posted a show that he was going to do on Staten Island. This, I thought, was big. He was finally going to be on my turf. That's why I figured if things didn't pan out in Florida, there is always S.I. I felt like the home team had an edge if Jeans Girl showed up. Claire and I had ordered our tickets before the venue was announced. Luckily, since he only mentioned it was on S.I. and details would follow, Claire and I knew there were only two places he could put this type of show on. She called them both. The first one was a no go but number two produced a winner. The girl was sweet enough to tell Claire that she would hold five seats for her and as soon as they went on sale we would get them. What could be better than that? Not good enough for me. I was still nervous. We followed the info as to when they were going on sale then called at that time to confirm anyway. I wound up speaking to Jessica. She was the poor bastard that had to deal with me for the next two months of her life. It all started

when I made the follow up phone call. The tickets were under Claire's name, but I would call Jessica every time my friends wanted tickets. I would call her and she filled them in next to us. We were on a first name basis. Before this was all said and done, I had purchased about fifteen tickets from her and stopped there one day to drop off a thank you card and cookies to our favorite ticket agent. Unfortunately, she wasn't in at that time. We continued to speak after that for various ticketing needs. All were Miles related, of course.

Everything was resolved. All my friends had their tickets, and then I went to Florida. During the meet and greet we had talked about his upcoming Staten Island show.

I spent the time between the Florida and Staten Island shows running like Forrest Gump and cleaning my house. My goal this time if he came over was to be able to turn a light on without feeling mortified. I set very high standards for myself. After I came home from Florida, I sent a friend request to Emma on Myspace with a message that read, "It's Piper from New York, the real slut in high school." She accepted me and we have since continued to keep in touch via email and Facebook. During one of our lengthy emails, she dropped a bomb on me. She said, "I almost didn't talk to you because I thought you were one of "those girls".

One of "those girls?" Me? I asked her what that meant and she said, "You know, the ones that are really pretty and too good to talk to the rest of us." I was shocked. From the time April and I were thirteen years old, we were always looking at and jealous of "those girls" and now I'm being told by the girl that intimidated me most that she thought I was one of them? I informed her that she couldn't have been further from the truth. She is not the first person to tell me that either. It just goes to show you how everyone else has a completely different perspective than you. Never in a million years did I ever think that I would have been considered one of "those girls."

In this time I also thought of Brandon. I've thought about Brandon ever since I laid eyes on him in the coffee shop. Since I didn't want to be pushy or seem like a stalker, I sent maybe one or two emails since I met him and that was it. From the comments on his

Myspace page it seemed as though he was having some new heart issues. It seemed pretty serious too and he no longer responded to my emails. My heart broke. All I kept thinking about was when he said, "If we never see each other again . . ." I couldn't stop thinking about him now. I couldn't get any information either. I sent him one or two emails just asking if he was okay and I never heard back. Finally a couple of weeks later I got a response. He had shingles and an infection had returned and had him hospitalized for over a month. He was optimistic and assured me he would beat this. I asked him if I happened to be in California this summer would I be able to see him and he said yes. *Well that's a good sign,* I thought. He was in bed for five weeks and unable to eat so he had lost a lot of weight.

I couldn't believe how much I was thinking about Brandon. I was still scheming about Miles but it was almost starting to feel like closure. Maybe Brandon was going to start a whole new chapter in my life. Shit, maybe a whole new book.

****

I felt extra pressure now because what does it mean if he is actually on S.I. and he doesn't come over? How much would that suck? Every Monday after work, which for me is 10:00 a.m., I talk to my friend Mike. Mike and I are always fooling around so when he sprung this on me I thought for sure he had to be kidding. He said, "So you heard they moved Miles' venue for the S.I. show?"

In my best Gary Coleman voice I said, "Whatchoo talkin' 'bout, Mike?"

"They moved him."

"Moved him where? Is it still on S.I.?"

"Yeah, but they moved him to a smaller auditorium."

"Oh, I don't give a shit about that, you scared me. I thought it was no longer on S.I."

"Well now I'm not sitting behind you anymore."

"Why? And how do you know all of this?"

"The venue called and said they moved to the auditorium and the seats had to be moved."

"Does that mean my seats are moved too?"

"Probably."

I called the venue. Jessica, my ticket bitch was not there, but someone else was going to attempt to help me. I asked her to please check my seats. "Hmm, yes, you are in Row B in the center but they are still great seats."

"How is it possible that the five seats you just moved to Row B were the first 5 seats sold and they got moved? Shouldn't everything after them be moved?"

"We wanted to keep the parties together."

"I understand, but those Smith tickets were the first tickets sold, shouldn't they be able to remain?"

"I'm sorry. That's the way it is and there is nothing I can do."

Luckily, I know everyone else in the first and second row.

It didn't really matter. How much closer can I actually get to him? It's almost ridiculous if you think about it. It was the principle. Whatever. A little while later I got a call from Jessica. She was calling to let me know the venue was moved. I told her I knew. She didn't realize it was me she was talking to at first because Piper is my middle name and the name I go by, but she was calling based on credit card information so, it had my legal first name on it. When she realized she was so apologetic. I told her not to worry about it, but asked how it happened. She didn't have a better answer but she did talk to her manager and said that was the only fair way they could think to resolve everything. I told her it was fine but she kept apologizing. I didn't want to let her know I've met him, I've seen him up close, and one row didn't matter. We hung up and I called Claire, who didn't take the news as well as I did. She flipped and I was laughing. I told her to calm down, "I've seen him naked, and one row won't matter."

"It's the principle."

I just found it laughable at this point because who else would this really happen to other than me? All of my friends were in the front row. It wasn't like hose bag central had set up camp on my turf. I was over it already. I said good, the further they go back, the more rows everyone goes back, so if Jeans Girl or any other hose bag shows up they could potentially be 10 rows further back than their initial seat. Fuck 'em. I'm fine.

An hour after that call I see the venue on the caller ID again.

"Piper, it's Jessica at the venue. I really feel terrible about what happened."

"Jessica, really, it's fine. It's not a big deal."

"I spoke with my manager and we really want to make this up to you. You were so nice and brought us cookies, and you were such a pleasure to work with so we called Miles Baker's people."

It was at that point that I threw up a little in my mouth, my ass clenched, and my stomach cramped.

"You what?"

"We called Miles Baker's people and set up a private meet and greet for you and your party. Would that make you happy?"

She was so excited to tell me. I was stammering. Thankfully she thought it was due to my overwhelming excitement to meet "my idol." She had no idea that I now had the hot-and-colds going on thinking he must think I am the biggest dick in the world. The biggest. And yes, in the world.

"Yes, I would love that but you really don't need to do this."

"Oh no, it's my pleasure. I just want you to be happy and to make this right."

I felt like saying, "Could you have him fuck me 'cause that, I think, could make things right."

"Well thank you again, Jessica," I said as my hands were shaking when I hung up. Oh my God, she wants me to give her a list of everyone's name in my party. All sixteen to eighteen of us that are going. He is going to be like, "Did you really need a private meet and greet?" Psycho me is now thinking this meet and greet could potentially cut into my sex time. When I called Claire, I thought she would pee herself laughing.

"Well, I'm glad you think it's funny." At least one of us is laughing. "We're still in Row B." That shut her up. "Not laughing now are you?" It was funny because then she started flippin' again.

Now I really need to clean my house. At least I was assured having contact with him after the show. Hopefully he will see that it would just make sense for me to drag him back to my house like a cave woman before he makes his way back down the parkway. Makes sense to me.

Because I second guess everything and worry about every stupid little thing, I was a wreck, worried that he was going to think I forced this meet and greet to happen. I know I put too much thought into everything. About a week before the S.I. show, he played a mall opening in Jersey. I thought this might be a good opportunity to feel him out so to speak. It was pouring rain and it was outdoors of course. They had a tent set up over him and his band and it was large enough to cover the very small crowd that was there. I did not see any familiar faces. I guess I was the only asshole, once again. After the show he came over and hugged me and it felt so good. I could have stayed like that forever. We talked for a minute before we were interrupted by a man crush. It was pouring so I said, "I'm going to get going." He hugged me and thanked me for coming. I felt like at least he seemed unfazed by me, as far as knowing about the meet and greet. I was okay with the quick good bye because I figured it was only going to be a week before the next show.

Gum Boy and Gum Girl and I had made plans to meet before the show for dinner. My kids were going to the show also, but they hung out at home while we went to eat. I was very excited that he was playing on S.I. but still equally as nervous and kept telling myself that everything was going to be fine and that I could explain this if need be. A few days before the show, I sent up a warning shot. A text that read, "I'm kidnapping you after your S.I. show so don't make any plans." I never heard anything, which was fine. I was working the whole "no news is good news" angle.

When we arrived at the venue, I had to meet Jessica at the box office. She told me where to go after the show. I could not believe this was actually happening. Instructions absorbed, we went in to take our seats. Felice gave me and Claire two of her seats cause she is a good biotch. I think she just didn't want me drooling down her back. I had a new video camera I was going to deflower with Mr. Baker. It really was a different feeling to watch him on S.I. Although it was a smaller group than anticipated, we were much livelier than his larger crowds in Brooklyn. I was impressed and hoped he felt the energy and would decide to come back. He had a large band with him. Some of the members of his band from The Event were with him as well as Mike Richards. I damn near passed out when he came on stage and just ate the whole night up. This night I didn't wish away. I just kept telling myself, he couldn't come to S.I. and not be with me.

I was still a little hesitant about what his reaction would be when he saw me at this meet and greet. I have no idea what the venue told him. Hopefully he doesn't think I demanded this. He knows so little about my personality and me. I would die if he thought I was pushy enough to mastermind this.

When the show ended, one of his guys was looking for me. He directed me and everyone else across the hallway to a lecture room. We entered at the back of the room so we all kind of just took seats in the back. There were a few people leaning against the wall. The five to ten minutes we waited were the longest of my life. I, of course, wanted to throw up. It's the feeling I do best with. All of a sudden the door opens and the man that directed us over to the room, announced, "Ladies and gentlemen, Miles Baker and Mike Richards." Everyone applauded, and I hid. I'm very mature. It was very uncomfortable because it was very quiet and Miles, it seemed, had to keep the conversation going. I couldn't even talk to him because everyone hung on every word spoken.

As soon as he walked in he said, "So I heard you all had front row, then we moved the venue and you got screwed." I could feel my face burning. Everyone started laughing and he said, "Well that's just what I heard."

He spotted my boys first and said, "Hey, what's up?" Then he looked over and smiled and said, "Hi Piper."

Mike kept watching and at one point he said to Miles, "Do you know them?" Miles turned to me and smiled and said, "We're friends." Finally, some validation and I'm no longer worried about that damn text. He could have said "No, I have no fucking idea who they are." My boys and Felice's son, Daniel, got some photos signed and I walked over to him while this was going on so it didn't seem so obvious. Like I said, you could hear a pin drop. I had a photo with me that I wanted him to sign for Jessica, as a thank you for everything she did. When I got over to him, he hugged me and in his ear I said, "You have to leave with me."

He looked at the picture and said, "This is a great shot." It is the picture I gave the S.I. Advance to use for the advertisement. He signed it and stayed another minute or so. I really felt bad because he was totally carrying the conversation. There was no indication from him that anything was going to happen. As soon as he left, everyone turned around and said, "Well?"

"I have no idea," I told them. Everyone started to make his or her way out and Felice said, "What should I do?" I told her to take the kids with her just in case and I apologized in advance if it is for nothing. "Don't worry about it," she said. We took our time leaving hoping he was coming out the same way. I pulled the car around and no Miles. Felice took the kids and walked to their car. I drove around to where they were parked. Seeing they made it okay, I pulled away. As I approached the light, I saw Felice in the left lane. I was going to drive up behind them and honk and be obnoxious, but there was also a car in the center lane. Instead, I pulled over to the right and when I pulled up, I looked over and it was Miles. I honked and he started to go because he thought I was hinting. When he realized it was still red, he put his head back down. I honked again and he looked over. I waved at him to follow me as the light changed. He looked ahead, then looked back at me, looked ahead again, then looked back at me. He waved goodbye and slowly drove away. I couldn't believe this was happening. Bad enough we weren't getting together, but the worst part is it's the only time he's on S.I. and it's still not happening. This is bad. I still kept hoping at some point there would be a text acknowledging me in some way. It never happened.

There were not going to be any shows until his annual show coming up, therefore, no opportunities. There was one small thing. It was a tree lighting ceremony in Brooklyn and his daughters would be with him. I took my boys because they like his girls, it was very convenient. It was also a nice Christmas thing to do with the kids. It was very cold this particular night. We toughed it out and went anyway. Not knowing exactly what time he was going on, we had to get there on time. I happen to know the DJ that was running the show, so to speak. I ran over to say hello to her and she pulled out the schedule and let me know what time he was going on. He was supposed to go on at 6:30 so we had a little bit more time. I was so cold, I said to the boys that we'd run across the street to Dunkin' Donuts to warm up. As my luck would have it, I looked at the time and we still had ten minutes to spare but I decided to just take a peek anyway. Sure enough, he had already started and was only doing one song. Again, one of those times you just have to laugh because if you don't, you'll cry. We ran over and caught the remainder of the song. I saw some people go over to him when they were finished. I felt a little uncomfortable going over to him while he was with his daughters. When he finished talking to them, he started to walk to a restaurant with his girls. I ran over and tapped him on the back. He and the girls turned around and he gave me a big hug. He smiled and said, "I can't believe you're here."

I'm getting a lot of that lately. "I just wanted to say Merry Christmas." He hugged me again and left with the girls. My boys were freezing, so I said, "Do you want to go?"

"Please."

We headed back home for a pizza, a movie, and a nice warm house. Although it was at least a happy meeting, I still couldn't help but be frustrated. I know what he told me over the summer but I can't help but feel that he wouldn't have said that if that whole thing didn't blow up. I don't regret saying what I said because it needed to be said. I'm just sorry about the way it was received. I can only hope that he said that coming from a place of a little guilt and not wanting to have to own what he had done. He is now able to live a life of not having to account to anyone and everyone lets him do whatever he wants. I didn't want him to think I was a doormat. He doesn't need to account to me but he should have to at least be respectful and not hurtful. Let's be honest, he knows how I feel about him, that's why I feel he holds back. But knowing that, he had to realize he killed me that day. At least respect my pain and don't be angry with me because you hurt me.

Social media adds to all of the drama and upset as well. The constant lingering idea of all of his female fans is unnerving. Thinking back to different situations at various shows is also a little unsettling, especially in Memphis. By the way, Whore was dubbed that based on several factors. The first is the fact that Joyce said she does the band, and Joyce knows this kind of shit. Second, I saw on her Myspace page several comments indicating that she was not essentially monogamous. Several pictures of her with various musicians and all the statements made pretty much alluded to the fact that she likes to dabble with said penis. Under a picture of her where she is lying down, Luke Michaelson commented, "Now that's the look I'm used to." *C'mon, are you kidding me?* I think she has very low self-esteem too. Look who's talking right? She has about one hundred pictures, all of herself, posted on her Myspace page, all in different poses. It looks like a Ford Modeling Agency portfolio. All of her friends keep posting how gorgeous and beautiful and blah, blah, blah she is. Are they looking at the same pictures that I am? She's not an ugly girl and she is photogenic, but these are not accurate subtitles for her photos. It doesn't matter what I think, though, because Miles has posted similar comments under his not-so-secret faux identity on her wall. It is what it is. I don't hate her. This hurts because I could see myself being friends with her. She doesn't seem phony, she seems fun. Don't get me wrong, that doesn't mean I want him with her. I have decided not to look at her Myspace page anymore as it only upsets me. I am just going to concentrate on how he treats me and try not to focus on anything else.

I got Sean and Jane tickets to his annual show as part of their Christmas gift. I knew if they just gave it a chance they would love it. I had to just get them, otherwise they'd never go. They weren't sitting with me and Claire, but they still had great seats.

Claire and I found a vegetarian restaurant across the street from the theatre that we were going to hit again. As I walked in, the first person I saw was Amazon. I figured Jeans Girl couldn't be too far behind. I walked back out and said to Claire, "I can't do this. What are we gonna do?" It was freezing outside and we didn't have a lot of time. I looked in the restaurant and there were empty tables on the other side. I said, "Alright, if we sit over there, I'll be good." We went back in and I walked passed her, no Jeans Girl in sight. I don't know what that meant. We sat by the window so we were able to see the comings and goings of our restaurant and the theatre. We rushed through dinner since we were late, as usual. I was really hoping that Sean and Jane were going to like the show and maybe Sean would see Miles in a different light. I would have been shocked if they didn't like it because it really is something to see.

Claire and I took our seats in the sixth row. This was bad for us because usually we are in the first or second row. The tickets went on sale when I was in Vegas. I can promise you, if I was given a choice between sitting in the front row at the annual show or the front row that I had on his lap in Vegas, I would be sitting right where I am in the sixth row. I was unable to get through to the box office at the airport. I had no problem settling for sixth row when the reason I couldn't get the tickets was because I was having sex with him. Sometimes you have to make sacrifices, you know what I mean?

I was hoping that Sean and Jane had gotten there in time to see the beginning. But I came to find out that they hadn't. I figured Sean, who is always late anyway, was dragging his feet, reluctant to see a Miles Baker anything. They texted me at the intermission to say they had to leave because their babysitter was leaving at 10:00 p.m. Another thing Sean probably planned before, assuming he wouldn't like the show. Not surprising, but they were sorry they now had to leave because they loved the show. I was at least glad they experienced it once.

When Claire made a bathroom trip, she came back with some info. Apparently, some of the usual suspects were chatting and Jeans Girl's name had come up. She was actually not here this evening because she had to go to a party. Thank God for small favors. What could she not have gotten out of for this? This, like I said, was announced in March and tickets were on sale in June. I can't figure it out but I'm not wasting another brain cell on it, especially since I can't even spare it at this point. I was just hoping this was a good sign, that perhaps things between them were not so close. I like to live in a fantasy world too.

It was a very long show, but good. Claire and I didn't hang around. We left right after. Part of my whole "cool and laid-back" scheme. Plus, I felt good knowing that Jeans Girl wasn't there.

Lori was planning on coming up for New Years. I always look forward to seeing her. She is always up for something and I love that. She was planning on going to see the ball drop on New Year's Eve with her son. I, however, was not. The thought of not being able to urinate and standing in the freezing cold for eight hours to look at a ball for one minute once a year? Please, it's too much like my sex life. I don't need to ring the New Year in like that as well. She planned to come to my house after she froze her ass off. Miles added a show at that small bar I had seen him at just before his Florida show. I knew Lori would love to see him. We spent the morning hanging out with the kids. That was short-lived since all they wanted to do was play video games. I was exhausted, Dad had gone into the hospital on Christmas Eve by ambulance. He had an intestinal twist, which now required surgery. Between spending days at the hospital and shuffling home attendants around, I was done!

Chapter 16

I took a nap before we went. Every year I fall into the same trap. I keep saying, *okay, this year is going to be different.* I also sometimes worry that New Year's Day is going to be an indicator of the rest of the year. In this case, God I hope not. I was feeling pretty good as we started down there. He was actually playing near his house. I was nervous but felt good that Lori was with me. I tried to be positive. As I pulled up, it was about 8:00 p.m. and that's when the doors opened. His car was parked right out in front and I had a bad feeling. He is always late, why was his car here now? Lori said I was crazy. I parked the car and we walked over to the bar. As soon as we walked in, I was finished. There were not a lot of people in there and Jeans Girl was sitting at the bar by herself. Miles was nowhere to be seen. This was bad.

My first thought was that she came with him. That's all I could think. She is never alone and they were both here at the time of opening. This was going to go south very quickly. We paid and I immediately ran to the bathroom because I thought I would throw up. When I came out I looked at Lori, who had a look on her face like she didn't know what to do. I looked over at Jeans Girl and Miles was standing with her. I tried to keep it together. "Don't let it bother you," Lori said. Nobody really knew how I felt since I just kept saying things like, "it is what it is," and "I'm not getting emotionally involved, don't worry." My heart was broken, again. I couldn't do this to myself anymore. It was time to stop. I don't know what hurt more at this point, the fact that he was with her of all people, or if it was because I knew this is where it had to end. For my own emotional and mental state, I had to walk away. They were sharing food and talking. He was standing and she was sitting. There was no real physical contact until she saw me. This is why I hate her. She didn't decide to start whispering in his ear and getting cozy until she saw me. I wouldn't care who was around if I was with him because I wouldn't even notice anyone else. I wouldn't be putting a show on for anyone. She is a phony cunt. A phunt, pronounced the same, but not to be confused with funt, which would be a fat cunt.

I could see him out of the corner of my eye and he was looking over. I couldn't even look at him. I was sick and I was also stuck. I couldn't leave because that would be immature and obvious. I had to now stay and watch this whole fucking, disgusting display. Display on her part because he never did anything. I kept going outside to get some air and it actually helped. He did a short set, thank God because then I could leave after. Lori always wants to get her picture taken with everyone she meets so, as if she was not a witness to all of this tonight, she says, "We have to go over there and you have to take my picture."

Slowly I turned to her and said, "Are you out of your alleged mind? I am absolutely in no condition to walk over there and ask him for anything. You, my friend, are nuts." She had a picture she wanted to get signed so I told her she could go over and get it signed, but there was no fucking way a picture was getting taken on my watch. She walked over to him after his set and they were talking and laughing. He signed the picture then the next thing I know, they are both walking towards me. I was making a mental note to kick her ass later. She was in front and said, "He's coming. You have to take a picture." That ass kicking was now getting upgraded to a beat down.

I stood up and he sheepishly walked over. We exchanged hellos and he hugged me and we talked a little. I was surprisingly calm. No more butterflies. Was that good or bad? Did I mature or not care? I was now staring through the viewfinder one last time. Lori got her picture, Jeans Girl got my man, and I left there a different woman. Again, I had to hold my tears back till I was alone. One problem I have, that's funny right? One of many problems I have is that at the moment, it's all black and white. That is why I can't send text messages at the moment. If I give it a day or so, I guess a defense mechanism kicks in and I tell myself, "He's not getting married. It's not over." Healthy? Who knows. As long as I can get up and function and take care of everyone I need to take care of without meds, then I guess, yes, it is healthy. I got myself into that mindset, and then checked his Facebook. There were five pictures of him posted two days after that awful New Year's Day, all with Jeans Girl. He did not post them, another friend in the picture with him tagged him. These could actually have been taken New Year's Eve. They were party pictures with two of his friends and their girls. This solidified the devastation I was still reeling from. I really was now closing the door. It was very sad for me but I knew it had to be done because I can't sit back watching this whole thing go on as if it doesn't bother me, yet I'm not allowed to let it bother me. This is not me. This is setting me back to the girl I was when I started therapy after my husband left. Clearly I had changed and evolved back into the woman I was before I met my husband when I caught Miles' attention.

Had I not doubted myself and felt as though the person he discovered wasn't good enough and thought I should change, maybe things would be different. Maybe they would be the same. I'm grateful for the experience. Not the experience, that sounds so clinical. It really was like a dream. The last four years of my life have been the most exciting, fulfilling, and enlightening years of my life. I've had many highs and many lows but I am the person I am today because of them. Miles may have been a functioning part of my life for the last five years, but he has been around for half of my life, whether I knew it fully or not. I have allowed myself the freedom to express myself artistically, verbally, and emotionally again and I credit Miles for being the catalyst.

I was in a very bad place the first time he looked at me and smiled. Things were never the same after that moment. I never would have had the confidence or drive to train for a half marathon, stand up to people who didn't approve of my life choices, get on a plane, or pin a rock star against a bar and tell him that I wanted him, then actually have him, had I not taken this chance with Miles. I know I would not have made it through the loss of my mother if it was not for him. He was more than a distraction for me. After my husband broke me down, he was the first man to truly make me feel like a woman again. I wasn't a mommy, a caretaker, or a receptionist. I was a sexy woman that a rock star wanted. Never in my wildest dreams did I ever imagine this dream would come true.

I met so many people and made new friends. I keep in touch with Brad, my two radio station buddies, and made other friends along the way. I've learned a lot about myself and most recently have gotten myself back out on the soccer field. These are not things I do in place of him. They are things I do because of him. Six shows have come and gone. I stayed home. I had never missed a local show whether he knows that or not. I'm lying, I missed two early on. I didn't stay home this time because I had a schedule conflict. I had an awakening. One night I played soccer, one night I hung out with

Anna, but four nights I stayed home and did nothing. The conversation I had with Brandon that hot August night will forever be embedded in my mind. That night I knew he was right, and he was completely honest with me. There was no pay off for him. One day Brandon and I will meet again and I will be a stronger woman when that time comes and Miles will not be a thought in my mind, merely the catalyst of my past. I will be able to look Brandon in the eye and tell him that I listened to every word he said that night and that I took his advice and stopped, and that a day has not gone by since that night that I have not thought of him.

Miles and I exchanged a couple of texts since that fateful, cold, January night, but he has not seen me. The Event is next month and I am planning to go but I will only be going to see my new friends, and most importantly, to see Brandon. Hopefully Miles will see a new Piper. If not then, maybe someday, but I'm not all that concerned about what he sees or doesn't see. That chapter in my life is closed. How ironic that the next time I will see him after my decision to no longer go to his shows will be where it all began: with a smile at The Event.

I wish he had really gotten a chance to know me. Me. Not the nervous, shy woman at the concert hoping for a look and willing to sleep with him on command, but the woman that would pack a bag in a heartbeat and hop a plane with him wherever he wanted to go. The woman that would run a 5k and keep up with the boys, then go home, shower, and put on a little black dress, and go to dinner with him. The woman that would work a double shift so that her sons could have their music lessons, then after that shift go out to a concert. Or even the woman that would stand by the man she loved and care for him when he could no longer care for himself. If only he knew.

THE END

About the Author

I'VE BEEN RUNNING FOR MILES . . . AND FOUND MYSELF is Jill's first novel. A lifelong Staten Islander, she has been published in The Aquarian/East Coast Rocker and S.I. Advance. With gallery showings of her work at The Cup (Staten Island, NY) for over 2 years, she has photographed STYX (Aquarian), Glen Burtnik (Staten Island Advance), Rick Springfield, Jefferson Starship, Bruce Willis, REO Speedwagon, Journey, Foreigner, and many more as a hobbyist. However, as her book has expanded, so has the demand for her services and her reputation as a talented photographer. Johnny Simms, previously of Jefferson Starship, personally invited Jill to shoot them when they played at BB King's, NYC, in 2008. Mark Hudson used two of her photos in two of his music videos. After meeting great friends in the music world, she has been given many opportunities to be in the company of some of the most talented people in the music business. Jill has gotten to know them on a personal level, which has given her a completely different perspective on where they are coming from, which is where she draws from for her writing. Jill happily resides in the Oakwood section of Staten Island with her two sons, Joey and Jack.

For more information,
Rubyjill18@gmail.com
I've Been Running For Miles...and Found Myself Facebook

Find more books from
Keith Publications, LLC
At
www.keithpublications.com

CPSIA information can be obtained
at www.ICGtesting.com
Printed in the USA
FFOW02n2205310316
22859FF